Limerick County Library

D1343470

NORWEGIAN
NG FOR REAL

WITHDRAWN FROM STOCK

LEOPARD VI

THE NORWEGIAN FEELING FOR REAL

Edited by Harald Bache-Wiig,
Birgit Bjerck and Jan Kjærstad

Introduction by Harald Bache-Wiig

0 0471800

LIMERICK COUNTY LIBRARY

THE HARVILL PRESS
LONDON

Published by The Harvill Press, 2005

2 4 6 8 10 9 7 5 3 1

Introduction © Harald Bache-Wiig, 2005
English translation of the introduction © Robert Ferguson, 2005
All material in this book is protected by copyright
Please see Acknowledgements, pp. vii—viii

This book is sold subject to the condition that it shall not,
by way of trade or otherwise, be lent, resold, hired out,
or otherwise circulated without the publisher's prior
consent in any form of binding or cover other than that
in which it is published and without a similar condition
including this condition being imposed on the subsequent purchaser

First published in Great Britain in 2005 by
The Harvill Press
Random House, 20 Vauxhall Bridge Road,
London SW1V 2SA

Random House Australia (Pty) Limited
20 Alfred Street, Milsons Point, Sydney,
New South Wales 2061, Australia

Random House New Zealand Limited
18 Poland Road, Glenfield,
Auckland 10, New Zealand

Random House South Africa (Pty) Limited
Corner Boundary Road & Carse O'Gowrie, Houghton, 2198, South Africa

The Random House Group Limited Reg. No. 954009
www.randomhouse.co.uk

A CIP catalogue record for this book
is available from the British Library

ISBN 1 84343 221 8

This book was published with the financial assistance of NORLA

Papers used by Random House are natural,
recyclable products made from wood grown in sustainable forests;
the manufacturing processes conform to the environmental
regulations of the country of origin

Typeset by SX Composing DTP, Rayleigh, Essex
Printed and bound in Great Britain by
Mackays of Chatham plc, Chatham, Kent

CONTENTS

CONTENTS

ACKNOWLEDGEMENTS

The Publisher would like to thank all those who gave permission for the inclusion of material in this anthology, as listed below. Every effort has been made to contact the holders of the relevant copyrights and to ensure that the information here is both accurate and complete.

Ingvar Ambjørnsen: "Skulls" from the collection *Sorte mor* © J.W. Cappelens Forlag as 1994. Translation © Don Bartlett 2005.

Kjell Askildsen: "The Dogs in Thessaloniki" from the collection *Et stort øde landskap* © Kjell Askildsen 1996. Translation © Agnes S. Langeland 1997.

Tor Åge Bringsværd: "The Man Who Collected the First of September, 1973" from *Karavane* © Tor Åge Bringsværd 1974. Translation © Oddrun Grønvik 1974.

Lars Saabye Christensen: "The Jealous Barber" from the collection *Den Misunnelige Frisøren* © J.W. Cappelens Forlag as 1997. Translation © Kenneth Steven 2005.

Gro Dahle: "Life of a Trapper" from the collection *Pelsjegerliv* © J.W. Cappelens Forlag as 1991. Translation © Katherine Hanson 2005.

Kjartan Fløgstad: "The Story of the Short Story" from *Fangliner* © Kjartan Fløgstad 1972. Translation © Sverre Lyngstad 2005.

Jon Fosse: "I Could Not Tell You", first published under the original Norwegian title, "Eg Kunne Ikkje Seie Dei Til Deg", in *Eldre Kortare Prosa* © Jon Fosse and Det norske Samlaget 1998. Published by permission of Rowohlt Verlag GmbH, Reinbek bei Hamburg. Translation © May-Brit Akerholdt 2005.

Karin Fossum: "The Pillar" from the collection *Søylen* © J.W. Cappelens Forlag as 1994. Translation © Robert Ferguson 2005.

Jostein Gaarder: "The Catalogue" from *Katalogen* © Jostein Gaarder 1998. Translation © James Anderson 2005.

Beate Grimsrud: "The Long Trip" from the collection *Det fins grenser for hva jeg ikke forstår* © J.W. Cappelens Forlag as 1990. Translation © Angela Shury-Smith 2005.

Frode Grytten: "Dublin in the Rain" from *Bikubesong* © 1999 Frode Grytten. Translation © Peter Cripps 2005.

Jonny Halberg: "The Cock and Mr Gopher" from *Gå Under* © Jonny Halberg 1992. Translation © Don Bartlett 2005.

Hans Herbjørnsrud: "On an Old Farmstead in Europe" from *Blinddøra* © Hans Herbjørnsrud 1997. Translation © Liv Irene Myhre 1994.

Ragnar Hovland: "The Last Beat Poets in Mid-Hordland" from *Vegen lang og porten trang* © Ragnar Hovland 1981. Translation © James Anderson 2005.

Roy Jacobsen: "Ice" from the collection *Det kan komme noen* © J.W. Cappelens Forlag as 1989. Translation © Kenneth Steven 2005.

Jan Kjærstad: "Homecoming" from the anthology *Vendinger* © Sverre Lyngstad 2005. Translation © Sverre Lyngstad 2005.

Merethe Lindstrøm: "The Sea of Tranquillity" from *Jeg kjenner dette huset* © Merethe Lindstrøm 1999. Translation © Don Bartlett 2005.

Øystein Lønn: "It's So Damned Quiet" from *Thranes Metode* © Øystein Lønn 1993. Translation © Steven T. Murray 1993.

Trude Marstein: "Deep Need – Instant Nausea" from *Sterk sult, plutselig varme* © Trude Marstein 1998. Translation © Don Bartlett 2005.

Hanne Ørstavik: "Love", excerpt from *Kjærlighet* © Hanne Ørstavik 1997. Translation © James Anderson 2005.

Per Petterson: "The Moon over The Gate" excerpt from *Månen over Porten* © Per Petterson 2004. Translation © Anne Born 2005.

Dag Solstad: "Shyness and Dignity" excerpt from *Genanse og verdighet* © Dag Solstad 1994. Translation © Sverre Lyngstad 2004.

Laila Stien: "Veranda with Sun" from *Veranda med Sol* © Laila Stien 2003. Translation © Katherine Hanson 2005.

Karin Sveen: "A Good Heart" from *Døtre* © Karin Sveen 1980. Translation © Katherine Hanson 1995.

Tor Ulven: "I'm Asleep" from *Vente og ikker se* © Tor Ulven 1994. Translation © Sverre Lyngstad 2005.

Lars Amund Vaage: "Cows" from *Kyr* © Lars Amund Vaage 1983. Translation © Nadia Christensen 2005.

Bjørg Vik: "A Forgotten Petunia" from the collection *En gienglemt petunia* © J.W. Cappelens Forlag as 1985. Translation © Don Bartlett 2005.

Herbjørg Wassmo: "The Motif" from *Reiser* © Herbjørg Wassmo 1999. Translation © Donna H. Stockton 2001.

PUBLISHER'S NOTE

This anthology was chosen by Professor Harald Bache-Wiig, scholar and critic, and his fellow editors Birgit Bjerck, the renowned Norwegian publisher, and Jan Kjærstad, critic, novelist and valued contributor to this volume, to whom our deep gratitude. It is published on the occasion of the visit of Their Majesties King Harald V and Queen Sonja of Norway to the United Kingdom in October 2005, a visit which is associated with the centenary of the peaceful dissolution of the union between Norway and Sweden.

The Publishers owe a great debt to the Director of NORLA, Norwegian Literature Abroad, Kristin Brudevoll, and her colleagues for their exceptional support and their administrative and financial contribution to the making of this book. We are grateful also for each author's and their publishers' unstinting help in making the texts and the permissions available, for the works themselves which make up this most admirable and entertaining collection of modern Norwegian literature, and not least to the translators whose scholarly and painstaking collaboration it is a particular pleasure to acknowledge.

In my lifetime of publishing translated literature – from 34 languages – no ambassador has done more for his country's authors than Norway's former ambassador to the UK, Tarald O. Brautaset. His support for Norway's writers, his insistence upon the seriousness of their cause, and his and his wife Elisabeth's hospitality to them and their publishers knew no bounds. His term of duty in London will be remembered with gratitude and affection, and this work is respectfully dedicated to them both.

CHRISTOPHER MACLEHOSE

INTRODUCTION

The writers of the stories in this anthology have two things in common: they are Norwegian, and they are – with one exception – living. Many of the texts have been created in a clear interplay between Norwegian sensibilities and a wider cultural horizon. All of them exemplify the ability the genre has to penetrate the surface of the everyday. Through the ocular nerve of the short story a hidden reality is revealed.

One strength of the novel is its ability to locate people in time and space. It moves along a linear axis and invites historical reflection. The short story operates as a cross-section. Its nature is often circular, even as it can open for a sudden expansion of perspective and insight. "A short story resembles a well-thrown discus," according to the novelist Jan Kjærstad. It lends itself well to existential introspection. An orientation to the everyday, to the norm, is abruptly upended and confronted by experiences of a quite different order. It seeks "to be authentic to the immaterial reality of the inner self,"[1] says Charles May, the American theoretician of the short story. Its drive is towards "the expropriation of the mystery".[2]

Given the inward-looking and contemplative character of the genre, published collections of short stories do not attract a great deal of attention, and their most outstanding exponents remain largely unsung. In Norwegian literary life, however, the genre has since the 1960s achieved a force and prestige that is unique and, in a nation with a documented fondness for writers of an oracular and socially aware turn of mind, even surprising. Maybe this is because practitioners of the form know that it has its own, unique ways of exploring reality. A good short story is like a marker float on the stream of time.

One who has perhaps more than most demonstrated greatness in the short form is Kjell Askildsen, the senior writer represented here.

[1] Charles E. May, "The Nature of Knowledge in Short Fiction" in *The New Short Story Theories*, ed. C.E. May (Ohio University Press, Athens, 1994), p. 133.
[2] ibid., p. 135.

As was the case with many of his younger colleagues, an early, modernistic phase in Askildsen's career presently gave way to realism and an engagement with radical politics. Since then there have been five collections of short stories, minutely realistic on the surface, modernist beneath, with their insistence on the impossibility of meaningful communication between human beings. There is a clear parallel to the minimalism of Samuel Beckett's "less is more", and his male characters often seem to be on some kind of self-inflicted, existential slimming diet, as the character in, for example, "The Dogs in Thessaloniki".

His colleague Dag Solstad underwent a similar evolution. In our anthology he is represented by an extract from his novel *Genanse og verdighet* (*Shyness and Dignity*) 1994. In construction it resembles a short story. As is the case with the other short novels Solstad wrote in the 1990s, the plot here centres on a decisive and shattering event in the life of a middle-aged man; these are tales that illustrate the inexorable nature of fate, the impossibility of retreat. Solstad's heroes search for a deeper meaning in their lives, and the search continues even when everything goes wrong and their lives become trapped inside "the absurd". A tragi-heroic insistence on "the impossible" emerges as the only valid measure of a human life, in a way that conjures associations with several of Ibsen's plays.

Beate Grimsrud, one of the youngest writers in our collection, shows a similarly trenchant honesty in her story "The Long Trip". The Russian Boris Eichenbaum once wrote that while the short story resembles a climb up a mountain, the view from the top of which is the entire point of the exercise, the novel also offers the trip down again and thence home.[3] In Grimsrud's text a mother takes her children on an arduous mountain climb, with clear reference along the way to some of the staple imagery of Norwegian folk-tales. The peak is reached, but the darkness there is complete and affords neither view nor revelation. Or does it? Perhaps the mother has, after all, introduced her daughters to one of the basic tenets of modernity: if all certainty about ultimate meaning is unattainable, then faith in the impossible is precisely what makes life worth living.

The impossible can also take the form of an encounter with something perfect, something that can never be articulated, never be realised, yet which can still give sustained meaning throughout a long

[3] "O. Henry and the Theory of the Short Story" in *The New Short Story Theories*, ed. C.E. May, p. 82.

life. This is the theme of Jon Fosse's beautiful monologue "I Could Not Tell You". Ibsen's successor as a Norwegian dramatist of international reputation here shows his mastery of the epic in miniature.

The short story's power to sustain a moment's sudden revelation in a kind of circular motion is movingly demonstrated also in Hans Herbjørnsrud's "On an Old Farmstead in Europe". Along with Kjell Askildsen and Laila Stien, Herbjørnsrud is probably the most dedicated practitioner of the form in contemporary Norwegian literature. He is as expressive and expansively prodigal with his words as Askildsen is ascetically tight-lipped. A farmer living in Telemark, the county where collectors of folklore in the days of the national romantic movement came upon most of their literary treasures, Herbjørnsrud appears on the surface of it to be an extremely "Norwegian" writer. It shows in "On an Old Farmstead in Europe"; but the conclusion comes to the reader through a whirlpool of modernist European sensibilities.

The Norwegian oral storytelling tradition is also present in Gro Dahle's "Life of a Trapper", as well as a naive, poetic sensuality in her treatment of language and content. The tormented mother who is the voice in this lyrical tale appeals in her despair and her prayers directly to nature. Finally she experiences a miraculous moment in which disaster turns to salvation for her two vulnerable children. Here the archaic sense of unity with nature that characterises the fairy tale is re-established, at least temporarily. We find a monumental expression of the same thing in Lars Amund Vaage's hymn-like prose poem "Cows", a text unique in Norwegian literature. Cows and milk are hailed dithyrambically as life-enhancing forces in a set of almost symphonic variations which would lend itself well to performance before an audience. Here too are elegiac passages. The ending of the short story is a turning-point that hints at the inevitability of loss, both of childhood and of an agrarian way of life that one might characterise as typically "Norwegian".

There is orchestration of a very different kind in Tor Ulven's "I'm Asleep", where the setting is as urban as it is pastoral in Vaage's story. The inspiration for the text is Edward Hopper's painting *Nighthawks* (1942), a desolate interior depicting a New York bar. In polyphony and dissonance the customers' interior monologues are counter-posed. It is the sound of a gunshot, a probable suicide, that brings matters to a conclusion here. Ulven, who died in 1995, was a sceptic who shared with Schopenhauer a rejection of the human fondness for self-delusion. Sometimes, as here, his texts convey a great and melancholy beauty.

Several of the female writers in our selection also strike a note of melancholy in their stories. The texts gravitate towards a condition of loss and separation which the women in the stories already inhabit. Not turning points, rather the inexorable nature of Fate is what is described. In Laila Stien's "Veranda with Sun" the loss is enigmatic in its imprecision, transformed into waiting for a realisation of the "promised joy", when the lived life has become an impossibility. In both "The Motif" by Herbjørg Wassmo and "The Sea of Tranquillity" by Merethe Lindstrøm, the women's loss is connected to an inaccessible father figure; in both it is a fatal road accident that occasions the feeling of loss. As substitute for a communication that is lacking, the two stories create talking pictures, visual memories in Lindstrøm's text, sketches of an unknown, dying man in Wassmo's. Both capture in words a wordless and impossible longing, something Laila Stien also achieves with her character's dream-projections.

A similar sense of longing, directed towards a man, is present in Bjørg Vik's "A Forgotten Petunia". A previous short story, "Aquarium of Women", has already been published in English translation, the title reflecting her involvement in the sexual politics of the 1970s. A second aquarium appears here in our short story from 1985. And despite the surprising turning-point in the story – the man she longs for, her lodger, turns out to be married – this too strikes a strong keynote of melancholy. The man and woman together achieve a kind of happiness in observing the "still life" of fishes in an aquarium. The aquarium no longer symbolises the prison of femininity; instead it has become a place of refuge, a silent world apart from the endless warring of the sexes.

The sexual perspective in Øystein Lønn's "It's So Damned Quiet" is also one of resignation. The point of view is that of a man who suddenly finds he has lost his economic footing in life. Instead of discussing it with his wife, who is planning expensive holidays in the sun, he climbs up a ladder and assumes the pose of the practical handyman. Impotent, in a meaningless and outdated male role, he remains in this pose for a long time, listening to the "bloody" silence. Roy Jacobsen's dark story "Ice" also illustrates the way a traditional and solid manliness can begin to break up when confronted by the unexpected and the unusual.

At several points in this collection we encounter the short story as dramatisation of the collision between the old and the new, the familiar and the exotic. The English literary critic Valerie Shaw has suggested that the short story moves in a borderland between two different worlds.[4] A diffuse territory like this is proffered as a *condition* in Per Petterson's personal essay "The Moon over The Gate", between "the one I was" and "the one I could have been". Here he explores a dark landscape which resembles the tension-filled borderland of the short story. There is greater definition and dynamism in Jonny Halberg's "The Cock and Mr Gopher", the tragi-comic tale of a small boy who is tempted by his encounter with a new and unfamiliar world. When at the end the boy crows like a cock, he is signalling his revolt against the dull normality and safety in which his father tries to keep him cocooned. The main character in Lars Saabye Christensen's "The Jealous Barber" similarly allows himself to be tempted into breaking away from a world that has become stale and routine: he switches allegiance to a new, more fashionable barber. But in genuine thriller-style, his former barber compels him back into the mausoleum of familiarity. The battle between the attraction of the new and the lure of the familiar is described with a tragi-comic ambivalence.

Lars Saabye Christensen is a virtuoso of the nuances of black humour; he has the modernist's eye for what is absurd. So too does Ragnar Hovland. The humour in his tale of two self-styled "beat poets" who astound the beasts as well as the human beings in their small coastal town is of a gentle sort, but it arises in the absurd juxtaposition of rural naivety against the world-weariness of the "cool" characters they are trying to imitate. The contrastive tension between local, "Norwegian" roots and the attempt to engage with a globalised culture characterises several of the writers in our selection, including Kjartan Fløgstad and Frode Grytten. Grytten's "Dublin in the Rain" is an extract from his short-story-like novel *Bikubesong* (*Beehive Song*) 1999.

Ingvar Ambjørnsen's "Skulls" describes a stylised and extreme meeting between modernity and tradition. Here two distinct, compressed moments are juxtaposed. One, the encounter with the ancient population of Orkney, is full of harmony and beauty. The other, an experience in a walled-up grave-chamber close by, is dense with claustrophobic anxiety. Its associations are with a modern, dehumanised rationalism. The short story's break with the normal can cover both what Charles May calls the "solidarity of life" and the

[4] Valerie Shaw, *The Short Story: A Critical Introduction* (Longman, London and New York, 1983), p. 192.

collapse into chaos and loneliness, both of which are depicted here.

Øystein Lønn has called the short story "a tale bigger than itself", [5] and for this reason it is also well able to provide a loaded critique of contemporary culture and mores. In his elegantly structured "Homecoming", Jan Kjærstad utilises the form's penchant for surprise and the inversion of perspective to satirical, anti-imperialist effect. Another master of the hidden surprise in prose fiction is the veteran Tor Åge Bringsværd. His fable about "The Man Who Collected the First of September 1973" casts unexpected and paradoxical light on the modern hysteria surrounding news as a consumer product. The mania for collecting which gets so out of hand in Bringsværd's story reappears in a global setting in Jostein Gaarder's "The Catalogue". Here mankind's urge towards ultimate knowledge and the consummation of history is posed against the certainty that our species is on the path to self-extinction. Sophie, in Gaarder's worldwide bestseller *Sofies verden* (*Sophie's World*) 1990, likewise sees the fable of the Tower of Babel as a bleak and foreboding commentary on our modern world.

Trude Marstein is the youngest author in this collection. Her contribution is ill-omened in a quite different way. The hyper-realistic writing style, with every detail registered, betrays a disgust with fellow human beings which, in its quiet way, is as powerful a critique of contemporary culture as is Gaarder's apocalyptic story.

"Descriptions of the short narrative are as manifold as they are confusing," writes Kjartan Fløgstad in his story about the history of the short story. Manifold, too, are the texts in this anthology. They are hardly likely to bring their authors reputations as truth-tellers amidst all the hubbub of modern life, but it is our belief that each of them individually creates its own oasis of calm, a space for contemplation, effectively clarifying the conditions of our common existence rather than further confusing them. Taken as a whole, we believe they are well able to show how contemporary Norwegian literature approaches life in the modern world. They cover a wealth of substance and expression which open up novel perspectives as well as confirming the existence of shared experiences of life common to both Britain and Norway.

HARALD BACHE-WIIG

[5] Øystein Lønn in conversation with Alf van der Hagen, in Alf van der Hagen, *Dialoger. Samtaler med ti norske forfattere* (*Dialogues. Conversations with Ten Norwegian writers*), Oktober, Oslo, 1993, p. 150.

HANS HERBJÖRNSRUD

On An Old Farmstead in Europe

The very first person known to have lived on our farm was Blind Margjit, who died in 1616.

In the 1620s a cottar named Jon made his home here. The sources give only one piece of information about him: Jon was in reduced circumstances, or, in other words, poor.

The tax ledger of 1645 indicates that Wise Ragnhild lived on the farm that year and paid six shillings in taxes.

The land registry of 1665 lists the farm as being leased from an estate. It owed half a barrel of grain and produced two and a half barrels, kept two cows, broke no new land and was charged with growing hops for beer brewing. In the census of 1665 the farm is not mentioned.

At the time of Blind Margjit, Jon and Wise Ragnhild, the farmhouses were located where we now call "Gamletun". The house site and the surrounding fields are low-lying, on the basement floor of the valley, and in the 1600s they were surrounded by bogs and wetlands.

Down at the old farmstead the houses were for centuries exposed to floods and water damage. Not until 1864 did they give up the hopeless battle against the water. At that time the main house, summer kitchen, storage houses, cowshed and barn were dismantled, log by log, and all the building materials carted higher up and rebuilt, house by house, on the ridge where our farm sits today.

But even up here, on the main floor of the valley, the houses sit so low that the great flood of 1927 would have dug out the ground beneath the foundations had it not been for the rock barriers they were able hurriedly to erect.

After the houses were moved in 1864 the foundations were levelled and the old farmstead converted into fields and meadows. This parcel has a deeper layer of topsoil and yields more than other fields on the farm. In our time the surrounding wetlands have been drained, cultivated and planted. Hydroelectric dams have tamed the once-sofrisky river, and the little creek that used to scurry about in the bogs has been channelled and now stretches like a taut plumb-line through its old meandering course.

These days we grow barley or wheat at Gamletun. And every time I till the fields there in spring, the harrow clanks against foundation stones forced into the light by the ground frost.

In earlier years these stones would always remind me of something absurd and alien. They would either be the colour of blue clay and flat like flagstone and resemble the plates and armour of an armadillo. Or the stones would be pale yellow and curved and look more like the weathered bones of dinosaurs. Three years ago I found two rocks that looked like ostrich eggs.

But early this morning, a windy April morning in 1991, when I heard two angry clanks from the harrow and jumped down from the tractor, I pulled from the teeth two head-sized stones and I immediately felt there was something strangely familiar and appealing about them.

With my nails I scraped the moist black soil from the foundation stones that it had taken the ground frost 127 years to bring to light. Both were bone-coloured and head-shaped and resembled the skulls sometimes unearthed by the gravedigger's shovel.

With the diesel motor idling, I stood there in the field with one stone in each hand. How strange: they had eye sockets and cheekbones and jawbones. Indeed they did, and when I looked a little closer, I could also make out nasal bones and ear cavities. I even imagined I could see a few amber-yellow teeth. The heads were evenly and smoothly curved from the forehead, over the crown and down the back. They resembled heads created by a sculptor more than they did skulls.

But still, how different they were, these two stone heads.

One had a high forehead with eye sockets close together in a narrow facial oval. It had to be Blind Margjit, I decided. This is how that singular woman might have looked beneath the skin. Her eye sockets stared at me with an empty, introspective and blind look.

The other head was broad-jawed and coarse, with high cheekbones and a bumpy forehead. It seemed to glare at me with a querulous and menacing look. This was how I had always imagined Wise Ragnhild without her gooseberry-green eyes and large, full-lipped frog mouth.

The stone heads were still caked with dirt. I knocked their foreheads together so hard that lumps of dirt and sand flew. The bumping of the heads produced an eerie stone sound that made me listen with excitement and curiosity. What was I hearing?

I banged the skulls together again. And again. And again.

And while I loudly knocked the heads together – clack! clack! clack! – I heard a heavy, dark, ancient sound, stone music that travelled up the bones of my arms – clack! clack! clack! – a bone music that sent electric sparks through my collar-bone and spine and reverberated throughout my limbs – clack! clack! clack! – a skeletal score for vertebrae and shoulder-blades, for hip sockets and shins, for hammers, anvils and stapes – clack! clack! clack!

I stood at Gamletun clacking and making skeletal music until my teeth began to chatter along. The heads seemed to knock out the beat of a mouldy old folk-song that centuries ago had come into being here from thundering floods and trickling brooks and tinkling rain. Soon the stone heads began to produce word after word of a refrain:

> And the Man with the Eyes
> Keeps searching for his sight.

I stood at Gamletun knocking out a folk-song that the ground frost had forced out of the field and into the sunlight early on this morning. When the harrow found it, the song was still dormant. I lifted it up and shook it awake. Music and words that had lain hidden and forgotten under the dirt for more than 170 years flew like sparks from the stone heads as they crashed together:

> And the Man with the Eyes
> Keeps searching for his sight.

At that point I had to stop. I didn't have the strength for more. Knocking the heavy stone heads together was becoming too hard and strenuous. I was able to uncover only the refrain of the song. Breathing hard, I sat the heads down on the furrow. There they suddenly began to resemble two women struggling in floodwater up to their necks.

I bent all the way down to Blind Margjit's head and gently stroked her brow while I began to puff like a bellows – whoosh, whoosh – into her eye sockets while I coaxed and urged:

"Whoosh, Margjit, whoosh, whoosh. I'm bringing you back to life. Whoosh, Margjit, whoosh, whoosh. Tell me what your song was about. Whoosh, Margjit, whoosh, whoosh."

At that moment a whirlwind as tall as a tree came reeling through Gamletun. The whirlwind had kicked up a veil of swirling dirt and it came towards me, careening across the field like a tall, ungainly ghost with a swarm of dry leaves for a head. The whirlwind swayed around the tractor and headed straight for me.

I was sucked into a mad reel and sandblasted by a hurricane of dirt. Abruptly the wind let go. Everything was still, deadly still and silent. For an endless moment I was in the quiet eye of the storm. The tornado sucked the air right out of me as if I was about to be vacuum-packed. Then I was wrapped inside a cocoon of perfect peace and calm. All around me the moments raged.

Right afterwards I was yanked back into the round dance and took a few turns with the wind.

When the whirlwind lurched on, I once again found myself in the field, exhausted and blinded by the dust. I sat on the furrow clutching the stone heads, unable to see a thing. And while I sat like that – disoriented, stunned and in total darkness like blind Blind Margjit – I saw for the first time Gamletun as it must have looked centuries ago.

On the farm, people staggered back and forth on the twenty-two wading stones across the wetland.

In late summer evenings a mist scented with white bog cotton drifted up from dykes and hollows and puddles, wrapping the farmstead in a woolly blanket until only the top of the ash tree in the yard peeked up out of the haze.

Sometimes the spring or autumn floods would snatch the broom from the front steps, extinguish the fire in the open hearth and toss hither and thither wooden vessels and the churn and leave wiggling carp behind on the dirt floor.

But the flood of the century left the houses completely submerged for days, those that were not set adrift and carried off along with a few outhouses and summer barns and logs and driftwood from huts and farms further up the valley.

My grandfather learned from his grandfather that during a spring flood in the 1560s the young girl Margjit sat perched for one day and two nights in the farmyard ash tree that stood there with trembling branches and parted the onrushing torrents.

Only the crown of the ash tree was visible above the flood waters, making it look like a bush. The rowan tree by the cowshed resembled an upturned broom. Above the main house the water simmered and bubbled like a boiling pot.

Margjit sat in the ash tree feeling as if the whole valley came rushing at her like a landslide. The water surface had no waves. It heaved, trembled and quivered like fine linen in the bleaching yard on a breezy day. Through the driving rain she heard the sound of the flood. It was low, rustling and almost inaudible, but as frightening and piercing as a hissing snake. A driving rain battered her hard, like a wet birch switch.

The seventeen-year-old Margjit was the only one left on the farm now. Her father and two younger sisters had succumbed to disease and illness in midwinter. Shortly before the onslaught of the flood, her mother fell dead while gathering herbs by the bog. She was buried on the day the drenching rain began to fall.

Legend has it that Margjit's mother was a medicine woman to the whole district. She was the one people turned to when evil crept in through a person's eyes and mouth and settled in the body as illness and pain. Her mother treated the sick with healing lotions made from bat blood, baby fat, beaver glands, corpse sweat, ear wax from virgins, semen from swains, werewolf spittle and many other things that only she knew to have healing powers. And she concocted potions for them made from henbane, celery, aspen leaves, juniper berries and other powerful herbs and plants that only the experts were familiar with.

Ever since she was a little girl Margjit had sat by her mother's side as she urged and beseeched the evil to let go of the tormented bodies. All the pain and misery of the victims that little Margjit saw fell like heavy burdens upon her soul. The little girl sat there observing, wide-eyed and attentive, taking it all in. All the pain and suffering, bitterness and rancour of others sank to the bottom of her soul and made her sullen and sad. Gradually she became snake-eyed and ill-natured. Her thoughts and gaze could injure others. Her mother was unable to exorcise the evil no matter how many of her balms, brews and incantations she tried. Nor did anyone else know of any remedies. She had seen too much evil and horror as a young child, they said.

As a result Margjit was feared and disliked by everyone. If she stared at a pregnant woman, the foetus died in the womb. If she stared at cattle, they began to milk blood. If she watched when anyone churned, the cream turned to water instead of butter. Her gaze could scorch a neighbour's green pastures. It could ignite houses and trees. It could stop birds in flight. That's how much she had seen.

So heavy was her heart. So piercing were her eyes. She lived under a blackened sun and could no longer shed tears. Thus she could not cry when she sat shivering and shaking in the top branches of the ash during the flood. Her life was as dark and empty and desolate as the rushing water she sat watching. Everyone avoided her.

Margjit sat in the farmyard ash tree and watched the roof of the house slowly disappear as the water rose. Finally the current sputtered white over the peak and lapped and licked like tongues of fire. Then it died down, and the house had vanished. She saw the water bulge over the house like a big black bump with churning swirls.

With each log of the house wall that disappeared into the water, she climbed one branch higher in the tree. It was raining. Her frock and blouse were dripping wet. Her numb, stiff hands gripped the tree's branches like claws.

When the flood swallowed the main house, she stopped screaming for help. Her cries had fluttered like the squawks of injured birds over the rapidly moving water. None reached shore. None arrived.

Eventually she kept silent and rested her tired head against the trunk of the ash tree and stared upstream. Her jaws were clenched, her mouth a gash and her protruding brow strangely white and shiny in her dirty face. She was so exhausted and weak that she could no longer scream. Only her eyes glowed with life. They were the colour of dewberries, hateful, burning. Poisonous. Her gaze hissed like red-hot iron in water when it fell upon the bulging current over the house roof.

At dusk on the first evening she saw a drowned sheep drifting downstream. The body was swollen but heavy in the water, and in the soft silvery light it resembled a floe of foam. Not until the sheep was close to her tree did she see the two crows on the cadaver – their claws buried deep in wool – pecking away.

When the rainy mist had wrapped itself around the sheep, she climbed another branch and settled down like a bird seeking shelter for the night. Darkness was falling. All around her she could hear the flood. It muttered and mumbled like tattles and tales; it sighed and sobbed like all the world's torment and torture, and its whine was as cold as a whetstone grinding against the edge of a scythe.

But whenever she stared down into the raging current below, she flew like a great loon, neck outstretched, over an endless field of water, alone and screaming.

In the middle of the night a big cowshed came bobbing towards her. The shed seemed even blacker than the pitch-black darkness from which it emerged, and the doorway gaped blacker than the blackest misery she had ever seen. It seemed like a nightmare: the cowshed emerged from the night and headed towards her, huge and eerie, like a mountain of solid darkness. When the branches of the ash tree began to scrape along the side of the shed she wanted to scream with terror, but she was so hoarse and cold that she was unable to make a single sound, not even a cough. The branches pushed at the shed, and it dipped and curtsied in the water before slowly it spun around and disappeared in the darkness.

In the morning, when she was so hungry that she began to nibble on buds and bark, she spotted a man astride a log coming hurtling right at her.

In the swirls of current over the house roof the log reared like a spooked horse, spun around, veered off to the side and rushed past the ash tree.

In a flash Margjit looked into a wild-eyed face. She exchanged a hasty look with the man, but no words.

Then he disappeared into the rainy haze.

She did not know him, and she never saw him again. From then on, everywhere she went she would ask about this unknown man who had ridden a runaway log in the flood. But no-one knew who he was, or where he had come from, or if he survived.

The man on the log had cast his eyes on her as he rushed past down the watery slope.

And she had accepted them.

He gave her the only thing he had to offer at that moment – his gaze – and she caught it in flight and kept it with her for the rest of her life as if it was a part of herself.

Legend has it that Margjit lost her sight in old age. She is said to have stated that it was not until she became Blind Margjit that she understood what she had so far only seen. That is when she truly realised the insight given to her by the nameless man from the spring flood in her youth.

She called him the Man with the Eyes.

In the summertime, when the old Blind Margjit sat on a stool under the farmyard ash tree, she told anyone willing to listen about the great flood when she was a young girl. Margjit's words must have been strong and durable, for some of what she told underneath the tree survived for generations – remembered for 375 years – and was not written down until now, by me, on a windy and rainy April night in 1991. And her words still have sap and substance, for when I close my eyes and try to think back, there is no face I see as painfully clear and obvious as that of the seventeen-year-old Margjit sitting in the farmyard ash, staring out over the shiny black water.

Blind Margjit recalled that the log that the Man with the Eyes rode was a log from a house, and that it made a leap into the air before it spun around in the swirling current over the house roof and tore past the tree where she sat. And she remembered seeing his back as it disappeared into the mist.

But how the Man with the Eyes looked, and how he was dressed, she had altogether forgotten. Or maybe in the rush of it all she never noticed. She didn't know if he was young or old, if he had light or dark hair, if he was heavy or slender. She didn't even know if his eyes were brown or black or blue. Perhaps his looks and age and manner of dress meant nothing to her.

The Man with the Eyes was simply two eyes on a runaway log in a furious current. And a back swallowed by the mist.

Yes, and the fact that he was a man, and probably just an ordinary man fighting for his life in the flood.

The Man with the Eyes was simply a glance to her. And their meeting became one single moment that she was able to wrest from the flood and hold on to all her life.

That was all there was to their brief meeting.

Yet, everything happened. To Margjit their meeting became a wide-open eye that lay buried deep in her soul, staring at her all her life.

But what really happened then?

Everything happened, as already indicated. Margjit and the Man with the Eyes exchanged glances, and faster than one dream can turn into another she was transformed.

She had been snake-eyed and mean-spirited. Her eyes were evil and could kill and torment. Her thoughts were evil and could bite and sting.

She had been a victim of the belief in the evil mind and the evil eye which was the basis for understanding fellow human beings in the old farming community.

But all at once she turned kind-eyed and mild-mannered. She had been hexed and shunned. Now she was released and became accepted and liked by all. She had been sullen and sad. Instantly she became cheerful and spirited. Her hair had been coal-black and her eyes dark as dewberries. Suddenly her hair turned the colour of corn silk and her eyes blue as cornflowers in a ripe wheatfield. From that day and that moment she was transformed. No-one recognised her. Nor did she recognise herself. She did not recognise her community and her neighbours at all. She saw everything and everybody with entirely new eyes. It was as if she had been held captive until that moment and was brought into the light for the first time.

But how did this happen?

I simply do not know. Nor does anyone else, perhaps. These things sometimes happen to young girls, or so I hope.

The legend may both see and describe what happened to Margjit in the top of the ash tree, but it doesn't explain or expound on her transformation. It may be that the legend knows itself as a legend, and it may be that it knows Margjit as a person, but it says or reveals nothing further about itself or her. Perhaps the legend understood and understands everyone who has ever heard it right up until the present. In that case the legend has served as a misted mirror in which generation after generation have dimly glimpsed their own reflection. Possibly the legend survived throughout the centuries because it was able to keep the wonderment of the listeners alive. It is precisely what the legend conceals and our own surprise and puzzlement which give the young Margjit the freedom she needs to become transformed in front of our wondering eyes.

According to the legend the light in Margjit's eyes burned slowly down until finally it died out. But when everything became pitch-dark inside her and around her, Blind Margjit called upon the sight she had kept hidden since her youth. And in the middle of her darkest night the eyes of the Man with the Eyes were kindled again; they flickered and shone and lighted her path. She was blind, but the Man with the Eyes gave her sight. He became her eyes and gaze. Blind Margjit saw better than when she had had her sight. She saw everything around her, and she saw herself from the outside. She both saw and was seen.

This is according to the legend, which also says that in the last year of Blind Margjit's life she became either mad or psychic. She withered and then rejuvenated herself. She broke into a thousand pieces which she scattered like stardust across the sky. She broke into pieces and made herself whole again. Perhaps she was both psychic and mad.

She began to see things that no-one could or would see. She swallowed the sun and crowed. She was everyone and she was no-one. Her gaze danced deliriously through the centuries.

It was then, in the year of her death, 1616, that she completed the ballad "Margjit & The Man with the Eyes", which she had been composing since the great flood in the 1560s. She could neither read nor write, but where she lived the oral folk-song tradition was still alive. Her neighbours listened to her and memorised the words and the tune.

The ballad describes a moment that grows and grows and becomes longer and longer and lasts and lasts until finally it spans her whole life, from birth until death. She is born and dies at the same moment. Her cradle is her grave, I think it says in one of the last verses.

Blind Margjit was consumed and possessed with the idea of time and mortality. She was not the only one among her contemporaries to feel this way. It was the early 1600s. Elsewhere in Europe the gods of war were about to be unleashed and go berserk for thirty years. Cervantes and Shakespeare died. The medieval geocentric world image collapsed, and soon Pascal would stare with horror into a desolate and ice-cold cosmos and exclaim, "The eternal silence of these infinite spaces terrifies me."

The 1600s was the obscure period between the Renaissance's confident and self-assured concept of time and the new notions of the 1700s and the Age of Enlightenment.

It was a century when the Europeans became aware of a chilling isolation, as the French philosopher Georges Poulet writes in his work about the perception of time from the Baroque period to Proust and Henri Bergson.

A world so far divinely ordered began to list and capsize. Time came unhinged. The individual was trapped in the moment or in his memories and became the victim of time and mortality. Someone once said that the baroque poets of the 1600s were nostalgic about the past and walked backwards into a threatening future. In their poems the word "history" is synonymous with decline and dissolution; life is compared to a shimmering soap bubble about to burst: the past becomes a lovely dream, the future something ominous and the present an open grave.

The Europeans of the 1600s were robbed of the sense of permanence and continuity. The strand was broken and the pearls scattered in every direction. Time no longer followed a straight line divinely determined. It overflowed its banks and flooded a large bog and carried everything away.

Poulet uses another image: the European of the 1600s felt at the mercy of a flood of disjointed moments. Time became a huge quagmire that must be traversed by stepping from one precarious foothold to the next, from one moment to the next, never knowing whether you would land on safe ground or in the quagmire and be pulled under.

In the outskirts of this Europe, on a swampy and impoverished little farm in Norway, the illiterate Blind Margjit circles the farmyard ash tree in the year of her death, 1616, leaning on her cane while humming and crooning a ballad that was to live on after her for 180 years. When she was finished putting the ballad together it was twenty-nine verses long, just as many as there were letters in the alphabet she did not know.

The first part of the ballad describes, interprets and explains what happened during the spring flood between the snake-eyed girl in the ash tree and the courageous, stalwart Man with the Eyes who rides on the wild current. Then the ballad goes on to describe how the blind Man with the Eyes doddered from farm to farm and from valley to valley in search of his sight.

Finally, when he is old and white-haired, the Man with the Eyes knocks one moonlit autumn night on the door at Margjit's farm. When Margjit opens the door and steps outside she sees an old, blind man underneath the ash tree. She recognises him immediately and walks over to him. At the moment Margjit takes his hand and looks into his moonlit face, she suddenly loses her sight and becomes blind. But the Man with the Eyes instantly recovers his sight and is able to see the stooping Blind Margjit standing before him.

The ballad ends with Blind Margjit saying she has lived her entire life within one incredible moment. In the end she sits folding baby nappies along with a shroud for an old man.

As the years and decades passed and the 1600s turned into the 1700s, people added new words to her ballad and left some out. New verses were added and old ones were dropped. The ballad became a folk-song.

But after 1790 the song began to disintegrate. It dissolved into stanzas, which then dissolved into verses and words, which in turn dissolved into letters.

When Norwegian folk-songs, fairy tales and legends were collected in the middle of the last century, only bits and pieces remained of the song about Margjit and the Man with the Eyes. Not one stanza had been written down.

The song finally returned to the Latin alphabet from whence it came. When I see the twenty-nine letters of the alphabet all in a row, they remind me of a cemetery where the song about "Margjit and the

Man with the Eyes" lies buried. Each of the twenty-nine verses has one letter on top as a memorial.

Perhaps the song also lies buried in the foundations at Gamletun. I was able to knock out the refrain with the help of the stone heads:

> And the Man with the Eyes
> Keeps searching for his sight.

Perhaps the song was not meant for life. It died, but the legend survived.

Everyone who lived on the farm after Blind Margjit heard about and may even have imagined the Man with the Eyes who was no more than a glance cast at a young girl in the great flood.

But there may also be those who have been touched, accidentally, by this glance from an obscure place in history.

We excavate foundations, and we study church registers and court records, and we try to uncover the past.

And sometimes we are caught by surprise when a glance from the past suddenly meets our own.

Perhaps we are seen.

Perhaps history sees.

Us.

Then the glance glides by and disappears in the rainy mist.

Whoever searches long enough in history will finally be found.

I am writing this one late April night in 1991. On the table in front of me are the two stone heads that my harrow found in the field this morning. From time to time I put the pen aside and lean over the papers to gently stroke Blind Margjit's brow. Her eye sockets gaze at me with a distant and vacant stare.

Before I began to write, I sat caressing her lovely head for a long time. And that is when the glance from the unknown man on the log quite unexpectedly met mine, sharp, piercing and painful.

The next moment his glance was gone into the mist and the rain.

History had seen me, and I could begin to write.

Translated by Liv Irene Myhre

KJELL ASKILDSEN

The Dogs in Thessaloniki

We had morning coffee in the garden. We scarcely said a word. Beate got up and put the cups on a tray. We might as well put the chairs up on the veranda, she said. Why's that? I said. It will probably rain, she said. Rain? I said, there's not a cloud in the sky. There's a nip in the air, she said, don't you think so? No, I said. Maybe I'm wrong, she said. She went up the veranda steps and into the living-room. I remained sitting outside about a quarter of an hour longer; then I carried one of the chairs up on to the veranda. I stood for a while looking over at the forest on the other side of the wooden fence, but there was nothing to see. Through the open veranda door I could hear Beate humming. She's heard the weather forecast, of course, I thought. I went back down into the garden and round to the front of the house, over to the post box beside the black wrought-iron gate. It was empty. I closed the gate, which for some reason or other was standing open; then I saw that someone had thrown up just outside it. I was rather upset. I attached the garden hose to the tap beside the basement entrance and turned the water on full force; then I pulled the hose along behind me to the gate. The jet hit slightly off the mark, and some of the vomit squirted into the garden; the rest got spread out over the tarmac. There was no drain nearby, so all I accomplished was to move the yellowish substance four or five metres away from the gate. But it was a relief after all to get the revolting mess a bit further off.

After I had turned off the tap and rolled up the garden hose, I didn't know what to do. I went up on to the veranda and sat down. Some minutes later I heard Beate starting to hum again. It sounded as if she was thinking about something she liked to think about; she may have believed that I didn't hear her. I coughed, and it went quiet. She came outside and said: Are you sitting here? She had put on some make-up. Are you off somewhere? I said. No, she said. I turned my head towards the garden and said: Some idiot had been sick just outside the gate. Oh? she said. A really disgusting mess, I said. She didn't answer. I got up. Do you have a cigarette? she asked. She got one and I gave her a light. Thanks, she said. I went down from the veranda and sat at the garden table. Beate stood smoking on the veranda. She threw her half-smoked cigarette on to the gravel in front of the steps. What's the point of doing that? I said. It'll burn, she said. She went into the living-room. I stared at the thin wisp of smoke rising almost straight up from the cigarette, I hoped it wouldn't burn. After a while I got up; I had a feeling of homelessness. I went down to the gate in the fence, over the narrow strip of pasture and into the forest. I stopped just beyond the edge of the forest and sat on a tree stump, almost hidden behind a thicket. Beate came out on to the veranda. She looked towards where I was sitting and called my name. She can't see me, I thought. She went down into the garden and round the house. She went up on to the veranda again. She looked once more over at where I was sitting. She can't possibly see me, I thought. She turned and went into the living-room. I got up and walked further into the forest.

When we were sitting at the dinner table, Beate said: There he is again. Who? I said. That man, she said, at the edge of the forest, just beside the big . . . no, now he's gone away. I got up and went to the window. Where? I said. Beside the big pine, she said. Are you sure that it was the same man? I said. I think so, she said. There is no-one there now, I said. No, he went away, she said. I went back to the table. I said: You couldn't possibly see that it was the same man at that distance. Beate didn't answer straight away, then she said: I would've recognised you. That's different, I said. You know me. We ate for a while in silence. Then she said: By the way, why didn't you answer when I called to you? Called to me? I said. I saw you, she said, and you didn't answer. I didn't reply to that. I saw you, she said. Why did you go round the house then? I said. So that you wouldn't realise that I'd seen you, she said. I didn't think you saw me, I said. Why didn't you answer? she said. It wasn't necessary to answer when I didn't think you had seen me, I said. I might well've been somewhere totally different. If you hadn't seen me, and if you hadn't pretended not to have seen me, this wouldn't have been a problem. Dear me, she said, it isn't a problem, is it?

We didn't say anything more for some time. Beate was continually turning her head to look out of the window. I said: It didn't rain. No, she said, it held off. I put my knife and fork down, leaned back in my chair and said: You know, sometimes you irritate me. Oh? she said. You can never admit that you're wrong, can you, I said. I certainly can, she said. I'm often wrong. Everybody is. Absolutely everybody is. I just looked at her and I could see that she realised she had gone too far. She got up. She picked up the sauceboat and the empty vegetable dish and went into the kitchen. She didn't come in again. I got up as well. I put on my jacket, then I stood a while listening, but it was dead quiet. I went into the garden, round to the front of the house and on to the road. I walked eastwards, out of town. I was really quite upset. The gardens around the villas on either side of the road were lying empty, and the only sound I heard was the fairly steady hum from the motorway. I left the houses behind and crossed the large level stretch of ground which runs right down to the fjord.

I arrived at the fjord just beside a small outdoor café and found a seat at a table right at the water's edge. I bought a beer and lit a cigarette. I was warm, but I kept my jacket on because I reckoned my shirt would have sweat stains under the arms. All the café guests were behind me; in front of me was the fjord and the distant, forested slopes. The buzzing of low-pitched voices and the slight gurgling of water amongst the rocks on the shore put me in a drowsy, vacant frame of mind. My thoughts followed their own apparently irrational paths and were not unpleasant; on the contrary, I felt an extraordinary sense of well-being. So it was all the more inexplicable that, without any noticeable transition, I was gripped by an anguished feeling of desertion. There was something all-encompassing about both the anguish and the feeling of desertion that in a way suspended time, although it probably only lasted a few seconds before my senses brought me back to the present.

I went home the same way I had come, across the broad level stretch of land. The sun was drawing closer to the mountains in the west; a haze was lying over the town, and the air was completely still. I noticed that I was reluctant to go home, and suddenly I thought, and it was a clear, distinct thought: If only she were dead.

But I continued on my way home. I walked through the gate and round to the back of the house. Beate was sitting at the garden table; directly opposite her sat her elder brother. I went over to them, I felt completely calm. We exchanged a few trivial remarks. Beate didn't ask where I'd been, and neither of them suggested that I should keep them company, which in any case I would have declined, with a plausible excuse.

I went up to the bedroom, hung up my jacket and took off my shirt. Beate's side of the bed was unmade. On the bedside table was an ashtray with two fag-ends in it, and beside the ashtray lay an open book, with the cover face up. I closed the book; I took the ashtray with me to the bathroom and flushed the fag-ends down the toilet. Then I undressed and turned on the shower, but the water was only lukewarm, almost cold, and my time in the shower was different and much shorter than I had intended.

While I was standing at the open bedroom window getting dressed, I heard Beate laugh. I finished dressing quickly and went down into the utility room in the basement; through the window in there I could watch her without being seen. She was sitting leaning back in her chair, with her dress rucked far up over her spread thighs and her hands folded behind her neck so that the thin dress material was stretched tightly across her breasts. There was something indecent about her pose that aroused me, and my arousal was increased by her sitting like that in full view of a man, albeit her brother.

I remained standing looking at her for a while; she was sitting not more than seven, eight metres from me, but on account of the perennials in the flower-bed right outside the basement window, I was certain that she wouldn't spot me. I tried to catch what they were saying, but they were talking too quietly, remarkably quietly, I thought. Then she got up, her brother got too, and I went quickly up the basement stairs and into the kitchen. I turned on the cold water tap and fetched a glass, but she didn't come in, so I turned the water off again and put the glass back in place.

When I was calm again, I went into the living-room and sat down to leaf through a technical magazine. The sun had gone down, but it wasn't necessary to put on the light yet. I leafed backwards and forwards. The veranda door was standing open. I lit a cigarette. I heard the distant sound of a plane; otherwise everything was quiet. I grew uneasy again and I got up and went into the garden. There was no-one there. The gate in the fence was standing ajar. I went over and closed it. I thought: She is probably behind the thicket watching me. I went back to the garden table, moved one of the chairs a little so that the back of the chair was facing the forest, and sat down. I convinced myself that I wouldn't have noticed if someone or other had been standing watching me from the utility room in the basement. I smoked two cigarettes. It started to get dark, but the motionless air was mild, almost warm. A pale crescent moon was risen over the hillside in the east, the time was just gone ten. I smoked another cigarette. Then I heard a faint creaking from the gate in the fence, but I didn't turn round. She sat down and put a small bunch of wild flowers on the garden table. What a lovely evening, she said. Yes, I said. Do you have a cigarette? she said. She got one and I gave her a light. Then she said in that childishly eager voice I'd always found so difficult to resist: I'll get a bottle of wine, shall I? – and before I had made up my mind what to answer, she got up, took hold of the bunch of flowers and hurried across the grass and up the veranda steps. I thought: Now she's going to pretend that nothing has happened. Then I thought: Nothing has happened, has it? Nothing she knows about. By the time she came out with wine and two glasses and even a blue checked tablecloth, I was almost wholly calm. She had put on the light above the veranda door, and I turned my chair so that I was sitting facing the forest. Beate filled our glasses, and we took a drink. Mm, she said, delicious. The forest was like a black silhouette against the pale blue sky. How quiet it is, she said. Yes, I said. I held the packet of cigarettes out to her, but she didn't want one. I took one myself. Look at the new moon, she said. Yes, I said. How thin it is, she said. Yes, I said; I took a sip of the wine. On the Continent it lies on its back, she said. I didn't answer. Do you remember the dogs in Thessaloniki which were stuck together after they'd mated? she said. In Kavalla, I said. All the old men outside the café yelling and carrying on, she said, and the dogs howling and struggling to get loose from each other. And when we left the town, there was a thin new moon like that one that was lying on its back, and we wanted each other, do you remember? Yes, I said. Beate poured more wine in our glasses. Then we sat silent for a while, for quite a long time. Her words had made me uneasy and the silence afterwards only increased my unease. I searched for something to say, something distractingly common-place. Beate got up. She walked round the garden table and stood behind my back. I got scared, I thought: Now she is going to do something to me. And when I felt her hands at my throat, I jerked away, throwing my head and shoulders forward. Almost at the same moment I realised what I'd done and I said, without turning round: You frightened me. She didn't reply. I leant back in the chair. I heard her breathing. Then she left.

After a bit I got up to go inside. It had become altogether dark. I had finished the wine and thought up something to say; it had taken some time. I took our glasses and the empty bottle with me, but after a moment's consideration I let the blue checked tablecloth lie. The living-room was empty. I went into the kitchen and put the bottle and the glasses in the sink. The time was just gone eleven. I locked the veranda door and switched off the light; then I went upstairs to the bedroom. My bedside light was on. Beate was lying with her face turned away and was asleep, or pretending to be. My quilt was turned down and on the sheet lay the walking-stick I had used after the accident the year we got married. I took it and was about to lay it under the bed when I changed my mind. I stood with it in my hand and stared at the arch of her hip under the thin summer quilt and was suddenly almost overpowered by sexual desire. Then I went quickly out of the room and down to the living-room. I had taken the walking-stick with me and, without really knowing why, I struck it across my thigh and broke it in two. The blow hurt me and I became less agitated. I went into the study and put the light on over the drawing board. I switched it off again and lay down on the couch, pulled a rug over me and closed my eyes. I saw Beate distinctly in my mind's eye. I opened my eyes again but saw her all the same.

I woke up several times during the night and I got up early. I went into the living-room to remove the walking-stick; I didn't want Beate to see that I had broken it. She was sitting on the sofa. She looked at me. Good morning, she said. I nodded. She continued to look at me. Have we fallen out? she said. No, I said. She looked at me with a compelling gaze I couldn't interpret. You misunderstood, I said. I didn't notice that you got up, I was sitting in my own thoughts and when I suddenly felt your hands on my throat, I realise though that you got . . . but I didn't know that you were standing there. She didn't say anything. I looked at her, met the same inscrutable gaze. You have to believe me, I said. She withdrew her gaze. Yes, she said, I do, don't I?

Translated by Agnes Scott Langeland

ROY JACOBSEN

Ice

Since the forest was on the other side of the lake all portage of wood during winter months had to be done over the ice. Even was in the habit of rowing over in the late autumn, cutting and preparing the wood he required and then letting it lie out on the hillside. Once the ice was sufficiently strong he would drive over with the tractor, carry the trunks down onto the snow and bring them back across in his trailer. It was the only forest of any size in the district, and most folk had to rely on the expensive option of electricity or else on coal.

"That's a fine lot of wood you have," they'd say.

"I bring it over on the ice," Even said. "There's enough for that."

He offered them the option of cutting timber in his wood. But they were not comfortable out on the lake in a tractor. It was all very well for him, a man who had lived by the lakeside all his days – he was used to such things; he could read the weather and could tell when the ice would be strong enough and when it would break.

"Come with me in the autumn," Even said. "We can get whatever wood you want and then you can bring it over once the lake has frozen."

The individual concerned hummed and hawed. Wouldn't it be possible for him to buy the cut wood and pay for Even to bring it over the lake?

Of course he could do that, but then the timber wouldn't be free like Even's, and nor would the fellow's house be so warm either. He'd be more careful by half with *bought* wood than with wood he had in abundance that had come free, gratis and for nothing.

"I always come back safe and sound," Even said. "Look, here I am, as large as life."

They looked at Even. He was big and stooping. He had red hair tumbling in curls down his powerful neck. An ordinary man. A farming man like all the rest in these parts. But not completely ordinary either. He had come back safe enough thus far from his expeditions over the ice, but that was no guarantee for what the future might hold. He was playing Russian roulette with his life, was more than a little crazy – though you couldn't tell that from looking at him.

In his father's time too the ice was like solid ground beneath the shoes of those who lived in the farm by the lakeside. It was almost a way of life, literally and metaphorically. But the other farmers wouldn't go out on it then either. When power was being brought to the community for the first time the cables had to be brought over the mountain. The poles had to go to the other side of the lake. The thought was to float them over, but Even's father offered to take them across on the ice – and at much less expense. They looked at his figures and gave it some thought. They couldn't say no.

Even's father met a crowd of startled onlookers as he prepared to be the first ever to go out on the ice with a tractor. It was one of the community's first tractors at that, and worth too much to lose. It weighed 4.3 tons. The creosote poles on the trailer weighed yet more. But the ice held. He drove back and forth in front of the crowd of gaping faces and had the miracle performed in a single day. He made good money, too, so much so that he also became the first of the local farmers to be able to build a silo.

The work of setting up gates and poles and fixing cables was to be done by a firm of entrepreneurs. But the hill itself was a wild and awkward terrain: the work would take time – years possibly – and the labourers had to have somewhere to live.

"I can take a house across on the ice," Even's father said.

"A whole house?" they wondered. "For twenty men?"

"Why not," he said. "You leave the building materials here. In the spring they'll be on the other side."

For that he made even more money. And with this he bought a bulldozer.

"What d'you want that for?" his neighbours asked.

"I'm going to plant a wood," Even's father replied. "On the far side. I'll clear the ground with a bulldozer."

"And how are you going to get that across there?" they wanted to know.

"I'll take it over on the ice," he told them.

And he did take it over on the ice. He cleared the ground and planted trees – pines so high that Even had his work cut out to keep the birches down so they could grow taller still.

*

But all this was long ago and no more than a memory to Even and pictures on his living-room wall. You would think that conditions had changed with the passing of the years – but one and all could read in their army handbooks that ice four centimetres thick would stand the weight of one man, and that ice thirty centimetres thick would bear the weight of a tank, and so on.

"And a Massey Ferguson's no tank," Even said. "Anyway, the ice here'll freeze up to sixty and seventy centimetres."

They just hummed and hawed. They would have no truck with ice.

"You can come with me," Even suggested. The older he grew the stronger the yearning to show these people that the ice would hold, that he and his clan did not consist of halfwits but of intelligent people who knew exactly what they were doing. But they didn't give him the chance. They cut his honour to shreds with their scepticism and their mindless prattle. He told them that everywhere else in the country folk went out on to the ice in the winter.

"Inland, yes," they replied, having always a good answer up their sleeves. "But we're by the coast. The seawater flows into the lake. There's salt. And a river runs into the lake a way in by the mountain – there's current."

And in the meantime a new generation was growing up – young lads who also called Even a mad carrot-top because their fathers had done so before them. But they also realised – when they were old enough – that perhaps Even was *braver* than their fathers, and not off his head. And one day a youngster turned up on Even's farm saying he wanted to go with him to get wood. He was fed up not having enough wood at home when there was more than enough to be had.

"So you've got the guts to do it?" Even laughed.

"Yes, of course," the boy said briskly.

They rowed over with the chainsaws on a still November day and cut the wood they required. They kept at it for just over a week. In the course of the winter they met up again – a bit later than anticipated since it had been mild and wet over Christmas, and thirty centimetres of water had risen over the ice. Then it froze once more. But it snowed again before the middle layer froze a second time. The boy was a bit concerned about this.

"It doesn't matter," Even laughed, and got himself ready.

"So we *can* drive over?" the boy asked.

"Oh, Lord, yes. If we sink through the first layer the next one's more than thick enough to support us."

LIMERICK COUNTY LIBRARY

00471800

They climbed into the tractor and drove down to the edge of the lake. Even swung on to the jetty and carried on out over the ice.

As they left land, it came to the boy that anyone can walk on ice, anyone at all can totter out even on a relatively thin bit of ice – but it's another kettle of fish entirely to drive on to ice in a tractor. They lumbered out on to a level white cloth. The dimensions changed. The vehicle became smaller. It seemed as though they lost speed, as if in the end they had come to a complete standstill in one small, weighty point – bearing downwards towards a drop.

"Why did you do that?" the boy asked when Even pushed open the vent above them.

"You always have that open when you're driving on ice," Even told him.

"Why?" the kid asked.

"No reason in particular," Even said. "You just do. It's written up there."

He nodded in the direction of a small notice on the inside of the tractor. It read "Driving on Ice" and set out various rules on how it should be done.

The boy realised his swallowing wasn't what it should be. His stomach had knotted and his knuckles had gone white. "I don't like this," he muttered.

"I don't like this."

Even kept driving. For ten minutes he drove straight on over a white sheet. There was nothing around them. Just a still winter day. And then they went noisily through the upper ice. The tractor dropped thirty centimetres straight down and water spurted up around the wheels. They didn't move.

Even revved the engine so it gave a roar, and slowly the tractor crept up on to the surface ice again. Twenty metres on they went through the ice again. Now Even began laughing.

"This is where the sun has had most effect," he shouted above the noise, and nodded in the direction of the mountains. "The gap up there means this spot has sun on it all day long."

"Would it be possible to drive around it?" the boy asked.

"It's a big area," Even said. "There's no need." They went through the ice a third time.

"What if the ice underneath doesn't hold?" the boy wanted to know.

"It'll hold," Even told him.

"How can you be so sure?"

Even smiled.

When they went through a fourth time the young lad jumped
down on to the ice and began running alongside the tractor, but
twenty or thirty metres off. Even thought this highly amusing. He
revved the engine and waved his arm through the open vent above
him.

No rescue from anywhere, the boy thought. He'd given his nose a
thump there where they'd brought the wood down. He ran so hard
he could taste the blood in his mouth. All at once he noticed he was
running in curves, that he *had* to run in curves if he was to keep that
gap between himself and the tractor. He turned round and looked at
his tracks in the snow. They resembled some steep descent.

He signalled to Even to stop.

"How d'you explain those?" he shouted, and pointed behind him
at the tracks. Even looked at them. He shouted back that the boy
should sit in the tractor again, now that they'd passed the "sun spot".
Once he was close to the shore he swung north again, in line with the
ridge of the hills.

"Look over there!" he called a couple of minutes later. A bit further
out a grey shadow could be glimpsed under the snow. The shadow
became broader and clearer the further north they went. And finally
it became dark, open water.

"That marks the course of the river," he said.

This was the place where the whooper swans tended to rest up on
their journeys north in the springtime. The boy looked all round.
They were on a shelf of ice a hundred metres across, between a
channel of open water and the steep side of the mountain. He jumped
off and began his running again. Because of the sheerness of the
mountainside he couldn't leave the ice, but had to keep running
beside the tractor. Even laughed.

Once they reached the spit of land there weren't more than twenty
or thirty metres of ice between the shore and the open channel of
water.

"There's no current here by the shore," Even said, once he'd backed
in and parked. "The ice is as thick here as anywhere else."

He went out to the edge and kicked snow into the water, began
jumping up and down.

"See," he said.

The boy saw alright. Then they went up into the forest and stacked
wood. From higher up where they sat and munched their sandwiches
they could look out over the water and the fjord. The tractor tracks
went in a precise arc around the dark javelin-like point – probably

neither too close nor too far out. The boy had begun to feel more like himself as the two of them worked away with the wood. Now what he saw made him feel weird again.

"On the way back I'll sit on the load of wood," he said. "Then I've got something to hang on to if we go through the ice."

"That birch is new wood," Even said. "It won't float."

The kid *ran* back too. Over the ice beside the channel of open water, round the point and past the "sun spot". But after that he couldn't be bothered running any further and had to sit on the trailer after all. He was rigid with cold when they reached the shore and had no wish to go next time round.

"You're nuts," he told Even and went off home.

But he came back the following day. He had lain awake during the night, aware of just how good it was to be alive. He wanted to feel that again. And this time he wasn't going to jump off and run around like an idiot beside the tractor. He'd be like Even – keep his peace and stay seated.

He sat in the tractor cab behind the front seat. But the minute they left the uneven ground by the shore and came out on to the level flatness of the ice that same paralysis went through him. Their speed dropped. They became something small in a great, white space.

"Don't do that!" he shrieked when Even opened the vent above him.

"Why not?" Even asked.

"I can't stand it," the boy said. But that was not what he meant. He couldn't explain what he did mean. It was a riddle. So Even opened the vent just the same. And when they got to the "sun spot" and went through the ice a first time, the boy had to retch. He tried to concentrate on the red curls that circled like snakes down Even's neck and throat, from his peaked cap to the collar of his overalls, and most likely down the rest of his craggy, trunk-like body too. He looked up at the clouds and at the sky through the vent above him. He looked at the shaft of the vehicle going up and down in the water and the slush of ice; the trailer they were towing that hung and dangled like some amphibious landing craft in the green water. He couldn't do it. And when they went through the ice the third time round he had to get out and run again. He climbed in once more when they'd passed the "sun spot", but had to get back off after they'd rounded the point. He couldn't make up his mind whether he should run between the tractor and the open channel of water where the river's current flowed, or between the tractor and the sheer mountainside. In the end he ran so close to the tractor that there was no point in his running at all. He clambered up yet again, but the feeling of dizziness was no less strong – he *had* to get off, he *had* to run.

Even didn't laugh now. He let the boy be, revved the engine and drove on. And when the youth finally caught up with him, pale and shivering, Even was looking at the whooper swans resting in the open water. The boy sat down too.

"I don't know what comes over me," he said. "I just can't do it."

"It doesn't matter," Even told him.

"How long does it take to become as confident as you are?" the youth asked.

Even had no idea. He had driven on the ice for thirty years and more – he was as confident as he was.

"It's so quiet," the boy remarked all of a sudden. "Now that the tractor engine isn't running. It's all that racket I can't stand."

Even made no reply.

They watched the great birds drifting across the open channel of water. They marvelled at how unafraid they were considering their proximity to human beings and one mighty, powered vehicle. These were birds you normally didn't get closer to than two or three hundred metres.

"I've never really seen them before," the boy admitted.

"I see them each winter," Even said. "Here".

They carried down another load of wood. They ate their sandwiches and loaded up the trailer. Even started the engine and began heading south, parallel to the swans. And the boy ran. He ran and cried. Even acted as though he were quite oblivious and picked him up again once past the "sun spot". But it was no use. He had to get off there too and run. And when they reached dry land he wouldn't even have his own wood. He hadn't deserved it, he said.

Even said, "Well, well," and nothing more. But he let the wood lie on the trailer. And when the dark came he drove over to the young fellow's place with it and left it outside his house. The boy lay awake that night too, but gone was that feeling of how good it was to be alive. He had a sense now of how awful it was. And the realisation that it would be more awful still to make another attempt and fail that too.

He didn't appear the following day. There was no sign of him that whole winter. Even had to drive over the ice with the wood himself. And the ice always held.

*

One evening at the end of April something strange happened. Even emerged from the byre after he had finished tending to the animals and noticed a red car out on the ice. It screeched round in a great arc, stopped, picked up speed again, drove straight ahead and then screeched again – first forwards, then backwards. He saw the evening sun shining on the red paintwork; he heard the roar of the engine and the hissing of the tyres on the ice. Then the car abruptly came to a standstill for two or three seconds – before slowly sinking.

Even had to do a few rounds of the farm and pull himself together before he could bring himself to go inside and phone. It was just another Saturday. His thought was that it must have been the young lad and some of his mates who had been out joyriding after a drinking spree. The first calls he made were to the doctor and the police. Then he phoned the boy's parents. But they hadn't the foggiest what Even was talking about; their son had left the place over a month before, and was safe and sound aboard a fishing boat on the North Sea. And by the time the ambulance men and the police turned up, Even was making no sense at all.

"It's my fault," he kept saying, over and over again.

They got hold of ice axes and all the two-inch board that Even could lay his hands on. One by one they went out on the brittle ice, each one of them equipped with a pick and a pole for balance. Even went first. After just a few metres they went through the upper ice. They waded through a slush of ice that reached to their knees. The surface ahead of them was covered with wet, grey splotches and it wasn't possible to differentiate between open water and surface water above the ice. The police simply could not understand how a vehicle would be able to drive out in such conditions. Even was no closer to an answer than they were. He said that perhaps they had driven out further south in the shadow of a small hill – that was something he did himself when he was driving out late on in the year.

They got themselves back on to terra firma, and a group went down to the south end of the lake to search for tyre tracks. None were found.

"It's my fault," Even repeated. "I should never have taken him with me."

The police shook their heads and went their way. A search was made for a red vehicle. All red cars in the district were traced. No word came back of a red car being missing further afield either.

*

On the fourth of May the ice went. Even put his boat on to the water that very afternoon and at his own expense rowed out with two divers to the spot where he had seen the car. The divers were friends of the young man. And although the boy had never told them a thing about what had happened out on the ice in the course of the winter, they were aware that Even had a screw loose.

They swam round down in the dark for something like twenty minutes and found no car.

"We'll try further out," Even said.

"We've already covered the whole area," they told him. But Even refused to give up. So they changed oxygen tanks and went down a second time, spending a further twenty minutes underwater. And this time they made sure they came up a good distance from the boat. They hadn't found any trace of a car this time either.

But even this wasn't good enough for Even. He was redder in the face than he had ever been. He shouted. The divers agreed to use the last oxygen tanks too. And when they resurfaced for the third time, as empty-handed as before, Even was beside himself with rage. He hung over the oars and shook.

"What do you want us to do?" they asked.

A couple of minutes passed, perhaps five. Then Even was all of a sudden himself again. He said there wasn't really much they *could* do. He said he was grateful for what they had done, and for their having managed to put his mind at rest. He settled up with them and let them go on their way.

In the weeks that followed, the farm and its labours occupied his mind. He ploughed a new piece of ground, planted potatoes and did the milking. Summer days returned, the beasts were grazing once more, he cut grass and hay. It was a summer like any other.

That August the young lad came home, and one evening he sought out Even, armed with a bottle of brandy. Even was pleased to see the youngster, and visitors to the farm were few and far between. They drank away, and the young man told him he had experienced storms out on the North Sea on several occasions and hadn't felt afraid. He had encountered many other things too since leaving home – without being aware of fear. And he didn't relish his memories of the ice last winter. He wanted to have one more shot at setting the record straight – that coming winter.

"Fine," Even said happily. He felt that this suggestion alone had almost established a friendship.

But when the swans flew south again Even felt it was a sign of just how long it would be till they could make the crossing, and he dreaded the thought of the drawn-out autumn. It was almost as though rheumatism had seeped into his body and frozen him, as though waiting for this friend whom he was to help become as composed as himself had acted as a break that had brought him to a complete standstill. He had always liked autumn when both the farm and himself were at peace: he could cut wood, do the milking, or else lie inside reading his magazines. Then when he was at a party in town he got to hear that the two divers had tricked him and had never searched properly for the car, and that got mixed up with all his other thoughts and rendered his friendship with the young fellow stranger still. He arranged last year's wood in neat stacks behind the barn, but neither its volume nor the security it provided gave him any joy. He kept thinking of the car and the sunlight that had shone with such clarity on the red paintwork before it sank. Of the divers and the boy. When the fellow did finally come back over Christmas and was there before him in the field as large as life, Even was so bamboozled that to begin with he didn't know what he wanted.

"I've enough wood," he said. Besides, the lake had frozen already, and that would mean breaking with tradition. Tradition dictated that the felling be done in autumn and the loading and driving over in the winter. The youngster looked at the stacks of logs by the barn wall – old, dry wood.

"Can we not do the cutting and driving at the same time?" he asked.

"It's new ice," Even replied. "We'll have to drive over with chains." He had never liked having to use chains.

"That doesn't make any difference," the youngster said.

"No, it doesn't," Even said, his voice clipped, and started to make his way over to the farm.

"What do you mean?" the boy asked.

"Oh, nothing," Even replied. He went into the garage and brought the chains out of a box. The youngster tried to find something humorous to say as they put them on – he hadn't liked Even's tone. As they got closer to the ice he remembered more clearly how things had been the year before. But Even didn't listen to his cheery banter. He hauled chainsaws and other equipment on to the vehicle and climbed up into it. The boy followed suit. They started down the hill and out on to the jetty. Out on to the ice.

The ice was like green glass. Stones and tree trunks stood out clearly underneath them, all magnified, with silt and bubbles of air. The bottom fell quickly away. They were driving across a swaying, black mirror.

Then a deep boom entered the noise of the engine. The echo was thrown back from the hillside. Two echoes. A white stripe hissed towards land from the far side. Another one ate its way northwards towards the water where the river came in, a third went backwards – parallel with the markings the chains had left.

"The ice is setting," Even said.

"Are you sure it'll hold?" the boy asked.

"It'll hold," Even said.

The young man looked at his knuckles. Once again they were white. He wondered if he'd be able to let go if they really did go through the ice.

"Are you not going to open the vent?" he asked.

"I'd forgotten that," Even answered. He opened it and revved the engine.

Translated by Kenneth Steven

JONNY HALBERG

The Cock and Mr Gopher

Villy was standing with his father outside the biggest hotel in town in the cool summer rain. His right arm ached. He had been carrying a bag of oranges from the supermarket. Today was "ten kroner day" and everyone was allowed to buy one bag of oranges each. He and his father had three bags because his father had accosted a young boy and promised him a Mars bar if he would pretend that he was Villy's brother and carry a bag for them. Now Villy and his father were waiting for the bus home to Enevarg.

To pass the time he peered into the hotel restaurant, at the candle-lit tables, the gleaming chandelier and the black piano. At the table closest to the window sat a small, fat man and two teenage boys. They were twins and had side partings; one boy's parting was on the left and the other boy's on the right. Their cheeks were red and they were listening to their father. When he was quiet they were laughing. Villy thought it was odd that they couldn't see him because he was only three or four metres at the most from the window.

They were eating off thick brown dessert plates with lots of small holes in. There was melted butter in the holes. They used something that was neither a fork nor a spoon to pick up the black things from the holes.

"What's that they're eating?" Villy said out loud.

"Don't stare," his father said.

Villy continued to stare. When almost all the holes were empty and they had finished eating, the father said: "They're eating snails."

"No-one eats snails," said Villy.

"*They* do."

In his mind's eye Villy saw the slimy, brown snails in the garden and imagined that he would eat them one day.

"Why don't we eat snails?" he asked.

"Only foreigners do that. In southern Europe they boil up all sorts of things. They're barbarians," the father said.

Villy liked the word "barbarian". He thought that barbarians came

from a land where men grew beards down to their knees and they
were all allowed to belch and fart while eating.

Inside the restaurant the man and the boys raised gleaming round
glasses containing a dark red liquid. They clinked glasses with each
other. The liquid shone. Villy could see the ceiling lamps reflected in
it.

"My God," the father said. "Drinking wine on a Tuesday. They're
not old enough yet, either."

At that moment the waiter pushed in a trolley. The waiter set light
to a piece of meat in a pan, and the boys and the man clapped.

"He's burning their food. But they clapped," Villy said.

"Don't stare," the father said, giving his son a clip round the ear.
"We burn it in butter; they set fire to it."

Villy went closer to the window. On the large plates, next to the
meat and the potatoes wrapped in silver paper, there was a vegetable
that looked like a big bunch of parsley. They poured a yellow sauce
over the meat. Villy had never seen a yellow sauce before.

"They're eating a disgusting sauce. And fat parsley," Villy said.

"They're called yellow sauce and broccoli," the father said.

Villy thought broccoli sounded exciting. Broccoli, broccoli,
broccoli. From the land of the barbarians. He could feel his mouth
watering. The saliva in his mouth tasted of nothing, except for saliva.
He smacked his lips and as he chewed it was like sinking your teeth
into a cloud.

The fat man acknowledged their presence outside and directed a
smile over Villy's head to his father.

"Got cement in your ears, have you?" the father said, cuffing him
harder. "Decent folk eat at the cafeteria on Saturdays. They eat
normal food."

A tall, lean man had joined them at the bus stop. He was old and
had bags under his eyes. Around his neck hung thin folds of skin
which made Villy think of a turkey.

"Yes, they do. Normal food," the man said.

"Uh?" the father said.

"You listen to your father," the man said to Villy.

"He's a bit of a handful," the father said, patting Villy on the head.

"My name's Gunther Gopher," the man said.

They shook hands. Villy liked the man's name. He decided to call
him Mr Gopher.

"Some folk don't know how to set boundaries," the father said.

"Absolutely correct," Mr Gopher said. "Some people want to push the limits, like those people in there. And some want to go even further."

"Yes, they're barbarians, the whole lot of them," the father said. "They want to try everything, but sooner or later it's down the slippery slope with them."

"You listen to your father. He knows what he's talking about," Mr Gopher said to Villy.

"He knew they were eating yellow sauce," Villy said.

"Well, well, yellow sauce," Mr Gopher said. "Let's suppose . . . Let's suppose that people like to try everything."

"Yes, let's suppose that," the father said. "You listen carefully now," he said to Villy.

"Let's suppose that when you're young you discover food you've never tasted before. Entrecôte with béarnaise sauce, for example."

"Go on," the father said.

"You discover that first and then later on other foods: lobster, turbot, pheasant. You become hooked on food. You decide to taste the best that culinary expertise has to offer. That's exactly it, taste. You want to become a gourmet."

"You want to become a barbarian," Villy said.

"What a smart little sprog," said Mr Gopher.

"Don't take any notice of Villy," the father said.

Mr Gopher went on: "You save up your money to travel, to experience food in its appropriate setting, in its natural habitat. You fly to Tromsø and sink your fork into dried codfish in a sauce, a fish which has been swimming in the North Sea. Outside the restaurant the polar night is at its blackest. But the cod is swimming in the rays of sunlight from the melted bacon fat."

"Oh, my goodness," the father said.

"In Japan you are served sushi, raw fish with crisp, red flesh and on small side plates they have fresh vegetables and hot, spicy sauces. You sit in a kneeling position and eat slowly with chopsticks."

"Raw fish?" the father said.

Villy decided he would eat fish au gratin, kneeling, next time they had it. He would ask his mother for raw fish.

"You order bouillabaisse in a little inn in Brittany. It is cooked according to a secret recipe, with vegetables, fish and shellfish fresh off the boats in the harbour. The soup is deep, darkly golden like the sea itself, and it slips down your throat like silk."

The father had gone quiet. He swallowed several times. His pointed Adam's apple bobbed up and down.

"You've come a fair way. You've become older, particular, you want more than mere food. Now the world of experience is no longer confined to taste but includes places and people. The sub-equatorial sky on a calm night or in a side street in Paris. But still you allow yourself to be impressed. In Argentina you can get pampas steaks from a local minor aristocrat who owns an area of land the size of the whole of the Akershus region. The kitchen could accommodate an entire local council. The meat from the gaucho's kitchen tastes like the pampas itself, like grass, earth, sweaty saddles and boundless plains."

Villy's stomach rumbled.

"I'm hungry," he said.

The father did not answer.

"But one day you have tried all that the culinary arts have to offer," Mr Gopher said. "What do you do then?"

"Down the slippery slope?" the father says.

"Exactly. You get up from the table and gravitate towards women. But soon you are being led by women, too. You have to turn your attention to men."

"Turn to men?" the father exclaimed.

"Have we ever eaten men?" Villy asked.

"Men too, and before long anything that can be devoured, because pleasure has become the only governing principle. After men you look for pleasure in wine, spirits, hash or cocaine."

"Put your hands over your ears," the father said to Villy. Villy cupped his hands over his ears so that he could hear Mr Gopher better. The old man's face had gone red. He pulled out a handkerchief and wiped his forehead and neck.

"You're finished, done for, sitting in the gloomy semi-darkness, a long way from trees and houses and an everyday life that is worth living. If you don't . . ."

"If you don't what!" Villy said.

"Hands over your ears!" the father said.

"If you don't take a mammoth stride forward and make a decision to become a normal human being again."

"Boring ending," Villy said.

He received a stinging slap.

"You should eat normal food," Mr Gopher said.

"Rissoles, creamed peas, sausages and mashed potatoes. Fish cakes. Soggy carrots."

"Normal food," the father said.

They stood there for a long time without saying a word.

"You've been drinking," the father said.

"It was just a supposition," Mr Gopher said.

"The man has been drinking. He's a sick man," the father said, dragging Villy away from the bus stop.

They stopped at the next bus stop, outside a kiosk.

"Promise me one thing," the father said. "Forget everything the man said. I'm off to buy some chocolate and a fizzy drink now."

While his father was talking to the woman in the shop Villy realised that they had left the bags of oranges behind. What Mr Gopher said had depressed his father and to cheer him up Villy ran over to collect the bags.

Mr Gopher was still standing in the rain. He was drenched; his grey coat had long black stripes down the back. Villy waved to him, and the old man waved back.

"I forgot the oranges," Villy said.

Mr Gopher bent down over the boy.

"Do you want to become a barbarian?" he asked.

"Yes."

Mr Gopher bent closer. His mouth smelt of something sour.

The smell was like the odour of the damp forest floor in autumn before the cold and the snow came.

"This must remain between you and me. Here's three hundred kroner. Save it until you are in town on your own."

"Have I got to eat something?"

"Eat at a restaurant. You sit at a table and ask for the dish of the day. You pay the money after you've finished eating. But don't tell your father or your mother that you have this money."

Villy took the notes. He imagined large piles of snails and steak and a dark broth, all mixed together to make a mountain of food. On the top he would pour a yellow sauce, the revolting yellow sauce. Then a waiter would empty petrol over the mountain and set light to it.

And he would be kneeling and would emit long belches.

"Stand up," a voice said.

It was the father.

"What did you say to my son?" he said.

"You'll have to ask him that," Mr Gopher answered.

"What did he say?" the father asked.

Villy gave it some thought.

"Mr Gopher said that he had tasted something no-one else had tasted."

"And what is that?"

"He's tasted an Egyptian mummy," Villy said. It was the first thing that came into his head.

"A mummy?" the father said. "That can't be true. You're lying. You're a fraud."

"No, I'm an archaeologist. I trained in Munich," Mr Gopher said.

Villy waited for a telling-off from his father. It never came. He didn't punch Mr Gopher on the chin, either. The father crumpled, his shoulders slumped down. His mouth was slightly agape, like the mouth of a dead fish. He clenched his fists and stared at Mr Gopher's legs. The old man's hand-sewn shoes were shabby and cracked; there was a tear in one shoe between the leather upper and the sole. Then the father stared at his own black shoes that he had worn for years. They were nicely polished.

As he pushed Villy in front of him across the road, it stopped raining and down in the park a few shafts of sunlight poked through the clouds. Villy had the sour smell of grass and leaves in his nostrils. He breathed it in and shook his father's hand off his shoulder. He ran out on to the grassland and crowed like a small cock.

Translated by Don Bartlett

JON FOSSE

I Could Not Tell You

There are things in life you never put behind you, at least it's true of my life, the life of a now-ageing man, there are things I have seen in life that I will always see, glimpses of things that have happened, illuminated glimpses, as I like to call them, illuminated glimpses that have taken root in me, that may have become so deep-rooted because they are filled with a meaning I don't understand, a meaning that perhaps is not even a meaning, perhaps the illuminated glimpses are without meaning, at least they are for everyone else. And now that I'm going to die before long, the glimpses are going to die with me, the glimpses will be gone, but maybe it won't matter all that much, because the glimpses have already disappeared, it's such a long time ago that these glimpses of something that happened existed in time, in space, at a point where time and space met, it is much too long since these glimpses existed, these glimpses are already long gone, the glimpses are already long gone. The way you too are long gone. The way you, who have taken root in me so strongly, through a few illuminated glimpses, where I see you, where I see you do something, are long gone too. Everything is gone. You are gone. The time when it happened is gone. And before too long I will be gone too. That's how it is. But I see you for the first time, I see you walk across the school yard and since then I've always been able to see you walk in that way across the school yard, there was something in your movements, in the way you walked, something in the way you leaned lightly forward, towards a pride, but at the same time it was as if you were ashamed and wanted to hide, I saw you walk across the school yard, with something in your movements, with your black hair, with a jacket that hung quite big around you. When I saw you walk across the school yard something happened to me. I don't know what it was, I don't know what it is. Well, it's utterly without meaning, it doesn't matter one bit, but exactly those sorts of illuminated glimpses, of what was in your movements then, when you walked across the school yard, at exactly that school, exactly that year, exactly that morning, your first day at a new school, in the middle of autumn sometime, exactly what was in your movements there and then took root in me so deeply, not just in my memory, but also in my own way of moving. I saw you walk across the school yard, an early autumn morning and I was changed by something in your movements that morning, when you walked across the school yard, in the half-dark. Well, you have to laugh. You just have to laugh. It means nothing, but at the same time I'm getting closer to the end of what I'm going to see, and that is you, walking across the school yard an early autumn morning, that's what I see most clearly in my mind's eye, that's what is most filled with meaning to me, that, together with another illuminated glimpse where you sit in a canteen at school, with a few others, but you're still not with the others, you sit with the others and you sit on your own, alone, you sit alone with the others, you sit there with your black hair, you sit at the end of the table, where you usually sit down, how often I saw you sitting there, but it's this one time I remember seeing you sitting there, and there's something in your eyes, something in the way you look up, there's something in the look of your eyes, something I can never understand, it was something there, in your eyes, that took root in me so strongly, I cannot understand what it was, or is, but you sat there, you sat there and looked up, you just sat there, looked up, and everything I say about that look sounds wrong, it's not possible to describe what that look was like, there was far too much in your look, that late morning, in a canteen at school, where you sat at the end of a table, sat alone, with the others, there was something incomprehensible in your look, for a moment, just there, just then. I cannot forget what I saw in your look then. It has taken root in me. It's in everything I have been. I don't understand why I never can forget what I saw then in your look. I carry it within me, deep inside me, it has become a part of my own look, because when I see, I too see with what I saw then in your look. It's the kind of thing it's not possible to understand, it's the kind of thing that actually says nothing, that has no meaning, but now, when my life is coming to an end, because it is, what I saw then in your look is among the most lucid things I've seen in my life. It sounds wrong, it sounds ludicrous, because of all the people I have loved, of everything I have seen, everything that has happened, there's something in your movements, something in the way your body moves, an early morning, in the middle of autumn, when you arrived as a new student at my school, that is the most lucid thing I have seen. It's terrible, in a way it's impossible. It's also impossible that something in your look, a late morning, in a canteen at school, where you sat at the end of a table, alone with the others, where you sat with those eyes of yours and then looked up, it's impossible that what I saw in your look then should be among the most meaningful things, utterly without meaning as it actually is, that I have seen in my life. I'm sure that if you'd known, you would've become embarrassed and then you would never have spoken to me again, it would've been too awkward, too difficult, because what might I not observe in your most mundane movements, in your most mundane looks, how would you feel then in my presence, like something hardened, like something that had to disappear, I'm sure that's how you would have felt if I told you what something in the way your body moved, that morning, your first morning at my school, an autumn morning, in a cold half-light, with a little light rain, with a little light wind, came to mean to me. You wouldn't have been able to understand, you wouldn't have been able to live with me. And if I told you what something in your look, that late morning, in a canteen at school, when you sat alone with the others, when you looked up, meant to me, you wouldn't have been able freely to gaze upon the years we lived together. I'm certain of that. That's why I didn't tell you. Or maybe I only make myself believe that it would have restrained you. Maybe I might just as well have told you. I held your hand when you died and I never told you, not then either. I heard your breath slow down, heard your breath come to a close, heard your breath cease, disappear for a long time, then saw life in your eyes, saw your breath return, then disappear again, then your breath was gone and then, just then, I saw what was in your look move through the room, together with what was in your movements, I saw what was in your look and in your movements change, in one illuminated glimpse, to something that became indistinct and then disappeared. I saw your look become empty. I saw your eyes for the last time. I closed your eyelids. And I heard your voice, a voice I've heard many times, I heard your voice the way I for ever, for as long as I live, before I too disappear and your voice, just there, just then, shall disappear too, with me, I heard your voice, it was an afternoon, it was some meeting or other in the assembly hall at the school we attended, someone asked you something, you stood up, you said something, you sat down again, I don't remember what the meeting was about, I don't remember what you said, but there was something in your voice, in the way your voice and your body belonged together when you stood up, there was something in your voice, something I've heard inside me always since, I don't know what you said, I don't remember it, it's without meaning, this, it doesn't matter one bit, but something in your voice, there, that afternoon, in the assembly hall, at the school we attended, something in your voice, when you stood up, with your black hair, something in the voice, something in your voice, I've always since heard inside me. I've never told you. I cannot tell you things like that. I cannot tell you that everything you've said since has not held such meaning as something in your voice exactly that afternoon, in the assembly hall, at the school we attended, where you said something or other that I cannot remember. I saw you walk across the school yard an early autumn morning, in a cold half-light, saw something in the way you moved, that I've always remembered. And I saw you sitting at the end of a table, in a canteen at school, you looked up and I saw something in your look that I've always remembered. And I saw you standing up, one afternoon, in the assembly hall, at the school we attended, and I heard something in your voice that has never left me. Now you are gone. When you died there was something in your movements, in your look, in your voice, that went through me and filled the room and spread itself across the darkening sky outside the window of the hospital room where we were. I don't know what it was, I don't know what it is. I would not have told you this if you'd been alive, that would've made everything more difficult for you, because all I wanted was your body to move exactly the way it did, when you woke up, tired and shitty, when you were angry, when you were happy, when you exploded in anger and called me a shit, I wanted your body to be exactly the way it wanted to be, I didn't want to tell you, tell you that I walked around with an illuminated glimpse, as I like to call it, inside me, walked around with what moved in your body, or moved your body, when you walked across the school yard, that morning, inside me. I didn't want to tell you anything about what I saw in your look. You had to see exactly the way you wanted to see, without worrying about me walking around with your look inside me, walking around with your look in my look. I could not tell you that. And I could not tell you how something in your voice had taken root deep inside me, then your voice would never become properly angry, in a sense, the way it could now, all the times you gave me a piece of your mind, all day, all the days, said that I was a shit, and fuck it all. You must be allowed to keep your voice to yourself. I never told you that something in your voice was deep inside me. Now you are dead. Now you no longer exist. Now your movements no longer exist, your look, your voice. They exist in me, for now. And I am not afraid to die.

Translated by May-Britt Akerholdt

LARS AMUND VAAGE

Cows

Cows. I will sing of cows. Surely they deserve a song. For I have felt their warm presence. They have given me everything. This then is a song of cows. Peaceful cows. Birds hop around their legs. They find food in the eternal buzz of insects and small flying things. Wagtail, sparrow and thrush, these know the meaning of justice. I will mention Frøya. She who had to endure the most. Thus she was the wisest of them all. In her best year she produced three thousand litres. They named her after the goddess of love. Except for the pain, what did she know about love? Humble she was not. She carried her chains with pride. She never reached for her feed, but waited until it was given to her. She was a queen. Such a splendid cow. She was large and well-proportioned. She had dark circles round her eyes, and her eyes were as black as the night. She lashed out with her heels if the machine was left on her too long. She did not yield her milk to just anyone. Humble she was not, ever. She of blessed memory. She always got the most concentrates. I would try to wash her teats. She slapped my face with her tail. No, she wouldn't have any truck with me. They chose her as their leader. She led them to where the grass was greenest. No-one tried to hurry her. She found the paths they must take, from the pasture and back inside again. They followed her without question. Udders and teats dingle-dangling. The long row of hooves so ladylike. And the unfathomable patience with which they strode along. A thousand days at a stretch. Until one day the cup was full. Madness struck. Oh, listen to my song. That quiet wistfulness with which they left the barn. That sniffing along the wayside although they knew each and every plant. The dandelion leaves they snatched out of an old habit. But they passed over the docks. They knew the law and the prophets. Then on to the pasture with the gate shut behind them before the dew lifted. And we went home for breakfast. And the long tongues curled around succulent grass, pressed up into toothless, rough gums and tore, and ground with their molars, and swallowed. And they lay down. And they dozed and chewed. And

swarms of fat flies, a murmuring pest they never escaped. And they
fluttered their ears. And they slapped their heavy heads over their
backs. And licked themselves a little. And flapped their tails. And ticks
came, and stuck to them, and sucked their blood, and went on
sucking. And so they got up, one after the other, and the whole herd
went somewhere else. And they grazed. And worms crawled into
their lungs, and the cough never ceased. And the evening that never
came. And milking time. And Frøya knew her place. She was always
the first through the barn door. The burst udders and the stiff hind
legs wide apart. And the white stripes of milk dripping across the
floor. Then a young cow, a first freshener. Took a wrong turn and ran
twice around the barn. Worked herself into a panic, and plopped shit
in surprise, for she had lost her sense of where the others were. Yes,
they were stupid, stupid cows. Blessed are the poor in spirit for theirs
is the kingdom of heaven. Old Frøya, she came in. Homing straight
to the stall. Waiting there for her turn. She stood calmly when we tied
her. I was nursed on her white, white milk. I owe my teeth to her and
my good health. Running with my cup I begged for a drop of her
strained milk. Frothy lukewarm milk. How sweet it was, how thick
with cream. I will sing of milk. For what was Norway without milk?
What was Norway without the milking stools? One long leg in the
ditch, the short leg in the stall. The stool was level. Yes, the milking
stool is a marvel. And the wives wore kerchiefs, for they certainly did
not wash their hair every day. And their bony hands are stroking the
udders. And closing around the teats, and pulling. Oh, dear God.
There was a flushing of milk into pails, the rhythm of it. So hard at
first, soft and full as the milk rose. And suddenly men were in the
barn, the milking machines had arrived. There was my father, the
thick, round stream when he emptied the milking machine pail into
the fifty-litre churn. Slowly, for it must not overflow the strainer. And
down into the holding pen with it, so it would keep, and two stones
on the lid. Evening came. Milk. Milk in all churns. Milk poured into
large bowls and carried into the pantry, with both hands, the bowl in
front of them, with care, to let the cream rise. They skimmed it off
with a silver spoon. In the barn the cows were left with empty udders.
What did they get as payment? No other reward than the grass silage?
They got our thanks. A sort of useless gratitude. Life was labour. The
scars legion. They waited in their stalls, for anyone who would come.
Come to them into that warm presence. And place an arm around a
lowered neck. And lay a head down close to their bodies. Was this a
kind of thanks? They did get some thanks. With a curry comb and a

stiff brush they got thanks. They made time for that, the farmers, and
their children made time. And believe me when I say that the cows
understood. They flipped their tails to one side. They laid one ear
backwards stretching their heads forwards. They turned and gazed
with dim eyes. You bet it itches, all that manure. They stand in the
barn with empty udders. Sleepy. They get sleepy. They stand there the
whole time until spring, with the chains around their necks. Stamp
and stomp in the same spot. Morning and evening it is shovelled
under them, and they get dry sawdust to lie on. The winters are so
long. They will have their song. The cow has a long tail. The cow has
four stomachs. The cow eats grass. The cow eats bread. If she gets the
chance. But she never does get the chance. The cow can eat paper and
turn it into food for people. At a pinch, that is. The cow lived off
leaves when times were hard. They have gathered seaweed and given
it to her. And herring offal. The cow ate it. She has eaten everything
she has been given. For a thousand years she has chewed the cud for
us. If indeed there was any cud to chew. After lean winters she has
staggered out into the spring sunshine. Scarce able to walk. She did it
for us. She has endured her countless births. She has borne both her
sorrow and her grief. She has borne all of this. Dingle, dangle. Days
went by. I helped in the barn. I shovelled and scattered sawdust. I
watered the calves. I gave the cows their grain. It made the milk settle
better. Seven tins for Frøya. Because she carried the heaviest burden.
Plomrei only got one. Half a tin to the heifers. We came into the barn.
Unlatched the door and turned on the light. There was Frøya. She lay
on her side with her legs stretched out. The patience with which she
lay there. Bloat. Rolling her eyes. They seemed larger. Red eyes. Her
mouth was open. She lifted her big belly at a slant. She kicked her feet
slowly. How fat she had become! It made me laugh. I ran after the cat.
She didn't get up. She was large as a whale. She breathed heavily. She
moaned with her deep, deep voice. She didn't stand up. The deep
voice of Frøya. I stood there. I thought, this was not something to
laugh at. What could I, a small boy do? My father said, that damn
grain. That damned, damned grain. He rushed backwards and
forwards. He couldn't find his barn jacket. I wanted to give them their
grain. He shouted that they shouldn't have any. Well, give it to the
others then, but not to Frøya. He hurried out of the door wearing his
barn jacket, and the door went on swinging behind him. The grain
had frozen in the barrel. He came back with Einar at his heels. Bloat.
They had to make her stand up. She kicked her feet slowly. Make her
stand up, for God's sake. Einar said, do you have any liquor? Liquor?

My father had brandy. Tell your mother that you need that bottle of brandy. She stared wide-eyed. My mother with the liquor bottle in her hand, wonderful to behold. There Frøya had gotten to her feet. Her legs wide apart. Her belly swelled up under her spine. Einar pulled a knife with a red handle out of its sheath, with a snap. He stared at the knife. He breathed heavily. The knife trembled in his hand. He poured liquor over it. They were costly drops. My father held the tail. My father kept swallowing. Einar was calm. He spoke softly, a hand's breadth forward on the bone here and a hand's breadth down. He stuck the knife in, quickly, plunged it in halfway down the blade; Frøya, her knees buckled, but she stood up again. He didn't pull the knife out. But held it there. He jiggled it. A careful whistling, farting sound. Then he closed his eyes hard, and twisted the knife. And she bellowed like an ox, a long, half-choked bellow. Give me the liquor! Air gushing out of the hole, a terrible smell. He poured over more liquor, and pulled the knife out. Then he put the bottle to his lips and drank. My father was laughing a lot. We had a Dairy Farmers' Association party. It was in nineteen-sixty. The tables were set for coffee and dry cakes. No cows came. Although it was their party. It all revolved around them, the seasons, the work, all the building work, the milk payments. Yet their spirits moved upon and moved among the rows of tables. The spirit was everywhere. That faint smell of cow. God help me, the strength of that smell. No, the faint smell of cow. Wherever two or three are gathered together. They tried to get rid of it with soap. Or shaving cream. Or drops of perfume, rarer than manna from heaven. But it persisted, the faint smell of cow, penetrating everything. It was shameful. And the smell of coffee could not wipe out the shame. The district agronomist came to give a speech. He had a car. He said that now the best cows produce three thousand litres. Three thousand litres, he repeated, leaving his words to sink in. That had to be enough. Yes, by God, it had to be enough. Poor, dumb creatures. The milk was four per cent fat. And that, by God, should have been enough. But for progress what is enough? And what is enough when instalments are due and loans have to be met? No-one consults the cow. No cup is full until it flows over. Now it is ten thousand a year. The records reported in the paper. What do they get out of it? Now the N.R.C. are in vogue, the Norwegian Red Cattle. The ones with horns and white spots. I am singing about the innocent N.R.C. I will mention the fleshy, the heavy ones, too big for the old stalls. And those that feed on concentrates. And the electric hoists and the silage grab and the installing of the milk pipeline. And the cooling tanks. I greet these unhappy ones who will never see daylight again, who will stand all year round in their stalls, under the white fluorescent light. One day they go outside again. That is when they have given enough. When they are free of milk fever, and when the final dose of calcium solvent has been injected into their blood. When the knots in the udders have disappeared, and the milk is again without lumps, and when they have received the last shots of penicillin, one in each teat, and the udders are no longer ravaged by infection. They will die now. Profiting from the feed, they have arrived at the right weight for slaughter. Morning and evening on summer days they eat green, fresh-cut grass. Their faces are long and sad. One day, sensing something behind them, they turn around; it is not a bull, it is a man in a white coat. Oh, sluggish, friendly mountains of meat. They are not aroused. Neither know they lust, for even lust has been taken from them, it is just as well for their peace. It is difficult to get them with calf, for they have given the farmer no sign. That is the difficulty, that is the difficulty, the difficulty with the N.R.C. I grew up with the randy redpoll cows. I could never forget them. They rode each other in the pasture. And any child could say, that now that one was ready for the bull. What a stir inside the pasture! The one who stood still, she wanted it, she wanted it! And it was around her we made a circle. And brought her in. No white coat entered our barn. It was all so easy. There was no shame. She stood still, that was all. It was her due. She raised her tail, she burned like fire, she swelled up. And by God she knew what was missing. That Frøya, she went right through the fence. She ignored the electricity. She went through the fence and ended up in Torpe, miles away, where the Association kept its bull. And the farmers laughed. They loved it! The old women, they came down the road. And old withered men came, a short rope in their hand, a cow on the other end! And young farmers walked the same way. And they hummed and sang. This was their means of life; the cow, perhaps, would calve in autumn! They came willingly enough. A gentle-mannered harem. And my father actually thought it important to take us young boys along. My father, a cow and all of us young boys. This was the crew that came to Torpe. Seven times a year. A filthy cow on pure snow. A wet and shabby cow in the rain. A glossy, gleaming cow in the sun. Away to Torpe they went! There the bull was quite a sight! Have you seen a full-grown bull? There aren't many of them now. It is the sex. The thick neck and swelling breast. The short legs that he toddles around on, and his hind end, which is nothing at all! This bull was named Trym. He had a ring in his nose. He walked slowly, turning back and forth. His whole body was covered in muck. He was not very bright. But he knew his work. We small boys crept into the bushes. And the cow stood still. She stood as if frozen. She stood as if she had lead in her hooves and would not budge. And the bull approached. He bellowed and licked and pawed the ground. Made a grimace with his nose. It didn't taste good. It wasn't supposed to taste good. It should be bitter. It didn't take him long. He slipped down and let his thickset head stroke the cow's back and belly, not without tenderness. And he stood still considering things. Should he? More? And he came again. And the farmers whistled at him, for they too knew what they had to do. They hadn't learnt this trembling monotonous whistling in Sunday School. For she had to have another round. And he came again and she stood there, she stood there. They led him away. He walked with stiff legs. And the ring pulled his nose out to a point, and he went along. I will sing of the redpoll cows. These that are gone. The beautiful heads without horns, gone. The colours, dark brown, rust brown, almost golden, gone now. They no longer trip light-footed along the gravel road. They don't run madly after dogs and cats. Because they are gone. And never again will they leap over fences. They have traded for the last time patience for a sudden madness and freedom. I remember the quickness in them, when they took off with their tails in the air. Panting hard they looked at each other, wondering what devilry they could devise. They ran to the apple orchard, and broke branches off the trees, and ate. They rummaged the potatoes. They tore up the strawberry plants, roots and all, and shat in the carrot bed. Oh, redpoll cows, you who built the nation. Who will write your history? Redpoll cows, I still see you, the reassuring red against the deep green of western Norway. Now you are only a gene in the confused, kind body of the N.R.C. cows. I salute you. I went to the calves when time passed slowly and sorrows came. And the road became hard to travel. I stretched my hand out. And you restored my peace. I wanted to pat you, but you just wanted to suck. Optimistic, strange calves. Many times I just had to laugh. Although it could hurt if they got too excited. Then I pulled my hand back, and wiped off the sticky spit with hay. Now I sing of calves waving their tails. Of their gangly movements, and of the strange attacks of joy. The slender bodies, the round skulls, the long legs, and the balance that was so difficult to maintain. And the head, so perfectly pointed towards the muzzle, and the dangling, flapping ears. And the mouths that never smiled. But they smiled with their bodies. And the gentle eyes, and long lashes, that they blinked with. I went to the calves. I lay down in the long feeding alley, and fell asleep there, on remnants of hay that was become too old. And they licked me. My cap fell off, and my hair they licked so it stood on end, and stiffly, and a cold tongue awakened me, like sandpaper against my cheek. The calves are always the same. Just as children are still children. It is life that has changed. Now you no longer see an old cow. Ten years was no age for a redpoll cow. They were allowed to live for ten years. You could see them dragging themselves along the road. The old girls, trailing their teats. And so full of days. And sometimes they would step on their teats. And their bellies sagged, and they became sway-backed, and their joints got bigger. The old cows, they walked toward the evening sun. Every step so heavy. Every movement was painful. But the sight of them filled me with joy. The thoughtful smile that came to my lips sometimes, when they passed. And did not look to the right. Nor to the left. Yes, it's true. They disappeared, and were turned into sausages. Before they had a chance to die. But they were allowed to grow old. Even if they gave less milk. They got some respect. Now they rarely get to be more than five before the truck comes. Who can feed old creatures nowadays? And they go out. And the driver knows how to take them. And if they don't want to go out, he twists their tails. Then they go, they go. And he pulls the back panel shut. And it is dark inside. And there are other cows headed the same way. And it is hard for them to stand when the driver turns out of the courtyard. And the male choir sang. And it smelled of cow. And when the last one, Johannes, came through the door, the others had already lined up. His hair was in his eyes and he was flushed and flurried. Then it smelled of cow like fuck and grass silage. Then they sang "Mother Sings" and "Singer's Waltz" and "Lord of Spirits". It was not tuneful. But it was the male choir, and they endured. When they came on, the room was almost empty. The marching band, on the other hand, did not smell of cow. They had uniforms, and I suppose they didn't wear them to the barn. And when they were out practising their marching in spring, all the children came madly running, for they thought it was the Seventeenth of May. Finally the actual, peculiar Seventeenth of May arrived. And the cows took part. There were cow-pats everywhere. Cows behind the fence along the road. They played their part. And was it the marching band then, that blew such life into them? Or was it the bawling and the parade that drew them? For they couldn't resist it, they ran alongside. Or perhaps they had a will of their own, and rushed around to celebrate the day. I mean, what else could they do, if they wanted to celebrate? And we all waited for the parade to start, and the weather was good and appropriate for the occasion. And he who played the marching band's euphonium, Leidulf, stood with the instrument around his head, like a shiny glistening snake about to strangle him, it ended up in a harmless bell, and, what the hell, it did not look dangerous. I had a balloon I kept throwing into the air, insofar as it's possible to throw a balloon; suddenly it slipped and drifted down into Leidulf's euphonium, and settled there. Oh, Leidulf's euphonium was awe-inspiring after all, with its valves and curves and tubes. It didn't seem as if he was going to play. They stood waiting. Then I strode over to him, and said that it looked as if he had my balloon in his euphonium, and he stood there leaning against someone. He gave me this smile, while he bowed gallantly forward, with the whole of his upper body, so the balloon rolled out. He said, my name is Leidulf, what's yours? Then I noticed the smell of cow. I stood there balloon in hand and that smell found its way into my nose, where it was immediately recognised, and I felt happy, on account of the day and the support around me. I managed to untie the knot, the air rushed out of my balloon, and it whirred away. The drowsy drunken shout of the day, it seemed to be coming from far away. Flags were being waved, and lures with paper tassels. The slow persistent waving of the Seventeenth of May. I found my balloon between two legs, and a drum, yes, it was dangerous terrain. I blew it up, wanting to see how big it could get. I blew until it burst. Explosion. At the same moment fear seized me, I felt a fine shower of spit across my face. When I came to, bits of rubber lay on the road. Suddenly girls gathered around me, girls who wanted to blow bubbles with the rubber, and I felt hot and I turned away. Empty handed. They didn't seem to mind the spit. The headmaster stood in the front with his tasselled cap, he held his hand high and his mouth was open. Start the beat, they told the drummer. Start the beat. I kept close to Leidulf. Now I no longer had a balloon. He smelled of something else too, something sweet and a bit sickly. And his lips had a dull lustre, and his hair looked as if it had taken colour from leaning against a cow's belly. That's what he used to do, of course. And his fingers seemed to be frozen stiff. But the sun shone and the leaves were out on the birches. A heifer kept howling, but no-one answered her. Start the beat, start the beat, everyone said. I saw that Leidulf had dropped his sheet music; I was quick and picked it up, for he smelled of cow and I knew his kind. He bent down too, and the euphonium fell over his neck. But then I had to leave, for I could not resist that sound of cymbals and drums, and neither could the cows. And the parade got going, in a pure chaos of piping and tooting, for the euphonium wasn't playing. And Leidulf was gone. On to the common. And on to the green. And the bells jingling in the outlying fields. And the tussocks we sat down on. And a freezer outdoors, where ice cream was sold. And the male choir up front on the platform. And "God Bless the Land of Norway". They faded away under the clear, blue sky. And we started noticing the chill from the ground. And without his white coat the dentist stepped forward, to make a speech. We speak of the old days so often. But what *are* the old days, he wanted to know. Two crazy heifers stood behind him on the platform. And one of them was Plomrei. And they were clean and shiny, for they had been out to pasture for two or three weeks already. The heifers. They were free and unworried. They started eating the birch leaves on the decorations. And it is the veritable truth that those cows had a sense of humour. One seized the first Norwegian flag, the other flag was left in peace. She shook it so the flagpole beat a stirring rhythm, across the platform. And some girls got up and started to dance, even though they were in their national costumes. They danced and twirled and looked down so coyly, humming and singing "Love me tender, love me blue". Or something like it. And suddenly the dentist's words without his white coat carried no weight. And Plomrei. Now she stopped and looked around. But she still had the flag which hung from her mouth. Leidulf, Leidulf, people cried, for it was his heifers who were the ones that were always going astray. But up the road Leidulf was still looking for his music book. It was my grandmother who saved the day. Perhaps also my mother a little. And where was I? I stood under the speaker's desk, way up in front. And the dentist turned around. Shoo, he said. And my mother and grandmother were in the organising committee. Shoo, they said, and made the movements they were so skilled at with their hands, but it all seemed strange in these costumes. And Plomrei, Plomrei and the other one, they came down off the platform. In passing they grabbed some grass that grew in such abundance and disappeared between the buckthorn bushes. And where the Hardanger embroidery was stitched so neatly on grandmother's apron, there was a smudge of manure. And that was all. And my mother said, with her hand grabbing mine, that she would run to the village hall, and fetch toilet paper. Oh no, said my grandmother, can't you see, the heifer is already over the hill. So just simmer down, my dear girl. And my

grandmother's smile, she was always smiling. Cow-dung never hurt
anyone. Bitter, jealous Plomrei. It was the Seventeenth of May and
she was still young. She rushed over the barren fields and down the
slopes, with the other heifer. And the speech went on. And their tails
were in the air. And they kicked up their rumps. She was a crackling,
blazing red. No spots on her coat. Our Lord had made her out of fire.
Her slender, strong body, her insolence, and all her tricks. What
became of it all in the end? She was an enigma. She came to us that
summer between harvests. An odd time to sell cows, if you ask me.
She arrived on the end of a rope, led by Leidulf. I didn't know her
name then, but it was Plomrei. It was Plomrei, the one that had seized
the flag so disrespectfully, and as it turned out she was the one who
came to us. They came along the road, and she started to run, and
Leidulf ran after as fast as he could, which wasn't very. He didn't have
a halter on her, and her tongue was dangling from her mouth, foam
dripping off her. There was a fence post below the barn; he tied her
to it. She lay her head flat on the ground, and went down on her
knees, as if she wanted to slip out of the rope, but she didn't manage
it. And Leidulf came into the barn, his lips had the same lustre, and
his hair was the same colour, but he hadn't brought his euphonium.
It always had a trembling tone as if he was almost out of breath. But
Leidulf did have breath. The euphonium and the drum at the back.
They were the band. They drove everyone else, the whole troop, in
front of them. Walk on. Rich blasts from the euphonium. And the
scales, from below and up, and down again, all the way, no-one could
go deeper, and the grin got into his mouthpiece when he breathed in.
And the timid cornets, perfectly red-faced. And the snare drum. And
Erling, who threw back his head and laughed. And Leidulf's jowls,
out and in. He smelt of a mixture of something and smoke. He talked
for a long time about how much milk the mother had given. He
looked as if he had fallen from the sky, and said of course he would
have a drink. She's called Plomrei, he said. He kicked his foot
ineffectively in her direction, and left. He walked fast along the road.
She was, as far as you could tell, in calf. In August, her udder began
to swell. A darling, firm, trembling udder, with tiny teats. It wasn't
her fault she was filling out. She became the heavy, round Plomrei,
maternal. A maternity that grew in her. Perhaps she hadn't wanted it,
but she filled out. Where did her anger come from? And her happy
days of youth. And her supple body. They were no more. I had never
laid eyes on a fatter cow. She pulled to both sides as far as her chains
would go, crazed with hunger, perhaps. She finished off the others´

food too. She ran and ran to where the best grass grew, and ate and ate, and she butted the others away. She bellowed like a bull and dug up tussocks with her head. But she was maternal. She kicked behind her if anyone so much as walked past. And she rolled her eyes. And we who put up the fences, drove down the poles with a sledgehammer and stretched the netting across, we laughed at her. Such rage. Maybe joy was still there, inside her. Deep down inside her, beneath the anger, there might be joy. Maybe this blind rage was the reverse side of joy, or the obverse, or perhaps they are one and the same thing. And we should praise anger, perhaps, as we praise joy. So let us give thanks, Plomrei, that you were not like the other cows. You were all fire. And those that are lukewarm will I spit out of my mouth. Oh, no, be lukewarm too. Be everything. Be the whole spectrum, from red to violet. One day she did not come home. So the others had to wait, for Plomrei was not there. For if a man has seven cows and loses one, will he not leave the six and look for the one that has strayed? And we went out into the evening. It was either a silent evening, or we couldn't hear anything. Only the rushing stream from the steep mountain. We walked across the pasture. It stretched into the woods. Further and further. We came to paths we had never trodden before. We found her in a valley where shadows of tall trees shut out the evening light. She had given birth there, by herself, and her son lay on the green grass. The child, the child that had torn her apart. But she did not notice it. The child lay on the green grass. A small bundle, as red as she, almost black. But then there was the slime. It made him darker still. She stamped and trampled the ground. It was as if her lively tongue was fastened to this bundle, trembling, a terrible compulsion. She licked and licked the only begotten son, that lay there shivering. There was no pride. There was no joy either. Maternal, insane, she howled hysterically while her tongue kept going, and she went on stamping. We came nearer, for we were on a legitimate errand. The calf was ours, and hers were the udders bursting with milk, the food and the countless days. We crept closer, quiet as cats. She didn't run away. She who was so skittish. She butted us, a sweeping movement with her head. She had to go on licking, but she was ready for a fight. Had to go on licking. I offered her grain. I felt the treacherous smile on my face. For why was I going to offer her her feed? She paid no attention. I just stood there. The calf struggled to stand up. And he did stand up. He wanted to get to the tiny teats. She turned around, she didn't understand, she wanted what was best, she wanted to lick him again, it didn't seem it would ever be enough.

And the fat rippled on her. And the calf collapsed. And he never got to the teats. My father took him. He gathered the calf into his arms and ran. The poor mother, she didn't understand, she was looking for her child in the green grass where the smell lingered. My father was on his way. And Plomrei, after him now, and her tongue kept going, for there were other laws raging through her. She needed to go on licking. My father flew like a bullet across an open field, and screamed and screamed at me, Plomrei blindly following him. My old man and the calf were through the gate, and he yelled, shut it! And I threw the bucket to the ground, spilling the feed, and I did shut it. And Plomrei. She went crazy. She ran right into the gate. But the gate stood firm. My father raced down the road, he had slung the calf across his shoulders, and the feet and head were dangling down. Plomrei was on the other side of the fence, she howled and whimpered, the slime still oozing out of her hind end. She couldn't take it. She fell silent, she thrust her round chest against the fence, and wanted to break it down, but it held out. The fence. She didn't care about the barbed wire that was making her bleed. My father walked on. He had a terrible expression on his face, and his knees were bending. Then the calf opened his mouth and let out a long, clear, innocent cry. So he did have vocal cords, they were pure and new. Plomrei gave a start; she abandoned the fence, trailing the fence on the other side, hopelessly, until she came to the rock face and she halted. We could hear her howling, we got the calf home and put him in the pen. It didn't seem to worry him. He tried to get up, and staggered; I gave him my hand, and he sucked. Come on, said my father, now we must find Plomrei. We set out again, my father with a rope in his hand. The evening was quiet. We couldn't find our way back when we had crossed the pasture, and somehow the woods had taken over. We called and shouted to her, but there was no sign of Plomrei. Then an old man with a knapsack came through the woods, and my father said to him, have you seen my redpoll cow? No, said the man, I have not, and away he went, but shortly after we saw him again. He too had lost his way and was walking in circles. Suddenly we were back in that valley of the shadow of death, and there was Plomrei. She was rushing around sniffing the earth and searching. But all she found was her amnion sack and her own blood drying on the ground. Then my father got the halter on her. But I tell you she now understood everything. So she came willingly, her anger turning into grief. She walked as if nothing was the matter. She nodded her head at every step. Then one day she was gone. She gave no more milk than what went into the milk filter, said my father, and that we give to the cat. I went into the barn one day, her stall was empty, and it was peaceful without her, I recall, with her chains abandoned in the feeding trough. Gone. But the hay barns remain and are still there. Most of them that is. Red barns. The calf grew up. And the slaughter weight was good. And there are the barns. Where the swallows still build their nests. It's noisy for them during silage harvesting season. But they fly in and out. The young ones must be fed. Each looks after his own. Time passes. But the swallows continue. The swallows still fly there. Are you still there? And the starlings sit on the roof ridge. They rush like a shower of living rain to a power line. And the fields around, they were once cultivated. The largest stones left lying. They mowed around them. There was no dynamite then. If the ground was too steep, they put up walls and threw earth against them. It was needed for the cows, all of it. The cows, the rain, the full grass crops. We rose out of this, stubborn, unknowing. Life was given to us. In a fashion. The harvesting season came. They never mowed in a line. A line needed more than one person. There were no lines on these small patches. But mow they did. When the day grew too hot they mowed in their underpants. And the scythe lost its edge because the dew had gone. The flash of the scythe as it rose. The whetstone's song. And the women spread the hay, and they carried it inside and stacked it, and they scratched the final number of the bundles on the wall. They wrote it down for the cows. To see if there was going to be enough to last until the spring. The grass mower arrived, and whirled around. And the gear box into which they poured oil. And the finger bar that chattered away, and the iron guides that whispered through the grass. The grass fell. So now stones have gone and old men swear after the fact. For old men have always sworn. Did you never notice this? They swear when they think no-one is listening. I had a calf that was all my own. We bought it at Nes. It looked so pale. No-one had ever seen a paler calf. Nes was a strange place, the flat peninsula out into the sea, the small pointed hills, almost like warts, and they mowed everything, the old-fashioned way. There wasn't a straw, a single straw in the courtyard. The old, small houses still standing. And their barn was as grey as silver. The fields went right up to the walls, and the animals grazed there. And the calf was on the doorstep when we arrived, and seemed to know what was coming to him. We knocked, however, my father and I, and they called us in, and they coughed and spat and cleared their throats. We opened the door, and were straight into the kitchen, for there was no hall in the house. We spotted Sverre sitting on the bench by the wall with windows. He lit his pipe, and the entire stem disappeared into the hole where his front teeth should have been. He alternately lit and sucked. I thought maybe the pipe kept him alive, for he sucked, sucked in as much air as he could hold, and then blew it out. He disappeared in a cloud of smoke. So you want to buy the pet calf, he said. And we heard him coughing. When the smoke lifted to the ceiling he was still where he was. Red in the face. Pine dark walls surrounded us. Pine that darkens with its warm lustre. In the evening we tied a rope on the calf and left with it. The calf did not want to come, he quietly resisted. No calf wants to be led. But we got to the gate. And Sigrun came to say goodbye; she had yellow, curly hair that lay close to her head. She was very quiet, Sigrun, and spoke softly. When she said something, a certain note hung in the air, a sound that refused to die. We thought we ought to wait; we turned around, we could see the black furrows on the ground where the calf had resisted us. Sigrun had pieces of bread in a bowl. This is bread, she said to the calf. But the calf pretended not to notice. It was easy to see that Sigrun was crying, and I didn't turn away for it was somehow soothing to watch, tears that trickled, and the red spots that appeared on her forehead. Keep well, then, my pet, she said, in a deep, steady voice, and her voice lingered. We had got as far as the road. But calves will not be led. Doesn't she know? I said. Of course Sigrun knows, said my father, and ruffled my hair; he did ruffle my hair, and the calf began to trot along nicely. He said it was my calf. He baptized her Hera. But she was no heavenly queen. And the earth was ploughed and harrowed. It is dug deeper now. Timothy comes up, and the clover. It isn't grass exactly, with harebells and buttercups, but the crops are plentiful. The pale green meadows with clover and timothy. And now we have to mow, for the grass has grown and soon the roots will turn yellow. And the forage harvesters start roaring, it is the same as always, all of it, because of the cows. Out into the fields with the trailer with its high sides, and connect the power take-off, and pull the hand-engine speed control down and let the clutch out as the engine speed reaches full power. And the flails rising and slashing, and the curving jet of finely cut grass. It is for the cows. And the dairy is still there and has become a clothes shop, where you can buy fur jackets incredibly cheaply, and where shoes are sold at rock-bottom prices. Where there was once a dairy. And we were out there with a horse and cart and two or three pails of milk. And the milk truck that had begun to run, and the stands that everyone was compelled to build. And then the milk-truck driver. And his blue Chevrolet, that he didn't get rid of before the cooling fan one day emerged through the bonnet, then he switched cars. And inside the milk truck he sat steering with a more extravagant circular movement than anyone ever did see. But he stayed on the road. And then the bulk tanker with the hatch behind, and the drum with the hose, and the measuring equipment, and the young men with attitude who mess up the roadsides, wearing clogs and jeans, and jumping out and jumping back in again, and driving off to town with the milk. It's always the same, almost. It is for the cows. Pale, friendly Hera, she was a small but strong cow. I used to go into her stall. Then she turned her head, and I stood there, her neck embracing me. I scraped the muck off her, and brushed her. She liked it. She stretched her head out. When she gave birth, I found the amnion sack. It lay in the dung trough in the brightest daylight, and was beginning to dry out. I asked myself how long it had been there. Her back was arched. She turned around and looked into my eyes. I had to help her. Help her immediately. What could I do? I was only a child. That sound in her, what could I do? I ran and looked for my father. We had to put our trust in him, Hera and I. He was so strong. He was on the lower road. He didn't say a word. But he started to walk faster. For we could hear the sound coming from her, all the way from out here. We could see the calf's hind feet. Damn, damn, he hissed, but he gritted his teeth. He rolled up his sleeves. Find some soap and put the water on. He lathered his arms and hands. He said I must go out for a moment. I turned and saw how he pushed the calf in. And I saw his hand slide in and disappear. I ran for it. But I had to come back. She was calling me. I would stand in her stall and I would scratch her. The legs had come out. My father's hair had fallen into his eyes. His arms were covered in slime and blood. They were steaming. But he was smiling. Hera, you pushed. You were a brave cow, and a strong one. My father started pulling. The yellow hooves were out, pressed together. He said the calf is lying the wrong way. Fetch a rope. I found the green rope in the dairy house. He threw it around the small hooves, the calf pressed them so defencelessly together, and pulled. You'd better pull too. Behind me. Behind me, for God's sake. A gurgling sound came from inside Hera's body. That sound inside her. And she was frothing at the mouth. Get Einar! It wasn't my fault, I was crying. Einar just let go of his dung fork, and ran. Einar, the slaughterer, came in. What position, he said? The wrong way round and on his back, replied my father, but he had turned him on his belly. Let's just pull. Hera fell over in her stall. Einar said, get her up. Couldn't they just let her lie? No, then pulling was so much heavier. He kicked her. I wanted to hit him with my little fist. I was crying. I had to go and fetch my uncle. The road had many curves. Where is my uncle? He had gone for a walk in the woods. In the middle of the day. He was standing up in the pasture staring at a holly. He whirled round. He was the best of them. He wanted to know if they had been pulling long. I said, they have pulled for an hour, at least. I couldn't keep up with him. The cord might have snapped. I went after him, into the barn. Hera was standing among the heifers. She was so small. Not a sound came from her. Einar said her pelvis was so narrow. They pulled. Twist it too, shouted Einar. They pulled. The lad, cried Einar. He handed me the end of the rope. But I didn't pull. If only I could hear a sound from her. She was so quiet. The hind legs were out, dangling from the cunt. Oh, heave. The calf came out. The joy of it. At that very moment Hera sank to the floor, and lay still. Now she could rest. The joy of it. My face was warm and tingling. She ought to have some grain, I said. But she wouldn't touch it. And she paid no attention to the calf either, not to anything. The calf in the trough, all legs and bones and covered with slime. He didn't tremble. The wonder of life for me, for us, is the trembling of a newborn calf, and the twitching, and the mouth opening, and the first gasp of breath, the miracle of life, it all hangs in the air. Life. And it was because of life that Einar threw himself down, tall as he was, into the slime and filth, and opened his huge jaws over the muzzle of this steaming, skinny cadaver, and blew. And wanted to blow the spirit into him, but it was no use. He let go of the head to which the ears were still plastered. It dropped on to the cement with a clunk, and Einar tugged at my father and said, you try. But my father just stood there. Damn it, do you want to lose the calf? Then my father fell on his knees. And he lifted the head with the half-opened, blind eyes, into his lap, and bent down and kissed it, blew, but the spirit had fled from us. And Hera, you should have stood up, you should at least have turned your head and cared. But she didn't care. She would never again stand up. She would try, but even if she had wanted to, her hind legs would have failed her. They lay to the side, stretched out, and she could not. She would die, that's all, having brought forth the dead calf that had killed her, as if the same higher power had condemned them both. She had not given him life. But he had given her death. We buried her in a marsh, my father and I, and shovelled the wet, stinking earth over her. And my father got up from the trough and wanted to pull the calf away. For what else could he do? Then Einar woke up and said, do you have a knife? What the devil, it's dead, said my father, and started to drag it away, but Einar grabbed his arm and held him. Baby veal, my friend, baby veal. But it's dead, my father shouted, on the verge, I think, of tears. Get a spade instead. My uncle was standing there, and he pulled out his knife and handed it to Einar and said, we won't go to Einar's for dinner for a while. Einar thrust the knife into the slimy, fragile chest. And the blood flowed out and ran along the trough. Yes, the cow. The cow will have its song.

Translated by Nadia Christensen

RAGNAR HOVLAND

The Last Beat Poets in Mid-Hordland

For a long time we were the last cowboys in Mid-Hordland. Long after the others had shot their last Indians and hung up their hats and pistols, and left the lonely prairie behind them for ever, we kept going as before. By we, I mean Gunnar and me. Who else? We always kept our powder dry and brought law and order to the forests and farms. We fought desperate gun battles with old farmers and ornery cats. We were the lone avengers from the mountains and woods, long after the others had grown out of that sort of thing. Perhaps we just grew up more slowly than them.

Before that, we'd been the last of lots of other things. We were always last. We got caught up in things, and couldn't untangle ourselves in time. We were hopeless for that.

So while the others were developing a taste for girls and beer and reading *Playboy*, Gunnar and I might be found behind a hen-coop in some lawless, hard-bitten town, waiting for the Jackson boys, or whoever it might be. We would get them. It was now or never.

We were something apart. No doubt about that. But where is the connection between all this and the Beat Generation? Well, it's not easy to find. But it does exist. When we talk about the Beat Generation today we think of it as an American phenomenon. Allen Ginsberg, we think. Then we think of Jack Kerouac and Gregory Corso. Neal Cassidy and Burroughs and full throttle down unending roads, and wine and Buddhism, and beards and berets, and as little soap and water as possible. That was the Beat Generation in America. But as a phenomenon that reached all the way to Mid-Hordland, where Gunnar and I were its foremost (and sole) exponents, it's less well-known. It is to correct this impression and to do us justice in the annals of literary history that I want to tell this story. I can't see any reason not to now.

I've classed us as the *last* beat poets of Mid-Hordland, but I could just as well have called us the first. But last sounds better. It fits in better with our previous history, and gives us some of the cachet of a doomed generation. And that's what we were, we who belonged to the Mid-Hordland Beat Generation. It goes without saying.

Gunnar was the moving spirit. Give credit where it's due. It had been clear for a long time that cowboy life was drawing to a close. It became more and more obvious to us with each night we spent on the moonlit prairie, with nothing but a log for a pillow and the howls of far-off coyotes. The farther off the better for a good night's sleep.

The mornings were dank, with mists driving in from the river and fields. The birds awoke and started hawking and coughing and cussing.

"It's dank," Gunnar said on one such morning.

"It's a lonesome life," I said.

"How long can we keep going?" said Gunnar.

When we were cowboys we always dropped our dialect and spoke city Norwegian the way the real cowboys did.

How long could we keep going? Yes, that was the question. On just such a morning full of mist and smoke, Gunnar stood waiting for me out in our yard. But what was he clutching? It was a newspaper.

"Here, have a read of this," he said, pointing to the page he had opened.

The cat rubbed against our legs wanting to be stroked, but undeflected we read a half-page article about something strange that was occurring in America. It had to be America again, of course.

It was our first encounter with the Beat Generation, and the last cowboys entered the pages of history. Disappeared without trace.

"They held out real good. Longer than anyone would have thought, I guess. May their souls rest in peace."

This was so interesting that we had to sit down on the doorstep and read it again. Even then we didn't understand it all. But we realised it was about people who wrote dirty poetry and books full of four-letter words, and who also lived wild lives, let their beards grow and rarely washed. If only we could have seen one!

"Do you think it's true?" I said.

"Well, it's in the paper, you cretin," said Gunnar.

We sat looking at nothing in particular for a while. Wasn't the mist going to lift? Yes, over there the sun had punched a hole in it and let some blue sky filter through.

"Well, what do you think?" Gunnar asked.

"About what?"

"About what's written here."

"Sounds really tough," I said.

And so, at one blow we became beat poets, but for the moment we kept it to ourselves. We still weren't well enough prepared to show ourselves to the world in our new guise. We needed more material.

And the material arrived. Firstly in the shape of Gunnar shambling up with two more newspaper articles. And we read and studied and sweated. Eventually we stumbled across an article in an American magazine that someone had. There was a picture as well. These beat people looked like hard men with their beards and dark glasses. But we needed someone to translate the article, so that we could understand it all. In the end we got Loopy Leonard to do it for us, in return for the loan of some of our records. We lent him the ones with scratches.

At last, we felt we had a good firm foundation. We were on solid ground, now it was just a matter of taking the plunge.

But first we had to think about what we needed.

"We'll have to grow beards," Gunnar said.

"Yup," I agreed.

Gunnar looked at me and I looked at Gunnar. Both sets of cheeks were pretty smooth. That was undeniable. And we couldn't count on anything happening in the near future, even with sufficient sun and plenty of rain. Doubtfully we rubbed our chins.

"Oh, sod it," said Gunnar, "there's no point sitting on our butts waiting about for years. We'll have to do without the beards."

"Yup," I said. "I dare say we'll manage fine without."

But we did have dark glasses, and we discovered some berets up in the attic of Gunnar's house. Four of the things were hanging up there, so some berk must have used them. We tried them on. To say that they suited us perfectly would have been a lie.

"This one obviously belonged to somebody with a lot of head and no sense," I said.

"Same here," said Gunnar. "It should be illegal to have such a large loaf. It should be a finable offence."

But we found the solution. We took all four berets and steeped them in boiling water well-laced with washing powder to see if we could get them to shrink.

Their colour certainly bleached out, and with a vengeance. But after soaking them for a while they did get a bit smaller as well. If we tucked them in a little, they actually could be worn without too much embarrassment.

"Okay," said Gunnar, inspecting himself in the mirror.

"Okay," I said.

Sunglasses we already owned. We hadn't exactly used them a great deal, but from now on we were going to make up for it.

"What about six-shooters?" I said. "Will we need those?"

"Are you daft or something? We're through with all that."

Yes, it was true. A beat poet used his mouth and not a gun.

"What are you pretending to be?" asked my mother when she came in and saw us.

"What?" we asked.

"What are you pretending to be now?"

"We're pretending we're dunny-diggers," I said. "Just off to dig earth closets for people."

She'd never have understood anyway.

"Well, I suppose it was bound to end up like this," she said. "The best of luck to you both."

And so we'd come out. With slouching hips and hunched shoulders, we thought we made quite an impression.

And who should we meet but old Konrad, hauling his cart.

"Hi there, Konrad," we called. "What have you got in your cart today?"

"Kohlrabi," said Konrad.

"Kohlrabi?" we said. "We really dig that, Konrad."

"What are you dressed up as? Bank robbers, is it?"

"No, we're not bank robbers, we're poets."

"Is that what they look like nowadays?" said Konrad. "Well, let's hear a poem."

"Just listen to this," Gunnar said:

"When cuckoos call from pine tree crown,
Girls' cunts are up and their knickers down."

"It weren't the pair of you who wrote that," said Konrad.

"No?" I said. "Well, just listen to this one then:

"Amanda lay on the sand a-
long with fifteen hundred men.
They all were going to scre . . ."

"No," said Konrad. "You didn't come up with those. I've heard 'em all before. And anyway, that's not poetry, that's just dirty talk, and you don't need dark glasses to do that. Go and read Bjørnson. You could learn a thing or two from him."

What old Konrad had said was true. They weren't poems we'd written ourselves. Because we didn't have any yet, and we thought these suited our style.

We carried on down towards the shops to buy some beer. O. Dale's was the only place that sold it, so we headed for that. There was a woman behind the counter wrapping two loaves for the policeman. *He* was buying a lot of bread. Were there so few thieves about that he could spend his entire day in the station eating?

Then it was our turn, but we waited until the policeman had left and closed the door behind him.

"We'd like four large bottles of Export," I said.

"*What* did you say you wanted?"

"Four large Exports."

"With straws, I suppose?"

"That's okay," Gunnar said, "you needn't bother with them."

"Do you *really* believe we sell beer to minors?"

We probably hadn't really believed it, but we'd clung to a slender *hope*. Now we'd been recognised and so beer was out of the question. We slouched out again carrying four bottles of Coke. It wasn't quite what we'd come for, but at least it did taste American.

We took the tops off and seated ourselves on the steps of O. Dale's shop. The weather was lovely and hot now, and we took great pulls from the Coke bottles and stretched out our legs. We were wearing sandals with no socks, and we could see that our toes were getting good and grimy. That was just how it ought to be. We were on our way, provided we overlooked the painful episode of the beer.

A bevy of three or four girls came drifting past, almost as if they'd been clouds. They'd obviously noticed the fine weather, too, as they weren't wearing a lot. Only blouses or short-sleeved cardigans and tight-fitting jeans, which emphasised everything we thought should be emphasised according to age-old tradition. We stared at them from behind our dark glasses, but they hardly even deigned to bestow a glance on us. They were haughty and obnoxious.

"Who was that?" asked one of them.

"Didn't you see?" said another. "It was that Gunnar and what's-his-name. They've got a screw loose. They probably reckon they're something special now."

"They're just getting nuttier and nuttier, if you ask me."

"Yes, and that's not easy when you were so nutty before."

But Gunnar and I were unperturbed.

"That bunch of fat tarts can just go and take a running jump back into the cesspool they crawled out of," Gunnar said.

"Best place for them," I said, letting the empty Coke bottle slip on to the gravel.

What did we care what people said about us? It was fashionable to be misunderstood. It was part of the job.

"I wouldn't touch what they've got hidden away in those pants even if they threw them at me," said Gunnar, trying to explore the theme a little further.

I wasn't quite sure if I agreed with Gunnar there, but I nodded anyway, and spat at the Coke bottle, lying there all green and nasty.

We sat on awhile, looking out on the warm afternoon with studied discontent, as now and again customers negotiated their way between us to enter or leave the accursed shop of O. Dale and his old woman.

"God, what a procession," we would mumble each time someone squeezed past.

When we had tipped all the Coke into ourselves, and all four bottles lay in a huddle near our feet, O. Dale himself came out and stood there quivering with rage.

"Are you two going to sit here all day?" he hissed.

"And why not?" said Gunnar, giving him a dark and inscrutable look.

"Move off, the pair of you, and make way for decent people."

"See any decent people here?" Gunnar asked.

"Nope," I said, "but they could've broken down on the way and got held up."

However, we got slowly to our feet and, chewing all the while, walked over to the steps of the bakery which was next door. Baking smells of the most delicious kind assailed our nostrils, and we realised just how empty the poetic entrails had become. Well, poetry would have to wait awhile, we now had more important and worldly things to take care of.

We went into the bakery, where three energetic, white-clad demons were pushing loaves into hellish-looking ovens.

"Got any end crusts today?" asked Gunnar.

"End crusts?" one of them queried. "What d'you want with them?"

"We want to plug up the hole once we're sick of screwing," Gunnar said. "So no unwelcome guests get in."

"Ha, ha, ha!" laughed the three blokes in white.

"Old Gunnar's not such a spastic after all," said one of them.

"Ha, ha, ha," they laughed again. "Spastic, ho, ho!"

"Go on, take some end crusts, then," said the fattest of the three, who was the baker.

We took everything we could find, even though it was enough for ten men, as well as their wives and children. But we'd got there first.

Then we sat on the step, eating crusts and making plans for our great new poetic movement, the one that was soon to emerge. By the time the sun began to sink our plans had grown as big and bright as a huge, spark-spitting bonfire.

Fortunately the year was well enough advanced for the summer holidays to be round the corner. That suited us fine. School was no longer the right place for us. But we stuck out the final few days, pacing furtively about by ourselves during breaks, walking with a slight stoop and a mildly springy gait. This last was a hangover from our cowboy days, but we found that it was still serviceable. The classes were horrendously long and tedious, and we sat there squirming, looking vacant, chewing paper pellets, answering every question with sloppy uncouthness, and longing to get outside so that we could go for a smoke behind the toilets.

"Gunnar, can you tell me how we'd go about multiplying these fractions?" the teacher asked.

They were a pair of hard-boiled, evil-looking fractions that seemed quite impossible to multiply.

"I watched the finest minds of my generation being destroyed by madness," Gunnar said.

"Something tells me there are one or two people in this class who are deep in the doldrums of puberty," the teacher said ingratiatingly. He obviously thought he'd said something really clever.

"They've both become Jehovah's Witnesses," said a girl, cashing in on some Brownie points as well. But we didn't give a toss. The summer holidays began in seven or eight days' time, and our school reports would already be written for sure. What the hell.

And we didn't exactly get fantastic end-of-year reports either, as we found out seven or eight days later, but that didn't bother us unduly, because now we were free to get on with the summer, the great beat summer.

We had written a few poems, or at least we'd made strenuous efforts to write. To be more exact, Gunnar had a whole pile of lengthy, crude offerings, while I had just one – one that I'd been sweating over for weeks. It was about a squirrel I'd once seen, and which had left a deep impression on me. At first I'd thought it was a stone, but then the stone began to jump, and so I discovered it was a squirrel. This was what I had tried to express in my poem.

In the beginning we read our poems at Gunnar's, until his dad came charging in asking what the bloody hell all the bad language was for. That left us with the choice of either reading our poetry more quietly, or going somewhere else. The first was unthinkable, so instead we traipsed up to an old grey sheep-shed that stood unused now that the sheep had been driven into the mountains for the summer.

From now on – and just as a point of information – this was to become the Mid-Hordland Beat Generation's headquarters. But no matter how far the sheep had wandered into the mountains, their smell was still very much present. Gunnar and I certainly didn't smell too great after days without soap and water, but this was something else. All to the good: we wouldn't be disturbed. We were the only ones with a real feeling for this kind of thing, the smell of sheep and sweat and steamy sex.

"Oi!" we yelled, "Oi, oi!" And Gunnar immediately mounted a pile of rotten planks that were strewn with old hay and began to declaim:

"I ROAM AROUND LIKE A RAMPANT LION AND DON'T GIVE A TOSS ABOUT SCHOOL REPORTS."

This was how things ought to be, we thought. When we had no more voice left we lay down in the hay and belched and wiggled our filthy toes. This was the life. And it seemed incredible we could ever have imagined that being cowboys was better than sliced bread. This was real *living*, and we were at one with everything that had flesh and blood and shit and muck in it.

Gradually we also discovered that it was only partially true that the sheep had gone. Occasionally one would pop in. It would stand for a moment in the doorway, eyeing us sceptically, as if thinking that we had turned its house into a den of thieves, or something similar. But then it would come in in its sheepy way and do whatever it had to do. Usually this involved something it had forgotten, like making sure the iron was unplugged and that kind of thing. And then it would go off again. The sheep were alright, never any unpleasantness.

One hot day while we were doing our stuff inside, we heard something strange outdoors. Were the enemies of poetry now ranging themselves for an attack? We peered out. The first thing we saw was a sheep. It had been before, and we were now on good terms with it. But a few yards off stood a couple of humans, if you could grace them with the name. They were tourists from the city, of all things, a man and his wife in their fifties. They stood there, cameras resting on their bellies, staring at the sheep, as if they'd never seen anything like it before and had only come across one fleeting reference in a nineteenth-century travel journal. The sheep stared back manfully and stood its ground. Then they caught sight of us, and all three looked relieved.

"Excuse me," said the woman, "but what sort of animal is that?"

"It's a sheep," said Gunnar. "A sodding sheep."

Later we regretted not having said it was a kangaroo. They'd certainly have believed us.

The summer drew on. We kept at it and felt more and more misunderstood. We got loads of stick at home because we wouldn't help with all that stupid stuff like mowing a pathetic piece of grass or driving a few shitty cows out to pasture. We considered it just wasn't our kind of thing. Occasionally we'd drift down to the town centre just to show people that we were still in business and that we couldn't give a toss. We'd go to one of the shops and buy bread which we ate in the sheep-shed, or we'd go to the bakery and beg end crusts. And end crusts we got, provided we were sufficiently foul-mouthed, and this didn't usually pose much of a problem for us. The bakery was just about the only place we found any recognition. If they were in a good mood after just pulling out a successful batch of teacakes, for example, they would even listen to a poem or two.

But apart from that we had precious little audience. Discouragingly little. That is, until one day when the rain came pelting down the mountainsides, across the fields, over the bridge and finally began hammering on our roof. Gunnar and I were inside the sheep-shed declaiming for all we were worth when the heavens opened.

"Rain," Gunnar said.

"Rain," I said.

We carried on with a recitation fit to shake the walls, but were soon assailed by an unmistakable smell which steadily grew in strength: soaked sheep. And now they came pouring in through the door, one after the other, shaking off the rain like dogs. Being out was good while the sun was up and shining, but when bad weather arrived it was quite another matter. Then it was home sweet home, as the lamps of their own haven lit up in their brains, their sheepy brains. Eventually, a group of about twenty cold sheep was gathered in the shed, all staring expectantly in our direction. It was obvious that they saw us as responsible for the entertainment in the house and that they were expecting great things. And we, fully aware of our duty, stood up and with all our energy and presence gave the flock a show the like of which they'd certainly never witnessed before, not even in the wildest hills. We gave them everything we had, our entire repertoire, even to the point of improvisation. Finally, we discarded anything resembling a manuscript, and just launched into whatever took our fancy. Our words became more pithy and grandiose, our sentences almost endless, while pauses and punctuation marks were relegated to the status of medieval anachronisms, from the time before the fresh air of enlightenment had come streaming in through the window. By way of a finale, Gunnar recited four and a half pages of the Book of Revelations from memory. We thought it apposite.

"Hear, you who have ears to hear," Gunnar shrieked in conclusion. Then he sank down, utterly exhausted. And the sheep were every bit as spent. They lay stretched out on the floor, their fleeces sticking out in all directions.

It may seen cruel to say this now, with the benefit of hindsight, but that day with the sheep probably marked the high point of our careers. Never again were we to attain the dizzy heights we scaled that day, and afterwards things went into a steady decline as the summer slowly began to fade. The final straw came one Saturday night at a bash in the Recreation Hall, accompanied by the usual endless accordion music. In point of fact Gunnar and I were too young for this event, but nothing could stop us and we pushed our way in, the stink of sheep hanging like some aura of legitimacy about us. At first we hung around by the door, shoulders hunched, frightening people away from that corner of the hall.

"Where's that sheep smell coming from?"

"Let's move, we don't want it clinging to our clothes."

In the interval between two numbers that weren't worth listening to we walked over to the far end of the room where the chairs were. One of these was occupied by a skinny girl with unkempt hair who hadn't danced all evening and wasn't likely to later on, either. Gunnar went up to her and she brightened. Was she going to be lucky enough to get a dance with this macho guy who might even almost pass for James Dean, and who smelled so gloriously of sheep? But no.

"Lend us your chair for a tick, baby," said Gunnar. And up he jumped.

"Hey, you bastards, listen here a moment," he called out. "ALL I CAN SEE, ALL I CAN SEE IS A WHOLE MASS OF STUNTED MINDS, PEOPLE WITH NOTHING IN THEIR PANTS . . ."

I think that was as far as he got. He didn't say a lot more. A phalanx of four men in shirtsleeves pushed their way through. They weren't going to have their pants called empty, and now they were going to beat us up. They made a pretty good job of it, too. A couple of minutes later when we came to ourselves we were stretched out on the gravel outside the Recreation Hall, well tenderised and with mouths full of blood.

"Get out and don't come back – and take that shitty smell with you."

This gave us a bit of a jolt. It was dangerous work, being a beat poet.

True, we did hold out a while longer, just keeping a slightly lower profile, not being too provocative. Except with the sheep, of course. And they were happy to be provoked. They had gradually come to look on us as a kind of spiritual leadership, devouring every word we uttered and viewing it as pure evangelism. But this didn't prevent them bolting into the hills as soon as the sun was out again. Presumably they felt that there was a time for poetry and a time for juicy mountain grass and rosy-cheeked shepherdesses.

The final nail in our coffin was driven in by Gunnar himself. He fell head-over-heels in love with a blonde from the city, a girl who lived at her aunt's during the summer holidays and had a room of her own in the basement. She hadn't much time for filthy, rustic beat poets who reeked of sheep, but was prepared to bestow her favours on decent country boys who washed and brushed their teeth and had passably trendy hairstyles. And so, one morning I found Gunnar seated on a stone in front of his house, clean of face, with a slicked-down Elvis haircut, and wearing a white nylon shirt and Terylene trousers. There was not a trace of the sheep-whiff, sunglasses or the beret.

"Hey, I've written a new poem," I said enthusiastically. And then suddenly his appearance struck me.

"But . . ."

"Have you really?" Gunnar said dreamily.

Well, I wasn't itching to become the sole surviving member of the Mid-Hordland Beat Generation. That was a step too far, even for me. So I left Gunnar where he was and went home and got straight into the shower. I stayed there for at least half an hour, and when I re-emerged I shone like a newborn baby. I'd just watched a great epoch run away down the plughole.

Translated by James Anderson

LARS SAABYE CHRISTENSEN

The Jealous Barber

All down the years Bent had had his hair cut at Frank's, at Frank's Salon. From when he was twenty-nine and had settled in this part of the city he'd gone there, on the last Friday of every second month. Each appointment lasted about an hour, even though he had a straightforward enough head that didn't get any harder to deal with over time – rather the opposite. Bent was now nearing forty-four, and if he worked it out he would realise that he had spent almost a hundred hours in the barber's chair at Frank's. Nonetheless he had no recollection of their having said all that much to one another, apart from the occasional comment about the weather forecast when it was completely up a gum tree, or about a sports event or a politician who – one way or another – had gone too far. Nor even did they speak a great deal about his hair, for Frank knew how he had wanted it right from the first Friday when he came into his salon almost fifteen years before. Bent hung his jacket on the stand by the door, sat down in the barber's chair which was then cranked up a couple of times, had the cape put round him and the slightly stiff paper collar, felt Frank's fingers against his temples and let him get to work – without either of them saying a word. For Frank liked to work away in silence, and Bent respected that – perhaps it was for that very reason that for better or worse he always went back there, because he didn't have to make conversation and say things he might regret about his work, for instance. Because he avoided having to answer questions about every-thing under the sun, at the same time as being able to look at himself in the shiny old mirror that was so flattering to his face, and to listen to the rapid snipping of the scissors round his head and the low hum of the electric clippers on his neck, and finally the soft chuckle of the brush as it swept over his neck. This was the language of the hairdresser. This was the salon's one eternal vocabulary: a dialect of hair. After all these years they knew little or nothing about each other. And perhaps that was for the best.

Bent lived alone, had two rooms and a kitchen three flights up, above a store that was open night and day. Now and again he would go down at midnight and buy four doughnuts from the girl who usually worked there – Susie, she was called, she had a badge with her name – and rent a Mia Farrow video. But it was seldom any use. The films were neither soporific enough nor sufficiently exciting. Instead he began to put on weight; slowly he began to fill out and just about all the clothes he put on became a tight fit. Bent was a porter at the royal infirmary. He had never been off work.

As he stood at his living room window he could see down into the salon. Often Frank was there until late in the evening. He swept the hair from the floor and took it out into the back premises. He rinsed the combs in blue water, cleaned the electric clippers, tidied up the old weeklies which everyone had long since read, or wrote out small signs to hang on the door the following day – Half Price for Pensioners. Now and again Frank just sat in the barber's chair for hours at a time, doing nothing, almost as though he were sleeping. Then Bent didn't want to watch any longer. He went into the kitchen and sat there instead with a coffee. But he wished he could watch Frank cutting his own hair.

Frank was a slender, fastidious gent in his middle fifties. He had taken over the salon from his father – an Oslo master hairdresser himself – who had given up when he was right at the top, and who had died just three weeks later. But the trophy was still there in a glass case next to the mirrors. And his son, Frank, had managed to hold his own all these years, while hairdressers with names like Hairport, Splitting Hairs and Spaghetti sprang up on every corner and all but invaded the district. And Frank had managed it thanks to a small but faithful band of customers who consisted in the main of middle-aged men with precious few demands in respect of inventiveness when it came to their hair. Men who – if they said anything at all – said enough with comments like "Same as usual", "Short back and sides". Maybe, if the summer holidays were on the horizon, they'd stretch to a whole sentence – "I think extra short this time round, Frank." Then Frank would say – in a slightly wounded yet superior tone which few ever completely got used to but which they accepted nonetheless, because they'd rather avoid taking their frail follicles anywhere else – "I know. Just take a seat." When it came down to it their whole vocabulary comprised one word – "surprise" – the word that defined their lives.

So the years passed and that's how things went – no sharp bends, no calamities, no exultation. There were a good many speed bumps in life and each morning Time was a comb full of blue hair. They grew older, but scarcely noticed the fact themselves. They chose their mirrors with care – they chose Frank's mirrors. The only thing they did feel that changed was the city around them. One morning they might get up to see yet another carry-out joint, and before they hit the hay again there might be a new billboard with its gleaming green, staccato letters above the tram stop. Not to mention the new hairdressers that encroached on the turf once occupied by grocers, ironmongers and drapers. It bewildered them; they lay awake and homeless, even in their own dreams. Yet they could sense a sudden jolt of luck too at these changes – like a laughter in their heads – because all at once it struck them, with real force, that they were the only unwavering anchors in their own lives.

And when their alarm clocks ring they get up at once (having slept just the same) and perhaps they clean the hair from their combs, since now and then one of them does comb their hair in their sleep.

They never meet each other, except in the doorway to Frank's Salon.

It was the last Friday in November, in Frank's month. Everything was wet and gold, and the rain could turn to snow at any time. Bent was on his way home; he walked in the broad and shining shopping precinct that led from the centre of town to the district he lived in. There had been a bit of a rumpus at work (no more than usual in respect of visits to the mortuary) but one of the staff – a young student – had been sick in the corridor, had vomited all over the wall, before collapsing in floods of tears. They were wheeling in a young child. Bent was tired of the comings and goings of all these temporary staff – it was not as it should be, it was not right. But he did not bark at the guy; instead he tried to comfort him and told him that sooner or later it would pass. He had gone down on his knees and wept himself once upon a time. It takes a while to come to terms with the number tag round a child's white foot.

Now Bent was standing waiting for the green man signal at the crossing by the tram stop. He wanted to get across to the other side. He wanted some shelter. The rain became sleet, heavy on his shoulders and hands. Then, to his amazement, he saw that he was casting a shadow – a clear, angled shadow – into the street. He turned and was dazzled by the great white light coming from Spaghetti, the newest of the district's hairdressers. And there and then Bent changed his mind; he went in there instead, to Spaghetti's. Afterwards he could not say why he had. He just did. His steps took him in a new direction. He could justify himself by true lies: that there had been trouble at work, that he was not himself, that he had not quite regained his equilibrium. For who can, hand on heart, get used to the number tag round a child's foot and the cold shudder that comes at such a memory? But that was not the reason Bent noticed now that his jacket was dripping, streaming rainwater onto the tiled floor that looked like a giant chessboard, and that in the few seconds since entering the place a pool had gathered round his shoes. There he stood, a man from the sleet, in Spaghetti's sharp glare. The smells here were different, mellow and full of a strange heaviness, almost like on a journey. Bent's hand swept his brow and he looked around. There were both men and women there; they sat together in ordinary seats in front of tall mirrors he didn't recognise. He heard music – a monotonous hammer of a beat – not unlike the noise of the generator in the hospital basement, and of sleepless nights. It was as though he had all of a sudden woken up. He could not stay here. He had to get out, had to clear off. This was a mistake, he was going somewhere else, he had to go. Outside the lights changed; Bent caught sight of the green light behind grey stripes of sleet, like the sickly flame at the heart of a dead television screen after a film (perhaps one starring Mia Farrow) is well and truly over. Now he did go. He was already on his way out. Then a young man, just a boy, in trousers with a check pattern almost like the floor's, came up to him.

"Hi, what's your name?"

"Bent," said Bent.

"Have you an appointment?"

"No, sorry, I'll be on my way. Sorry."

The boy slowly weighed him up, studied at length the pool round his shoes and stopped, with a smile, at the crown of his head.

"We'll manage to fit you in alright, Bent. Bags of cancellations, because of the weather. Horrible weather to be out in, right?"

"I can come another time. I'm sorry."

The boy took his arm.

"Nothing to apologise for. Just take a seat, Bent. It'll be fine."

The boy helped him off with his jacket and Bent was put into a chair, a perfectly ordinary chair, in front of the mirror in which he could barely manage to meet his own gaze. On either side of him were women, or rather girls– schoolgirls – so shamelessly young, getting their hair done for the weekend. *This isn't like a hairdresser's*, Bent thought, *this is like a theatre; this is what it must be like at the theatre, behind the scenes.* Hair was examined, hair was burnt, hair was dyed –

everything possible was done with hair there apart from cutting it. Bent clasped his hands and shut his eyes, and an old angst rose within him like the fear he had experienced on his first day in the city. It was in June and he had got off the train at the Østbane, having travelled for two days, and he stood there alone on the platform in another world. There with a brown suitcase – all he owned in the world – and the heavy weight of expectation in his other hand, a shadow that would not leave him. To say nothing of that first shift after he had got summer work at the Royal Infirmary; he lay on all fours outside the mortuary gasping for breath, pissing himself – the shit, the vomit – and then the laughter up in the canteen later. "He'll not last all that long," they said. "A week at the most." But Bent was the one who lasted longest. He came to the city to begin his training in the bank and ended up in the hospital instead, in the underworld – the catacombs and the mortuary. Bent was the temp who stayed. He got a bedsit in the centre of town, sold his textbooks to a second-hand bookshop, and did not have far to go to work. Later he moved to his flat above the store and started to get his hair cut at Frank's. He never went home again.

The boy put a black gown round Bent, stood behind him and raised his head, just a fraction.

"It's a while since you've been to the hairdresser's?"

"No, I had it cut . . ."

The boy interrupted him.

"To the hairdresser's, I mean. Is it long since you were last at a *hairdresser's*?"

"Two months. Why?"

"No, no reason. I just wondered, you know. How do you want your hair, Bent?"

"Nothing special."

There was no way back now. Now it had begun. He looked at himself in the mirror. He had put on more weight than he realised. He had to stop seeing those Mia Farrow films.

"Nothing special," the boy repeated. "Nothing special?"

The other stylists looked over at them, the other customers too, the schoolgirls. Were they laughing? No, Bent could not see that they were; they just nodded quickly before meeting their own reflections again and conversing, the mirrors acting as middlemen.

"Yes," Bent said. "As it is now, just a bit shorter. That was the idea."

This was more than he'd ever said to Frank, and the thought of Frank unsettled him, was almost a shock. Now Frank would be waiting in his salon, already starting to look at the clock because it was after half past four, while Bent sat here under different hands. *What am I doing?* he thought. *What have I done?* The boy's fingers pressed against his temples.

"Now, we really need to keep that head still. I've got to work in peace."

"Sorry."

The boy stood behind him, apparently lost in his own thoughts, letting one finger trail through Bent's wet hair.

"That sounds really boring to me," he said at last. "Nothing special, I mean."

And then Bent said something he never imagined he'd come out with:

"Do whatever you think's best."

The boy raised his hand and pointed into thin air as if to begin with he was not believing what he'd heard. But right away he gave a smile and snapped his fingers.

"You won't regret this, Bent!"

The boy pressed his ears to the side of his head and looked at him studiously.

"Are we leaving the chops or not?"

Bent gave a quick glance into the mirror. That was the place to talk.

"The chops?"

"Your sideburns, Bent. Are we leaving them be or not?"

The boy let his ears go. Evidently he thought he still hadn't heard right.

"Do whatever you think's best," Bent said again.

It took less time than it would have at Frank's, but he had to pay twice as much. The boy even gave him a card, wanting to follow things up (as he put it), and a shampoo sample. When Bent came out it was almost like having a new head. The lights changed to red. It was still sleeting. He managed to catch a taxi at the next crossing and went straight home. When they came past Frank's Salon he had to tie his laces. He couldn't face being seen now. Fortunately the driver said nothing, although he looked at him in the mirror now and again. Bent settled up and hurried into the store where he put milk, a loaf, a magazine and half a chicken into one of the baskets and carried the lot over to the counter.

Susie stared at him as she put everything into a bag.

"You're looking good," she said.

Bent scratched his forehead.

"D'you reckon?"

"I wouldn't have said it otherwise, would I?"

"No, maybe not."

Susie gave him the bag with the shopping and very obviously stared again – not at his eyes but somewhat higher up.

"Maybe? I said you're looking good. Much better than before."

"Right, thanks. Thanks a lot."

Bent was moving towards the door. It was then that Susie called to him. He turned in her direction. But suddenly she was silent. Bent grew perturbed.

"What is it?"

"The films. You haven't returned those films."

"I'll bring them in."

Susie took a sweet from the bowl on the counter and popped it in her mouth.

"Not that it bothers me. No-one else wanting them. But it'll be expensive."

"Don't worry about that."

"I'm not. Are they any good?"

Bent shrugged his shoulders.

"They don't put you to sleep at any rate."

Susie laughed.

"They sound really exciting."

And for the second time that day Bent said something he never believed he would say.

"We can watch them together one evening. If you'd like to, you know."

Susie leaned against the counter and slowly sucked her sweet. He could hear her right over where he was standing.

"Maybe, as long as they're not boring."

Bent got to his stairwell. There was no mail, just something from the butcher offering Christmas bargains. He took the lift up to the third floor. A neighbour was struggling over by the rubbish chute. She glanced quickly at him, drew away and continued her battle. Something smelled – fish, or maybe a tin of cat food. Bent let himself in, set the bag of shopping down in the kitchen and went out to the bathroom. He stood there for a long while, in the half-darkness, in front of the mirror. The plumbing gurgled – the intestinal workings of the building, the Friday rumbling. His face seemed smaller, narrower. *I have to slim*, he thought to himself. *The rest of me is out of proportion with my face. That's an end to the night-time doughnuts*. He put his hand on his head – smooth, that's how it felt, completely smooth. He sniffed his fingers and the smell reminded him of something he couldn't quite remember: a forgotten holiday, a present he had never opened, some fruit perhaps. He washed his hands and put the little bottle of shampoo in the medicine cabinet.

Then he moved through the flat, put out the light and peered through the curtains. He could not see anyone down there in Frank's Salon. The window was dark. There were no handwritten notices on the door offering reductions to the district's pensioners. Bent grew restless. He ate the chicken cold; had to pull off the tough, clammy skin and throw it away. It was things like that which could lie around the place, stinking, if you didn't pay enough attention – the legs too, those thin chicken legs and the breastbone. The mustard bottle was empty; he rinsed it in boiling water and scraped off the label. He watched the news, but afterwards had no recollection of what he had seen, or what the weather was going to be like, or who the weather-man had been. His films lay in a pile beside the television. He sorted them in such a way that those he liked best (or the ones he reckoned Susie in the store would like best, if they had the same taste) were lying on top, in case she took up his offer and came round. He had to go out to the bathroom again and press his ears to the side of his head – now his face looked thinner still. Much better than before, she had said. He drew his comb back through his hair; it was difficult, like pushing one's hand through water with spread fingers. He inspected the comb afterwards in a stronger light. He couldn't see anything. Then he wandered through to the kitchen to make some coffee. His shift list was up on the fridge; he was on duty the following day at eight in the morning. Working weekend shifts did not bother Bent – something the temps did everything to avoid, despite the fact that it meant a few extra kroner. The weekends were fine; they tended to be quiet times, for one reason or another. It was as if death only operated from Monday to Friday, as though death kept office hours and charged an hourly rate. The angel shift, that was how they termed weekends. He put the card from the hairdresser's into the basket with all the other adverts and lifted the kettle from the stove.

The phone rang.

He let go of the kettle and ran through into the living-room. No-one ever phoned. He waited. It kept on ringing. He snatched up the receiver.

"Bent? Are you ill?"

It was Frank.

Bent had to sit down. He swapped hands and took a deep breath, as unobtrusively as he could.

"Ill? No, I'm not ill."

Now he'd said it. Now that lie was used up already.

"You never came," Frank said.

"I was late home from work. Had to do an extra shift."

"I waited for you for a long time, Bent."

"I'm sorry. Really. I should have let you know."

"You're welcome to come now."

"Now? What d'you mean?"

"That you're welcome to come now. I'm here."

Bent stretched in the direction of the window, as far as the cord would allow, and peered out. There was a blue light down in Frank's Salon. He could see Frank, sitting in one of the barber's chairs – the middle one – with his back to him, a cordless phone to his ear. He was wearing his white jacket, with all its combs and a pair of shining scissors in the breast pocket. He made a sudden movement and the chair swung slowly round. Bent let go of the curtains and retreated. He could hear Frank's low laughter.

"I thought you weren't home," he said. "Your place is so dark."

"I haven't got around to putting the lights on yet."

There was quiet again.

"Are you coming?"

"Can't I come next month instead? Friday of next month, perhaps?"

Bent heard the heaviness of Frank's breathing and something that fell to the floor and shattered. He did not dare look to see what it was.

"Next month? December?"

"Yes, the last Friday in December. Would that be alright?"

Frank laughed again, strangely, as if he had something in his throat.

"No, that won't be possible."

"Why not?"

"Why not? Why can't you come now? I'm here."

"I'm tired."

"Quite sure you're not ill?"

"I'm just tired. It's work. There was a child today. Two children."

Bent heard himself saying the words. He sank down on the chair. For the third time that day, he thought to himself, he had said more than he should have. Two things he had not believed he would ever say and one thing he never should have said. He wanted to take the words back. He wanted to deny them altogether. Only temps talked about the dead.

"I'm tired," he said again. "It's this weather."

"You can come tomorrow."

"Saturday. But you're closed."

"I'll open for you."

Bent squirmed on the chair.

"I'm working tomorrow too. I've a double shift."

"Well, well. A busy time, isn't it?"

"I've no idea when I'll be home. It's always busy."

Frank was quiet a long while.

"I'm here now," he said at last. "Just so you know."

He put the phone down. Bent stayed where he was, the receiver in his hands, then carefully he replaced it as though frightened he might waken someone. He did not dare go over to the window. He did not dare put on the light. Instead he went out to the bathroom, took off his clothes and showered. He washed his hair, not with the shampoo (he left that where it was) but with the old soap he had always used. He scrubbed his scalp really vigorously, as hard as he could; he shook under the slender and uneven stream of water. It was not sufficient for his body; like a projector that cannot light the whole of a screen but just sections in turn – the hands, the stomach, the shoulders, the knees. He saw the water taking with it trails of hair in a black circle down the plughole.

Afterwards Bent tried to watch a film, the one at the bottom of the pile, but he could not follow the plot. The cast became too overwhelming and he did not know who had done what or why. After quarter of an hour he gave up, checked that the cooker was off, and the door locked, and went to bed. He could not sleep. He knew it. The sheet underneath him was not right. The strange smell from his own head was more powerful now, as though it had spread over his whole body when he showered. It was like lying somewhere else entirely, in a different bed, in a hotel room where someone immediately before had got up and left behind their own fat shadow like a hollow in the mattress. The noises from the street were distinct: shouts, music, engines, something smashing – either a bottle or a window. Then everything was quiet, almost – it was never completely quiet.

And Bent woke with a start. The phone had rung. It rang again. He staggered over to it. It was past midnight. He reached out his hand. It kept on ringing. He answered it.

"Bent Samuelsen?" said a voice, a man's voice.

It was not Frank; it was someone else, a stranger's voice. It was just some wrong number, Bent imagined, some drunk. But it couldn't be a wrong number; someone had just given his name, his whole name. Someone was dead – his father, it had to be his father. Somebody was phoning Bent to tell him: the minister, the police, a neighbour – most likely the neighbour from the white house at the back of the boat sheds, where they used to play on the beach.

"Yes," Bent said, almost impatiently. "Yes?"

"We're disappointed in you."

"What?"

"We're disappointed in you, Bent."

"Who is this I'm talking to?"

"We have a common friend. Short back and sides."

And it dawned on Bent – it was one of Frank's customers, it had to be one of his customers. Someone he had met either on the way in or out, someone he'd held the door for or nodded to or greeted, but never really talked to. Bent struggled over to the window; it was dark down there in the salon, apart from the pale blue light above the mirror as it might be in some great, empty aquarium.

"What do you want?" Bent hissed.

"What do you want? That's the question."

Bent suddenly realised that he was getting really angry. He could not keep still. Something rose within him – a rage, a violent rage. It was a long time since he'd felt that, yet it almost felt good. He could have shattered something.

"You woke me up!" he shouted.

"You didn't answer my question."

"And you didn't answer mine! What is it you want?"

He heard the breathing at the other end of the line – somewhere else in the same city, the same district, maybe even the same street. Something fell – a glass or a cup – something that spilled.

"Are you scared now?" the stranger asked.

"Scared? What d'you mean?"

Before any response came, there was a weak sound of laughter.

"D'you think you're something special now? Huh? Better than us?"

Bent didn't reply. His feet were freezing. There was a draught coming from the hallway. The noise of a siren drifted through the city, an ambulance – two folk had gone and beaten each other senseless just before closing time. A dog barked in a flat above or down below.

"Bastard!" Bent exclaimed. "Bloody bastard!"

He heard a click in the receiver, a pip, as if the noise of the siren had been trapped by the apparatus and now was extending outwards in every direction. Then the voice came again.

"We have to take care of Frank. That's all I have to say. We have to take care of Frank."

The line went dead. Bent let go of the receiver; it extended to the floor, just and no further. He let it hang like that. He gave it a kick. The receiver smashed into the wall. Furious, he went into the kitchen. *Now I won't get to sleep,* he thought, *now I really won't get to sleep.* He ransacked the food cupboard and the fridge. *But I said it all the same – bastard, bloody bastard.* He could have used stronger language, that he could have done – words he had all but forgotten. He was not going to button his lip if the situation demanded it. He spat into the washing-up foam. Finally he found what he was on the hunt for – a doughnut – at the very back of the breadbin. He sat down at the kitchen table and ate the doughnut slowly. It was dry and hard. It made no odds. He ate it and it broke up in his mouth like thick dust. He drank a glass of water and it tasted of mustard; then he went back to bed.

He lay there, awake and frightened – really frightened now. He felt it like a heavy weight in his stomach; the other side of rage and fury: fear. He had broken out. He had betrayed them, this band of silent men to which he himself had belonged. Frank's faithful customers. One Friday in November he had ridiculed them, and on a whim – in an utterly unpremeditated manner and without heed – he had made fools of them. Bent tore at the duvet. He was burning. He pressed his face into the pillow. But sleep he did nonetheless; he dreamed something or other about Susie. She was waiting for him while he rewound all the films, but they never got there, they kept dragging. He dreamed of the shells on the seashore, that their names were given to farm animals: cow, sheep, goat – the mussel was a cow, the cat was blue. And he dreamed of the black eye of the plughole that sucked hair and skin into itself. Sleep was a metal link of vision that rusted solid in a new day.

Bent woke up in a different light. Amazed, he got up, in a different light. He put on his dressing gown and went over to the window, looked out. Winter. He wished he could have seen it, that precise moment when sleet turned to snow, when grey became white – that transition from heaviness to lightness. But he had not once seen rain turning to sleet, even when standing in the midst of it feeling the weight of the wet cold. Now he could see footprints leading along the pavement from Frank's Salon, crossing the street by the store.

Someone had been there already. Bent whirled round. The phone was hanging over the floor, still swinging slightly like a slow pendulum. It was half past seven. He put the phone down, then quickly lifted it again. He could hear the dialling tone. He called the Royal Infirmary to say he was sick. He could not come to work . . . he was ill . . . it was his stomach . . . there would be more to report the following day . . . he was ill and whatever it was was infectious . . . it was more than likely something infectious. He banged the phone down. He just stood where he was, out of breath, as if waiting for them to call straight back and expose his lie. Now he had done it. Now he could not call to say he was alright, thereby doubling the lie with a half-truth. Why was there no such thing as a white truth? It was the first time he had been off work. The dead would have longer to wait that day. The dead were in the minority. The dead had nothing to say.

He put on some coffee and cut a slice of bread for himself. But he wasn't hungry and left it. He swept up the crumbs from the table, put the knife back in the drawer. Winter blinded him. Whiteness pressed in from every side – snow, disintegrated light. He went into the bathroom and looked at himself in the mirror. Yes, he really had to go on a diet – the previous night's doughnut was the last. He was totally out of proportion; he was an inverted exclamation mark with far too small a dot on top. He had to become an "i"; it was high time he became a bog standard "i" who slept every night and did not go munching doughnuts instead. He drew his fingers through his hair. It was no longer smooth but dry, dry and stiff. He looked at his hands; a sprinkling of dust fell from them.

At that moment the doorbell rang. Someone rang Bent Samuelsen's doorbell. It was long enough since that had happened last – then it had been the Jehovah's Witnesses. He hurried out to the door, then stopped. What if it was Susie, and there he was standing in a hideous dressing gown and in bare feet, barely out of bed on the first day of winter? What an impression. But all he could do was open the door. He did. It wasn't Susie, it was Frank. There was Frank standing there staring at him, with a plastic bag from the store in each hand.

"Are you not going to ask me in?"

Bent stepped to one side and let him past. Frank put the bags down on the floor, took off his shoes and coat, and turned to face him. Frank stared at Bent's forehead and smiled, almost imperceptibly.

"You can be honest with me, Bent."

"How d'you mean?"

"Haven't we known each other a long time now?"

Bent didn't answer. The door clicked shut. Frank's eye was everywhere. It was on him.

"Haven't we? Known each other a long time?"

"I reckon so. Fifteen years."

Frank moved closer. Frank was almost touching him.

"You're ill. Why didn't you say you were ill?"

"I'm not ill."

"I've just phoned your work. They said you weren't there. They said you were ill."

Bent grew cold and afraid, more frightened still.

"You phoned the hospital? Why did you call the hospital?"

"I'm worried about you, Bent."

Frank lifted the plastic bags and smiled again.

"I bought some goodies for you. Shall I put them in the kitchen?"

Bent took a deep breath.

"Yes, in the kitchen. On you go."

Frank took a step backwards, stared at him again, and shook his head a long while – just so as not to be in any doubt.

"You really look in a bad way, I must say."

"There's nothing to be worried about."

"And here was me thinking you were just skiving."

Frank gave an abrupt, high laugh. Bent looked away, agitated.

"I'm not skiving."

"There are plenty who do, there are plenty who do."

Frank whistled a tune from an old television series while he went out to the kitchen and put milk and various spreads in the fridge, and a loaf in the breadbin. Finally he thumped down a big paper bag on the table and grinned.

Bent was standing in the doorway.

"Doughnuts," Frank said.

Bent said nothing.

"You like doughnuts, I believe. Isn't that right?"

Bent nodded. Frank took one out of the bag and gave it to him. It was warm and fresh, but it swelled in the mouth like a mushroom. Bent swallowed and swallowed. Frank's eye was on him the whole time. Frank never let him out of his sight.

"Are you not going to show me the rest of the flat?"

They went back to the living room. Frank trailed a finger along the length of the bookcase, peered at a photo of Bent's parents – taken the day before he left home – and picked up some magazines lying strewn about on the floor beside the television.

"May I take these, Bent?"

"Yes."

"Sure you've read them?"

"Yes, I've read them."

"Absolutely certain? I don't want to take them if you're not finished with them."

"I've read them all. Just take them."

Frank put the magazines in one of the empty bags.

"In times gone by the salon subscribed to a couple of weeklies and took a daily paper. Gone are the days."

Frank sighed and stood over by the window, peering out through the curtains.

"Good view," he said. "Funny to see the salon from here, look down on it from up above."

Frank kept standing there, his back to Bent, silent – a thin shadow set against all the whiteness. The curtains breathed gently on both sides of him. *Now I'm off*, Bent thought. *I'm off and I'm leaving him here, and I'll not come back before he's gone.*

Frank began to speak, quietly.

"I used to come with Dad sometimes, when I was a boy. In the days when a haircut was three kroner and everyone wanted Brylcreem and a cheeseline cut. I sat on a stool in the corner and wasn't allowed to say a word. Dad wasn't to be disturbed while he was working. But one day I nodded off. I fell asleep and tumbled right off the stool. I gave Dad such a jump he cut half an earlobe off a customer. It poured blood. Oh, Lord, what blood there was. But that customer came back just the same. Next month he was back in the chair again and his ear had healed. Have you ever had any reason to complain about me, Bent?"

"No."

"Have you ever had any reason to be dissatisfied with the manner in which I've carried out my work?"

"Never. Never, Frank."

Frank turned to face Bent and he leant forwards.

"I won't manage much longer."

"What d'you mean?"

"The years don't make us any younger. Soon we'll all be pensioners getting things half price. It's best to quit while you're ahead."

"You're not serious?" Bent said.

"Am I not? I have three barber chairs down there, but only use one of them. It wouldn't make any odds if you all took it in turns to come to the house and I cut your hair in the kitchen."

"The pensioners could pay full price," Bent said. "Just like everyone else."

Frank laughed and smacked his own brow.

"Here I am inflicting my insignificant problems on you. As if you didn't have enough to worry about."

Bent grew uneasy. Frank didn't take his eyes off him.

"How much do I owe you?" Bent asked. "For all the groceries."

"Don't worry about that now. I think you should go and lie down, get better. Would you like me to make you some tea?"

"There's really no need."

"Alright, I just wondered."

"Thanks," Bent mumbled. "Thank you very much."

Frank went over to the television and began putting the Mia Farrow films into the plastic bag with the magazines. Bent was about to stop him again.

"I've paid for them," Frank said. "It costs a fortune if you just let them lie like that."

And Bent didn't stop him. He watched Frank put the films into the bag, one after the other, and carry them out to the hall. Once there he put on his coat and shoes, and when he stood tall once more he stared at Bent again with that look that bore down on him.

"Just come whenever it suits you. I'm there regardless."

Frank opened the door and hesitated, almost as though he was on the point of changing his mind and turning.

"That's all I wanted to say," he finished. "Get better soon."

Frank went. Bent hurried over to the window, and after a moment he saw Frank go into the store. When he came out again all he was carrying were the magazines. He went obliquely across the road and unlocked the door to the salon. Once inside he put on the main light and disappeared for a few minutes, most likely into the back premises. Then he reappeared in his white coat with his father's gold lapel. He sat down in the barber's chair, the middle one, and swung round on it as he sat there, looking up at Bent's window.

Bent let go of the curtain and backed away from the window. He just stood like that, motionless, until he grew cold. He had never heard it so quiet; the snow soundproofed everything. He padded through to the kitchen and ate the doughnuts, as quietly as he could. But it gave him no peace of mind. He tore up the card from Spaghetti and threw it in the bin. Already he could sense a vague whiff from the chicken bones. He slammed the cupboard door shut and was startled by his own loudness. He had to go back to the window. Frank was sitting down there, looking up at him. Bent could stand it no longer. He dressed, took the lift down, and when he came out the whiteness of the light went right into his eyes so he had to shield his face behind his hands for a few seconds. Then he ran across the road and went into Frank's Salon.

Frank got up, adjusted his jacket, and smiled.

"I knew you'd come," he said.

"Yes, I've come after all."

"You're not cold, Bent?"

"No, I'm fine now. Shall we get started?"

"There's something I want to show you first."

Bent went out with Frank to the back premises. There stood a whole line of black bin bags, all of them full, standing against the wall. And on each of the sacks Bent could see that a different year was written, right the way back to 1974.

"My life's work," Frank said softly.

Bent didn't quite understand what Frank meant. He began to wish he could go.

"What is it?"

"I couldn't just throw it all away, could I?"

Frank toppled over one of the sacks and emptied the contents over the floor. It was hair, a veritable stream of hair that whirled round before finally coming to rest.

"1982," Frank said. "D'you recognise your own?"

He waded out into the hair, plucked a few tufts, and looked at them more closely.

"Here we are, I think."

Frank nodded to Bent.

"You've got a bit greyer since then. But otherwise it's fine."

Frank laughed, clapped his hands and stood in a cloud of hair.

"Right, we should think about getting started."

They went back into the salon again. Bent sat down in the middle one of the three chairs, and Frank cranked it up a couple of times, put the cape round him and the paper collar into place. Then he positioned himself behind Bent, took the scissors from his breast pocket, snipped the air once quickly, and just stood there with the shining scissors in his hand, as if pondering something. He then stuck them in his pocket and got the electric clippers instead. Bent closed his eyes and heard the buzzing close to his ear, really close. He felt the tug at his neck, the blades ever so slightly pulling at his skin. Frank bent his head forwards, then worked the razor through his hair, right to his forehead, slow and steady.

Bent opened his eyes wide and looked at himself in the mirror – in the old, smooth mirror that erased more than it revealed. He could see his skull – the thin, dented cranium became visible – and the white line that outlined the person he was. Frank laid his hand there, on his bare head, as the razor still hummed in his other hand.

Bent sensed a sudden queasiness. He twisted round. He tried to get up. But Frank held him down.

"Are we friends now?" Frank asked.

Translated by Kenneth Steven

KARIN FOSSUM

The Pillar

Father walks with long strides, plants his feet firmly on the ground.

A fresh breeze blows towards him from the sea. It lifts the thin fair hair from the scalp and blows it backwards in a little white tuft.

The boy stumbles along behind on thin legs. His sandals are a bit too big. The knees are knobbly, the red shorts flap around him like a skirt on a girl.

Vemund. Father takes the name in his mouth and tastes it. He pushes it to the side of his mouth as if it were a strange fruit. Vemund isn't a man's name, he thinks. It's something weak and frail, there's something girlish about it, something that swishes. The boy is so insubstantial. Pale and thin, his features much too delicate. Not like a son should be, solid and well-built, like himself. He can never find the right way to speak to him, doesn't quite know who he is, this skinny body trailing along behind him. A pale something that shivers and whines. Says the water looks cold and that he doesn't want to. Whereas he, he had always run on in front.

"You can't tell what temperature the water is just by *looking* at it!" Father is irritated. A schoolboy who can't swim – that's terrible. And he won't learn either.

"But it looks so cold!"

Vemund looks at the dark breakers with their foaming white tops. A week before mid-summer and the water is leaden grey. They haven't had any sun.

He knows that the water is ice-cold, and it's not true that he can't swim. He can just about stay afloat and move forward a couple of feet; but his legs dangle down in the water and act like brakes.

His arm movements are good, so are his leg movements. It's just that he can't do them at the same time.

Father turns towards him. "If you fell in the water, out of your depth," – he stares at him – "then you'd drown. You'd panic. You're not confident enough. Seven or eight strokes isn't swimming. We live by the sea, Vemund. You can't live where we live and not be able to swim. You shouldn't even be allowed out in the boat, do you realise that?"

"But I've got a lifejacket."

"Yes, yes. But you've got to learn now. It's this summer or never. We can't carry on like this for years. Make an effort now, boy." He walks on. They're on the top of a smooth, sloping rock, and now the path drops steeply towards the beach and the jetty. Vemund thinks that if he fell in out of his depth then he'd swim like hell. Because he would have to. When they practise he keeps to the shallows. The bottom is never far away. His legs get heavy and sink by themselves; he starts swallowing water. And it's so cold. He struggles to keep up. Father has long legs, and he is annoyed.

Vemund sees the beach now, where the water is shallower and paler. It looks friendly, with the yellow sand and above it a belt of polished round pebbles in different colours, strewn like pearls, white, grey, pink or pied. And he sees the jetty beyond, black and wet, a road that runs straight from the land into the sea. The deep water begins at the end of the jetty. Three metres, his father said. A little way out is a blue island, bare and fairly large. When the water is warm the bigger boys swim out to it.

Four hundred and fifty metres. The grown-ups measured it. The name of the island is the Pirate, they've been there in the boat.

Father stops suddenly and stands stock-still, a hard-contoured man, a dark sculpture against the pale sky.

"When you can swim out to the Pirate and back, then you can swim. Nearly a kilometre. You should be able to manage at least that. I mean, after a while. Since we live by the sea and have a boat and all that." He turns round. "Take off your shorts. There's an onshore wind. That means the water's warmer."

Vemund starts to wade out. It is freezing cold. The shock is the same every time, even though he knows it's cold and is prepared for it. The bottom is soft, the sand is like velvet, with here and there a shell. He whips up a little sand as the water rises up him in little jabs, to his knees, halfway up his thighs, to the swimming trunks with the blue and white stripes. Then he reaches the belt of pebbles and shells which he has to cross to get far enough out, so that the water is up to his waist. Just above the navel.

"Stop now, Vemund!"

He raises his arms up in front of his chest, but he doesn't want to put his hands in the water. Father sits on a large rock, the same rock every time, watching and gesticulating and instructing.

"Yes! That isn't so bad now, is it?"

He doesn't answer. He tries to stand on tiptoe. He's thinking it'll soon be over and they can go home again.

"Right then, let's begin. Into position and dive. On you go, Vemund!"

He sags a little at the knees. The water glides upwards over his chest and the waves break over his arms, his legs shrivel in the cold water. Reluctantly he allows himself to fall forward, with his knees bunched under him, the little hands splashing away furiously four or five times, until a wave breaks over his face and he has to stand up again. His teeth are chattering. He takes several little steps and doesn't understand why he can't do it. What kind of secret is this that he isn't in on? He's got two arms and two legs like everyone else. Maybe he wasn't meant to swim. And the water's so cold anyway, and anyway you can always just stay in the shallows. Father shakes his head. Stares down among the stones and tries to summon up a few fragments of goodwill until he has enough to offer encouragement:

"You're doing well, Vemund! You've been under now. In a little while you'll get used to the water. But make a bit more effort. And slower strokes, boy, not so fast. And don't forget to breathe. Fill your lungs with air and then you'll float, just like a balloon, OK?"

Vemund takes a deep breath and throws himself forward. He parts the water and kicks out a bit with his legs, one stroke, two, three. Then he breathes out again, then in again, swallows a mouthful or two of salt water this time, coughs and splutters, but his arms are working away, four strokes, five. His legs grow heavy, they begin to sink.

"Legs, Vemund! Legs! Very good, kick out, give it all you've got!"

He disappears under the water then rises up again, the icy water pouring and rilling off him; he rubs his eyes and spits.

"That's better now, Vemund! Better now, don't you think?"

After ten tries Father is satisfied. He managed nine strokes. But he wasn't using his legs, and he didn't move through the water. Clumsily Father dries his back and helps him pull his shorts up over the wet swimming trunks. Vemund's teeth chatter, he shivers and his lips are blue. There is a deep line in Father's forehead, a furrow of worry.

He doesn't like to look at it.

"Come on. Let's sit on the jetty for a minute."

He sees how chilled the boy is and it makes him uncomfortable.

Vemund follows hesitantly. Father sits at the very end and lets his legs dangle.

"That's it. Sit down. You won't fall in, I'm here. Come along, boy."

He glides down on to his backside and scuttles the last little bit. Feels Father lightly rub his back.

"Remember when you learnt to ride a bike? That little red bike?"

He nods.

"Remember how difficult that was?"

"Yes, but not all that. I learnt it in three days. Then you said I cycled too slowly. Now you say I swim too fast. Cycling's easy. Swimming is a lot more difficult."

"No, no. But you have to . . . cross a barrier, in a way. Do you see what I mean?"

"No."

Father sighs.

"Being able to ride isn't so important. Not really. But swimming, Vemund! It could be a matter of life and death. Look at the sea."

Vemund looks.

"Most of the sea is deep. Maybe several hundred metres. It's only along the edges that it's shallow."

He shivers and begins to get goose-pimples.

"Lots of people drown, every summer. Grown-ups and children. Because they can't swim. Quite frightening, isn't it?"

"I think perhaps dinner is ready now soon."

"Are you listening?"

"Yes."

"If you fell in here," – Father leans forward and stares down into the black water – "you would drown, right? Three metres, Vemund! Not all that deep. You'd drown in two metres too. Even one and a half. Do you know why?"

Vemund isn't quite sure what the answer is.

"Because you're only one metre forty tall."

Father stares and stares down into the water. He puts a careful hand on his shoulder. Everything goes quiet. The water ripples lightly in front of the jetty.

Vemund waits. Something is wrong. He wants to get up but can't work out how. If he leans forward he'll fall in. With his father's arm round him he can't scuttle backwards and save himself that way, not with the strong arm blocking him in like that. And he can't swim, the water is ice-cold and deep, three metres deep.

His father is peering at a point some way out from them. Vemund searches between the breakers and sees a pale orange smudge floating.

He stares at it. A stinging jellyfish. It bobs and sways from wave to wave without getting any closer. Vemund stares, concentrating hard on the jellyfish. It seems to him the hand on his shoulder gets heavier. He can't feel the toes inside his sandals. It's as if he's shrinking. From the corner of his eye his father becomes indistinct. A dark, diffuse shadow that can no longer talk.

"In the old days," he says suddenly, "they used to throw the children into the sea with a bit of rope around their waist. They had to splash about as best they could. A bit brutal, maybe, but at least they learned to swim, without spending a whole summer on it." He smiles sadly. There is silence again.

Suddenly the jellyfish rocks wildly and vanishes for a few seconds.

This is the moment at which Vemund falls in. He falls slowly and softly, the little body almost upright in the air, but with legs bent and fists clenched. With a cautious splash he hits the water and sinks slowly towards the bottom, almost surprised, but his body feels nothing, he is on his stomach there in the deep water and it is so cold he feels the pain in his temples. His body isn't big, he's just a wisp of a kid. A breaker rolls in and obliterates the little fleck of foam floating on the surface.

A gasping second goes by before Father reacts.

Then he gets up quickly and looks around. Sees nothing and dives into the sea with a splash. It's a shock; the water is much colder than he thought. His body seems paralysed, it almost disappears and he is just two pained eyes peering stiffly through the dark water, searching for a thin white leg, a little hand, or the blue and white stripes, something that stands out in the smudged darkness, but he sees nothing, just his own flailing hands, drained of all colour. So he pushes off and shoots up towards the surface again. Of course the boy isn't on the bottom, he thinks, he's much too light, but when at last his head breaks through the surface he still sees nothing; he stares out towards the horizon, listening, but he hears no scream. Panic seizes him for a moment before he ducks back down again. He swims round the jetty, sees the slimy black pillars and something black shooting along the bottom, and thinks: he has to be here, he fell straight in, straight off the end, and there's no current in the bay; a small child can't just disappear like this however big and deep the sea is, because he can't swim, so he must be lying right in front of the jetty, maybe just a metre from the pillars; he should be visible, pale as he is, but there's so much bloody seaweed all over the place, great forests of greeny-black bladderwrack and other stuff he doesn't know the name of, he pushes aside something slimy and soft to look underneath it – the boy's so little, he doesn't take much room – but he sees nothing and can't hold his breath anymore; he's afraid he'll faint and kicks off again, bursting through the surface like a torpedo, and can't believe this is really happening, it must be a bad dream.

He treads water and spins round, silently, searching for the fair hair, looking for air bubbles, dives down again, because time is running out, he can't go for help, it's too far, he'll have to do it himself; Vemund is somewhere down there in the cold water; just keep going, he thinks, but his eyes are fading, the salt water is too much for them, he can hardly see any more, just splashes aimlessly, almost panicking, hardly feeling the cold and the water anymore, just a fierce exhaustion that slows his arms and legs down, and he rises up again, gets his chin just out of the water and gasps in disbelief. I can't find him. It's not possible. He swims towards the jetty and holds on to one of the pillars. Hangs there by one arm, slightly rocking.

Silence.

His clothes feel like lead. He walks slowly and unsteadily up the steep path, constantly turning and staring out over the sea. All the time he wants to turn, but there's nothing to see, nothing he can do. Now and then he stumbles over a tuft or a stone, even though his gaze is riveted to the ground in front of him. Because if he lifts his head then maybe he'll see the house that is getting closer and closer, the sharp white gable amongst the black pines, the house he will have to enter. Maybe the windows will be open, maybe she'll be looking out and see from afar that he is alone, so he walks quietly and holds his breath, walks like a thief in the night, thinking: this is not possible.

But his steps bring him ever closer. Soon he sees the roof. And because the kitchen window is open a light-coloured curtain flaps soft and playful like a sail in a carefree dance, but inside is dark, and the front door a black gap.

He is at the steps. At that moment he sees a naked shoulder pass the window, hears her quick footsteps inside, then she opens the door. He raises his head heavily and meets her gaze.

"What's happened?"

His head droops again, his clothes are cold as ice, the wind drives in from behind, and he shrivels when he hears her voice, there is rebuke in it, with a touch of uncertainty.

"Well, tell me! Good God, you're dripping wet!"

"No," he mumbles, and supports himself against the jamb, "I don't know, it happened so fast."

The rest is just a whimper. And when he looks up again he sees fear in her eyes.

"But you do watch out for him, don't you? Good God, he's just a little boy."

He leans his head against the jamb again and realises that she doesn't understand. He closes his eyes and feels weak. He sees the future disappearing behind a fuzzy darkness, and the road isn't there anymore, it stops right where he's standing, there is no way forward.

Then he sees Vemund. In a blue tracksuit, half-hidden behind his mother.

His hair is wet. Mother turns and strokes his head.

"I swam underwater, Pappa," he says nervously. "And I couldn't see you anywhere."

Father tries to take a step, but his knees fail him. The big man topples forward, and Vemund stares in alarm at him, at the pillar of dark granite that is always reality, the way it suddenly collapses in the middle and loses its colour. The face is grey, the mouth gapes in such a strange way.

"Is Pappa ill?"

Mother shakes her head and bites her lip. And finally he falls.

The chin hits the floor with a resounding crack.

Translated by Robert Ferguson

JOSTEIN GAARDER

The Catalogue

What matters our creative endless toil,
when at a snatch oblivion ends the coil.
GOETHE, *FAUST II* (MEPHISTO)

I

The Catalogue is global. It envelops the world like a fine net, a net that gets finer and finer as time goes on. The whole of humanity helps in its creation. Not a single uninspired soul is excluded. And yet it is written in vain.

I began working for the Catalogue when I was just seventeen. Then I was a messenger in the small seaside town where I still live today. Now I'm seventy-three and have been national editor-in-chief for a generation. And so, in attempting this assessment of its importance, I have a certain amount of experience to draw on.

The Catalogue is the diary of the entire human race. It is published every four years (in leap years), and every citizen on the planet is duty-bound to produce a statement of between seven and fourteen lines in length for the Catalogue each time it is published.

So, once citizens reach the age of eighteen they must know what they want to say to the world. Careful thought must be given to it since the Catalogue is studied with the greatest veneration in schools and homes, and it is preserved in perpetuity.

Statements may be reprinted from one edition to the next, but everyone has the right to insert a new one every four years. The latter is certainly the more popular option. But many people elect to keep the same article for years, sometimes all their lives – perhaps because of apathy, monomania or lack of invention.

I have already pointed out that the Catalogue covers the entire globe. On exactly the same date (29 February), a Catalogue is published in every locality. Within it, the local inhabitants (anything between 100,000 and half a million) are listed alphabetically. And every home gets a copy of its own local Catalogue as soon as it comes out. As a result it's easy to consult the Catalogue and find out what friends and neighbours consider important about the world. Each local area must have the whole country's Catalogues available, and a national register enables any individual to be traced to their local area. In addition, several national centres have large libraries containing every Catalogue in the world. Such libraries are identical no matter where on the planet they are situated. When you walk around such a library you are in contact with every person on earth, because all the Catalogues, as well as being printed in their original tongue, also have an edition in a universal language. Thus it is the work of very few minutes to trace the words of anybody in the world.

As can be seen, the Catalogue is entirely democratic in structure. Everyone is treated the same. Everyone has the same rights and responsibilities with regard to the Catalogue, no matter where on the planet they live. And all the local Catalogues are identical in appearance. There is no meta-Catalogue, no anthology or Catalogue of Catalogues with selections of the "best" quotations. It is true that, at an early date in the history of the Catalogue, the idea was mooted of giving preference to great women and men – such as heads of state, writers and philosophers – and providing them with more space in the Catalogue than more modest and less significant souls. But the idea was rejected by a considerable popular majority. Even the more modest proposal of allowing a selected few the opportunity to put their Catalogue entry in a wider-spaced type was turned down. To quote a popular saying: "We're all equal in the Catalogue."

This equality does not mean to suggest that it is equally simple for the Catalogue's staff to wrest an offering from each citizen. I, who have worked for the Catalogue for more than fifty-five years, can assure you of that. Many people – the large majority, in fact – are very punctual when it comes to sending in their contributions. The average citizen not only performs his civic duty with pleasure, but is almost "aroused" by the idea of spreading his manifesto. But a number of citizens do indeed require some coaxing before a maxim appears. If, ultimately, this fails his name will appear in the Catalogue without any entry. And this is regarded as the deepest shame. Living life from one leap year to the next without anything important to say is viewed as an abject humiliation. Insignificant folk like these are often described as scroungers. At regular intervals motions are put forward to confiscate their homes and stop their food supplies.

Taken as a whole, the individual isn't asked to do so very much. All that is required is seven to fourteen lines every four years, and what is that? We don't believe that a human life is validated by its physical processes alone. Animals and plants are every bit as good at living life from conception to death as we are. Many regard physical existence merely as a tool or organ for an inner life, and this the Catalogue helps to reflect. At least once every four years people must pull themselves together and think about what they want to do with their lives. One might say that they are forced to take the food out of their mouths and ask themselves why they are eating.

Although there should be plenty of time for everyone to think about what they want to convey, there is a remarkable variation in quality amongst the Catalogue's millions of statements. But all are given the same modest treatment, whether they express the most profound sentiments or the tritest of banalities. On the same page you can read clever conundrums, subtle paradoxes, political satire, clumsy attempts to solve the mystery of life, determined efforts to express the quintessence of the Catalogue, a farmer's experiences with stock-raising and a housewife's recipes. To this extent the Catalogue bears witness to the victory of democracy. There are no requirements regarding style or content. Each submission is of equal value. Philosophy and horse-shit are all one.

Nobody lives in vain. Every name appears in the Catalogue. Everyone gets the chance to say and believe something that will be preserved for all time.

II

Reading the Catalogue is like skimming the cream of history.

How many profound meditations, how much worry, how many human souls lie behind each edition of the Catalogue? Today the word culture is synonymous with the Catalogue. Culture in its archaic sense died out at the beginning of the twenty-first century.

There are still individuals who study that culture, but only out of historical interest.

In contrast to pre-Catalogue culture, it is the immeasurable practical importance of the Catalogue that stands out more than anything else. Right across the globe it is possible to get an idea of what any particular person considers important. The practical use humanity makes of such a forum is obvious. Many people read the Catalogue in search of a friend or a spouse. And even when meeting a stranger, it sometimes happens that one remembers the piece he or she wrote in the Catalogue. The topic of conversation suggests itself, and the acquaintanceship gets off to a flying start.

Many others read the Catalogue in their search for Truth. There are examples of people travelling to the other side of the world to meet a particular individual for whom they have formed an interest through the Catalogue. People are constantly making contact to discuss a particular aphorism in depth. Study groups and schools of philosophy are starting up by the dozen. The whole world is one big family.

The Catalogue has always been enveloped by the buzz of speculation. Innumerable dissertations have been penned about how it should be read and understood. The most seductive current interpretation is the "arithmetical" one. According to this school the Catalogue may be read – according to certain arithmetical principles – as a coherent whole. This whole reflects the history of reality, paints a picture of the development of life on earth, paraphrases various philosophical systems, and so on. Above all it links the Catalogue's millions of statements and turns the whole of humanity into one soul – into one single narrative subject, in fact.

Indian mystics have used this school in support of their ancient doctrine of Brahman, or world soul. We are all fractions of the same consciousness, impulses within the same soul or facets of the same eye. This eye is the Catalogue. And the Catalogue is God's eye.

In the West, too, pre-Catalogue anticipations of the arithmetical method have been alluded to. A philosopher like Hegel comes close to the arithmetical method on a purely speculative basis. He actually applied this method to history, just as today we can use it on the Catalogue. Hegel also pondered randomness, and the single individual. He saw history as the story of how the world soul is arriving at a consciousness of itself. Today the arithmetical school believes it can see that idea set out in concrete form. The Catalogue is, to borrow a term from H.G. Wells, the world brain.

To just what extent the arithmetical method is true or false is naturally of the most absorbing interest. It is just now, in our own times, that it's being tested. But it is still too early to give judgment. Our children and grandchildren will have the final verdict.

III

So everything should be rosy. Everyone is proud of humanity's communal property. But when you get down to it, what use is the Catalogue? What aim has this culture in the perspective of eternity? As an ageing man – my life is, of course, a once only phenomenon – I feel the deepest regret that my answer must be negative.

The Catalogue is completely worthless. It is no more than a monstrous expression of human conceit. I have already allowed it a certain practical value. It is a forum for people, a market for souls, an address book for the realm of the spirit. To this extent it is more serviceable than the old culture. But it hasn't made it easier to die.

The idea behind the Catalogue was that all human beings should have their names – and their reflections – etched into something everlasting, something beyond time and space. Just as earlier generations preserved the names of people like Buddha and Aristotle, the Catalogue was to sustain the memory of every member of the human species.

I myself have been hugely enthused by the project. But the truth is that the Catalogue fails to live up to the essential core of its purpose. For what we write in the Catalogue is writing in the sand. Let me explain in more detail.

Three billion years ago the first primitive signs of life appeared in our solar system. And now, today – just as we're in the process of forming a coherent picture of the development of life on earth – we're receiving a series of warnings about life's nemesis. After three billion years in the dark, life has awoken to the consciousness of its own evolution. In this respect evolution has fulfilled its aim. We've reached our goal. And the goal is consciousness of development towards the goal.

So what's left? Does life simply go on and on? Can it? Should it? Are we not at journey's end?

The purely technical liquidation of life is another matter. And that doesn't concern us. It's occurring at this moment. With systematic thoroughness man has begun to destroy the biosphere. We are at the end of the road. Only the very last act remains, the collective suicide on the stage of life, before the curtain falls to the blind and mute applause of the universe.

We are virtuosi in the art that is *ars moriendi*. If one or two of our suicide attempts go wrong, there will always be others ready to take the place of the ones that failed. If we do not celebrate the world's last New Year's Eve with the fireworks of atomic weaponry, we will almost certainly suffocate each other like bacteria in a sugar solution. And if life takes too long to die out like this, sooner or later we will fling aside the curtains of the ozone layer, admitting ultra-violet rays into life's living room on earth.

The methods are also a separate issue. Just *how* we make an end of life is immaterial here. Of far greater importance are the mental preconditions. The ring has been closed. Evolution is at an end. There is no need for more history, there is no room for more history.

But still the Catalogue continues. It grows in size from year to year. Its repositories grow ever bigger, soon they will cover large areas of the earth's surface. With each passing year it gets harder for the living to find space. The Catalogue must be accommodated first. History must come first. But is there room for more history, is there room for more culture? Will we be able to keep track of more thoughts and ideas? Aren't we approaching saturation point? Is history not full of days?

Even if we could imagine a civilisation that was everlasting, the Catalogue would be a hopeless project. At best we would drown in culture. The problem is that we create more history than we are capable of digesting. In the end we become buried in paper. We expire in the excrement of our own past. (It is a long time since human beings lived lives that left no other traces but their own skeletons and a few shards of pottery. Over the last fifty years alone more books have been written than in all of the rest of human history.)

The Catalogue may have a hundred or a thousand years left to run. But what is a thousand years? In my final days on earth, surely I may be allowed to open up the perspective a little? Civilisation – the thin ice upon which we tread – is ultimately merely an island in a sea of chaos. If nothing else, we have a finite number of years – the actual number is immaterial – until all life in our solar system ceases because our own star has burnt itself out. And for me, who has at best fifteen or twenty years of life left, a thousand or a billion is much the same thing.

There is no eternity. That is the basic point. There is no straw to cling to in this ocean on which we're drifting.

I am no longer afraid of dying. I'm resigned to the idea that my visiting time is limited. But I cannot come to terms with the fact that everything – absolutely everything – will cease to exist. I have nothing to hold on to, nothing eternal, nothing that is raised above the level of our transitory flotsam.

Perhaps the Catalogue will survive me. But it will not survive. It, too, is a function of time and space.

As yet the universe – on a speck of which we live – is still conscious of its existence. But this is a very fleeting phenomenon. And even if the arithmetical school were correct in its contention that the Catalogue is the eye of God, it is cold comfort while this eye remains an island in the midst of nothing.

There is no hiding place from time. Time finds us everywhere. The whole of reality is suffused by this restless element we operate in.

Why am I writing this? Perhaps it is one last attempt to wrest control. I don't know. But I have no interest in forcing my tedium on others. Whether or not these lines are found and read after my demise is of no concern to me. I shall be gone by then anyway, I shall be gone the way everything else goes. Look at it how you will, no statement is so crucial that it cannot be dwarfed by the wider context. We belong to a word-spawning race. The most sensible thing a person can do is to keep quiet.

In a few days' time I shall hand in my notice to the Catalogue's international secretariat. Not only am I unfit to be national editor-in-chief, but I'm unfit to be a human being. When the next edition of the Catalogue goes to press, my name will not be followed by the obligatory encomium.

I have finished with the world.

Translated by James Anderson

KARIN SVEEN

A Good Heart

Out from a black chimney on a little brown house with white window frames on the outskirts of a green pine forest and a flat quiet city float little clouds of cobalt blue smoke and silently they cling to the trees.

As if someone were smoking in there, puffing and smoking and blowing! Outside it's raining, a fine drizzle upon the city, the forest and the roof and in the grass which glistens with moisture. And up from the walls of the house rises the heavy smell of logs and pine tar. Stacked in the yard are a couple of cords of gleaming birch; the split wood is the colour of cream, almost golden against the black-stained wall of the woodshed, the grey sawhorse and the grey axe and the grey saw.

There is no fence around the house and no wood thief in sight, nor is there anyone who expects there to be, even though the times are more grey than golden and more and more are having trouble making ends meet while others do better and better and speak louder and louder.

Some get together with friends and talk quietly. They sit in their little houses and puff on their pipes, formulate thoughts and think them out loud.

Standing next to the fire wall, the wood stove sends its scant warmth into the room and its blue smoke up through the chimney and out into the cold.

Sitting around the round table, Olaf and five or six other men are reading pamphlets aloud, passing books across the tablecloth and leafing through papers; smoke is pouring out of the kerosene lamp that is hanging by a chain between their heads and the voices rumble through the body of the fifteen-year-old Synnøve, who is sitting on the divan under the window, listening and watching. Out in the kitchen her mother is watching the coffee pot and sitting on the wood box in her brown Sunday skirt, chewing on granules of coffee. She has a little silver cross in the throat of her blouse and is religious in her

own way and a good singer – everyone asks her and she expects that
to happen any minute now.

And the men call to her and beg; she stands in the doorway
between the living room and the kitchen, gives in to them and folds
her arms behind her back. Sitting over in the pale light under the
window, Synnøve listens to her mother's deliberate, billowing voice,
like an emerging dawn, or steam that rises from the earth after chilly
nights:

> *Wealthy folk are often feasting at home and with their friends*
> *And rarely do they give a thought to the working men!*
> *They should take the crofter's place, if only for a year,*
> *So they might understand his lot, the life he has to bear!*

When she has sung all the verses and her face is red and glowing,
one of Olaf's friends, who has spent several years logging in the Soviet
Union, walks over to her and kisses her on both cheeks and whispers
"comrade" in her ear. The mother's eyes fill with tears, she looks
down and over at her husband and at Synnøve and says:

"Terrible manners he's picked up in the woods!"

Because people might just as well appear stark naked as kiss each
other while someone's watching!

But the men just whoop and clap their fists, suck on their pipes and
pack up their papers; and the mother puts on a clean tablecloth and
brings out the coffee.

Olga Berg has faith in common folk and in a people's God and she
sings at all kinds of meetings; everyone always wants her to sing and
she enjoys it and likes to be asked. At the prayer house and the
community hall and even at a strike meeting at the market place one
time. That was when the seamstresses in the town were threatened
with dismissal because they had organised. She had stood in the
picket line and sung; why shouldn't she?

Olaf Berg says the same, and even though he's not exactly religious,
he'll go so far as to say that there's more devilry between heaven and
earth than the Lord could have dreamt up – damned if it isn't other
lords who have done it, he'll say. And Olga Berg is pleased that he says
that. And is satisfied.

The two of them have agreed that every other child should be
baptised and since Synnøve is the eldest and therefore baptised, she
shall also be confirmed. Today is the Sunday before catechism; Berg
and the men are going off to a meeting across town and Synnøve and

her mother clear the table, open a window to air the room and wash the dishes.

Synnøve dries. The cups scrape against the bottom of the zinc wash basin. The water is steaming and condensation forms on the little kitchen window.

It's quiet after the men. Synnøve likes to listen to them. One time one of them had asked what she was going to be when she grew up, and she burst out that she was going to be a communist and she would have twelve kids and all of them would be communists and loggers just like the man who'd been in the Soviet Union.

And the men had slapped their knees and laughed and asked: "And what if you have girls?" It was all quiet for a minute, because at the time that hadn't occurred to her, but she found her tongue and said that that made no difference! Loggers they'd be, the whole pack of them! And while the laughter pounded against her and her face reached boiling point, she decided that she would rather have strange ideas than be taken for being shortsighted.

Her mother draws breath a couple of times as if she intended to say something, and then she says it: "I wish I were in better shape."

"How's that?"

"So I could earn a little more money and you could get a decent confirmation dress."

"It doesn't matter," Synnøve says. There's nothing more she can say and nothing more she does say.

"But I did get some nice bleached sugar sacks from the store which I'll try to use. If all else fails."

"I'm sure that'll be fine," Synnøve says, and tries to imagine what she'll look like.

Outside it's raining and the loggers are at a meeting and inside the living-room it's chilly and the kerosene lamp casts a yellow reflection against the low ceiling.

It's raining the following day as well, all day long, a wet, watery rain that splashes and washes everything it comes in contact with. In the late afternoon when the ground is squishingly soft and soggy and the grass can be peeled loose from the earth, along comes Mother's aunt, puffing down the road.

No-one really knows if she is the sister or half-sister or foster sister of Olga Berg's mother or if they have simply grown up under the same roof. However it is, she's so old that no-one can remember her as a child, and so spry that it's inconceivable she'll ever pass away. She has lived forever, and since Olga Berg's mother is dead, she regards herself as her successor and everyone's mother for all eternity.

She has a crimson silk dress, a brooch and white hair and she's so round and stout that she doesn't fit in the armchair but has to sit on the divan.

With fervent motherliness she calls the mother Bitsy and Synnøve Little Bitsy. She always looks as if she's come straight from the prayer house; her heart mild – yes, truly! – and her eyes tender from sacred songs and the soul's sincere prayers for life and nourishment for friend and stranger alike and for itself.

She always has good ideas and now she's brought one of them with her. In her strong matronly hand and bulging out from underneath her snug, light-grey rain cape is a large handbag. She walks right into the living-room beaming her hearty smile; Mother helps her out of her wraps and boots and into a shawl and rag-socks. They hug each other and look so wonderful that Synnøve almost feels ill at ease because she doesn't have Jesus in her heart too! She's almost at the point of wishing that she had Him there!

Then Synnøve gets a hug as well and it's exactly like having a whole clothesline of warm rustling clothes fall on her head.

"To think you wanted to go out in this weather," Mother says.

"Nothing can stop me when I have a mission," Auntie (everybody calls her that) replies mysteriously and lowers herself onto the divan with a contented grunt. Tiny raindrops glitter in her little curls and her eyes shine grey; she folds her hands across the ample crimson silk stomach and gazes at Synnøve with friendly, almost loving eyes and says, "Well, well," with a long, cheerful breath.

"My, but you're getting big, Little Bitsy!"

And when Mother comes in with coffee and a plate of cakes, and the convivial aroma seeps from the spout, she sighs again her cheerful sigh and says:

"Oh, but you are a blessing, Bitsy; first you clean and cook and sew for others and then you do the same at home, and He (that's Olaf) is always at work or out running around. Yes, it is true what is written: He who will eat must work in the name of the Lord."

Mother just smiles with her big lips and her big melancholy eyes. In the grey light of this rainy day she looks like a narrow shadow of the rotund aunt.

And now, leaning over the cake dish so that the silk ripples, Auntie grabs a *krumkake*, crumbles it in her round paws and puts the crumbs in her tiny mouth, just like a squirrel munching on a pine cone.

Synnøve chooses a piece of *julekake*, saturated with the fragrance of fresh yeast, and when the clatter of coffee cups has stopped and the raindrops have disappeared from Auntie's hair, her full voice floats through the room as if she spoke for the congregation and for God:

"To think that I, an old sinner, should live to see you, Little Bitsy, stand before Jesus and confess your childlike faith. He who has saved us from damnation and death. Stand forth like a white-clad angel among your loved ones. Oh, how happy I am! Can I be anything but thankful that I shall experience such a glorious day!"

Auntie takes a deep breath and continues with a fervour that makes Synnøve's ears burn. Her voice low and almost intimate, she says: "I have prayed to Jesus about this!"

Then she takes a new *krumkake*, crumbles it between her hands and blissfully eats like the squirrel munching the seeds in a cone.

It's steaming on the inside and pouring on the outside of the windows. Synnøve picks out the raisins from her piece of cake, looking at no-one but knowing she is looked at. Her tongue presses against her mouth and she feels the words growing inside her until she becomes quite speechless.

"And then I hear Bitsy say that she doesn't know how in the world she'll ever get you a dress, and that's when I decided that you could have my wedding gown. She doesn't think she can take it, but I said, Yes, indeed, Little Bitsy is going to have the finest dress I have and be every bit as good as the other girls in the church. A better-looking confirmand no-one has seen, you can be sure of that!"

Synnøve feels her heart beginning to move inside her. Auntie stops to take a breath and then she pulls from her bag a huge lace thing, as big as a pile of curtains, as big as an entire laundry, with the unmistakable smell of mothballs. With gathers and pleats and scallops, embroidery and lace, and a train, swishing like bird feathers and wind through the trees. Before she gets the whole thing out of the shopping bag, Synnøve bursts out: "I don't want it."

The bridal rustle stops momentarily.

Everyone stares at the dress and Auntie says, her voice suddenly metallic: "Nonsense, of course you do! Get up now so we can try it on."

"Aren't you happy?" Mother says. "You'll be so pretty. Of course it has to be altered, but I can do that and no-one will be able to see it was Auntie's wedding dress."

Synnøve stands up and screams with a fury and an astounding

desperation that do not come from her head or her thoughts and that she did not know she had:

"I don't want it! It *is* Auntie's wedding dress! I don't want to wear it! I'd rather run away, I *will* run away if I have to wear it!"

Auntie stares at her as if she'd fallen off the roof, her mouth is open, her eyes the colour of pewter. Mother begins to cry, a terrible, sad sobbing and Synnøve feels the rain and grey weather eating into her and she stomps on the floor and shouts, "No! I don't want it!"

Now Auntie takes control and gets angry. She hoists herself up from the divan, holding the bridal finery in her hands.

"You ungrateful child! Now, you listen here: Bitsy can't afford to get you a new dress, can't you see she's crying! She can't *afford* to, I'm telling you, and you can't appear naked at your own confirmation. Use a little common sense, girl, this is going to be a big and joyous day for all of us – let's not have any nonsense."

"Not for Father!" Synnøve holds her arms in front of her face, waiting for a slap. But it doesn't come.

"No, not for Father, the heathen, but for us and for you and everyone else."

"Besides, I didn't ask for a new dress. Mother said she was going to make a dress from sugar sacks and that's good enough. Isn't that good enough?"

All of a sudden Auntie has started to pull the dress down over Synnøve's head and gasping she tries to fight herself loose. Mother sits straight up in the chair crying and Synnøve screams and Auntie scolds like one not yet saved. And Synnøve, Synnøve doesn't have one good reason to say no, but her whole self says no, her toes and her arms and her body, everything in her cries out. And it's pouring rain and you can't see out through the mist and steam and smoke. She jerks and tugs at the fancy dress and Auntie lets go, horrified, and says, almost snarls:

"Are you out of your mind, girl! You mustn't rip to pieces the most precious garment I own!"

Synnøve hears from her voice that that's enough. Twisting and turning she yanks the big white net off and scurries out before anyone manages to stop her. And she runs, runs down the road until she is sure no-one can see her and find her and bring her back.

And she cries over her mother and she cries over herself and curses those wretched kroner that are forcing her to be confirmed in a wedding dress.

And she hates herself because she's alone with herself in that eternal rain, among the dripping trees, in the empty streets and the muddy gravel and the soggy earth. She can't go to anyone and tell them and she knows she has to go back, always and forever back.

Later on when she again stands outside the house and her face is streaked with the stinging rain and she's sure that Auntie must have gone and Mother is alone, then she feels compelled, by despondency and defiance, to silence, and she feels sorry for her own mother.

When she comes in neither of them say anything. The table has been cleared. The dress is gone. Mother doesn't look at her and she doesn't look at Mother. She changes into dry clothes. She goes over and stands in front of the window by the divan.

After a while she has to say something.

"Look at this weather, every day."

The air is oppressive.

Olga Berg is looking out through the other window and replies:

"If you'd like, I can try to make something with the sugar sacks."

"Yes," Synnøve speaks to the windowsill.

She should have done something or said something.

"I've been thinking you should get my sewing machine as a present," Mother says.

Synnøve wanted to hug her.

Translated by Katherine Hanson

HERBJØRG WASSMO

The Motif

Hot? For this time of year anyway. Enormous broadleaf trees with buds ready to burst into bloom. And a faint odour of decay. Or decomposition?

A telegram from home? It was in my hotel room. Nevertheless, I sat at a pavement café and read it word for word. I could hardly believe it. Nothing is so unbelievable as reality.

Grandmother, my father's mother, had probably been there for a while before I noticed her.

Her smile made her face crack. Her skin was white, with a net of innumerable fine wrinkles. Like the backs of old, crackled porcelain plates, or wind-blown desert sand at first light. Shadows in soft folds of living, moving planes.

At first I said nothing. Just let the tip of my shoe scrape against the pavement.

"Do you remember when? When we sat under the birch trees back behind the house, smelling the catkins? And we said that the light had the same colour as the sandy bottom when we rowed over the shallows to spear small flounder?"

"I remember that I was burning to tell you all about how the light looked from the bottom of the sea. When I lay there and looked up at the sky through six feet of clear water. With my eyes wide open to the smarting, salt-watery light."

"Why didn't you tell me?"

"I was probably afraid that you would forbid me to do that kind of thing."

"Would that have stopped you?"

"No, it would have given me a guilty conscience. That would have disturbed me when I was trying to find out how long I could lie that way without losing consciousness."

"How long could you hold out?"

"There was never anyone there to time me. It took so much concentration that I couldn't have anyone hanging around. I had to have complete control of myself. From the moment when I felt that my lungs would explode until just before I lost all sense of awareness."

"Have you stopped doing things like that?"

"Exactly that, yes."

"Maybe you'd like to talk about the telegram?"

"I would rather tell you about the art exhibition I went to after I read the telegram."

"Is that more important to you?"

"There were three large rooms filled with larger-than-life spirit figures, boomerangs and murals. Created from dreams and myths. The artists were descendants of the original inhabitants. The exhibition was called 'Dream Time'. They say their ancestors come to them in their dreams. That each person recognises himself in these dreams, and from that self-recognition creates his art. Carves it out of tree trunks and decorates it with glowing natural dyes. Red dots and black lines, for example. At first glance, I found it disturbing. After a while I sensed a feeling of peace and power. Even justice and retribution. The brochure described the works as primitive art. It also stated that the art form had most likely been under continual development through the entire history of the indigenous people. No-one knew how far back. These spirits of wood communicated with me. They commented on my innermost, my most acute, problem."

"The telegram? The words: 'Died suddenly'?"

"Grouped together, the sculptures were a frightening army with war-painted faces. Though maybe that was the point. However, the one standing alone in the corner made the most powerful impression. It was holding a boomerang in one hand while it pointed straight forward with the other. Its face was nearly as big as its body. Its cheeks were as white as chalk, and its chest was covered with red, asymmetrical dots."

Grandmother looked at me for a while, then finally said, "To the living, death and dreams have no substance. So they erect statues."

"The boomerang was almost aggressive in its decoration. An ingenious projectile for which we have no equivalent in our culture."

"It takes a sure hand."

"I was never any good at throwing. I didn't practise. I was a runner. I'm going now."

*

Whenever Grandmother appeared, she helped me organise my thoughts. But today she didn't quite manage.

She was the most travelled of us all. Not because she had been in more parts of the world or in more cities, but because her journey was more solemn, more inevitable.

"I should have thrown the telegram away as soon as I read it, then I wouldn't have to see it when I go back. Things like that should be cleared away before they ruin the day."

"That isn't always wise. Sometimes it's better to pick things up and look at them one more time."

"I haven't seen him for five years. I thought I would die before he did."

"People don't die any sooner just because someone chooses not to see them for a while."

"He had that air about him. The eternal life on earth."

"That only makes one old."

"He collected so many things. He was afraid of losing his things, afraid that someone would take them from him. That he wouldn't get as much as he could have."

"Those are traits that often crop up along with sudden wealth."

"Didn't he get enough when he was a child?"

"Who does?"

"I remember when I got the German measles. He promised me a present if I didn't cry. But I cried."

"After all, it's only a funeral to decide about. An expectation with fixed limits."

"Should I go home and act like nothing? Just because everyone will ask why if I don't turn up? It would be sheer hypocrisy."

"I have attended many funerals where the corpse was the only one who wasn't a hypocrite. There are ceremonies. People restrain themselves. They say words of tribute and cry if they can. The bravest reflect upon the fact that their own turn will come. There is a certain kind of order to it."

"I can't do it!"

"You didn't come to my funeral either."

"That was different. I was shattered. Young, and . . . afraid."

"I think the real reason was that you were more like your father at that point in time."

"But I painted a picture of you! The first picture I could acknowledge artistically."

"Which your mother had hanging at my funeral because you weren't there. Oh yes, thank you very much. There is something about the living that I don't like . . ."

"That we don't turn up?"

"No, this smell of decay."

"Do you mean that we are sitting here rotting away?"

"Not me, I'm all done with that."

Grandmother spoke with the same voice which she used when she spoke to her houseplants. She used to say, "Hey, you there. You look like you're going to die."

Traffic roared by incessantly. It began to bother me. I paid for my wine and prepared to leave.

Suddenly, the man was standing there on the other side of the street. I saw him just as I raised my glass to drink up. If I had dropped something on the pavement, for instance, and had bent to pick it up, I would have never noticed him.

His face was huge. His eyes. All the features of his head were enlarged. His body was only an attachment. A figure all too strongly backlit, placed beside a random lamppost in a city.

The traffic light had just turned red. The traffic roared by in a tight stream. I could barely get short glimpses of him between the cars.

Then it happened. He raised both arms and opened his mouth to shout something. To me?

Even if his voice drowned in all the turmoil, my day almost seemed to be good. And with an unexpected feeling of anticipation I started to plan what I would say when he had crossed the street.

"Isn't it a beautiful day? It's spring!"

I raised my arms and waved.

The impact! Hard, yet soft at the same time.

Then, suddenly, he came flying through the air and landed on the bonnet of a car. Only to fly in the next instant with outstretched arms over a passing car. For a moment he travelled in a graceful arc towards a windshield, which turned into myriad shooting stars.

Smashed bumpers and headlights. It sounded like being in a kitchen when all the cupboards fell off the walls at once.

Afterwards came the silence. For how long?

The car parts lay there and glittered like stranded seashells in the sunlight. Two coins escaped, rolling in different directions over the asphalt. They winked at me before they were hidden in a stinking veil of exhaust.

Then the air gradually cleared. A sign on the opposite side of the street advertised three pairs of socks for the price of two.

People were already flowing between the cars. With tremulous, wavering movements. Opened doors and windows. Came from pavements, houses. Where did they come from? Had they lain in wait there all along? In anticipation? Just for this?

A stream of arms, hair and flowing garments. Mouths opened and closed, like fish in an aquarium. In rhythmic movement towards the bundle in the dirt. Slowly, like a film in slow motion. Or a dream?

Crushed? Was that the way it was? One day suddenly: crushed.

He lay on his stomach. It seemed as if everything were just a misunderstanding. As if he had been given a little push, just for fun. He looked almost peaceful.

His right hand was resting on a banana peel. His arm was strangely twisted, and was soaked in bright red. One of his feet was stretched backwards at an angle it had never been in before.

A few yards from my table lay what a moment before had been a pair of glasses.

I wanted to get up from my chair and pick them up. At least support myself on the table, so that in one way or another I could start to move. But it seemed pointless.

The police and ambulance were on their way. Sirens in blue auras. Cars that started up and drove off. Voices. Shouts.

The ambulance parked on the pavement barely a yard from my body, and four men bounded out. Two of them did a kind of quick, rhythmic dance while they tossed a stretcher in the air as if it were a folded envelope.

I sat in a theatre and watched the film *Amadeus* on a large screen. Up close. A slow procession of people moved in time to Mozart's *Requiem*. Streaming from a place off to the left side of the screen. Like a river. Towards the right. Always from left to right.

The people floated out of the picture. Arms and legs were like helpless tentacles in the sunlight.

No, in torchlight. Of course, it was night. And torches! The shadows danced. The dying composer rose and sank, as if in burning water.

High above all, the music floated.

They came with him in triumph. Strong arms were already waiting, and the ambulance doors were thrown open.

They had covered him up. Only his face was visible. Sleeping peacefully. Closed.

But moist, red beads in various sizes dropped rhythmically on to the pavement. Surface membranes tried to form an enclosure, but the contents became too heavy. The drops trembled an instant before they joined together and ran down on to my feet.

Red towards steel-grey stone. Red towards a white receipt for a half-bottle of wine, which the wind had blown down. Red towards black leather.

It ran towards the gutter as if from a soggy watercolour.

A police officer pulled me up from my chair. Shoved the table and everything further along the pavement to make room, while he pushed the curious away.

They held a tourniquet twisted tightly around the man's foot. Or arm? It dripped anyway.

If it had been dripping so evenly all the time, since it had happened, then many pints were gone.

How many pints were there in a human body? I didn't know any more. It was one of those things I didn't think I needed to remember. Now it was my responsibility to find out how much blood a grown man needed to hold on to, so that he could keep his place in reality.

Grandmother was still there: "He decided to hasten his decay."

"Decided? He didn't decide anything. I waved. I enticed a man to walk right out in the street when the light was red!"

"You overestimate your own importance. For whatever that's worth."

Rage has often made me capable of action. Or maybe it was just my usual tendency towards hysteria which made me take the arm of one of the men dressed in white and say in a foreign language, "I'm his friend; I have to go with him!"

He didn't understand right away, so I repeated myself, too fast and with too much urgency. Finally he nodded, and pushed me into the front seat.

"Now you're in trouble. But maybe that's the point? You should have sat down and waited until the credits with the cast of characters had rolled off the screen and the lights were turned up. Your part is definitely finished, no matter what."

I opened the window and let the old woman disintegrate somewhere outside. Then I breathed in deeply. Exhaust.

I felt a sickly remembrance of lead being melted down on the black kitchen stove.

Lead? I was nine years old, and was moulding anchors for my boats. The shape was carved out in half a raw potato. It hissed when I poured in the hot, glowing mass. The potato whined and shrank around the cut. I suddenly understood that potatoes were also living things. Cut in two and tattooed with a cavity.

The smell of lead. The taste in my mouth when I had run more than I was good for. Blood?

The floor was a chessboard. I was directed to a chair on the periphery. Most of the pieces which moved on the board were white. We on the edge were a dull, and more or less static, mass of colour.

The corridor had a strange echo. It made me feel as if I were just a negligible little part of the whole. In fact, as if I never had been any more than a part of someone else's echo.

I sat on a box down at the fishing wharf.

Even if ice-cold water continuously streamed over quickly moving hands, splashing down on to the cement floor; even if guts, waste and blood were continually hosed off and driven away; even if salt scoured out the tubs; even if the grindstones turned and the wheelbarrows and the rinsing tubs were painted white; even if everyone wore oilcloth aprons and pale white faces while their knives glinted below their face masks – it still smelled unmistakably putrid.

Decomposition's race against humanity.

A continuous jangle of metal from hooks, cranes, wheels and knives drove everything onward, hour after hour. Through a stench of salt water, sweat and not yet coagulated blood.

I became aware that I was staring at the swinging door directly opposite. Doctors and nurses came and went. They made their moves towards us who sat and waited each for our fate.

Afterwards they disappeared with the same expression as a librarian who has just placed a book in its correct place on the shelf.

"Why did somebody decide that this corridor should be a chessboard? How many twisted minds decide what stages, what sets the world is supposed to have?"

"Now you're exaggerating. When this floor was laid they weren't aware that an accumulation of squares could make people feel as if they were going crazy."

"Do you think that man back home knew he was going to die?"

"Possibly. Or maybe he, too, used his final minutes to blame somebody because he was sick."

"But forgiveness, Grandmother. What if he called out and got no response."

"Then it was too late."

"Too late . . ."

"Right, each of us has to make sure that it doesn't get to be too late. That's why we exist."

"What did you think about when you were near the end?"

"Oh, that I would have loved to have gone out in the spring night and smelled the fragrance of new leaves. Just one last time. But I was sensible enough to admit that I had overseen a number of springs in my life. And I settled up a few things – in time."

"Am I crazy following a man here whom I don't even know?"

"You probably have a reason."

Someone dressed in white came over to me and spoke to me quietly in a foreign language. I understood very little. Finally she pulled me out of the chair and dragged me away.

I was a defenceless rag doll. Right out of childhood's attic and over the chessboard, I hung over the arm of the person in white and tried to make friends with her by tickling her on the cheek with my hair of yarn.

The rag doll had holes in her head and dirty linen hands which swung a bit helplessly here and there. There were visible marks left by hard hands that had flung her into a corner.

I was placed in a chair at a table and had a glass of lukewarm water held to my lips.

A staccato voice tried to get me to understand that my husband was seriously injured. He had not regained consciousness. The severed peripheral arteries and serious multiple fractures would most likely heal. The problem was his head.

"But his head wasn't injured."

"It appeared that way," said the person in white, discreetly checking her watch.

Then it all began. I was placed in a cubicle and had to fill out a form.

"I can't do it, I don't even understand forms in my own language."

"Well, it's too late not to understand."

So, now I had to take final exams. Take a test on the biography of a man I didn't know, and whom I had carelessly enticed out into the street and under a car. A double offence.

In numerous spaces I was to place name, birthplace and date, plus all kinds of other things.

I bowed my head, trickling with sweat, already hearing the metallic voice of the examiner: "Failed."

No-one could help me list the man's personal details. He had simply let himself be run over without carrying identification papers.

They understood that the examinee was useless. Someone else appeared and tried to convince me to cooperate.

"This won't be easy, but even a dunce can make something up when he's forced to."

I got an idea. Scribbled down his name and pushed the paper away.

"Amadeus what?" they persisted.

Then I started to cry. It is unbelievable what can be gained by crying. That is, if the recipient isn't already fed up with tears. This is what women sometimes miscalculate.

This one hadn't seen me cry before. Didn't know what I could take, and therefore didn't know how much trouble I could make. So she made the expression in her eyes turn friendly and helpful.

I sat at my desk the first day of school. I had many squares of paper with letters in a pile in front of me. Es and Fs and Ks and As. A whole bunch of Ss. These were supposed to go together and make a word.

But I knew that no matter what word I made, it would be wrong. They would put me in jail because I tried to falsify a man's identity.

This would all end up in a jail stinking of decomposition. I could already hear the jangling when the guards unlocked the door and shoved in dry bread and a metal cup with water.

"If you got away now and took a taxi straight to the airport, you could still make it."

I saw before me the frosty white face of the man as he, accompanied by Mozart's *Requiem*, was carried in triumph to the ambulance. The cold from his face made me shiver.

"Frost!"

I wrote it on the form: Amadeus Frost.

In one of the spaces he was placed under the sign of Cancer, and he was given an address that was within reality.

I thought I had done it.

But then they wanted to know where he had left his passport. What hotel he was staying at, etc.

"Use your hysteria, girl."

It ended up with a pill and more lukewarm water. The rag doll was placed on a cot.

Afterwards I exhaustively and incoherently told the long-suffering aide that my husband and I had got into a fight while we were on the plane. He had walked off and left me. Until he saw me at the pavement café, crossed the street and was run over.

To my amazement I understood that a lie had saved me – again.

I was served a sandwich and bitter coffee in bed.

"Grandmother, why did he do it?"

"It's easy to step out into traffic."

"That man back home wasn't run over."

"No, he saw to it that others were."

"People's tragedies don't affect you very much, Grandmother."

"I am excused from worrying about death. But an accident could reveal a few things for you."

"Pseudo-psychology."

"It would seem you resemble your father more than you like."

I stared at the wall.

"He too had the habit of punishing others when he himself had acted impossibly."

"Why do you keep bringing up that person? Not only did he ruin my life, but he also . . ."

"That gives you no excuse to imitate his bad behaviour."

"Do you think I have to hate to be able to survive?"

"Hating is exhausting in the long run. It just doesn't seem to leave time for anything else. What you need to do is focus on something so powerful that you forget yourself."

Just then it happened to me. I slid across the chessboard and into the hospital room.

As soon as I saw him, I was aware of the emptiness of the scene. I was a figure staring at another packaged figure.

He was something in a cocoon. Was I a spider lying in wait?

One of his legs was elevated towards the ceiling. His right arm was bandaged and in a cast. But his head looked undamaged. His hair was black, with threads of silver. His face was smooth and bluish, and his eyes were closed. As if he was already dead.

The lights in the room were carefully dimmed. The light from a single lamp illuminated him. When I stood at the edge of the bed, I could see the veins in his eyelids.

I stood there, looking at an unconscious person who could not hide himself. Just as I used to look in windows at people when I was taking a walk.

Sometimes I would stand outside thinking, "I'll paint them right now. While they, with their faces half turned away, dedicate their entire lives to the blue light of the TV, not noticing that they are being watched. Like spoiled children at a circus. Faces that reflect anticipation, thrills, tedium, melancholy and apathy. And on a rare occasion, when the show affects them, insight into happiness and sorrow. Always with the distant gaze that reveals that they are watching a circus."

But when I got home and tried to sketch what I had seen, it was never the same.

"Get out your sketch book."

"I can't."

"Of course you can. That's why you're here."

*

Was this the motif? The subject that would release me from the pain of feeling no grief?

One of his hands was stretched out on the blanket. Long fingers. Strong thumb. Even while he lay quietly with his eyes closed, he had an air of restlessness about him.

I sat down by the bed.

"You could use charcoal."

I reached out my hand and touched his fingertips. They were cold.

"Maybe that is what he will use me for. To die."

"Death has sympathy for you. It's only natural that you use it."

I covered his entire hand with mine. His skin still had a kind of clammy warmth. As on a newborn. He smelled that way, too. A bit sharp, sweet, stale, and somewhat fresh.

"That is the scent of a portrait of discreet decomposition."

His beard had grown. It already formed a dark, hard frame around his face.

I wondered if he had been standing in front of a mirror this morning, shaving. Without my knowing about it.

Had he already decided what was going to happen to him? Why did he bother to shave then?

Maybe he hadn't shaved at all. Maybe his beard didn't grow very fast. It could be more than a day since he had drawn the razor across his skin, making all those idiotic grimaces that men make when they shave.

I raised my hand and placed two fingers carefully on his cheek. It felt prickly. I formed my hand into a warm cup, and covered his whole cheek. His mouth. So far, I found nothing that repelled me.

The difference between his bearded skin and his lips was unexpected. Lightly I caressed his hand. His eyelids twitched. Maybe he wasn't as unconscious as they thought.

The artery on his neck was working. A restless flickering under the skin. Most likely he wasn't aware of anything. Nevertheless, the new blood they had given him danced around in his veins. The brain was still giving orders.

I felt a budding agitation, a kind of longing. For brush and palette.

Suddenly there was a change in him. His breath, which until then had slipped quietly between his lips, now came in irregular spasms which made his face break out in beads of sweat.

Feeling as if I were a mechanical aide, I buzzed for help.

*

I understood that they were discussing whether to connect him to a respirator. But soon he began to breathe evenly.

They looked at me with friendly suspicion, then said that I shouldn't disturb him or try to wake him.

I didn't reply.

"You are rude and arrogant towards them. They are trying, after all, to keep him alive. You could have managed a smile."

"I'm tired."

"You don't need to sit here and wear yourself out for a stranger if you don't care."

"He is probably just as lonely as I am."

"In the condition he is in right now, loneliness isn't very relevant. He is going to die."

"Be quiet."

"An impending physical death is a rare subject. You can make some quick sketches right now, then come back tomorrow for the finale."

"That man back home, do you think he died suddenly?"

"Why don't you call and ask, if you're interested."

"Then I'll get all sorts of questions. Like when am I coming."

"So what? A mother should be close enough to take an honest answer."

"And what should I say?"

"That you have used most of your life to get over the fact that she made a mistake when she chose a father for you. So now others can take care of the body. You don't want it. Besides, you've found something more interesting. He is truly picturesque."

"I can almost see them. The moral judges. The righteous. Those 'you-shall-love-your-enemies and honour-your mother-and-father'. They'll cast me into the fires of Hell and turn everybody against me."

"So what? Meekness and cowardice cause more unhappiness than denunciation and defection."

In a strange mood of controlled fury I took out my sketch book and some sticks of charcoal.

The man had stopped sweating and was breathing fairly evenly. Still with his eyes closed.

Grandmother demanded attention, and I found it useless to object.

"The truly beautiful are rarely pretty."

"You're right, Grandmother. Pain, for example. The broken-hearted? Brutality? All that which hurts so much that we close our eyes to avoid seeing. That which makes everyone who sees turn away. Maybe it's when we recognise our own pain that we shrink away, falling back on emotional declarations: I don't like it, I don't understand it, I don't want it, it's horrible, disgusting."

"You have the ability; you're just missing a bit of courage, to carry yourself and others over the threshold."

The stick of charcoal caught the curves of his cheekbones. The deep furrows. The prominent veins on his hand, visible as if under a thin layer of ice. His heavy, porous nose. Steel-grey beard, which with his dishevelled hair added a frame of decline. And vulnerability.

The shadows falling on his skin made me think of a winter landscape. Soft, lit by a dull light with no visible source. Naked yet mysterious in the midst of this merciless realism.

A faint tremor in the corner of his mouth was transmitted through my hand. It made me believe that I was capable of making visible the landscape of pain. If only for the few who could truly see.

I don't know how long I sat there. Perhaps a couple of hours. They came in now and then. First they stared in disbelief. Then there was acceptance.

The soft scraping of charcoal on paper was the only thing that happened. That and my own laughter. Like a sigh from deep within me.

I made sketch after sketch. I used colours, too. They glowed. The winter landscape was transformed.

Then it happened! He opened his eyes. He looked at me.

It was the first time anyone looked at me! Sombre and unwavering, yet infinitely mild.

His fingers moved on the blanket. As if he wanted to say something and weakly tried to gesture.

I let go of the pastels and took his hand.

"He's smiling! It's a smile!"

"More like a grimace, to be honest."

I thought about an infant who confuses his parents when in eager anticipation they look for the first sign of contact, asking each other:

"A smile?"

"Or tummy ache?"

"Pain?"

"It's over now."
Grandmother was so close.

I sat on a suitcase on a dock in the rain, because Father had gone in somewhere and run into some pals – and forgotten us.

An enamel sign on the wall of a warehouse advertised chewing tobacco. A fisherman with a beard and a yellow raincoat. The enamel was knocked off on the right corner, which was covered with rust.

When Father came back, we were dripping wet and Mother's face was grey.

Later, while we sat in a waiting-room waiting for the night boat, I came down with a fever.

We had to stay at a boarding house, even though we couldn't afford it. It smelled like mildew and fried fish.

An angry-looking woman sat up on a podium behind a counter, and shouted towards the back of the house to someone we couldn't see.

I followed Mother, who was carrying the suitcase up some steps. She had beads of sweat on her face, and she stopped to take off her coat. Her dotted red blouse was soaked under her armpits.

Father was already up on the podium with the lady behind the counter. He was talking about how my fever was wrecking his vacation.

I thought that when I grew up he would surely be dead. Was that the first time I had that thought?

When we came into the room, there was only one narrow bed. Father had a big fight with Mother, who said nothing because she was putting me to bed. He was angry because she had let me catch a cold.

I trembled violently with every word he said. Because his hands were like weapons, grasping the bedposts.

Mother's face was as white as the face of the lonely spirit at the exhibition. But I didn't know that then. And her blouse cried red dots down on to my face.

I wonder why I thought about that incident at this moment in time. I hadn't thought about episodes like that one for years. Because I refused to.

"Let's say a prayer for him," said Grandmother.

Obediently I folded my hands, because she told me to. And because I didn't want to be alone.

"I will never find out who he was."

"A good subject always has rooms where no-one else can enter."

I was standing in Grandmother's yard, watching her work.

She had such a distinctive profile. I could have drawn her profile with a stick in sand and everyone would have recognised her.

Now and then she stood up and straightened her back, while she looked around. Far out over the forests and the mountains. The sea. Sometimes I sensed that it wasn't nature she was looking at, but her life.

She had been a widow for many years. She worked as a cleaning woman, and her family and their relatives would always come and spend their vacations with her. They used her house like a bed and breakfast, with three meals a day.

I couldn't recall that I ever saw one of those visitors bring a house gift.

Father never did, either.

Every year all her brothers came to spend the summer, bringing their wives and children and grandchildren and their friends and acquaintances. She didn't have room for herself in her own home. So she had to go out to the garden to look at her Siberian poppies and straighten her back.

I sat and held him for a while. Then I pushed the button by the bed.

Two nurses came. Efficient. Did what they were there for without bothering about me. Took his pulse. Looked under his closed eyelids. Lowered his leg from the ceiling and straightened him out.

They didn't want me in there while they cleaned and washed him, but I made a scene. They retreated for a while, mumbling as they went, then returned with renewed efficiency.

Thus began an ice-cold but technically perfect performance by two experienced nurses and a dead body. Routines and orders were followed down to the smallest detail.

Their project was to completely undress a body after death had taken place. While the limbs were still warm and flexible.

A final ritual of cleansing. Not performed with love and care, maybe not even with respect for the deceased. They had learned the routine for such occasions. To wash death's body.

And I? Was I a vulture?

I longed for my slightly shabby but large hotel room with the two big windows. I longed for blinding white light. Turpentine. To mix a shade of blue. For the nose. Pale pink with touches of grey around the eyes. Not too much grey. Not too much red. Not yellow. Brown, instead. In the furrow at the corner of the mouth.

Slowly, I put my drawing materials back in my bag. Then I leaned over and lay my face close beside his. Just for a moment.

The touch. Like drinking from a mountain stream before continuing with a metallic taste in the mouth. Of earth and ice, of remains of dead plants in bogs. Of one thousand years of decomposition. Transformed into fresh water.

And in the interim?

The moment? Daybreak coming in the window. A void. An awakening.

Grandmother was there.

"Remind me when I forget it! How it strikes – happiness, grief, love. Stupidity. Malice!"

"Like a boomerang: a force – or a blow – which always comes back."

Translated by Donna H. Stockton

FRODE GRYTTEN

Dublin in the Rain

Just as I'm about to go to bed, the phone rings. I've tidied the house and turned out the lights in the living-room. Only the TV is on now, bathing the room in blue light. I pick up the phone after the first ring, wanting not to wake the family.

Hello.

No reply from the other end. Just some static and a soft whistling sound.

Hello, I say again. Who is it?

No reply. My first thought is burglars. They're calling to check if we're at home.

Who is it? I ask.

Still no reply. Using the remote, I turn the sound down on the TV. I think I can hear breathing, soft breathing from a mouth close to the receiver at the other end. Maybe it's my imagination. Maybe just some noise on the line.

I'm hanging up now, I say, and remain standing.

I wait, listen. There's an ad showing on the TV. A bee landing on a flower. A car driving through the desert. A mannequin with long, blonde hair walking down a catwalk. It all happens in slow motion, with fast cuts.

It's strange to watch the ads without sound. I've seen them a thousand times and know exactly what they're saying. It's as if I can hear the words even with the sound off.

I'm hanging up, I say.

Just as I'm about to hang up I hear a familiar voice.

It's me, says the voice.

God, you scared me, I say. Where are you?

Dublin, he says.

God, how you scared me, I say.

Can you talk? he asks.

I say I can. My husband's asleep. He's on the morning shift and went to bed early. I've been watching a film on TV, flicking through the paper.

How are you? he asks.

He has a dark, low voice, a voice from somewhere far away.

I don't know, I say. As usual. And you?

I don't know, he says. As usual.

We laugh.

How was the journey over?

Fine. Just fine.

Silence. No-one speaks. All I hear is the whistling sound, and I picture the phone signals coming all the way from Dublin.

Where are you staying?

A place called Finbar's Hotel.

Nice place?

A dump. An utter dump. You wouldn't believe it.

You got a view from your room?

Sure.

Tell me what you see from your window.

Oh . . . just dirty old Dublin. I can see the river, the docks. Kingsbridge Station. A couple under an umbrella. It's raining. It's always raining in Dublin.

I like hotels, I say. They're so full of life.

Well, here's a hotel you wouldn't like.

I picture him in the hotel room in Dublin. Standing at the window. Raindrops on the glass. And outside, an unknown town. With different smells and different sounds. I wish I was there. Walking hand in hand with him, from the hotel room, down to the lobby, out into the town. Dublin in the rain.

I miss you, I say.

He doesn't answer. A new series has begun on TV. A pack of police cars is chasing a silver Ford with broken windows and loads of dents.

He says nothing.

Say something! I beg. Say something . . .

I don't know what to say, he replies.

Silence. From the children's room I hear one of the children cough. In the flat upstairs the neighbour shuffles across the floor. Outside in the street a motor revs.

You know? he says at last. The morning I left, I could smell you on my hands . . .

*

I sit down on the chair beside the phone, shifting the receiver from my left to my right hand. I can hear my own, fast breathing. He tells me how it was to sit on the plane with all those business travellers.

I sat there with the smell of you on my hands, he says. Your hair, your perfume, your skin . . .

He holds back. I want to say something, anything, but I don't know what.

Are you there? he says.

Yes, I say.

All the way to Finbar's Hotel, I could smell you.

I swallow, take a breath.

Then I went into town, out in the rain. And bit by bit, you disappeared.

And now? I ask.

Now I can only smell the rain, the smog, and fish'n'chips.

I miss you, I say. I want you to come back.

I'm not coming back, he says. I can't.

How come?

It's too late.

What's too late?

Everything.

I stare at the TV. As if in a trance I switch channels with the remote. A man kisses a woman. With their arms round each other they disappear down a rainy, foggy street.

Good night, then, he says from the other end.

Good night, I say.

Neither of us hangs up. We sit there, listening to the whistle on the line. We listen to each other's silence.

Don't hang up, I say.

Then the line goes dead.

I sit there, and notice my heart is beating fast. Upstairs, someone turns on a tap. I can hear the sound of water even down here. I get up to turn off the TV. The phone rings again. I lift the receiver.

Hello, I say.

Silence.

Are you there, my love? I ask.

No reply. Just the same, ethereal whistle as before.

Don't hang up this time, I say. Please, don't hang up . . .

I just wanted . . . he says. I . . .

He holds back.

Go to the window, he says.

What? I ask.

Go to the window, he repeats. Is the phone cord long enough for you to stand at the window and talk at the same time?

Why? I ask.

Just do as I say. Does it reach?

I'll see, I say, and try.

It reaches. I stand at the window with the phone in one hand and the receiver in the other. I can see my own face in the reflection, blue from the light of the TV.

Turn on a light, he says.

Where are you? I ask.

Turn on a light, he says. I want to see you.

Where are you, dear?

Do as I say. Turn on the light. I want to see you.

I turn on one of the floor lamps.

Where are you? I ask.

Now I can see you.

Where are you?

In a car down in the car park.

That's not true, I say. You're kidding.

I'm not kidding, he says. I'm sitting in a car outside Brick House. Now I can see you.

This isn't true. You're not here. You're at Finbar's Hotel, Dublin.

I got back yesterday. I had to see you. I was going crazy at Finbar's. Silence.

Then he says: You know, I've been following you all day.

You haven't. That's not true. You're not here. You're not here.

Wave to me! he says.

I'm staring into darkness. All I can see is Odda covered in black. Plus some yellow light from the streetlamps, and my reflection in the window.

I notice a man. It's just the neighbour out for a smoke, staring at the sky.

You're not here! I say.

I'm here.

Prove it.

You've been to the dentist today. And down at the Domus café.

Oh, God . . . I say. Oh God oh God oh God . . .

Wave to me! he says.

I lift a hand and wave.

I can see you waving, he says.

I wave at him out there in the darkness.

You know, those arms of yours, he says. You remember the restaurant where I met you?

I say I do, of course I remember.

I remember how the autumn sun was shining, he says. I remember your blouse, the grey one, with short sleeves. You know, I fell in love with your arms, your arms there on the white tablecloth, your arms, the tiny hairs on your arms.

I lean my head against the window, feeling the cool glass against my warm forehead. I could stand there like that until I fell out of the window. Right until I fell out, out, out.

Show me your arms, my love!

I don't know what to do, so I put the phone down on the window-sill. I hold my arms up against the silent night window. I don't know how long I stand there like that.

Finally, I lower my arms, pick up the phone again.

Where are you? I ask. I can't see you.

He doesn't reply. I turn off the light and the TV, and the living-room turns completely dark. Still I can't see him.

Get out of the car, I say. Get out of the car so I can see you, my love.

He doesn't answer. I'm afraid he'll hang up again. I can hear the children coughing, and my pulse throbbing in my ears.

I almost lose my balance, and the receiver slips out of my hands. It remains hanging from the window-sill, swinging back and forth in the darkness. As if from somewhere far away, I can hear his voice.

Come out and find me, he says. Come and find me.

Translated by Peter Cripps

I'm Asleep

I like to sit like this in the dark and see without being seen. But not when I cannot sleep. I detest not being able to sleep. Consequently, I detest sitting like this in the dark and seeing without being seen.

The ash is long, it's beginning to lean, a leaning ash tower, grey and growing, it's about to break or tip over (sort of like a stack of dinner plates). She has stopped sucking on her cigarette, merely holding it vertically in front of her as she stares absent-mindedly at the blue smoke that rises from the light, twisting and turning like a Möbius strip in response to chance air currents, before it dissolves into an indeterminate haze. It looks like she doesn't care whether the ash falls or not, whether the tobacco burns up between her fingers or not, as though she were a dummy in a window display someone had rigged out with a cigarette.

About time, too, for the gentleman to ask for it, he thinks, and bends towards the shelf under the counter, says please and puts it before them. When someone has left a whole one lying across the circular stainless steel: a negative cigarette of greyish-white ash, broken at the edge, the filter at a downward slant, on its face, he thinks, a dead cigarette, quite unsmoked and still gone forever. The opposite – that the ash, from the filter onwards, slowly transforms into paper and tobacco while the smoke rises, and the light at last goes out at the tip when the cigarette is whole and new again – no-one will see, he thinks. When nobody talks to him, he must think to while away the time, he thinks. He glances at the clock.

And what is such an old bloke sitting here for, now, at this hour of the day? When he only drinks coffee and doesn't chew on hamburgers or sausages, it's probably because he has gobbled up enough food already; he has long ago grown, no, spread, no, gorged himself out of that suit, which is likely to suddenly burst, tear in the back with a sound like a fart and fall off like the skin of a caterpillar (shamelessly exposing what is underneath: glistening, quivering, sweaty worm fat), but still, doesn't he look rather strong, he thinks, more bull than pig, more rhino than walrus (typologically considered), and vicious, indifferent and vicious, perhaps a bandit who has seen better days, perhaps armed. (But how to find room for a weapon under that nearly bursting jacket? Wouldn't it get squeezed flat as a flounder, as if it were made of crunchy crackers or the rotten rubber of an enema syringe?) And she – now she's trying to look cool and dignified, playing a professor's wife being bored in style at some preternatural cocktail party, staring at the cigarette smoke as if it were seeping out of the Platonic cave, a philosophical cave dweller's smoke for blasé females who smother the soul the moment it is released from pouting lips in the guise of a yawn. In reality, a sour, angry and empty-headed woman, he thinks, no, not empty – her head resembles her handbag, which rattles with lipsticks and eye liners, make-up pencils and mirrors, and chinks, with money? No, with unpaid bills and obscure religious tracts, while her handkerchief just lies there, mute, dutifully folded, waiting to be sniffled into as she overacts a straight part; youth doesn't help, she should have a broom in her hand, curlers in her hair, and a rolled cigarette in the corner of her mouth, he thinks. He lights his own cigarette. He asks for an ashtray.

If only I could turn on the radio. But no. Or if I could read. But no. For if I turn on the radio, however low, the monster awakes. And if I am to read, I must have light, and if I turn on the light she awakes. After all, her door must be left ajar, in case she were to have an attack. A little. Anyway, I don't like listening to the radio. It's mostly bad music. And then all that talk. True, some voices can be nice, at least as long as you don't try to hear what they are saying. In the hour of need there is company in a nice voice that foolishly chatters on and on. Especially if you can choke it off by turning a knob. To read is tiring. Your eyes constantly become larger and larger, while the letters become smaller and smaller. The best thing is to sleep. I like to sit in the dark and see without being seen. But the best thing is to sleep.

*

Coffee – it's smart to drink coffee before going to bed after a spree and not go to bed with a rising intoxication, you have learned that much in the school of life. Well, spree, he thinks, correcting himself, is an overstatement; a few pints of beer in a reasonable place, a cheap place, is better, in spite of everything, than to sit at home in front of the TV, and then, afterwards, a coffee to top it off, in a reasonable, cheap place, with just one sugar lump (the other three you can put in your pocket, at a moment when the waiter isn't watching). The real is what's sober. Unfortunately, he thinks. Besides, it's interesting to observe people, even talk to them now and then, but not, he thinks, now, not here, they sit too far away, almost at the other end of the counter. But you can look at them, not too frequently, not too directly, but look anyway, noticing, for example, that the young man is well-dressed and that the young lady who is with him (she could be his wife or even his sweetheart) is pretty, very pretty, or better, perhaps, handsome, he thinks, with that rich red hair, and he glances over at the young man and thinks that he's lucky, he must have money, and he has that attractive young wife (or sweetheart), a nice couple, maybe she is his sweetheart, but they will soon be getting married; thanks to support from rather well-to-do parents, they can afford a house in a nice residential quarter, perhaps they'll get married already on Saturday, and now their thoughts are taken up with the wedding. He suddenly understands that he wishes he were that young man and not himself.

The ash from the brown thing (the tobacco) turns white, grey, greyish white, like old people's hair, as if their hair burned up as time passed, but not this hair, she thinks; red hair is aflame without burning up, but the head is ice-cold, ice-cold for once, though he thinks, I'm on the verge of tears and hysterics, ha-ha, she thinks, ha-ha, my insides about to be blown up with tears, like a balloon you hold under the tap and fill with water until it bursts – which is what he's waiting for, his tactic being the water torture of silence, second after mute second dripping, but he hasn't understood that so-called emotionalists can be the coldest of all once they are cold, she thinks, and now she is cold, as cold as he, she can feel her own coldness and warm herself by it, and he can just sit there and flick the ash needlessly often, while she can let her own grow till it threatens to break and then, at the very last moment, lean the cigarette against the ashtray, with the result that the grey column falls of itself, fully ripe, so to speak, and he can just sit there drumming with his rag-and-bone man's fingers, drumming on the counter with those dirty rag-and-bone man's fingernails of his, and believe that he has got her under his thumb. What else could he be, she thinks, but a rag-and-bone man, a rag-and-bone man dressed up for the occasion in jacket and tie and hat, whereas it is among rubbish that he is happy, he is happy among rubbish and feels ashamed. Wasn't there a woman, she thinks, who murdered one of those revolutionary leaders in the bath? She pretended she was bringing a letter and stabbed the naked man with full intent, and his blood flowed into the water and turned into smoke-like swirls and mist, the same way his consciousness became smoky and befogged as he was dying, and his revolutionary rag-and-bone man's nails helplessly clawed the edge of the bath; wasn't there a poet, she thinks, who wrote a poem in praise of this woman before he himself was sent to the scaffold? But these things are only thoughts, she thinks; why do most things occur only in your thoughts?

Ten minutes past three. Still, two hours and fifty minutes to go. If only they had been well-paid hours, but they are poorly, no, pitifully, miserably, wretchedly, scandalously paid. At least there's someone there, it's worse when nobody is there; if he then should fall asleep, they might take it into their heads to clean out the till while he slept, and then he would as like as not be finished in this job as well, unless he managed to cook up a credible cock-and-bull story, he thinks, casting a professionally appraising glance at the fattish one, who actually looks rather insecure. He, with his dexterity, his great knowledge of wine, and his past as a conjuror, should of course have landed that job at the hotel, he shouldn't have been here at all, slapping ketchup on *pommes frites*, tossing raw onions over grilled sausages, and packing hamburgers into rolls, he's a waiter, not a cook for pigs. Or a soldier. If it hadn't been for that miserable missing lung, he would have become a soldier, and he would rapidly have advanced to officer's rank. Or, in the hotel, to *maître d'*. But why does he bend so low when he reaches down for something, he thinks, and why does he thank with such exquisite courtesy for the most miserly tip, and why doesn't he speak up when young rowdies pour salad dressing on the counter, but only quietly wipes it off as soon as they're gone, and why does he only smile apologetically to those who abuse him when he serves the wrong dish or doesn't come rushing up quickly enough, he thinks, concluding that it must be because the one who wants to get ahead in the world has to treat his superiors with respect, and his superiors are in this instance the patrons, and you cannot command others before you have yourself obeyed. But perhaps he would have to be someone else in order to succeed? Could *he* have been that young man in the fine suit? Could he have stood inside the counter? And served him a coffee? And handed him an ashtray?

Up through the floor and through the walls. No. Obviously not during the night. At night it was quiet. But during the day. The plunking of guitars and the blasts of tubas were bad enough. The rumbling of double bass and big drum as well, not to mention the snare drum. And those ghastly howls of the trombones! But the violins were the worst. Not loudest, but worst. If the violin were an egg slicer, I would be the egg. She, naturally, loved it. That's because the monster is unmusical. She would say, just imagine, we're getting music for free. But it was only noise. Now the music store is closed down, thank God. Bankruptcy. The question is only what will move in there now. A clinic for pets, perhaps. Then we'll hear the screams and squeals of the animals about to be castrated or killed. How strange that it's always easier to remember unpleasant sounds than the beautiful music you may have heard. But then I really don't like music. Only what it reminds me of. And there's not much entertainment to be made out of the three miserable creatures sitting down there in the café. But I have to see in order not to hear the disagreeable sounds.

And constantly, he thinks, this reckless over-symbolisation of every-thing, even of the most commonplace objects and facts; she never stops spawning clusters of words with no *raison d'être*, figments of imagination that come to a pitiful end from drought in the light of day; like here, he thinks, this ashtray on the counter in front of me, a simple round ashtray of stainless steel, with some scratches after steel wool or the like and a hint of burned black edges at the dips, the result of certain raw materials formed in a certain process of production for a certain purpose (to be able to be used as an ashtray) and nothing more, not an emblem of the round, enfolding earthly atmosphere, the recurrence of the seasons and the years, the wheel of fate, the cycle of life, death and new life, the vast circuit of the incarnations, the movement of the planets around the sun, the twelve-part circle of the zodiac, or whatever she might take it into her head to bubble up from the bottomless, inscrutably simmering depth of her soul. She can never, he thinks, let things be what they are, period. And always, he thinks, these complacent ideas about the cyclical, maternal element associated with biology, with no sense of the cycle of *things*, like that of iron, from its being extracted, alloyed, tempered, rolled, stamped and welded until it becomes, for example, an oil drum, which at last, after many years of service precisely as an oil drum, cracks and rusts and ends up at the rag-and-bone man's, to be sold and melted down again; continuously this talk about the cyclical aspect, but why isn't the movement ever represented as going from death to new life to new death? he thinks, and if it's only women who can give life, then it's also only women who can give death, for the one supposedly doesn't exist, he thinks, without the other. But this is logic, and logic is exactly what's missing. And then, he thinks, this transmigration of souls, why all these interesting previous lives, all these princesses, ladies-in-waiting, priestesses, witches, why never a profusely perspiring, cursing and swearing waitress in a filthy, greasy, dark and stinking medieval tavern, wading in sawdust and vomit all her life? He, he thinks, could for that matter easily imagine himself being born again as a waiter, say, in a modest all-night café like this, and work like that waiter over there (who's now righting an overturned pepper-mill and wiping off the mess with a cloth). A subordinate, to be sure, but also with no responsibility for other subordinates, a simple and uncomplicated life as a waiter, alright with him, he thinks, stubbing out his cigarette in the ashtray with a slowly crushing mortar-like movement of his hand.

Well, actually no, but rather that it was he himself who sat beside the young woman, and that it was him she was in love with, he thinks, or no, he further thinks, that it was himself as a young man she sat beside and was in love with. But if it had been himself as a young man, he wouldn't have been sitting beside her, and she wouldn't have been in love with him, she would've avoided him like the plague; already as a young man, he thinks, he was a pest and a nuisance to women, it appeared, at least to the women for whom he didn't want to be a pest and a nuisance. He always began to touch them (if he ever got that far) in the wrong place at the wrong time, and he always put the wrong question, as, for example, whether he was bothering them with his overtures; a question that definitely answers itself: if you have put the question, the answer will always be the same regardless, for either 1) the sincere answer is Yes, and then you are a nuisance, or 2) the answer is No, but Yes all the same, since the question itself is a nuisance. Or he asked if they thought he was too stout (a big mistake: self-absorption instead of focusing your attention on her, or acting as if you did, and complimenting her on her looks or attire or other manifestations of her soul, or simply on her soul itself); incidentally, he always took a rebuff for a rebuff (he was utterly blind to the difference between the false and the true ones, he had later come to realise) and bowed politely out of the lady's life for ever, he thinks, so if he now were to be sitting happily beside the young lady with the red hair, it wouldn't have helped to be himself as a young man, he would have to look and talk and behave like the young man who was now sitting beside her; but then, he thinks further, he would quite simply be the young man in that smart suit, without as much as a shred of his own personality, and he would himself continue to sit there by the counter as the one he was, a hopeless superfluity that refuses to disappear. And that was, as a matter of fact, the way things were right now: the young man was sitting beside the young woman with the red hair, and he himself sat, alone, at the other end of the counter. But to say, he thought, that he was alone, he was too weak, he was lonely, he was sitting there lonely, in contrast to the handsome young couple, and in contrast to them he had nobody, nothing, to go home to, except, it suddenly struck him: one thing.

Nothing is happening in his thoughts, she thinks, nothing other than what is ingrained and worked out in advance, what has previously been rehearsed and calculated; his way of thinking is a completely mechanical one, she thinks, in which thought resembles a ball that rolls through one of those tortuous and labyrinthine toys, down spiral chutes, over tilting bridges, doing sudden jumps but continually rolling until it always, every single time, without exception, ends in precisely the same place, and the only thing you can do is to pick up the ball and set it rolling again, down the same spiral chutes, over the same tilting bridges, doing the same sudden jumps, rolling in exactly the same way and ending in exactly the same place every time. In a way, she thinks, his head is nothing but such a ball labyrinth, or perhaps all of him is something of the sort – yes, she thinks, he actually brings to mind one of those curious ready-made sculptures she has seen, he is junk incarnate, having arisen and emanated, every trashy atom of him, from his own junk heap, like a grotesque machinery of rusty, worn-out parts which, when you push a button, begins to live, soullessly, mechanically: it hums, bumps along, vibrates, shakes and pitches, squeaks, grates and grinds, she thinks, and all of this huge machine produces nothing, absolutely nothing, it only consumes power without giving anything whatever in return, until it stops; and nothing has happened, the result being nil, except for a bit of wear and tear of the machinery, a wear and tear that one day, however, will wear it all out, making it stop for good. But hasn't she, she thinks, heard about a variant on such a machine that was built to self-destruct? Yes, she has. And, she thinks, remembering, it actually did self-destruct, after a series of complex operations whereby it lighted a fuse with an explosive charge that put it out of commission, destroying it in a mechanical suicidal explosion, definitively. So in that instance the consumption of power led to a result, she thinks, namely, the annihilation of the consumer of power.

Is the pause in the snoring too long? No, there it begins again. The monster is alive. And down there nothing is happening, as usual. Only three patrons. Nothing doing. They sit there drinking coffee in the total absence of eventfulness. A youngish couple, unfortunately seen from the back. And an elderly gentleman, a trifle on the plump side and humpbacked, or rather stooped, in profile. There's something familiar about him. He probably lives in the neighbourhood. The waiter tidies and wipes the counter. Even an old woman like myself needs more entertainment than that. If something happened there, I could at least ring the police. Even if she should wake up. For then it would be a matter of life and death, of course. It would have been amusing. The monster is even older than I am. Soon I myself will be a monster for someone else, most likely. It's hereditary. I like to see without being seen. But the best thing is to sleep. Accordingly, I do not like to see.

A cloud of dust. Or a thick swarm of insects, or it could even be a star cluster, probably sprinkled on the counter intentionally (strange he didn't notice), although the pepper-mill lies overturned nearby, he thinks, deciding that black pepper is never, in a ground condition, black, but looks, if anything, yellowish grey against the white counter, nearly sand-coloured, and with a consistency like fine powder. A storm of ground pepper would be terrible to meet up with, a truly supernatural judgment, he thinks as he wipes away the spice with his damp cloth, you would shed more tears than in any funeral. Go to where the pepper comes from, someone will snap at you – he would gladly, if he could afford it, if he'd been well paid instead of poorly, have gone to where the pepper comes from, to the tropics, and if he'd been as well off as the young man in the smart suit, he would certainly have gone to where the pepper comes from, on holiday, and wandered about among the pepper plants and the palms, instead of standing here and serving poor food to poor patrons in a poor joint. If he now, by a stroke of magic, as they say (the word makes you think of another kind of stroke and of heart failure, he thinks, hence: dead from a stroke of magic), well, if by a kind of miracle, in other words, he suddenly were the man in the smart suit, he could simply walk out of here and go away. But is that really what he wants? he thinks, that is, really to *be* the other man? Because then, first, he would have to lose himself and, consequently, no longer have any perception whatsoever of being the one he is now, and then, he reasons, he would in a manner of speaking be as good as dead: to become the other he must himself die, and he doesn't wish to die (as the one he is), so the answer to the question (whether he really wanted to be the man in the smart suit) is, after careful consideration, an astonished No. He did not, he thinks, want to be the man who now, after failing to leave a tip, gets up from his seat and (followed by the woman) walks through the room, past the only other patron, the length of all the empty seats, towards the door. He wants to be himself, but to have the other man's money.

And then this abnormal, wax-like silence of hers, contrary to her customary frenetic jabbering, he thinks; she is presumably on the verge of a crazy outburst, or a crack-up, a nervous breakdown, so-called. It can become unpleasant, it occurs to him (and he stuffs the cigarette packet in the pocket of his jacket, finishes his coffee and looks at his watch, it's nearly twenty past three); once she unbuttoned her blouse, tore off her bra and stripped to the waist in the street. Hooked, to get hooked, isn't that, he thinks, an old expression for falling in love with someone, biting off more than you can chew, or biting off less than you had expected, something quite different, like the disappointment when you raise a glass with a liquid you think is alcohol, say, and your palate is left with the flat taste of, say, lukewarm water, which, however, has a quite shattering effect. A metaphor, a sort of photograph. That must be what he originally was caught by, this face framed by the rich red hair, he thinks. No, not an ordinary photograph, not even a still, however elegant. A funfair picture. A sort of flat with painted figures, preferably in amusing situations, gaily dancing, brandishing bottles, or half-naked, with coconut palms in the background, or something else amusing, and where the heads of the figures should be there's nothing, that is to say, holes, holes where all who want to can, for a modest sum, stick in their heads and be photographed, as carousing optimists or cannibals in hair skirts and with bones in their hair, for example. But in his case, it looks as if the picture hailed from a funfair of sobriety, where the painted stage set figure she had chanced to stick her alluring face into appeared to him, at the start, to be wholly serious, sympathetic and attractive, whereas, under his infatuated glance, the picture was gradually, so to speak, not developed, but counter-developed, brought back to its initial funfair vulgarity, until she emerged exactly the way they do in such pictures: as a poorly painted cancan dancer in garish colours, but with a real woman's face, misplaced inside an empty hole where in five minutes there will be someone else – not amusing. The fat man over there is peeping at her on the sly, he notices. Or at both of them, possibly, with the hint of an ingratiating smile. He may well be a retired bandit or burglar, he thinks. She doesn't look at him. She is as silent as ever. He gets up, determined, and walks towards the exit. She stubs out her cigarette. He doesn't know, he thinks, what will frighten him the more: that she comes along with him or stays behind. She cannot secrete a double; there are only two possibilities. He nods to the waiter and does not look back.

Yes, one thing. Strange that he never thought of that, he thinks. As if what in an emergency should be a defence against others couldn't be turned against himself. A middle-aged or elderly man, who is ugly and boring and without charm to boot, and endowed with a merely middling intelligence, can certainly find an attractive and charming youngish woman, not to mention someone of roughly the same age, to be his wife or mistress, but only if he (he surreptitiously counts on his fingers) 1) has money, or 2) has power, or 3) is a well-known public figure, or, preferably, if all these three factors are present together, which is the case amazingly often, as though there existed a kind of natural magnetic attraction between them, plus the fourth, he thinks: the woman. When, on the other hand, you are, like himself, middle-aged or a bit more than middle-aged, and ugly, boring and without charm, and only endowed with a middling intelligence (as he assumes), and are penniless, powerless and completely unknown to the public, then the prospects are (on the whole) more than poor. He is surprised that this hasn't been clear to him before right now, this evening, this night (which proves, he believes, his mediocre intelligence), when, happening to be sitting here, he caught sight of that happy young couple, who will presumably soon get married, or they may be having a secret rendezvous; now they are on their way out, not hand in hand (most likely too bashful, he thinks), but the man first and the woman next. A little bell rings, and the door closes after them. The coffee isn't sweet enough. With a resigned hand in his pocket, he works a sugar lump out of its wrapping, and as the waiter turns his back, while the *pommes frites* emit a protective hiss on being lowered into boiling oil, he slips it hurriedly into the cup and starts stirring. The man in the white waiter's cap clears the counter after the young couple. With the help of the teaspoon, his sight and his experience with this phenomenon, he can feel how the sugar lump, now saturated with coffee, gradually dissolves, first into smaller bits, afterwards into swarms of free-floating crystals, like ordinary sugar, circulating in the form of artificial whirlpools produced by himself in the half-emptied coffee cup, until these too (the crystals) are completely dissolved in the lukewarm brownish-black liquid. There was something he read in the Sunday paper once, about a philosopher who had lived a couple of hundred years ago and who didn't believe in the soul or in any form of immortality; he was of the opinion that everything consisted of atoms, and when he died he would himself be dissolved into atoms, but his mistress died before him, and then he thought that his (the philosopher's) atoms, when the time came, would mingle with hers. If he now begins to stir the other way, counter-clockwise instead of clockwise, as he does, the sugar won't thereby begin to condense again and turn into clouds of crystals, nor cluster together to form clumps, and the clumps won't join together and form a sugar lump, which the coffee will retreat from so he can fish it out, just as white and whole as when he slipped it into the cup. The hissing of the boiling oil is now the only sound in all the room. It's so quiet that he doesn't dare tap the spoon clean against the edge of the cup, so he places the dripping eating utensil on the saucer, where the coffee forms a small pale-brown puddle, which after a momentary slow, tremulous motion seems to settle nicely and not stir at all.

I cannot sleep. But she's sleeping. There are few sounds. Someone is flushing the toilet. That won't do. If only I could hear them talk down there. Though it doesn't look as if they are talking. Or rather: if I could hear their thoughts. It would doubtless be mostly nonsense. Time wasted. (Though, to be sure, my sleepless time is wasted anyway.) To me, they are and always will be mimes. Strangely enough, not even those who are sitting beside one another down there hear one another's thoughts. Only their own. The perpetual buzz of your own thoughts. It's worst of all when you notice it. It disappears only when you sleep dreamlessly. I wish I could somehow bless those who are down there. What am I saying? I'm tired. As if I had the power for that sort of thing. Not even the monster does. As if anybody did. As though there were any point to that sort of thing. Now something is happening. The young man gets up and walks to the door. The woman sits a bit longer. Then abruptly she gets up and follows the man. Well. They're gone. They are probably going home to sleep. I don't sleep. I'm sitting sleepless in a dark room, looking out of the window. I detest it. How long will I be able to endure it? It's three twenty-five. And then there is the date, the month, the year.

His silence. For once, she thinks, she has managed to answer his silence with silence. And women who are dumb enough to believe in their silence, believe in it as in a miraculous egg they can hatch; or they secretly believe, she thinks, that his silence will open up, little by little, creaking like a secret door to a treasure, and reveal the depth of his soul, that unfathomable space of thoughts never entertained, with the sonorous echo of the strength of undreamed-of feelings welling forth, as long as she can show a little patience, and she is patient, but the door doesn't open, and she will never get to know him – she lives (at the worst) her whole life glued to an unknown human being who is placed inside a suit of armour with the visor lowered, his head in a helmet from which occasionally a few words are rumbled, commands or tactical instructions for the daily struggle, never anything more. Or the door slowly opens, she thinks, squeaking dramatically on its huge rusty hinges, but there, inside, the floor shows not a glimmer of the coloured spots from the pretty stained glass she had imagined; the

light there is wintry, cold and sharp, and it doesn't fall on long rows
of thick, old volumes of wisdom in parchment and calfskin, nor on
glittering astrolabes and enigmatic hand-coloured star charts, or on
sparkling flasks and retorts and multicoloured bottles with
mysterious chemicals – there isn't as much as a fireplace with crackling
logs, so she could restore the circulation, she thinks. The only thing
the wintry light, cold and sharp, reveals is, in a corner, a meagre heap
of half-rotten root vegetables; no, she thinks, not even that, nothing
that once was alive, no, in the corner stands, she thinks (while pulling
a fresh cigarette out of the packet with the tips of her nails, so that the
filter gets marked by a sickle-shaped line), only an old workbench,
and on the walls hang the most commonplace tools, the same rulers
and squares, hammers and saws, dull from wear and tear, used by
innumerable generations before him for the same routine work
operations. No, she thinks, not even that, no, the room is full of junk,
old scrap iron, from which nothing whatever will come. Nothing
interesting. No inherited treasures, no inventions of genius. Only
trash. Or the room is empty, she thinks, quite simply empty. Before
the door a face, behind the face a door, behind the door nothing. You
can be terribly disappointed, she thinks, at not getting something you
have wanted for a long time, but you feel even more disappointed at
never getting a human being; it's like receiving an advertising leaflet
instead of a letter. She's tired. She envies, she thinks, those who are
asleep in their beds now. She puts the unlit cigarette in the ashtray
while looking for the lighter in her purse. From the corner of her eye
she registers that he suddenly gets up and begins to walk towards the
exit. She sits for a second without moving, with her purse open, then
slips the lighter into it, snaps it shut and walks after him to the door.
The unlit cigarette is left behind in the ashtray.

For that matter, as good an hour as any. Or as bad. You have to take
each second as it comes. And above all not count them. But we reach
a point where we think you can't hold out any longer, not for a week,
not a day, not an hour, not a minute, not a second longer; but we tell
ourselves, just one second, one minute, one hour, one day, one week
more and it's over, we'll give up; but it's never over, we don't give up,
we hold out, not only weeks but months and years and decades, we
stand for too much, we bear up all too long, that's the trouble. Now
the fattish old man is leaving the café as well. So now it's empty, apart
from the waiter, who isn't to be seen at the moment. And I, strange

to say, begin to feel a bit sleepy. I detest sitting like this in the dark, seeing without being seen, when there is nothing to look at. I lie down in my bed. As if I could sleep like the monster. I close my eyes. I'm sleepy. It must be one of those everyday miracles. I hear a bang. It sounds like a pistol shot, but as though wrapped in foam rubber and corrugated cardboard, like a fragile gift. It can just as well be a poor exhaust valve. I won't let myself be disturbed now. I'm asleep.

Translated by Sverre Lyngstad

HANNE ØRSTAVIK

Love

When I grow old we'll take the train and travel. As far as it's possible to go. Gaze out of the window at mountain and city and plain, and speak to folk from foreign lands. Be together always. Never arrive at journey's end.

She gets through three books a week, often four, five. She'd like to read all the time, sitting in bed under the duvet with coffee, loads of cigarettes and a warm nightie. She could do without the television, too, I never watch it, she thinks, but that probably wouldn't work for Jon.

She pulls out for an old woman who's waddling along the icy road towing a grey, wheeled shopping bag. It's dark, it's the roadside snowbanks throwing everything into shadow, Vibeke thinks. Then she realises that she's forgotten her headlights and has driven almost the whole way home in a car without lights. She switches them on.

Jon tries to stop blinking. He can't manage it. It's the muscles round his eyes that twitch. He kneels on his bed looking out of the window. Everything is quiet. He's waiting for Vibeke to get home. He tries to keep his eyes open and still, he stares at the same spot outside the window. The snow's at least a metre deep. Down on the ground, beneath the snow, are the mice. They have passages and tunnels. They visit one another, Jon thinks, perhaps they give each other food.

The sound of the car. When he's waiting for it to come, he can't remember it in his head. I've forgotten it, he thinks. But then it comes, often when he's stopped waiting for a moment and isn't thinking about it. Then she comes and he recognises the sound, hearing it through his stomach, it's my stomach that remembers the sound, not me, he thinks, and right after he's heard the car, he can see it, from one corner of the window, her blue car behind the snowbank down by the road, she turns in by the house and drives up the small slope to the front door.

The engine is loud and quite clear inside his room before she switches it off. Then he hears her slam the car door before the front door opens, he counts the seconds before it closes again. The same sounds every day.

Vibeke shoves the carrier bags into the hall and bends to undo her boots. Her hands are swelling from the cold, the car heater isn't working. A woman from work to whom she gave a lift home from the shop last week mentioned someone she knew who repaired that kind of thing cheaply. Vibeke smiles at the thought of it. She hasn't got a lot of money, and she's certainly not going to spend it on the car. Provided it goes, she's happy.

She picks up the post from the table under the mirror. She feels a slight stiffness in her shoulders, just right after an active day, she stands rolling her shoulders and stretching her neck before leaning her head back and letting out an "aah".

She's taking her things off, he thinks, he imagines her in the hallway, in front of the mirror, taking her coat off as she looks into it. She must be tired, he thinks. He opens a box of matches and takes out two. He puts a matchstick in each eye socket to keep his eyelids up so that he cannot blink. You'll grow out of it, Vibeke says when she's in a good mood. The matches are like great tree-trunks, it's difficult to see. He thinks about the train set, he can't help it, no matter what he thinks about, a train comes tearing into his thoughts, leaning into a curve with screaming whistle, rushing past. Maybe he can give her a facial massage, he thinks, massage her forehead, cheeks, they've learnt how to do it in gym, it's supposed to be good.

She carries the bags into the kitchen, dumps the post on the table and stacks the food in the fridge, places some tins on a shelf. The engineer from the Technical Department, the dark-haired one with the brown eyes, sat opposite her while they were presenting the Culture Plan, her first task as the new cultural adviser. She'd insisted on having the front cover printed in full colour, an inspirational picture by a local artist. She stands by the work surface drinking a glass of water. It went off very well, people came up to her afterwards and said they were glad to have her there. They'd had visions, seen new possibilities. Those brown eyes had smiled at her several times during the presentation, during the summing-up he had remarked that he was extremely interested in increased interdepartmental cooperation.

She pushes her hair away from her face, gathers it all over one shoulder and strokes it, pleased that it has at last grown long.

He hears her footfall on the floor above him. Her shoes. Vibeke always wears house shoes. Summer shoes with a low heel. He takes the matches out. He strikes one on the box, doesn't blow, wants to hold it for as long as it burns. Skirt and lipstick, to work. When she gets home she changes into a grey tracksuit with a zip at the neck. Perhaps she's changing now. *It's so soft inside, come and feel.* She gave him slippers when they moved here. Came home from work with them, on one of the first days, wrapped in paper with a flower pattern on it. She threw them to him so that he had to catch them mid-air. Woollen slippers that reach to the ankles, with leather soles. They're supposed to be fastened with a metal buckle. When he doesn't do up the buckle the slippers jingle as he walks.

Vibeke puts her glass down on the table. She looks out of the window. It's dark. The street lights are lit, they light up the road between the houses that stretch along it on both sides. To the north the municipal road joins the trunk road. It's a sort of circle, she thinks, you can drive into the centre of the community, past the council offices and the shops, through the built-up area, turn on to the main road further up, follow it southwards and drive into the town centre again. The living rooms of most of the houses look out on to the road. We must do something about holistic architecture. In the background in every direction there is forest. She scribbles some catchwords on a piece of paper: identity, pride. Aesthetics. Information.

She goes into the living-room. On the sofa is a grey woollen blanket with white circles, on the other side it is white and the circles are grey. She gathers it up and pulls the armchair over to the radiator beneath the window. She picks up a textbook from the small round table.

The book has a waxed dust-jacket, it feels pleasant to the touch. She caresses it with her hand before opening it. She reads a few lines. Then she sits there with the book open on her lap, leans back, closes her eyes. She sees faces from work, people who drop into her office, which looks really nice now. She goes over events in her head, repeating her own gestures.

Jon stands in the living-room doorway, watching her. He's trying not to blink. He wants to ask her something about his birthday, tomorrow he'll be nine. Now he thinks that it can wait, she's sleeping. A book on her lap. He's used to seeing her like this. A book, the clear light from the standard lamp. She often has a lit cigarette, and then he usually watches the smoke coiling up towards the ceiling. Her long, dark hair is fanned out across the back of the chair, some of it hangs clear of the edge, stirring lightly. *Stroke my hair, Jon.*

He turns and goes into the kitchen, takes some biscuits from the cupboard. He puts a whole biscuit into his mouth and tries to suck it soft without it breaking.

He goes down to his room again and kneels on his bed. He lays the biscuits in a row on the window-sill.

He looks at the snow right outside the window, thinks of all the snow particles that go to make up a mound of snow. He tries to count up the number in his head. They were learning about it today at school. Snow crystals they're called. No two are quite the same. How many are there in a snowball? Or on the window, in a little speck of snow?

Vibeke opens her eyes. Through the large living-room window she can see the red lights of a car disappearing down the road. In her head she goes through all her acquaintances, to see if it could be one of them. The engineer, she thinks, maybe him.

She sits up and looks at the clock, then she goes into the kitchen and puts some water on the stove, chops up half an onion. When the water is boiling she takes the pan off the heat and adds sausages, opens the fridge and puts the rest of the onion inside. She turns the radio on. It's an interview, she doesn't listen to what they're saying. The alternating voices make a kind of melody. She clears a used bowl from the table. There are crumbs around the edge and dregs of milk at the bottom. She's still wearing her short skirt, it's an old one, but it rides so softly around her thighs and bottom. Thin stockings are a luxury she allows herself. Most women dress for the weather. Thick tights, and an extra pair on top which they take off in the toilet when they arrive. Life's too short, she thinks, not to look nice. It's better to put up with being cold.

She rinses the bowl under the tap, uses the brush to scrub loose the crumbs that have set fast. Jon usually eats when he gets home from school. Biscuits or cornflakes. Often he has the radio on while he's eating, and he can forget to turn it off. Sometimes she's come into the hall after work and heard low voices from the kitchen, thought that there were people there.

The interview is finished, they're playing a song and she knows the group is famous, she's sure she knows their name, but right now she can't think of it. She feels a hankering for a good book, a really long one, the kind that seems more vibrant and real than life itself. I deserve it, she thinks, after my efforts at work and everything.

Jon sits down. His bed is close to the radiator under the window.

When he's lying down he can feel the warmth along one side of his body. At the head end of the bed there's a blue-painted shelf with some things on it, including magazines, a roll of tape, a torch and a water pistol. He presses a button on the radio on the shelf and tunes it until he finds some music. He tries to pick out the various instruments. Airy guitars, he thinks, he's heard someone say that. Airy guitars.

He lies on the bed and closes his eyes. He thinks that when he's not thinking about anything it must be completely dark inside his head, like a large room with the light off.

Suddenly she remembers what the group is called. Of course, she thinks. A scene from a graduation party: another student, younger than herself, with a pony-tail, they'd danced to this very song; he'd stood rocking his pelvis against her bum in what was really rather a vulgar way. She smiles.

She's got a packet of potato cakes out of a drawer and a fork to fish out the sausages. She leans out into the hall and calls Jon. Finds a mat for the saucepan, and lays it on the table. She wants to light a candle and searches in the drawer, but she's obviously forgotten to buy any. Isn't he coming? She calls again, then goes down the stairs and across to his room.

He's dreaming that he's playing basketball with some mates, it's sunny and warm and he gets lots of shots in, he's happy and runs up to the house and goes in to tell Vibeke. She comes slowly out of the kitchen. He begins to speak to her, but she's smiling so strangely that he turns to go down the stairs to his room. Just round the bend of the stairs there's a woman who looks exactly like Vibeke. She's whispering softly to him as if trying to coax him to her. Just as he's about to embrace her, a third woman comes up the stairs. Perhaps she's Vibeke. He just stands still.

He wakes to the sight of Vibeke standing in the doorway, there's light all around her, she says that food is ready.

Jon follows her upstairs, they sit down at the kitchen table. Vibeke switches the radio off. She looks through the post while they eat. Jon sees that there are advertising leaflets from furnishing chains and large supermarkets. On one sheet there is the headline: FUNFAIR. He asks what else it says. Vibeke reads out that a funfair has come to the sports ground next to the council offices, it has a UFO ride and a centrifuge. A funfair isn't your kind of thing, is it Jon, she says. Jon asks if they've got 3D simulators. Vibeke doesn't know what he means. Spaceship machines and that sort of thing, Jon says, computer games where you sit inside a machine and steer through space and have to overcome obstacles. Vibeke reads the notice again, she can't see anything about them.

He looks at her, she goes on eating and leafing, he hears the snap as she bites through the tight sausage skins.

Jon gets another sausage ready. They're piling up in his tummy like tree-trunks in a forest, you can always squeeze another one in.

A path runs into the forest, from a secret, forgotten place.
If you can only find it, your body will follow its trace.
Past trees and flowers and anthills and up to a castle so rare,
In the castle sit three damsels, fabulous, fine and fair.
For the prince they sit there waiting, maybe he'll come one day,
They're singing a song in the meantime, a lilting, lugubrious lay.

What did it look like in there, Vibeke always asked when the princess had fled into a strange castle. Say, Jon. He remembers sitting on her lap and describing great, empty rooms with open windows and long, flimsy curtains. Lighted candles and soft carpets. You've got good taste, Jon, she would say. I'm so fond of large, bright rooms.

He looks out of the window. The house directly opposite belongs to an old man. His driveway isn't cleared of snow to its full width, because he hasn't got a car. The old man scrapes out a path in the snow with a spade. When he needs to go shopping he uses a kick-sled. He's very slow, Jon has watched him stop and sit down on the seat to rest. He hasn't seen him leave his house for the past few days. It must have been too cold. The path has hardly been cleared. The woman from the shop called round in her small van. She kept the engine running while she waded through the snow to get to the house. Jon saw her deliver a couple of carrier bags through a chink in the door before trotting back down to the van on the road.

Vibeke looks at her hand as she reaches out to take another potato cake. Her fingers are long; with her eyes she traces the tendons on the back of her hand. The air inside buildings makes her skin dry, nothing really helps except Vaseline. And then there's her nails. Her hair. The cold dries it out.

The town isn't far off, and yet it feels like an age since she's been there. She tries to recall when it was. Don't do that, Jon. A little over a week ago. The Saturday before last. The bookshop, naturally. She and Jon had cake somewhere that was non-smoking. What else? God, what a place, a plastic tearoom. The town hasn't one decently designed café, it's like a house without a proper hall. Stop that now,

Jon. It's actually been quite a while since I bought any clothes, she thinks. She could really do with a new outfit, she deserves one, too, after all that work with the move. Stop puckering your eyes up the whole time, Jon, you look like a mouse. She thinks of the narrow, plain beige skirt she once saw a woman at a seminar wearing.

Jon is looking at a picture on the wall next to the window. It's an aerial photograph of the community in a black frame. It was there when they moved in. He looks at it while he eats another sausage. The houses stand in rows along the road. The road is a regular line. Although the photograph is old and beginning to yellow, there is no difference between then and now, only that everything was newer when the photograph was taken. He tries to work out who owns the various houses, but he only knows the ones where somebody in his class lives. If he stares at the picture long enough they'll come out of their houses and begin to move about like in a cartoon film.

One of the boys in his class got a fighter plane kit for his birthday a fortnight ago. Jon wants a train. Märklin. He only needs a few parts to begin with, a simple layout and, more than anything, a locomotive.

There's a book of raffle tickets for the sports club in his satchel. When he's finished eating he'll go round the houses he's looking at in the picture and sell them.

Vibeke gets up and carries the plates and glasses to the worktop. Jon kneels on his chair leaning across the table, she sees that he's trying to spear the last sausage using his fork as a prong. He tells her a joke he's made up about a man who throws himself out of a window and never hits the ground. She can't see the point of his jokes. He gets hold of the sausage, breaks it in half and gives her one piece. She smiles. They always have the last bit like this, sharing, eating it just on its own. Then he lolls on his elbows awhile, as if waiting for something. He talks about a torture picture he's seen in a magazine, a man suspended just above the floor, a hood over his head. His arms tied to a pole, he's been hanging there so long his arms have almost come loose from his body, Jon says. Why don't you just go, she thinks. Find something to do, play a bit.

"It's good that you think about people who are suffering," she says.

"If everyone did that, maybe the world would be a bit better."

She reaches out a hand and smoothes his hair.

"Are you starting to make friends here?"

His hair is fine and soft.

"Jon," she says. "Dear little Jon."

She repeats the movement, looking at her hand. She's put on a light beige nail varnish with a touch of pink in it, she likes being discreet at work. She remembers the new combination that must still be in her bag, plum, or was it wine: dark, sensual lipstick and varnish in the same tint. Trappings to match a dark-haired man with brown eyes, she thinks suddenly with a little smile.

Jon fetches his satchel from the vestibule. He takes out the book of lottery tickets from the small compartment at the front where he usually keeps his packed lunch. He pulls on an extra pair of socks before lacing up his grey boots. He puts on his jacket and his blue scarf. Cap. He looks at himself in the mirror. He tries to stop, but he can't help himself. He feels in the pockets of her coat. Amongst receipts and an old bus ticket he finds some money. He shouts into the hallway that he's off.

He opens the front door and stands for a moment on the doorstep. As he breathes through his nose, he can feel how cold it is.

Translated by James Anderson

TOR ÅGE BRINGSVÆRD

The Man Who Collected the First of September, 1973

I

Ptk discovered that he was about to lose his grip on reality. In fact it had been building up for years (he suddenly realised) – without his caring, without his giving it a thought. Perhaps he hadn't even been aware of it. Now the grey film had thickened to a crust, a stocking cap stretched over and encasing his arms, a sagging tent-like umbrella dimming out the outside world. The hands of his wristwatch flamed, and he no longer knew on which side his hair was parted: the mirror said the right, his hand the left. In the paper he read about a Frenchman who for various reasons had had himself imprisoned, naked, inside a small chamber three hundred feet under the earth's surface. When he returned from isolation after three months, scientists were able to affirm that man has "a natural rhythm – a built-in timekeeper" and that this timekeeper "is not adjusted to the sun, but counts thirty-one hours in the day-night cycle, instead of twenty-four." But no-one dared to make the inference, the only logical possibility . . . that man is a stranger, that Obstfelder was right, that our real home is another (and slower) globe – which, lighted by an unknown sun, takes seven hours more than the Earth to rotate around its own axis . . . that this is the genuine Eden – the garden we have been turned out from . . . Ptk pointed in amazement at his own mirror image, and neither aspirin nor Valium were able to make him think otherwise.

2

Ptk decided to face his every day, to try to orientate himself in the reality he was stranded in. He went out, bought all of that day's Oslo papers (Saturday, the 18th of August, 1973), and went home. He read them thoroughly – page by page, column by column. When at last he felt that he had got some sort of grip on Saturday the 18th of August, in the meantime Tuesday, the 21st of August, had arrived – and reality had changed its face three times. Ptk realised that the sum of information was too weighty for any single man to balance on his head. News fell in heaps around his feet, clung like ivy to his legs and tightened like a belt round his stomach. He fought in despair against Wednesday the 22nd and Thursday the 23rd. He dared not blink for fear that Friday the 24th might weigh down his eyelids. And even so . . . despite the best will in the world . . . Saturday the 25th went over his head completely.

3

Ptk realised that he had acted in haste. He who consumes too much news has no time for boiling, frying, or chewing it over, but is obliged to swallow everything raw and whole. Having considered political digestion and protective fatty layers of tissue, he decided to attack the problem from quite a different angle. Confronted with reality as a hydra-headed beast, he resigned, chosing instead to cut off one of the heads in order to get under the creature's skin by means of a detailed study of one single head. He selected the 1st of September, 1973. In advance he had equipped a corner of his bedroom as a laboratory, and was all set with a typewriter, scissors, glue, paper, and a twenty-four-volume calf-bound encyclopedia at hand.

4

By the end of October Ptk had finished all the Norwegian papers from the 1st of September (including weekly papers). Without hesitation he delved into the study of papers from the rest of

Scandinavia, primarily Denmark and Sweden. He had his fixed seat in the university library, and at night he stuck cuttings, notes, and Xerox copies on his bedroom walls. He developed an interest in curves and diagrams.

5

Soon his bedroom grew too small. In order to make his material for study as complete as possible, Ptk wrote to papers all over the world and asked for a copy from the 1st of September, 1973 – whether he had command of the language or not. He went to evening classes in Spanish and Russian.

6

Four years later his flat had been utilised to the full. Apart from a cooker, a fridge, a bed, a coffee table, and a wooden chair there was no furniture, no ornaments. The rooms were divided with hundreds of partitions, and the passages were so narrow that Ptk had to walk sideways (very carefully) when he wanted to remind himself of an important cutting or add a new note. Working hours apart (Ptk was an accountant), he spent all his time in his historical archives. He neglected friends and relatives, and when he met one of them in the street (going to or from his office) he found it hard to carry on a sensible conversation. He grew more and more appalled at how little people knew of the 1st of September, 1973. In the end he cut himself off altogether, ignored invitations, had the telephone removed, and made detours.

7

Twice he had to find a bigger flat. By 1982 he knew – more or less – twenty different languages and dialects. But all the time there were more things to learn. The subject turned out to be almost inexhaustible. Who would have guessed that so much had happened on exactly the 1st of September, 1973? "What a coincidence!" Ptk said to himself (he hadn't talked to anyone else for six years). "What luck I had, choosing *that* particular day!" He still used the partition system, and busied himself organising it all as systematically as possible. Not all subjects required the same amount of space. Some subjects, like temperature and wind, only needed half a wall, while others, for instance business and finance, covered the whole dining-room alone (all in all thirty walls, that is, about 4,050 square feet).

8

On a grey and cloudy day in February 1983 a fire started in the games and sports department. Ptk was on his way home from a private lesson in Mongolian dialects. When he opened his front door the whole heavyweight title fight was in flames, and champion George Foreman struck a powerful right hook when the Puerto Rican challenger as well as the picture curled up. It was an absolute storm of fire. Nothing survived. Before the fire brigade got there, the whole archive was in ashes. (Apart from the two basement storerooms, of course. But here he had mainly deaths from the personal columns and unsorted obituaries. All of peripheral interest.) Ptk was badly burnt, and spent the rest of his life (two years) in a hospital.

9

During these two years both doctors and patients tried in vain to get through to him. But whenever anyone spoke of the war in South America, Ptk talked of South-East Asia. If anyone mentioned the E.E.C., Ptk replied that he thought there was still a Norwegian majority against it – *he* certainly was. If the other patients talked about games, Ptk always shook his head and mumbled something about an illegal punch and the first world championships in synchronised swimming starting in Belgrade. Now and then he talked about two Englishmen rescued after being trapped in a mini-submarine on the floor of the Atlantic, he referred to the king as the crown prince, and always spoke of the president as "Nixon", if he was willing to reply at all. Most of the time he was not. "A hopeless case," the doctors said. "There's nothing we can do."

10

And when no-one tried any more, Ptk was allowed the peace he so ardently yearned for. He spent his last three months lying happily on his back. One by one he brought forth the fragments, one by one he painstakingly put them together, starting at the back right-hand corner of his brain and working leftwards. The picture of the 1st of September, 1973 slowly grew in his mind, getting bigger and clearer day by day. Names and numbers melted into maps and diagrams. Border disputes and cinema advertisements merged. Ptk smiled. The picture filled his head. Certain bits were still missing. He found them. His head became too small. The picture shattered his head and filled the whole hospital. Still bits were missing. A few. He found them. The picture shattered the hospital and filled all of the park outside, unfolded like a transparent film and became one with the trees, the birds, and the sky. But then he'd already been dead . . . a quarter of an hour, one doctor said. Ten minutes, said the other. And neither noticed that it was autumn.

Translated by Oddrun Grønvik

BJØRG VIK

A Forgotten Petunia

"Piano tuning must be interesting work," she said. The falsetto voice cut through the air, as it always did when Maggi was animated. And she very often was.

"Interesting?"

He gave the impression that he was considering the idea for the first time.

"It's bound to be so interesting," Maggi said. "You must be so gifted," she added firmly. She continued to stare intently at the burly man. After the last assertion her mouth hung half open. The powerful lenses of her glasses magnified her eyes. She always wore glasses. Even when she came out of the bathroom in the morning, with her bright-red dressing-gown and golden slippers, she wore glasses.

"It's no more interesting than anything else," he said.

"You must be tremendously musical," she said. She was sitting with a straight back and legs apart. Her supple kneecaps were visible.

He downed his tea, turned the teacup upside down on the saucer, as he usually did, and pushed it to one side. He insisted on using the same cup for lunch. He pulled his pipe out of the pocket in his home-knitted pullover.

"You must have a special talent," she asserted.

He shook his head slowly. "The talent thing is superstition," he said. "It's just a kind of memory."

"Memory?"

"It's all about remembering tones. Pitch. That's all there is to it."

The kitchen was small. As she walked from the table to the sink, she brushed against the chair he was sitting on. And when she opened the fridge, it was so cramped that there was hardly room to pass by.

"You're much too modest, Tremmel. I'm sure you are."

He had lit his pipe, sucked deeply and released the smoke through the corner of his mouth and his hairy nostrils.

"If I am," Paul Tremmel said, "it's because I have a lot to be modest about."

Maggi Svendsen's laughter tinkled, pure and wholesome, quite different from the falsetto voice with which she spoke.

Over the three weeks that the piano tuner had lodged with Maggi Svendsen, the evening rituals had become fixed patterns. When they were both at home, they ate and drank tea in the kitchen. As soon as the food was cleared away, the pipe was lit, and Tremmel, as she called him, would withdraw to the room he was renting. It was an attractive room, a bright living-room with two windows facing freshly-painted detached houses and small gardens. One door led out on to the small balcony, the railings covered with sheets of corrugated plastic in the process of disintegrating. The remains of Maggi's summer plants were still in the window-box with a few weeds and a couple of obstinate white petunias which refused to concede. A poplar hedge, which had grown astonishingly quickly, had been planted alongside the road. The poplars still had shiny, green leaves well beyond autumn. Maggi lived in the bedroom; it wasn't particularly large, but she thought it was more than sufficient. "Anyway, I hate housework," she used to say when colleagues from the department store wondered why she rented out one of the rooms of her small flat. Maggi was out several nights a week; she went to meetings at Save the Child, the Residents' Association, the Housing Cooperative, Plant-a-Tree, and she was a member of the Gym Club, where she participated in keep fit classes for women once a week.

She loved going to meetings.

Why should the flat be as good as empty for half the week when an unhappy piano tuner, for example, was going through a difficult patch and needed a roof over his head? Anyone could see that Paul Tremmel was in a tight spot. A middle-aged man who suddenly moves to another town, who takes a rucksack and a fish tank containing six or seven goldfish with him, and who inserts the following advertisement in the local paper: "*Help me!* Quiet, older man needs place to live for brief period. All offers considered. Urgent."

When Maggi Svendsen read the advertisement it struck her that something was missing at the end, something more drastic, or at the very least an exclamation mark after "Urgent". And she had imagined someone considerably more down-at-heel than the man with the abundant hair who rang the bell one late September afternoon, a polite man with a soft voice, in a light poplin overcoat and well-polished, robust brown shoes. There was a suggestion of ill temper in his facial expression; she couldn't really work it out – he seemed to be both brusque and reserved at the same time. There was a dark smouldering in the small brown eyes, a little glow in a dark recess.

She liked him.

And Paul Tremmel of the dark eyes moved into Maggi's bright living-room. What he got up to in there she didn't actually know, but at any rate he wasn't a trouble maker. In the evening he switched on the old black-and-white TV and watched the news. Afterwards he switched it off. And then it was just as quiet in there as before.

Maggi's husband was prominent in an unframed colour photo on the kitchen wall beside the department-store calendar, wedged in diagonally behind the spice shelf. The picture showed a bony man in a white shirt, possibly in his sixties. She had explained to Tremmel that he was a ship's engineer, and frequently away on long trips.

"It's best like that," she said. "Basically, I'm almost a widow," she added cheerfully. "How old do you think I am? No, no, don't guess. In two years' time I'll be half a hundred. Isn't that dreadful?"

She hadn't asked him how long he was thinking of staying.

"Just use the bathroom as and when," Maggi said as usual, after clearing the table. "Perhaps you'd like to take a shower or a bath?"

Tremmel thanked her. Then he said what he usually said before wishing her goodnight.

"I suppose I'll have to toddle over to see my little friends."

The little friends were the fish. Tremmel had introduced them to her. It happened one evening when he was changing the water in the aquarium with a siphon and Maggi had lent him a bucket.

"I don't want to get any green algae," he explained. Maggi ventured to say how nice the aquarium was looking.

"It's almost like a piece of furniture," she said, bending over the tank. She held her glasses in place as she bent her head over the illuminated glass cabinet. He manoeuvred the rubber pipe over the bucket and drained away part of the water.

"It's a little world all of its own," he said.

"What are they called?"

He pointed and explained while keeping hold of the siphon. His fat index finger tapped against the glass side of the aquarium.

"That one's a guppy. Viviparous carp with teeth. Most lay eggs but these give birth to living fish."

"Really?"

"When they're hungry, they can sometimes eat their young. And there, can you see the little silver fish with the black stripe? A genuine venus fish from China."

"Venus fish," she repeated, enthralled. "They look like bloodstains, the stains on the fins. Which fish do you like best?"

His index finger ran across the glass, the water trickled into the bucket, the finger stopped by a leaf-shaped fish. It was shiny with diagonal stripes and elegant fins.

"The scalar fish. You see, it doesn't eat any other fish. A peaceable fellow. It just gets a bit too big."

"There are such nice plants, too," Maggi said. She leaned against the table that the tank was standing on. Her arm touched his.

"Once I had a wonderful fish, a West African moon fish. Yellow and black, very elaborate pattern. Its eyes were strange, with a green ring surrounding the pupil. All goldfish look lugubrious, but there was something insane about the moon fish's gaze that I liked."

"What happened to the fish?"

"White spot disease, sadly. It died. It seemed to understand me. You probably think I'm mad, don't you?"

"We all need someone to understand us," Maggi said with emphasis. She straightened up. "I hope you'll feel comfortable here," she said.

"You become so calm inside," he said. "The serene fish, the plants, the Java moss, the water. There is a peace in there which is special."

"Despite the fact that they eat each other?"

"That's part and parcel of it," the piano tuner said.

For a moment Maggi appeared to have misgivings. Then she laughed – a quick, tinkling laugh. At that instant the doorbell rang.

The widow stood outside.

She had moved into the flat across the corridor in early summer. A young woman with narrow eyes and high cheekbones, and a kind of torpid, almost expectant expression on her cat-like face. She had two small girls who used to curtsey to Maggi on the stairs.

She asked if there was anything wrong with the reception on Maggi's television.

"I really have no idea," Maggi said. "I never watch television."

Tremmel came out into the corridor with the bucket. He threw the woman in the doorway one of his imperturbable, ill-tempered glances. Then he put the bucket down and offered to investigate whether the black-and-white set in the living-room was working. It turned out to be working as it always did – the same worn, drab, grey picture.

"I thought perhaps there was something up with the transmitter," the widow said. "The children wanted to see *Our Planet*, or whatever it's called now, and I'm just so unbelievably cack-handed."

It was not easy to discern whether it was the mention of the planet or the expression "unbelievably cack-handed" that triggered the change. Perhaps it was Maggi's hall lamp casting its yellow light over the young woman's face with the tinge of expectation over it. The widow smiled apologetically. The piano tuner seemed alert all of a sudden; he stood up straight and ran a hand through the mass of hair.

"Perhaps I can be of help," he said. He went with the widow into the flat across the way.

Maggi put the bucket in the bathroom. She tidied up the kitchen. A couple of times she went into the hallway to listen at the door. She began to wipe the small spice jars on the shelf. She watered the potted plants in the kitchen window. She washed the bread bin. Finally, she sat down at the kitchen table. She yawned. She went to the bathroom, turned the light off in the kitchen and went into the bedroom. She lay reading for a while. As she was on the point of falling asleep she heard the hall door being opened and the piano tuner going into the living-room.

When Maggi returned home from the keep-fit classes, she was flushed and in high spirits, and her hair was damp. She hung up her tracksuit in the bathroom and drank a lot of cold water. It was an opportunity to demonstrate to Tremmel some of the activities she had been practising in the kitchen: neck exercises and hip gyration. She also showed him one of the dance steps, and imitated a couple of the less graceful movers in her class.

"Do you understand why we're here on this earth, Tremmel?" she asked him out of the blue. "When I see all these creatures humping and thumping about in the gymnasium I really have to wonder."

"Difficult to say," Tremmel said. "But I think a lot about it. When I'm with my little friends."

"The last thing I do on this earth will probably be something daft like washing a cup or watering a stupid potted plant."

"It's already got too much water," he pointed out.

"And if I die suddenly, my last thoughts are bound to be about whether the iceberg lettuce in the fridge has gone off, or whether I've paid the electricity bill. Isn't that terrible?"

"Show me that dance step again," said Tremmel.

*

That autumn Maggi was promoted to floor manager in the department store. Her progress had taken in the cash-till, the cheese counter
and the vegetable section. She was well-known throughout the store,
and being the bright, energetic person she was, it was no surprise that
Maggi Svendsen was picked out for promotion. The new status
brought with it a higher salary, more independence with regard to her
duties, and considerable responsibility, she felt. Previously, she had
scurried between the shelves at a pace that displayed commitment and
remarkable fitness; now she strode between departments, always with
the shop's coffee-brown pinafore dress open while the other sales-
women buttoned theirs up. The open skirts conferred something
dignified and dashing on her person. Fru Svendsen's bearing was a
direct reflection of her new position.

One day she found a bag of rotten bananas in her locker. She
observed her colleagues one by one as they came into the locker room
to change clothes. No-one noticed the bag she had placed on the
bench by the mirror. A couple of the young cash-desk girls strolled
past the bench and lit up cigarettes before they took off their shop
pinafores. Fru Moe, from vegetables, brushed her hair in front of the
mirror. Fru Jacobsen, who exuded her own special aroma of cheese
and sweat at this time of day, took off her pinafore dress and sprayed
the armpits with a deodorant. It mingled with all the other smells in
the room – smells of food, perfume, tired bodies, tobacco, bread and
the day's papers.

"What's this?" fru Jacobsen asked, lifting up the bag. "Who does it
belong to?"

Maggi waited for a while. The eyes behind the strong lenses of her
glasses swept from one woman to the next in the locker room.

"Rotten bananas," Maggi said. "They were in my locker."

The women looked at her; they looked at each other. Fru Moe
went on brushing her hair. Fru Jacobsen shrugged her shoulders.

"Odd," she said.

"Isn't it," Maggi said.

And fru Jacobsen dropped the bag in the waste-paper basket under
the sink.

Maggi was in an indignant frame of mind as she walked home. It
was about twenty minutes on foot, a walk she generally enjoyed. Now
she was becoming more and more indignant with every block of
houses she passed. She was so upset that she almost tripped over the
cycle stand outside the post office. And as if that wasn't enough, she
almost slid on the slippery leaves in front of the post office entrance.

The elm tree had lost all its leaves and the caretaker hadn't swept them up yet. The lazy man was waiting for the poplars to lose their leaves, too. But, actually, he was waiting for the snow so that he wouldn't have to do any raking at all.

It wasn't until she was in the kitchen that the real disaster occurred, and there was no-one she could really blame. Maggi was angry and she was hungry; as she waited for the potatoes to boil she gnawed furiously at a carrot. There was a dull, almost imperceptible sound, a muted little crack which made her back run cold and her earlobes hot. She spat out what was in her mouth, bounded towards the sink and looked in the mirror. The tip of her tongue had already discovered what would soon be revealed to her gaze in the mirror. One front tooth, broken off close to the base. She dashed into the hall and banged on the living-room door.

"Tremmel! Tremmel!" she screamed.

The piano tuner didn't open immediately. There was music coming from his room, some sort of symphony or other. She knocked again. Tremmel came to the door.

"What's the matter?" He ran a hand through his hair.

"God," Maggi shrieked. She held her mouth, her skin all aglow. "I've had such a disastrous day!"

At that moment, she caught sight of the widow. There was a portable radio she had never seen before on the table, and two small tumblers. The young woman was sitting on Maggi's faded moss-green sofa with her thin legs drawn up underneath her. She slanted her head and looked at Maggi with her oblique eyes.

"You can't imagine what has happened! It's so dreadful!"

The piano tuner had problems comprehending what she was saying behind her fingers. In one dramatic movement she removed her hand from her mouth, stared at Tremmel, tight-lipped, then snatched up her top lip and pointed:

"Thee," she lisped. Maggi thrust her face up into his and pointed again. Then the piano tuner did something he had never done before. He stroked his landlady's cheek.

"Poor little girl," he said.

Maggi took off her glasses and burst into tears.

The autumn was unusually beautiful that year.

As mild and forbearing as only the last season of the year can be. There were days with rain falling gently against the windows, and days with limpid air and bright sunshine, and short days with cottony mist sweeping the tops of the fir trees, making the houses and the fields indistinct and softening the ridges around the town. Yellowing leaves still hung from the birch trees and shone in the autumn sun with a pale vigour all of their own.

A flock of thrushes collected, chattering, in the poplar hedge.

Paul Tremmel had a few jobs, one of which was for a piano and organ dealer. He tuned the grand piano in the Town Hall, the piano in the Salvation Army hall and the piano in the Athletics Club clubhouse. He was away for the odd day or two, when a piano tuner's services were required for concerts of various kinds. He set off wearing his light poplin overcoat and carrying a battered leather briefcase, in which he kept his tools.

Tremmel paid his rent, pottered about with his fish and rarely went out in the evening. He washed his clothes in Maggi's washing machine. For lunch he usually ate at a fast-food bar by the taxi rank. Occasionally he went to the widow's across the corridor to "lend her a helping hand", as he called it. He often took his old leather briefcase with him – Maggi thought she could hear something clinking in it, but that was none of her business, of course. And she had seen him coming home with bags of beer bottles which he took straight into the living-room. There he stayed, just as quiet as the fish.

After the tooth episode – it had been put back, by the way, using a porcelain crown – Maggi and Tremmel were on more intimate speaking terms. Maggi was and remained convinced that the unfortunate incident with the tooth was closely connected with what happened in the locker room at the department store.

One Thursday evening she returned home after a long day at work. Tremmel bumped into her in the hall. She seemed upset.

"There's someone *after* me," she said, rattling the clothes hangers and kicking off her ankle boots. "Someone's got it in for me! My God, I must have a shower!"

He could hear her rummaging about in the bathroom, things falling on the floor, the water striking the bath, the steam escaping into the hall. It was as if Maggi's fury were being driven out through the crack in the door, hot and steaming and tearful. Through the kitchen window, Tremmel saw a large autumn moon hanging over the ridge and the rooftops; it reminded him of an old-fashioned watermelon. Eventually Maggi appeared in the kitchen in her dressing-gown, with her glasses all misted up and a towel wrapped around her head. The shower didn't seem to have calmed her down.

Tremmel went to the living-room on an errand. Immediately afterwards, he returned to the kitchen and placed a bottle on the table.

"Today, I think you could do with a snifter," he said.

Maggi was cleaning her glasses with the lens cloth. Her eyes were smaller now, and possessed an innocence that he had not noticed until then. He found two small glasses in a cupboard.

"Envy," Maggi said. "Pure, undiluted envy. I'm not in the habit of drinking."

"*Skål*," the piano tuner said

"People are nasty," she said. Her hand was shaking.

Tremmel nodded serenely. "We have to take them as they are."

Maggi had sat down. She finished the glass.

"They all steal like magpies," she said. "I don't know who steals more, the customers or the employees. As it happens, I've got eyes on me. And *that's* dangerous, that is!"

"It's always dangerous to see too much," Tremmel concurred. "We should see what we're supposed to see."

"Could you give me some more?" Maggi said.

Tremmel filled her glass.

Maggi began to talk about her previous lodger, herr Mikalsen, as she called him. He had worked in the storeroom, a really good man, quick-witted and funny. Everyone in the department store had liked him. And he had done up the bathroom for her, by the way. Kind and helpful in every way. Quite a different sort from young Bull Hansen who just lay on the sofa, played rock music and went out to collect his dole. Yes, Bull Hansen rented the room *before* Mikalsen. Thank God, he disappeared one day and the *way* his room was left. But what was it she was going to tell him about?

"Mikalsen," Tremmel said.

"Oh, yes, right."

"And so?"

"And so –" Maggi paused after the two words; the pause came between them like a misting panel of glass. She had forgotten to do up the top buttons of her dressing-gown, her skin glowed against the red material.

She continued: "Herr Mikalsen was caught in the storeroom with his pockets stuffed with wrist-watches – there were several dozen – and his shirt bulging with cassettes and packets of cigarettes. Thank God they didn't find anything here – that would have looked good! But they did come here. That was all. And such a good man. And such a nice job he made of my bathroom. Of course, he got the boot."

Maggi looked pensive.

"We don't know very much about other people, do we?" she said.

"No," Tremmel said. "Not much about ourselves, either." He drank his vodka and stared at the moon.

"Is it true that you've given concerts?" she asked suddenly. "The chairperson of Plant-a-Tree, lovely lady, a music teacher, she says that you've played at big concerts."

A whale-shaped cloud floated slowly past the moon. He followed it with his small dark eyes.

"That's a long time ago," he said. "There's nothing to talk about."

Maggi stretched her lips into a strange smile, a caricature of a smile.

"Do you think it's alright?" she asked. "Not too white?"

He furrowed his brow.

"The tooth," Maggi said as she repeated the bizarre parody of a smile. He gazed at her thoughtfully.

"Superb," he decided finally. "Perfect."

"Do you mean that?"

"It looks as if it's always been there."

"Well, it cost a fortune, too. Ugh, we're not going to talk about money." She waved her hand dismissively, before pouring from the bottle. "*He's* always talking about money." She flicked her head towards the little colour photograph behind the spices shelf. "He's obsessed with saving money. Can you make out people like that? What fun it'll be telling him what this tooth cost in my next letter!"

Maggi laughed a loud, tinkling laugh. Tremmel chuckled along with her.

It was a wonderful evening. The vodka, the moonlight, the flushed landlady, the small, quiet kitchen. The piano tuner was enjoying himself. A vague haze from the steam of the shower and the aroma of Maggi's herbal shampoo lingered in the air.

"So you're actually a pianist," Maggi said.

Tremmel took the pipe out of his pullover pocket.

"People gossip behind my back," she said. Now her eyes were enlarged, her cheeks gleaming. "Since when has it been forbidden in this town to have lodgers? Do you know what they say? They call me "that Svendsen slut"," she burst out. "What do you think about that?"

Tremmel blinked. Then he coughed.

This confidence released a torrent of words. Either Maggi regretted saying what she had and was trying to bury it under more words, or the vodka had gone to her head.

She set off: "Fru Moe does *not* keep the vegetable section tidy. She does *not* remove the rotten grapes or keep the boxes looking appetising. Who's going to buy grapes when half of them look rotten to the core?"

"You certainly know your job," Tremmel said.

"Please pour me another glass. 'You shouldn't let it *bother* you, fru Svendsen,' fru Moe says. 'I do my job, Lady Muck,' she says. The truth is that she brushes her hair, cleans her nails and gossips with fru Jacobsen for most of the day. And I'm absolutely convinced that they both steal as much as they can carry! And, you know, there are always *hairs* in the tomato basket. Fru Moe's hairs, I swear to it. What do you think?"

"Yes, well," he said, "whether it's sales assistants or customers who steal, perhaps it's all much of a muchness."

"Do you *mean* that?" Maggi said.

She was stressing more and more words now. The vodka didn't make her slur her words; on the contrary, she was more articulate now than ever, but she was putting greater emphasis on an increasing number of words.

"Probably," Tremmel said. He looked a little sleepy.

"And today," Maggi continued, "today the *following* happened. I had the audacity to ask after Anita, as no-one was serving at the perfume counter and several customers were waiting. Then fru Eliassen turned up – *she* works on the tobacco counter – and started serving in perfume. '*You* are not supposed to be here,' I said. My God, if looks could kill. I was as *cold* as *ice*. Afterwards Anita arrived and I asked her if she was taking lunch-breaks when it suited her. And this was the Anita I had been so happy with. Nice-looking young girl. I've given her all the perks I can. Once I said to her: 'You are *not* allowed to chew chewing gum.' I said, 'You don't stand there ruminating like a *cow* when you're selling nail varnish.' And *that* job in perfume is a cushy number. *Do you know* how she answered me back today? 'You're a dragon, fru Svendsen,' she said. 'My little one's ill and I had to nip back home. I suppose that won't *do,* will it?'"

Maggi blinked behind her glasses. She sniffled into a handkerchief she found in her dressing-gown.

"I didn't have any lunch today," she said. "I'm not used to drinking."

Tremmel reached out over the table and patted her arm.

"It'll sort itself out," he said. "The girl will be sorry and apologise tomorrow."

She blew her nose and straightened up.

"Some of the women drive me round the *bend.*"

"Listen," Tremmel said. "Some people have a piano, but there's never any point in tuning it. Do you know why? Underground water channels. There's a channel of water under the house. You're one of those channels, Maggi. You're strong and pure. Some people can't take it. It's as if it withers their souls."

He filled both glasses. The air in the room was thick with pipe smoke; she peered through it and pondered what he had said about water channels.

"Strong and pure," she mumbled.

He stood up, laid a hand on her shoulder and said firmly: "Come on. I know what you need."

She peered up at him apprehensively; her eyes had that same shiny surface of innocence.

"Come on," he repeated. He took both glasses and went ahead of her into the hall and the living-room. She noticed the dressing-gown buttons that were undone, held the dressing-gown together with one hand and followed unsteadily. He pulled the two armchairs up to the fish-tank, bade her sit down with a commanding gesture of his hand and sat down in the chair next to her.

"Forget your woes," he said gently. "Let's sit and watch the fish. It'll do you good."

He passed her the glass.

"Easier said than done," she sighed.

"Shhh," Tremmel whispered. "Those small creatures, they can't utter a word to each other. Do you think they miss that?"

"Right now I really do wish I were a little *fish*," Maggi declared. "And that everyone else was too, and would *never* be able to say another word."

"Good," he said. "Now let's be quiet. Now we're fish."

The fish swam around in the yellow light, in the slightly turbid water between small stones and moss and green plants. Now and then they remained stationary in the water, vibrating their transparent tailfins, staring through the glass walls with their small, expressionless eyes.

"Strong and pure," Maggi muttered. She was having problems focusing her eyes. The fish were swimming in front of her eyes in two senses. She pointed to the biggest fish.

"What's that one called?" she whispered.

He craned his neck. "The scalar fish," he said in a low voice.

She nodded sluggishly. "That's the one I'd like to be," she mumbled. "Large and shiny. And completely still."

He was lost in his own reverie, following the fish's soundless movements with his small, burning eyes. Maggi put her hand over his, stroked his veined wrist, then she drew his hand towards her bosom and filled his palm with a warm, heavy breast. He continued to stare into the aquarium. Neither of them said anything. One of the small, sparkling fish floated motionlessly in the water, watching them through the glass wall with its flat eyes. Occasionally one of the aquatic plants swayed gently, a movement as light as the quivering of eyelashes. After a while, he realised that Maggi was asleep. Her head hung down limply towards her side. Carefully, he removed his hand.

He let her sleep.

He smoked his pipe, observed the fish, cast a few distressed glances at the sleeping landlady. He put down his pipe. He emptied the glasses. Afterwards her head fell down on to her chest and she awoke with a start. She looked at him, perplexed. Then she stood up without a word, staggered into the hall and closed the bedroom door after her.

The piano tuner remained seated, looking into the illuminated space behind the glass walls.

Maggi went to her meetings.

The autumn was still mild.

In mid-November it was so mild that Tremmel could spend time on the balcony in a coat. There were afternoons with a shimmering of yellow after the few hours of sunshine and the piano tuner unfolded a collapsible chair to gaze at the bare black trunks of the trees against the golden afternoon sky. The air had a special clarity; it was the weather for clear thinking and unhurried decisions. In the window-box there was still some life in one petunia, a leggy, bedraggled plant, desperately stretching outwards for light. The poplar hedge still retained some of its leaves.

He could sit, motionless, on the balcony for long periods, with his veined hands on his knees, with an introspective concentration, as if listening to something. It was only when dark, reddish features moved across the sky and the trees lost their definition that he folded up his chair and went indoors.

He asked Maggi a couple of times if any post had come for him. It hadn't.

One evening Maggi came across the widow in the basement.

The woman was making a lot of noise in the storeroom, groaning, dragging heavy objects across the floor, mumbling to herself. Maggi thought she would have to peek into the storeroom to see what was going on.

"Goodness me, you frightened me!" the widow exclaimed upon catching sight of Maggi. Then she gave a desperate laugh. "I've got to be the clumsiest person in the world. I'm trying to shift this chest of drawers out, but there's so much mess in here."

Maggi surveyed the situation.

"I'll help you," she said. "A seaman's wife is used to coping," she added, not without pride. "We'll have to move these chairs," Maggi explained. "Such a shame to have such nice chairs standing around in the basement," she said sympathetically. The widow shrugged. They moved the chairs into the aisle in the basement. They moved an old mirror and slipped in past bureaus which smelled of elegant furniture polish and linen. They tried to move the chest of drawers, but it was like concrete.

"Oh God," the widow said. "I'd forgotten that. The porcelain."

The drawers were full of cups, dishes and plates. The fragile porcelain with the straw design had been packed hastily in Christmas wrapping paper and any other packaging that had come to hand, such as towels and silk tablecloths.

"Good God," the widow said. "Is this where my tablecloths were? I don't need them," she said apologetically, emptying the drawers. "I want to live a bit more simply now."

Maggi, who, unlike the widow, was an organised person, found a couple of cardboard boxes in her storeroom in the basement. As they filled the boxes with the porcelain, Maggi made admiring comments about the beautiful objects. The widow, for her part, uttered exclamations of despair. "What on earth am I going to do with all this? Perhaps I can sell some of it?" she said in a daze. "My husband was a hoarder. What good's all this stuff? Both our mothers heaped things on to us. Some people try to kill you with objects."

Maggi straightened up and gave her a sharp look.

"These things," she said with a flick of her head, "these things represent a fortune."

The widow looked at her with her apathetic, cat-like face. "Do they really?"

The drawers were empty. They carried them out into the aisle.

"I could have asked Paul, couldn't I?" the widow said. "He's so kind to me, but he's got a bit of a bad back."

They had reached the steps with the chest of drawers before Maggi realised whom she was talking about. She was talking about the piano tuner, about Tremmel.

She had called him Paul.

One day, Tremmel turned up at the department store.

He seemed to be searching for Maggi. He was still wearing the thin poplin overcoat, although it had begun to turn cold.

"I'm glad I found you," he said, smiling one of his rare smiles. Maggi moistened her lips with the tip of her tongue, straightened her glasses and thrust her hands into the pockets of her pinafore. Out of the corner of her eye she could feel her colleagues following everything that was unfolding.

"I was looking for some mackerel fillets in tomato sauce," Tremmel explained. "In this circus of yours it's impossible to find anything."

Maggi followed him to the tinned goods section with a smile. Tremmel studied the tins and to Maggi's astonishment he gathered up a whole pile of tins of mackerel, seven or eight; they weren't even on offer.

"Would that be all?" Maggi asked.

"What do *you* like best?" he asked in a confidential way, using intonation she had never heard him use before.

"What was that?"

"I'm happy," Tremmel said candidly. "And I feel like making someone else happy. What do you like?"

Maggi seemed to be caught off guard. She mulled it over – apparently trying to remember something she had long forgotten.

"Nothing in particular, I don't think." She automatically tidied the shelf, squinting at the price tabs. She seemed embarrassed, as if consideration coming from another person were unfamiliar to her.

"Give it some thought," he said, patting her on the shoulder once. "And one more thing," he added with a gleam in one eye. "Mosquito larvae. Where can I find some mosquito larvae?"

"Some whatdidyousay?"

"Mosquito larvae," he repeated.

Maggi burst into shrill laughter, she put her hands on her hips and roared, it almost sounded hysterical and she couldn't stop. A number of customers stood still with their trolleys. The saleswoman at the vegetable counter was weighing onions and oranges inordinately slowly. Maggi was bent double with laughter as Tremmel regarded her with an imperturbable smile.

"I have absolutely no idea what you're talking about," Maggi gasped. "But that's the funniest thing I've heard for a long time."

"I'm not trying to be funny," Tremmel explained. "I need them for my fish. They need mosquito larvae. All this dried food isn't good for them."

Maggi was laughing as she shook her head and wiped her glasses on her pinafore. The saleswoman in the vegetable section had at this point completely stopped serving customers and was staring uninhibitedly at Maggi Svendsen and the middle-aged man with the mass of hair.

"You must be slightly mad," Maggi said.

He was serious. His head glided round to face hers; he whispered into her ear: "Yes, happily. Goodbye."

Maggi's laughter sliced through the music playing in the store, it sawed through like a thin blade cutting dry wood. Tremmel picked up the pile of mackerel tins and walked towards the cash-desk to pay.

How long does the piano tuner think he's going to stay in Maggi's living-room?

She asks him to his face. He has just been across the corridor putting in double glazing in the widow's flat. Tremmel appears surprised, as though he had never given it a moment's thought.

"*He* may be coming home for Christmas," Maggi says. "And he doesn't like me taking in lodgers. By the way, isn't it time she got herself a job? Her over the way?" She nods in the direction of the widow's flat.

"I haven't got a clue."

"When herr Mikalsen lived here there was a terrible scene when *he* came home. I must have forgotten to tell him that I was renting out a room. On top of that, he gets all sorts of whims into his head. Old men have such strange ideas."

"Is he old?"

Maggi nods emphatically.

"*I* think so, at any rate."

Tremmel sits down on a kitchen chair and pulls his pipe out of his pullover pocket. He appears to be brooding over something.

"I really don't want to throw you out," she says. "Please don't misunderstand me."

Tremmel lights his pipe. The small dark eyes glow in the flame from the match.

"My situation is somewhat unclear," he says at length. "I don't want to cause you any trouble."

After this conversation, Maggi takes the rubbish bag out. She meets the widow, who has just been to the rubbish bin, and they greet each other as they pass. Maggi opens the lid; at the top of the overfilled bag which has just been pressed down, there are several empty tins of mackerel.

The weather has turned.

The days are cold and drab with hoar frost. There is an inviolable beauty about the frozen trees; the narrow strip of grass around the block has a grainy quality, as if coarse salt has been strewn across it. The dusk brings pale blue colours with it, like the light in marble. Three or four crows are installed in the elm tree.

When Maggi comes home in the afternoon, Tremmel often stands by the living-room window staring out. He seems alone. How often the widow with the hungry cheekbones visits him, or he her, is difficult to say. Someone who has to stand watch over a large department store, where customers and staff vie with each other to pilfer, has other things to do than spy on gentle-mannered lodgers who have problems of their own to battle with. She has an inkling that the widow's refuse bags contain the odd empty tin or two, and a small, dark pain tears at her.

It is Sunday morning and Maggi is restless.

She has no meetings to go to; the store is closed. The town lies still and the day is as uneventful as only Sunday in a small Norwegian town in winter can be. Maggi pads around in her dressing-gown and listens at doors. When she opens the front door she can hear music coming from the widow's flat. Otherwise everything is quiet. A car starts up in the road outside. Once she hears the cawing of crows.

There is a ring at the door.

Maggi opens.

Outside stands a small woman with large eyes and a white face. She is dressed normally. Her ankle boots are wet. She has a brown knitted hat pulled down over her hair. Her hair is grey and reaches down to her shoulders.

"My name is Anne Tremmel," she says. "Is my husband here?" The voice is small and melodious, like the sound of a delicate instrument.

Maggi is startled and backs into the hall. Then she raises her shoulders, straightens her glasses and politely shows the woman in. Maggi points to the living-room door.

"He lives in here," she says. "I'm not sure if he's in at this particular moment."

The woman turns her white face away from Maggi, approaches the door, knocks briefly and enters. She looks at Maggi.

"Do you know where he is?"

Maggi considers this.

"No," she says initially. "I'm afraid not," she adds. There is something about the wide-open eyes in the small face looking at her. It is the face of a person who has made up her mind to confront the realities, whatever they are. And Maggi Svendsen changes her mind.

"He may be across the way," she says. "With a neighbour," she adds, as neutrally as she can.

She opens the door again, watches the little woman walk towards the widow's door and place a finger on the doorbell. This time she rings long and hard as if she suddenly knows where the person she is looking for is to be found. Maggi waits.

The door opens. The widow stands there in a green tracksuit. She is barefoot.

"Who are you?" she asks.

"My name is Anne Tremmel."

"Really?" The widow smiles her slow, thin smile. "That's interesting. Paul? There's a lady here calling herself Anne Tremmel." She moves to make way for the piano tuner. He pulls at the grey pullover to straighten it; he is not wearing a shirt underneath.

"What are you doing here?" he asks.

"I want to talk to you," the woman says.

Tremmel coughs. He sweeps his hand through his hair.

"I didn't think there was anything left to say."

The woman shifts position. It looks as if she is going to move a step closer, although, in fact, she is only shifting the weight of her body from one foot to the other. She stands erect in her dark woollen cloak, which is slightly too short.

"You've got to come back home," she says.

He looks at her. "You threw me out," he says.

She nods in silence.

All three of them look at her, the widow, Maggi and Paul Tremmel. They all stare at her as if the little woman in the woollen cloak were a revelation, an answer to the mysteries of life.

The widow lowers her gaze first. She steals a glance at the piano tuner, standing there in his knitted pullover with his grey chest-hair on show, and at Maggi in her dressing-gown, and at the little lady in the knitted hat pulled down over her hair.

Suddenly the widow begins to laugh.

Her laughter is awful to hear as her narrow eyes flit from one person to the other. She laughs as the tears begin to flow. The stairwell causes her laughter to echo cruelly. She continues to laugh while clutching her stomach as if in pain.

"Stop that," the piano tuner says.

"Are you coming?" asks the woman who calls herself Anne Tremmel.

The widow continues to laugh. Bent double with laughter, she backs into the hallway. They can still hear her laughing in a room inside the flat. Tremmel casts a glance after her.

"Women," he says.

He says this as if he were pronouncing the final diagnosis on a long, incurable illness.

The little woman does not move, but she seems to be gaining in height, growing where she stands in her cloak, hat and wet ankle boots.

Maggi, who remained quiet during the whole episode, stands there with a flushed face, feeling she ought to do something. If only she knew what. Then it hits her. She clears her throat to make her presence known and closes the door to leave the Tremmels alone on the stairway landing.

The same Sunday, a couple of hours later, the piano tuner takes his leave. As quietly as he moved in, he packs his things and moves out. He has no more than it takes to fill the taxi that fru Tremmel returns in. She sits in the car and waits while he carries his things out: the rucksack and some plastic bags. He collects the fish-tank last. He has placed it in a cardboard box.

Maggi holds open the door for him.

"I'm going to miss them," she says. "Your fish."

"I'm going to miss you," he says. "You're a good woman. Strong and pure."

Tears form in Maggi's eyes. He holds the heavy cardboard box with both hands. She looks into the small dark eyes; she cannot see whether he is happy or unhappy. She kisses him firmly on the cheek.

"Thank you," she says in a flat, dry voice with its own particular passion. "Thank you for being such a . . . gentleman."

The piano tuner looks at her glumly. But somewhere in the dark eyes there is a sparkle. He kisses her on the mouth.

As the taxi rounds the corner by the poplar hedge Paul Tremmel cranes round in the back seat and looks at the block of flats he has been living in. There is still a flower in the window-box on the balcony, a tough, leggy plant stretching out for the wan December light, a forgotten petunia.

Translated by Don Bartlett

Deep Need – Instant Nausea

Some sad human beings keep pumping the jukebox with money and putting on lousy music. Her glass is empty. He still has three or four centimetres left. For every beer she has drunk she has had to wait until he has finished his and each of them paid for their own beer each time. She cannot remember if they have had three or four large beers. "Have we had three or four beers?" she asks. "I've only had three," he says. He is tapping his index finger on the tabletop, almost in time with the music, but not quite. "You were nursing one when I came in," he says. "So you must have had four." She has long come to terms with his chat-up line – "Do you come here often?" – but now it is irritating her again. She thought that he was being wry, that he was playing on the cliché, but he wasn't. He was perfectly serious and waited for an answer and she had to say, "No, not that often." She doesn't feel like another beer, she can't afford it, and she doesn't feel in the least like sitting and talking to him; everything has been said, the conversation is going nowhere. And the last thing he said was that he liked the sounds in the bar. Must be compassion, she thinks to herself, but she can't even muster that for the music. The simplest thing would be to say, "Let's have another beer"; not only would it be easier to say than "Let's go, shall we?", but it would be easier than sitting there one second longer with an empty glass. "Shall we have another beer?" she says in a suitably interested tone of voice; she looks at him as she speaks, but then at once coolly looks away. "No, I'm just so tired," he says with a smile. "I can't manage another beer." And then he begins to tell her about his nephew. Tells her that the boy could read fluently when he was four and now at the age of eight he reads Knut Hamsun. He's an obnoxious boy, he says. She laughs, not out loud; she forms a broad smile with her mouth and forces air through her nose twice. He doesn't laugh. She cannot fathom why he won't have another beer. It crosses her mind that she has to do the dishes before going to bed. He suggests going to the cinema tomorrow. "Maybe," she says. "I promised I'd go and see my father.

I'll ring you." The barman comes to take away the dead glasses. They get up and go out. He stands outside with his hands in his jacket pockets. "It's quite early still," he says. "Yes, it is," she says. "Do you like listening to music?" he asks. "Would you like to come to my place and listen to some music?" She hesitates for a few seconds, but without actually giving it much thought she looks at him, smiles and says, "Yes." They start to walk. "Shall we take a taxi?" she says. "No, let's walk," he says. "It's not that far." She is wearing new shoes and they are beginning to chafe. He walks at an abnormally fast pace. Once he is almost run over because he charges across the road without stopping to look. Despite walking so fast, he talks all the way to his flat, first of all about social issues: about the advantages and disadvantages of immigration, about whether prostitution should be legalised or not and about the quality of Norwegian kindergartens vis-à-vis Swedish ones. Then he talks about himself, about the jobs he has had and his plans for the future. She has more than enough to deal with just keeping up with him and is quite out of breath. It is all she can do to say "Uh-huh" and "uh?" "You're a bit shy, you are," he says with a smile over his shoulder. "No, I'm not," she says. "Perhaps you're just not very talkative," he says. Her heels hurt. It feels as if the blisters have burst now. He practically stops dead in his tracks in front of a door. "This is where I live," he says. The key is already in his hand; he unlocks the door and goes in ahead of her. She looks at his back as they go up the stairs. He lives on the fourth floor and neither of them says a word. He has quite a cute bum, but his trousers are not up to much. She is not sure that she actually wants to sleep with him. In the hall she bends down to undo the laces of her shoes. "Please take off your shoes," he says. He opens a door. "Here's the bedroom," he says. She can feel a pee coming on. The bed is quite narrow. There is a magazine on the bedside table. "It's a bit messy," he says. Two or three items of clothing hang over a chair. She stands there with her arms crossed, her weight on one leg and her head thrust upwards; she can feel that her sweater has ridden up and her stomach is visible. I need a pee first, she thinks. The bed wear is flowery, a pastel shade and the duvet nicely folded over. He leaves the room. She follows him. "This is the sitting-room," he says. The walls are a burgundy red. There are green plants and pleated yellow lampshades, with reproductions of Van Gogh and Munch on the walls. He waves his hand towards the stereo system and three shelves of CDs. "I spend much too much money on music," he says. Now a whisky, she thinks, a whisky first. "Where's the loo?" she asks. Not content with pointing to the door, he goes right over and opens it, gestures with his arm into the bathroom as if showing her around. On the edge of the bath there are glass jars of pink bath salts and round, light-blue capsules of bath oils. Towels, also pastel-coloured, are arranged in neat piles on the shelves according to size. She has a pee and cleans herself carefully with moistened toilet paper. The floor is spotless; there isn't a hair or any dust to be seen. She kneels down and peers under the bench; nothing to be seen there, either. There are cans of hairspray and bottles of moisturising cream on the shelf under the mirror. When she comes out, there is a CD playing. She asks what it is, but she has never heard of the music and she takes an immediate dislike to it. There is a diploma hanging on the wall, black letters on mint green paper; the paper looks old and faded. She reads it. It is from 1979, with his name on, third prize in downhill skiing. "I beat my brother," he says. "We were competitive about everything. He was the eldest and always came top in everything. He was more popular than me, better at school and generally better at sport. But that time I won." He points to the diploma. "My brother had a cold and came fifth," he says. He moves something from the sitting-room table. "He had more luck with girls, too. I hated him." He comes over to her. He is carrying a bowl with a spoon in. There is something brown in it and it has set; chocolate pudding perhaps. "When he died I realised that I didn't hate him that much," he says. "But it was absolutely fine that he was dead." He goes to the kitchen. She hears him putting the bowl down on the steel sink unit before returning. "When did your brother die?" she says. "In April," he says. He goes over to the sofa and starts arranging the cushions, systematically; he gently pats the square cushions into position, working from one end to the other. Then he goes to the toilet. She wonders whether she should sit on the sofa, waits a little, remains standing and then looks at the CDs. He returns so quickly that without thinking she says, "Have you already been?" He walks past her and positions himself on the other side. "He had dreadful taste in music," he says, "but he would never admit it. I played in a band for a few years, but I've given up." On the shelf above the CDs there is a photograph framed in glass and held with clips, resting against a brass candlestick. Three pale, skinny boys with unnaturally twisted limbs lying on their backs on a carpet. "The one in the middle is my son," he says. "He's got cerebral palsy. He lives in Tromsø. I haven't seen him for eight months. He'll recognise me when we meet." He puts two glasses down on the sitting-room table. "Would you like a glass of Coke?" he asks. She says, "Yes please," and moves towards the sofa to sit down. He goes into the kitchen and returns with a large bottle of Coca-Cola and sits down in an armchair. He fills the glasses, passes one over to her, lifts the other one up and, while looking at the wall, holds it in his hand without drinking from it. Set in one wall is a closed door. "What's in there?" she asks, pointing. "My sister's room," he says. "We share the flat. She's not here right now." "When will she come home?" she asks. "Not until tomorrow," he says. "Now I can understand the hairspray and the skin cream in the bathroom better," she says, smiling. "I'm not one for one-night stands," he says. "I like to get to know a girl before I go to bed with her." She looks at him, doesn't say a word. "If that's fine by you," he says, "that we don't sleep with each other." He looks at her. "Of course," she says. "I hadn't thought about it, either." "No, of course not," he says. "But it would be nice if you would stay the night." She nods, smiles, takes a swig of the Coke. "You're good to talk to," he says, smiling. "And you're good-looking." He knocks back the whole glass in one and puts it down on the table. She can see by the way he bends his chin down towards his chest and opens his mouth that he is belching noiselessly.

Translated by Don Bartlett

KJARTAN FLØGSTAD

The Story of the Short Story

The short story as a literary form is an oriental invention, wholly unknown to the Greeks and the Romans; it came to Europe through Mohammedan and Spanish intervention, together with imaginative accounts that eventually turned into parables of a moral nature.

There is reason to believe that the short story left the Emperor's palace in Beijing one warm August afternoon in the twenty-fourth year of the first Ming dynasty, together with the imperial official Tzu Sun. Their journey took them first through the notorious Gobi desert, where the short story suffered many hardships due to sandstorms and an acute lack of drinking water before reaching a camp in the Kara-Shahr oasis, where it served to frame the tragic end of the imperial official Tzu Sun at the hands of the Mohammedan Afif the Bloodthirsty from the Bokhara region.

A few days later, incredibly enough (when one considers the distance), the short story witnessed the shameless use of the tax money which Tzu Sun had so painstakingly collected in the red-light district of Samarkand—scenes so licentious that Feisal, head censor of the Baghdad caliphate, could find only one word to describe them, namely, "filth", before giving orders to burn the short stories which dealt with the fortnight-long carousal of Afif the Bloodthirsty and his Kirghiz bandits in the red-light district of Samarkand, after the successful attack on the imperial official Tzu Sun in a camp at the Kara-Shahr oasis.

Due to this resolute and ably executed violation of the freedom of expression, we know little about the subsequent fate of the short story until, four years later, it turns up in a Tashkent marketplace, together with the beautiful slave Zama, who, by means of trickery and an immense ambition, had worked herself up from a dubious origin, to put it mildly, to become the favourite wife of the provincial governor, the wealthy and good-natured Aranki, and also his foremost counsellor, so that, at the height of her power, Zama, the former beautiful slave, was far and away the most powerful woman in Central Asia.

With Aranki, the wealthy and good-natured provincial governor, the enterprising Zama had no fewer than twelve sons. Nabil, the next eldest of them, was as a young and prosperous tax collector sent to Baghdad to make his career at the caliphate. But the young, inexperienced provincial soon fell prey to court intrigue and spent the few years that remained of his young life in the ghastly torture chambers underneath the Al-Hallaj palace in Baghdad – under circumstances that made it perfectly natural, not to say inevitable, that the caliphate should try, with all the means at its disposal, to suppress the short story depicting the details of young Nabil's ill fortune in the cold and damp dungeons under the Al-Hallaj palace. So it must be called a minor miracle that the short story managed to leave Baghdad without being confiscated, made its way on its own up the River Tigris among hardy oarsmen and huckstering traders, and after many hardships finally managed to cross Mount Sidon in three feet of snow and get down to Beirut, where the short story bummed around for four years among outsailed Vikings and seedy little spies from the Holy See and from the sultanate in Cairo.

Under such circumstances it is obviously almost impossible to follow the further development of the short story, and we know nothing more about its fate until one spring day many years later when, right after the *reconquista*, having tossed off over eight (the English historian A.H.P. Sledgethwaite-Jones thinks over nine) *aguardientes*, the young, depraved, Andalusian nobleman Lazarillo de Tormes took it into his head to go to North Africa and bring the short story across the Strait of Gibraltar by force, in order thereby to renew European prose. Together with three other young rogues, Don Lazarillo set out from Algeciras at the darkest hour of the night and returned with a short, melodramatic (and untrue, as it later turned out) story about prodigious fights and bold abductions in the Moorish port of Ach-al-Ghazal (Ceuta).

Since then, many have followed the example of Don Lazarillo: in particular, I'll mention the Norwegian Bjørnson and the Russian Sologub. This, among other things, has led not only to a flourishing of the short story in our part of the world, but also to its becoming more respectable. Some important exceptions from this rule will be mentioned.

In the early summer of 1839, the North American journalist E. Allan Poe, otherwise so excellent in many ways, one morning, to his own and his friends' great surprise, awoke sober in his own bed and without a hangover. Poe resolutely got out of bed, put on his dressing-gown and in the course of a few hours wrote the theory of the short story. Only long afterwards did the victim recover from the shock, and then took a cruel revenge. On October 3, 1849, the unlucky Mr Poe became the central character in a short story in which he – "who, like Shelley in his verse, like Keats, / had kept the rhythm of the tameless azure, / and in stories had borne up with / hermetic cadences, the machine as torture" – was found near dead from alcohol poisoning at Ryan's 4th Ward Polls in Baltimore and died a few days later, "to the wind's litany of tarps, / awnings, chimney pots, and company flags".*

Viewed metaphysically, this cruel and paradoxical incident is reminiscent, to the point of confusion, of a similar instance in Paris, where another North American, Professor Merle P. Sparrow of Columbia University, was staying on a grant from the Guggenheim Foundation in order to explore the influence exerted by the environment on the development of the sub-plot in the short stories which had fallen into the hands of his countryman, Ernest Hemingway. After drinking two glasses of absinthe in a now extinct bar in rue Akrut, Professor Sparrow, who had come to Paris on a Sunday, was overcome by an insurmountable homesickness, took the first plane back to New York, was the sole surviving passenger after the greatest aeroplane disaster in the history of L.A.C.S.A. (*Aéronaves de Suriname*), came back to Columbia University safe and sound, spent four years transcribing the notes he made in Paris, and published the result with Schuster and Rinehart under the pseudonym Johnny Weissmueller. Thus, in the end the nostalgic Professor Sparrow, too, fell prey to his own misdeeds.

We live today in a time when sightings of the short story are as numerous as they are confusing. It is reported to have been seen in the Congo, been heard in the mouths of central characters in the novels of the Rio Plata, and been lost in the papers of an overworked master at Bryne Rural Junior College, who searches his brain in despair for material to fill the regular Wednesday short story in *Stavanger Aftenblad* with events that are sufficiently bizarre and horrible. All of this, of course, simply to conceal the fact that the short story, an oriental invention that was wholly unknown to the Greeks and the Romans, is snugly blanketing two young people who are making love on an overcrowded beach on the Pacific coast of North America, while the ocean sits motionless in the background looking on, close-

up and beautiful like a photographic scenery in a film by Elliott
Silverstein.

[*] The two quoted passages are from the poem "Poe's Death", in
Thorkild Bjørnvig's collection *Figur og Ild* (*Figure and Fire*) 1959, pp.
46–7.

Translated by Sverre Lyngstad

GRO DAHLE

Life of a Trapper

For Christmas Louie gets an airgun from his father. With one hand Louie's father shows him how to load, aim, and fire. In the other he's holding a glass. Louie is standing alone on the steps. There's been a frost, but no snow. Ice on the fjord thick enough to drive on. The ducks are frozen stiff in the pond. He loads, aims, and fires. Hits the window on Mrs Jensen's outhouse.

Louie buys a snow-blower in July. Thunderstorms in October, and finally in February it snows. Like seagulls or angels. He's too late to do the driveway before work. And when he comes home, everyone has shovelled their own. Everyone except Mrs Jensen. But he can't be bothered with her. It has to be for people with a little money.

Louie has gone behind the hen-house. His tracks are in the snow. Concealed by the red wall, he pisses May-Britt's initials in the snowdrift. Two hours later it snows again.

Louie has a moped. It's not the same as last year's. This one's even nicer. Besides, it's red. That means something, Louie thinks. He gets someone he knows to paint a tiger on the gas tank. Doesn't turn out right, so he has to take it off with paint thinner. There's nothing wrong with mopeds. If you don't take girls into account. But Louie has an extra helmet. Just in case. The warmth of another body against your back.

Louie doesn't think his mother loves him as much as she should.

Apart from Mrs Jensen's window and her randy dog, it's mostly been crows. Now and then a seagull. But they're tough to bring down. He hangs up the crows in the woodshed. Sees how the carcass gradually dries out. Withers. The hollow eyes. The feathers that lose their sheen. Occasionally he skins a squirrel, nails the fur to the wall. Later he might get twenty kroner for it.

Louie hears about Roy. They used to go swimming together at Klopp. Rode their bikes with the others, three in a row. Louie usually stayed in shallow water, looked for flint in the sand. While Roy swam out to the big boats anchored in the cove. Now Roy's become a seaman.

No-one drinks as much soda at work as Louie. Mostly Coke. For every twenty cases he carries, he opens a bottle. Counts to twenty, takes a break. Counts to twenty. Every morning at seven Louie's on the job, and he's the last one to leave.

The ferryboats meet midway and glide past one another, each to its own harbour. Louie is walking along the public dock. It's Sunday. He's wearing his new black slacks with grey stripes. And his white windcheater. The islands farther out where the fjord opens up hang in the air like blue ovals. He has binoculars, but there's nothing to look at. Apart from the ferryboats and the expanse of water between them. It's Sunday. Ten-thirty. The ferry docks. The cars drive off. The ferry pulls out. A half-hour later the ferryboats are once again midway, gliding past each other, slowly.

Louie goes with his parents to Nesbyen the first week in July. He's wearing a dark green turtleneck, gets carsick and throws up in the back seat. Sun against the windshield. Goddammit.

First Louie hung out with Roy who was the same age. Then it was Tom who was five years younger. Now Louie hangs out with the seventeen-year-olds over at the petrol station.

When Frode and Louie talk over the fence, Frode presses his white stomach against the wire fence so it makes a waffle pattern. It's repulsive and fascinating. Just like the deformed girl at the end of the street.

Frode knows May-Britt too. It turns out.

Who can walk on their hands under willow trees that sing? Louie can. Who can make the dog talk? Louie. Who can lift Jørgensen's anchor?

If Louie could choose a gift, he would choose healing hands. And he would lay them on May-Britt's breasts. She would bend over backwards and touch the floor. He knows her cropped haircut from all the others. The arch of her back. The curve in her neck.

Louie has to go with his parents to Benidorm. Just when it's starting to be exciting to be home. It rains the whole week. His father reads Norwegian newspapers. His mother writes postcards. And Louie. Louie looks at walkie-talkie equipment.

The walkie-talkie doesn't work when he comes home.

Three dry afternoons. Red dust from the gravel. Clothes-lines with sheets. He doesn't know where she lives. All the houses are alike. The fourth day it rains.

May-Britt is a nice name for a girl.

His brother's girlfriend tries her hand with the scissors. When he leans back, he touches her boobs. He could fall asleep like this. And she is nice and warm. "Not the moustache," Louie says. He grew it out on the Costa del Sol. Enough hair for a soccer team.

May-Britt smiles. He's belching, but is happy.

Louie leaves the moped at home when he goes out on the town. This time the grey slacks with black stripes. The white windcheater. He doesn't run into anyone he knows, but nods at two people he thinks he recognises. Others borrow chairs from his table. On the way home he trips on a chain.

The sinking feeling in his stomach when he sees Frode on the lawn. And her in a white dress. That night he shoots a cat and nails it to Frode's door. Two blows of the hammer. Iron through the cat's eye.

The most irritating thing about May-Britt is that she talks through her nose. There's a heatwave and mosquitoes. Louie is lying behind the hen-house with a fever, reading porn.

Union meeting. Two show up early. One comes late. Louie takes off his hat for the foreman. There are refreshments, a vote and resolution. Louie walks home alone to the bird under his pillow.

Louie has a dream that comes true that summer. Window shut to keep the mosquitoes out. He dreams that his mother is sick and lying under a spruce tree with a cone in her breast. He forgets all about May-Britt until October. Then his mother comes home with one breast missing.

On Father's Day all the children come home. Three brothers, one sister. They talk about the inheritance for the first time.

When he sees May-Britt again, winter has set in and he has earned two thousand from his snow-blower. She has snow in her hair, sores on her mouth. She isn't so pretty any more.

She's just as pretty. Just different. Frode comes to the door. Louie opens up, scarf around his neck, with a cold. They've made up again, are equals and without a god. Go to the movies together. Eat potato chips. But both become a little thoughtful when she sits two rows in front of them.

Frode tells him he's going to America. And here Louie had been thinking he'd teach Frode how to skin squirrels that winter.

He shoots birds haphazardly and can't be bothered to pick them up. His father lies on the sofa with sciatica. And the cat has kittens.

Louie gets glasses. When he was little he became dehydrated from vomiting and diarrhoea. This went on for three weeks. So long that he developed allergies and astigmatism.

That spring Louie puts all his effort into getting his driver's licence. And before he turns twenty-eight he's driving his own car with Annette. Annette with the short blouse. Black bra. And a birthmark across half of her face. When she sits next to him in the car, he only sees the pretty side.

Louie and Annette walk through the forest to the burial mounds. There are no secrets there any more. They've been filled with sand and rocks. Light filters through the treetops. He thinks about May-Britt then. Her short hair. Her chapped lips. One blue eye, the other green.

The horsemen come back across the fields without their horses. The hare slung over a shoulder by the ears.

Louie falls asleep on the sofa. He has a dream that his father pulls him down under the water. Carries driftwood back to the sea. Fills a container with sand.

That summer Louie and Annette sleep in a tent on Torger Island for two weeks. Louie has hay fever. It turns out that Annette is pregnant, but not by Louie. Autumn. The yellow-white grain has been cut to the ground. He strangles the cat with his mother's stocking and takes long drives at night.

Translated by Katherine Hanson

ØYSTEIN LØNN

It's So Damned Quiet

He came home early and stood by the window in the living-room as it started to rain. A flock of starlings swept over the fields across the road and settled on the lawn in front of the house. It was autumn, and he stood motionless at the window, looking at the rain, and he saw that the glistening birds were snatching at earthworms under the grass. He had seen the birds on the lawn in front of the house all summer and had watched the young birds grow up and learn to fly.

When he was a boy the teacher had told him that the starlings could hear the earthworms. The worms made long burrows and channels down in the dark earth, and the starlings could hear the worms when they moved. He imagined that he could see how the birds listened, found a worm, waited until the right moment, struck with their beaks, and gulped down the worm.

He stood quite still and watched it happen.

He didn't like birds, no matter what kind, but he had never told anyone that.

"Did you pay the bill?"

He heard the voice clearly through the kitchen door. She stepped into the room and flicked the ash off her cigarette.

"Look at them," he said. "Look at the way they're stuffing themselves. This autumn they're really voracious."

She went to the window and looked at the birds. "What's wrong with you, anyway? Did you pay that bill?"

"It's so damned quiet," he said.

She followed him with her gaze as he went downstairs to the cellar and got the toolbox. He rummaged around in the compartments and threw her a glance that meant there was something he couldn't find. She got up from her chair, went to the window, lit another cigarette, and looked at the birds. The ones closest to the window managed to fly in under the trees before they carried on gobbling up worms. She drew the smoke deep into her lungs and blew it up towards the newly-painted ceiling. "Why didn't you pay that bill?" she asked.

"Which one?" he said.

She looked at the birds.

"Take your pick," he said. "We have five bills that are about the same size, and we can pay one of them. Our creditors are participating in the monthly lottery. Instead of sending nasty letters they ought to be grateful."

"So you didn't pay it," she said.

He went out the back door, got the ladder from behind the garage, and leaned it up against the gutter. It was drizzling, and he got his hands wet as he climbed up the ladder.

The first autumn storm arrived a week ago. It was a typical storm and it made the pine trees behind the house sway. Above the garage hung a heavy branch that swept over the roof. He had been standing in the bathroom shaving when he heard the roofing felt beneath the tiles flapping in the wind. By the time he had finished shaving, he could see the rain trickling in between the slabs of wallboard in the bathroom.

He climbed the ladder, wriggled loose five roofing tiles that had turned porous with age, and climbed with them all the way down the ladder to avoid hearing the sound of them falling to the ground. The dry sound of roofing tiles shattering would have been more than he could stand. He gathered the dark-red tiles in a plastic sack and brought in new ones from the boot of the car.

From the radio in the kitchen he heard a band playing marches. They were ordinary German military marches that invited you to march along in time. He went into the house, turned off the radio, and noticed that she was still standing at the window looking at the birds. It was so quiet in the house that it was palpable. He drank some water, and when he passed her she put her arms around him, pressed her face against his neck, and he pushed her away so that he wouldn't make spots on her blue blouse.

"Are you alright?" she asked.

"Not bad," he said.

"You came home early. Did something happen at work? You don't usually come home early."

"No, nothing," he said.

"What'll we do tonight?"

"No idea," he said.

"Shall we go to the cinema? I saw in the paper that there's a good one in town."

"Sure, fine," he said.

He went out to the back of the house again, hoisted the new tiles on to his left shoulder, and went carefully up the ladder. Some of the rungs were quite slippery, and he braced himself with his left hand. In the distance he heard a dog bark; the cars down on the main road rolled noiselessly by; and he saw the exhaust of a tractor hanging like a white stripe across the field. He wasn't afraid of climbing ladders, but he didn't like it, and he was glad that he didn't have to go up on the roof. It was sufficient to stand on one of the top rungs and push the tiles in until they were in place in the grooves. The gutter was half-full of pine needles that had turned to dirt, and he put on his work gloves, thoroughly cleaned the gutter and carefully lowered the rust-red sludge to the ground. It would have been better to run the hose along the gutter, but it was so late in the autumn that the gardening things were already stored in the shed.

He didn't hear a sound as he stood on the ladder; everything was quiet, not a breath of wind, not a sound from the road, and inside the house she wasn't moving around. He didn't hear her rapid steps going from room to room, and there wasn't a sound from the radio. He liked it. It couldn't be quiet enough for him. He stood on the ladder a long time, far too long, before it dawned on him suddenly that it was raining and he was getting wet.

"Are you still up there?"

He looked down at her.

"Do you realise that you've been up on that ladder for almost half an hour?"

"Have I?" he said.

"Why are you standing up there doing nothing? You're just standing up on that ladder and staring."

"It's so quiet here," he said.

She went into the house. When he came in the front door he could smell that she had started dinner, and he opened the door to the cellar, went down the stairs, and put the toolbox back on the shelf. It smelled mouldy down there, and he closed the window that had been open all summer. Then he carefully wiped the white fungus off the wall and sprayed on some mould spray.

"Are you coming?" she shouted.

"What's going on?" he replied.

"Nothing's going on."

He heard the voice through the cellar door.

"Is someone coming?"

"No," she shouted.

She opened the cellar door. "Dinner," she said.

He washed, changed his shirt, went up the stairs and over to the window. A flock of starlings had gathered in the apple tree, and they sat motionless until he raised his arms. The ones sitting on the closest branches fluttered off across the fields. But the braver ones stayed in the tree and moved reluctantly from branch to branch. He watched as the birds took another turn over the field, flew around the trees on the other side of the road, approached the house, and came back and settled under the redcurrant bushes. He saw them hesitate before they came on to the lawn, then approached the window, and flew back under the bushes when he moved.

"Damned birds," he whispered.

"What did you say?"

She stood in the kitchen doorway. She followed him with her eyes as he watched the birds under the currant bushes.

"Nothing," he said, facing the window-pane. "I didn't say a thing."

It was still raining, drizzling, the lawn was green and slippery, and the first leaves were falling from the trees.

"Are you coming?"

"OK," he said.

As they ate she talked about their holiday and where they ought to go and about the guy she knew at the travel bureau who could get them a special deal. She took a pile of brochures from the newspaper shelf, spread them out on the table, and told him how it was cheaper to travel off-season. "Everything's better in the autumn," she explained. "Everything's cheaper in the autumn." He listened to her eager voice: "Nobody in their right mind travels in the summertime," she told him, "it's much too hot. But if we go south after high season we can find a little hotel where we can get away from the German tourists. In the villages there are little restaurants, more like cafés," she went on, "where we can sit in the evening and drink wine and play cards. The tables are outside on a concrete terrace, the wine is served in small carafes, and in the picture you can clearly see the ocean and the white houses on the hillside," she said. "Look at the rust-red earth, the palm trees in front of the hotel, and all the birds, and a tanker floating along on the horizon."

"What kind of birds?" he asked.

As she poured water into their glasses she explained that the holiday resorts were cheap because times were bad and almost no-one could afford to travel on holiday. "It's so expensive, far too expensive," she said. And he could clearly hear her voice turn shrill, a little too excited, and he thought that he ought to sneak out to the back yard and climb back up all the rungs of the ladder.

"What sort of deals?" he asked. "You have so many kinds of deals. Sometimes I can't follow you."

She gathered up the brochures. "Oh, come on."

"Do I know him?"

"Of course," she said.

"Who is it?"

"Your cousin," she said. "Did you forget that he works at a travel bureau? He's the one who gave me the brochures. This summer he lived on one of the Greek islands. He bought a house there."

Suddenly he went out on the porch and tried to scare off the birds. He waved his arms and shouted that they should go to hell, to the south, to Hellas, or anywhere. There wasn't a soul on the road; he shouted loudly and no-one heard him. He watched how the glistening birds flapped out of their hiding place under the bushes, up from the branches of the apple tree, and how some of them had hidden in the tall grass by the shed. They flapped up, not making a sound, and gathered in a thick flock that flew over the house, into the woods, and came back over the road.

He settled down and rolled himself a cigarette.

"Do you want to have coffee out here in the rain?" she smiled. She had opened the door to the porch.

He went into the living-room, sat in the leather chair in front of the television, got up and went out in the kitchen for a drink of water. He saw the birds sitting in a row on the telephone wires, at least fifty greyish-black starlings, none of them moving, and for a moment he was convinced that they would sit there forever. The dishwasher hummed, and he heard her clear her throat impatiently in the living-room. She was just as attractive as ever, and he couldn't help looking at her narrow hands and the hair next to her ear.

"I'm coming," he said.

"Do you agree?" she asked.

"I think so," he replied. "If I knew what you were talking about."

"I'm talking about our holiday. It's a good deal."

"It's so damned quiet," he said.

"Isn't that good?" she said.

He turned on the radio to hear the news, but changed his mind and went upstairs to change his trousers. Then he came down again and heard the newspaper rustling from the living-room. He went down to the cellar and got a carton of orange juice, opened it with a pair of scissors and poured a glass of juice. He stared at the yellow juice for a long time and had no idea what to do. He went into the living-room and looked at her for a long time. She took off her reading glasses and looked at him.

"Do you hear something?"

"No," she said. "Not a sound."

"Are you quite sure?"

"Yes," she said. "I'm quite sure."

"You're right," he said. "It's completely silent. Not a sound. There's no way it can last."

Translated by Steven T. Murray

Veranda with Sun

It's a different landscape. A totally different trip. The bus isn't like the other one either. All the same, there's something that makes her remember, remember that particular trip so clearly. It happened ages ago. She was just a little girl. A brave little girl sitting all by herself on a crowded bus. Her mother found a seat way in the back, but she had to sit in the front, right inside the door. There was a single seat there. All the others were for two. Her father had to stand. He stood in the aisle and held on to a strap hanging from the ceiling. Or was it a pole? She doesn't remember, but she remembers the white shirt-cuffs. Or rather *the* white shirt-cuff, just one, the one she saw when she turned around and caught a glimpse of his arm and the hand that was holding tight so he wouldn't lose his balance when the bus lurched forward on the winding road. A bright cuff under the sleeve of a dark suit jacket. Sometimes it was there, and other times, when she turned around to look, it was gone. Her mother was gone too, her bangs and curls, her whole head, forehead, nose and mouth. What if they've got off, she thought. There was another door in the bus, farther back. What if they'd forgotten she was there, forgotten they'd brought her, and got off the bus without her when they got to where they were going? In all the commotion on a crowded bus it was easy to forget. Anyone could do it. She was so tired, tried to stay awake, but couldn't. She was holding a bag in case she had to throw up. But she didn't throw up; she fell asleep, nodded off, and the bag fell to the floor. And when she woke up, she couldn't find them, she didn't see them, her mother and father, they were nowhere to be seen.

She used to be carsick, often was, but didn't throw up that time. She was good. They said that. That's what they said when they put her on a seat all by herself. "Don't go," she'd said, but they didn't hear. "Good girl," they said.

*

This time she's travelling alone. She has shoved her suitcase into the luggage compartment and put her small bag on the rack.

It's not full. Far from it. The seat next to her is empty. She's put her jacket there. Folded it and placed it beside her handbag.

It's warm, but not too warm. Might get warmer later on, it's still early. Early, but no haze, clear blue sky.

She's breathing normally. Sitting on the bus. She's finally sitting on the bus.

She remembers more. A fjord with a boat. Cows on a meadow. She tries to grasp what's whizzing by now too, wants images, something to remember. She's got to remember this.

But all she sees are blurs. Everything runs together. Fogs up. She's not able to concentrate, can't decipher anything. Sees, and yet sees nothing.

She has a good seat, though. She feels the firm pressure of the cushion behind her back. And it's cool; she's stopped perspiring now that she's taken her jacket off. There are several passengers on the bus, but not too close. They are sitting a few seats away. She'll be left alone. Good seat. Her palms are dry. She's calm. Leans back and breathes normally.

It's not far. Five hours, not quite that long. One ferry *en route*. There were two before. Now there's a bridge. She'll buy herself coffee on the ferry. Maybe something to eat too. Thinks: *Maybe I'll buy something to eat – that's very possible.*

The steady hum from the bus. Some people are talking a couple of seats behind her. That's fine with her. They're talking about the weather. That it's good. Has been for a long time.

She has watered the flowers on the veranda the whole time it's been so hot. Has taken care of that. Fertilised too.

It was nice to get a veranda. She'd wanted one for a long time. They hadn't had one where they lived before. "Veranda with sun," it said in the ad. She wanted to have an adjustable deckchair out there. The kind with a reclining back. Two chairs like that. There's room. One for each of them. Good chairs for relaxing when you're off work, or sunning yourself in summer clothes.

Veranda with sun. That's what the ad said.

She'll buy a cup of coffee on the ferry. Maybe something to eat. She's got to eat.

She also wanted pots – on the veranda. Large pots filled with herbs. That you can go and pick, a little of this, a little of that, to put in things you're making. In salads and other things you make. "Shall we go out and buy some pots?" she has suggested.

It feels so foolish now. So pathetic.

It won't be long until the ferry now. Can't be far.

If they have waffles, that's what she'll buy. If not, she'll buy a hard roll. With cheese maybe. Or ham. Ham is good. She will eat. She will.

She's talked about pots. Herbs and sun-chairs on the veranda. The tiny little veranda with flower-boxes along the edge. White flower-boxes with red petunias. "Don't they look nice?" she has asked. "Big and nice?" "Oh yeah," he replied. And then she has chattered on. About pots, and herbs for salads. "Mint is good," she said, "and basil. They only cost twelve kroner and they grow for ever, keep on growing."

And she's talked about the chairs again, that the cushions shouldn't be too gaudy. Blue maybe. If they have that. Marine blue.

She's gone on and on about this. "Do we need that?" he's asked. "Don't you think it seems a little – *staid*?" "No," she answered. "OK," he said then.

She could have taken the car and driven to a place where they have things like that. Gone out there one afternoon. Any day at all.

This landscape is completely different from the landscape that time. She doesn't know what it is. It's rural here too. But more open. And flat. Straight road. She could have read. With such straight roads you could read on the bus without getting sick. She doesn't get sick so easily any more. That was before. She's brought a book along. It's in her handbag. It can just stay there. She lets it stay there.

Fields. Fields on both sides. Cultivated land. Someone has planted. Soon they'll harvest. Cut and bundle and get under cover. Before autumn. Before it starts to rain. There's a lot of mist and rain here.

But today it's absolutely clear. Not a cloud, that she can see. It's almost too clear. She has sunglasses, fortunately. Remembered those. She's remembered most things. And if there's something she's forgotten, she can borrow. Or buy. She needs a jacket, maybe a cardigan. Something to throw over her shoulders when it's a little chilly. Something lighter than what she's brought.

The bus driver is sitting in front of a wall of plexiglass. It's a thin divider between him and the passenger seat right behind it. His head is bare. He's not wearing a cap. They hardly ever do now. She sees his head and back through the glass wall. He has broad shoulders.

Her parents had been way in the back of the bus that time. She could only catch a glimpse of them now and then. Crowded with people who blocked her view.

Her sister hadn't been born then. She was the only one. She and her parents.

Nothing had happened. There wasn't anything else. She'd sat there, still as could be. And she wasn't sick. Not carsick. It was just that – that she didn't see, and didn't know.

Adjustable reclining chairs on the veranda. That's what she'd wanted. Put the back down, almost lie down. Maybe have a little table in between. Room enough for two cups, or glasses. Sit like that – leaning back. In warm sunshine, bare skin. On her own veranda. The enclosing walls are fairly high. Flower-boxes at the top. Open enough to see in though. Partially in any case. Partial view. But she can't remember that that made her feel uncomfortable. All you're doing is sitting there. With a cup of coffee. Or something else. Wine. Tea. It never occurred to her to think about that.

There are a lot of things she hasn't thought about.

The look in his eyes. She sees it now. Remembers it now. Vacant look.

They'd been to the theatre one evening. It had been her idea. He hadn't wanted to, but agreed to go. During the intermission they met a couple from their apartment building, same age as they were, a couple they'd talked to occasionally at work parties and other things. Nice people. But there, in the foyer, he was clearly trying to avoid them. And when they bumped into them on their way back into the theatre, he acted strangely. Just stood there, fumbling with the tickets.

After the performance they were offered a lift. He stopped the car, the neighbour, and offered them a lift . "Thanks, we . . . we'd rather walk," he'd answered. He was so quick. Lightning quick. She didn't manage to say anything. But she smiled. And thanked. Thought she should be polite for both of them. Waved and smiled when they drove off. And she had smiled too, from the car.

It's a good thing she didn't get her way with the chairs. She would have used hers. Undressed. Taken off her blouse or T-shirt. On a really warm day. Just sat there in her bra. Bare skin.

The shivering starts when she thinks about it. That horrid shivering. It shows. Other people see it. He's seen it. Seen her. Shouldn't have seen it.

But nobody's here now. She's alone. When she breathes deeply, it helps.

Yes, she's got to be happy they didn't buy the chairs.

Happy that she never got around to planting all kinds of herbs.

She'd thought about painting the little table. She's happy she didn't do that. On her knees, out there on the veranda, paintbrush in hand, sweaty.

She's got to be happy about all of this.

Perfectly calm outside. No movement in the tall grass. They have left the fields. The fields of grain with their golden, upright stalks. Mostly mountains now. Steep mountains. Mountains blasted away for roads. Narrow passages. A long tunnel. The ferry ride a little way ahead is short. Short enough that she can stand by the railing. Stand in the sun. Just remember to put her jacket on when she leaves the bus.

But she must eat. She must go down to the cabin, buy something to eat.

There's a whiney kid who wants ice cream. Not a hard roll with cheese. Ice cream is what he wants. His mother grips the child's arm firmly, pulls him away from the counter, plants him at one of the tables bolted to the floor. He's furious.

The bite of cake swells up in her mouth. She's got to leave. Up and out. Where there's sun – and air.

She gets dizzy on the first step. An older man who's right behind her takes hold of her arm.

"Are you sick?" he asks.

"No," she answers, "I'm fine. Thanks – thank you. Stood up too fast," she smiles.

He doesn't let go of her arm. Holds her a little longer.

Then he lets go.

The foam is churning around the bow. A light, delicate spray. The water is glassy, like a mirror. Just the white foam against the side of the boat – and the waves, gliding away.

She is welcome. Knows that she's always welcome. That's what her sister has always said. "Just come. Come whenever you want."

She'd been at her sister's then too. A short trip. Weekend. Girls' weekend. That's what he'd called it. Kissed her on the cheek goodbye. Waved. She took the car that time. He said he didn't need it. Was just going to be at home. "Bye," he said. "Drive carefully."

It was after that trip that she couldn't find her slippers. Found them several days later – in the back of the closet.

"Did you tidy up around here?" she asked.

"Got a little restless."

He laughed.

He'd tidied up. But not everything. Why would her slippers make such a big difference? Pretty stupid to think that. How was it *possible* to think that? There were other things. Lots. Everywhere. In all the rooms. Big things – and small. Jars of cream. Pillows. Clothes. Her jewellery box. The jewellery box her parents had given her when she was a child . . .

She went into the bathroom and hid. Hid her face and her hands. He came and tried the door, but she didn't open.

Restless, he'd said. And laughed. The corners of his mouth always twitch when he laughs. She noticed it the very first time. When they met each other. A hundred years ago, almost. Thought it was charming. When he smiled he was extra good-looking.

The churning foam against the side of the boat. When she leans over the railing she sees it. Sees the pearls lifting themselves up from the surface of the water—to foam. Light and white. The boat cuts through the dark, placid water and lifts it.

This is the image she wants to have. To remember. The image she must take with her. From the trip. She will not forget this trip.

It's a nice image. It glistens.

She is welcome. Her sister is there. Will be there when she comes. Her sweet, little sister. Grown-up now. She's there. Waiting for her. When the bus arrives, it will still be early in the afternoon. They can sit on the veranda. Each in her own chair. If the sky is still clear, she can take her clothes off. Pull her T-shirt over her head. Sit quietly, completely relaxed. Take almost all her clothes off, lean back in the chair and let the rays of the sun warm her body.

Translated by Katherine Hanson

JAN KJÆRSTAD

Homecoming

First the landing, the expectation, the nervousness as the wheels touch the ground. And already as I walk down the aircraft steps and feel the heat coming at me, I sense that it is like coming home – well, not home but back, back to something pristine, forgotten. I notice how my senses open up during the drive to the capital, how pictures that I have stored within me are getting confirmed: the red earth, the ornamental trees, the flowering, the veil of yellow, blue, orange; the cornfields, the smoke from the huts, the people walking, *walking*, everywhere, talking together everywhere, people who have *time*, the cluster of booths along the road, crocheted rugs, baskets, handicrafts, the faces, the gaiety, not clichés but something deep, true, images, an atmosphere that is part of me; a landscape, Africa, the cradle of humankind.

And, finally, how I was not able to hold back – that is, the whole situation overpowered me. And at the same time my consciousness became strangely lucid, so that I could register almost curiously, scientifically, how this – could it be called irrational? – element was flowing from far away, as though it were being pumped out of some never-ceasing spring, a kind of heart of darkness deep down. I noticed, half annoyed, half applauding, how it grew and grew and became something irresistible and overwhelming, until it finally overflowed – for lack of something better I have to say like bodies of water plunging over a high precipice and forming a mighty waterfall, so that I had to resign myself and let myself be swept away by this primeval drive, which in addition represented the opposite of everything that I was striving for. And since I, who wanted to bring out what was white and soft, was forced to be black and hard lying here in the dark, it was in a state partaking of wildly triumphant enjoyment and the crystal clear self-contempt of an observer that I allowed this deep something be poured forth, like a jet stream, like a last line that epitomised the evening's defeat, misunderstandings and lack of communication. As I let it happen, I mumbled a wordless no, and because the moment seemed to stretch out, as in a nightmare, I repeated it: no, no, no.

And then, almost immediately, a lovely dream, on to Victoria Falls and this famous, tradition-steeped hotel, a white palace redolent of vanished elegance, the old railway station in Edwardian style directly opposite the main entrance, with giant locomotives and masses of steam outlined against the boulevard of fragrant trees that leads to the city centre. I am welcomed, respectfully, by the doorman, red coat plastered with medals, top hat, piloted to a splendid blue room through long corridors by attendants in white jackets and white gloves, friendly remarks, a feeling of being wealthy, important, indeed unconquerable. I drink tea on the wide terrace and see the waterfall for the first time, or not the waterfall itself but the spray, a veritable cloud rising up from the chasm where the bodies of water crash together, and also that faint rumble, a beast of prey in the guise of water, a divinity, Africa itself, something powerful, majestic, something utterly incomparable. I sit there with my cup of tea, an afternoon in Africa, take in the view, the green hills on the other side of the border, and in the centre of the picture the railway bridge across the dizzying chasm, so near the Falls that the windows of the carriages are showered with spray. I sit there a long time, a cup of tea, afternoon in Africa, let the landscape, the quiet, the green hills, slide into me, until, after dusk, we are at last called together by the signals from a kudu horn and torches and escorted to a fenced-in arena with some huts in the background, a big bonfire, men drumming, men dancing, hot rhythms, muscular bodies, suggestive movements, an Africa Spectacular, complicated rhythms all mixed up, faces hidden behind expressive wooden masks, loins covered with goatskins, storytelling dances, ritual dances, war dances, I am impressed, carried away, knowing that this is not primitive but true, authentic, I feel it in my whole body, I'm open, I'm home.

And before that, how the door to her room was open, sure enough, and how I stood in front of it for a long time, as at a sort of Danger Point, weighing the pros and cons, while at the same time cursing this desire which, against my will – despite the fact that I obeyed an order,

like a slave – was running riot in my body, until my hand, ostensibly
in the midst of the very process of thinking, acted on its own and
pushed wide open the door. It was dark in the room, and I must say
in my defence that I hesitated anew, but when I heard her breathing
and deduced from the rapidity of her breaths, not without a certain
satisfaction, that she must be somewhat aroused, it was once more as
if my legs reacted independently of the reasoning of my head and
walked over to the bed, where she resolutely clutched me and pulled
me greedily down so that I met her eyes, which seemed to glow in the
dark and almost scared me, because I sensed a desire that demanded
something I could not possibly fulfil, an impression that was
confirmed as she pressed or clung to me with a desperation or a
passion, or an explosion of lust, that was as overwhelming as . . . I
must once again have recourse to the waterfall for comparison. After
the decision was irrevocable and, following a usage that required that
if you say A you say B, I had rid myself of my garments with
remarkable dexterity, I could, however, have wished for some
foreplay, to sort of underscore our shared breeding, but she wanted
me, as it were, to go full speed ahead, betraying an impatience which
astonished me, indeed, also in fact irritated me a little since – frankly
speaking – I had expected something more sophisticated, something
more along the lines of my own notions of worldly-wise European
women, who, in a manner of speaking, had certificates in sexual
technique, as distinct from our women's more, dare I say so,
backward and simple guidance on how a man is most easily satisfied,
which in my eyes unfortunately tallied perfectly with the cultural level
of our country. And since she now dispensed with any introductory
manoeuvre, I wouldn't at all have objected to a modern or virtuoso
tactic, such as her getting on top of me and engaging me in slow
figure-of-eight movements, but she was obviously thinking of
something else, if indeed of anything, for lying there on her back she
more or less made a grab for me and pulled me down upon her,
shouting something that could, at best, be interpreted as the lack of
an adequate vocabulary in English. And so I slipped into her with a
feeling approaching sorrow, thinking that I had come back to do
some drilling, alright, but not in this way. Nevertheless, it was at this
moment that I perceived a change in my own body, perhaps because
the friction could not fail to have its effect, for from having a sober
conception of doing this out of a sense of concern, or fatalism,
abruptly I became angry, beset by a wild desire to penetrate her, as
she, or her race, had penetrated my continent – if I may express myself

symbolically. All of a sudden, emotions emerged that I had difficulty acknowledging and that were not devoid of such ignoble elements as revenge, yes, revenge pure and simple. At once I caught myself pumping her, as I believed she wanted to be pumped. She begged for it, and I pushed my way into her as far as I could, violently, as if I wanted to crush the whiteness of her, or something I was experiencing then and there as white guilt: a wish to be taken and used. I was playing a role. I was an avenger. I knew she wanted me to play that role. Or rager, she believed this was what I was like, that this was me, us. At the same time I realised quite clearly that I ought to have desisted, but I continued to push hard into her, pounding away; I felt I was about to tear her apart, but dign't give a damn, partly because I was overcome by a disillusion as heavy as lead, the certainty that it was no use anyway, that you were fighting so many prejudices and myths and wishful thoughts that you might just as well pound away, to no avail, because she, by some magic metamorphosis, transformed this violence, this hate, too, into unmatched pleasure. While I lay there, trying as best I could to tear her to bits, I had all the time to ask myself whence she came by this continual rapture, this gasping, distorted, madly blissful expression, this incessant whispering in a language I did not understand, this demand for more, more, more – more of something that was not me, that was but someone I debased myself to play, a stranger.

And then the walk around the place, the body in good shape, senses wide open, all that was unfamiliar, previously encountered only in *National Geographic*, and now here I am, in the middle of it, the smells, the colours, the sounds, the suspense at every step, all that I cannot identify, the things in the curio shops – I hold it up, examine it, ask, they laugh, joke, say I can have it cheap, I buy a few trinkets, a wooden giraffe, some pieces of jewellery, postcards, a T-shirt, before I enter Falls Craft Village, a kind of museum, an introduction to how people have dwelled in this country, their way of life, clusters of ancient huts, straw and clay, kitchen utensils, the meeting with something half-repressed, a workaday world distinguished by simplicity and naturalness, articles on exhibit, more special things, from receptacles made of ostrich eggs and necklaces of snail shells to penis sheaths and a *mbira* hand piano. And there, most exciting of all, a man dressed in hides, with an odd head ornament and sundry conspicuous necklaces, and in his hand a kind of sceptre with an animal's tail, I know right away that he is a *n'anga*, a medicine man, a soothsayer, a shaman, I feel my heart beating more rapidly, he smiles, missing teeth, wants to tell me about the future, invites me into his hut, it's dark, a glimpse of articles, I am curious, trembling with curiosity, but do not dare go in, it is coming too quickly, I do not feel prepared, and yet that is the purpose of my being here, in this country, the reason I received the grant, the *n'angas*, the hunt for the dark, the black, the alternative. I do not dare, decline politely, try to show respect, consoling myself with the thought that these are merely preliminary skirmishes, the task will take several years, the field work will start only later on, and yet the incident tells me that I have made the right choice, my whole body shows that I am confronted with something instructive, enormously important, I know I shall be ready at the next meeting.

And before that, how I met her again in the evening on the terrace, whereupon she, perhaps because of the surprise, invited me to sit at her table. She obviously thought I was from the area and seemed disappointed when I told her why I was here and how I occupied my time generally, a reaction that, due to the tacit disapproval I sensed in her, caused me to hold forth about my hopes and visions, without, however, making any particular impression on her. Nonetheless she betrayed, by a couple of remarks, that she was of above average intelligence, and I'll confess that she looked attractive in her fashionable suit, evoking images of the proficient female politicians of Europe. However, I became doubtful at the buffet, which consisted of grilled food of every variety, when against my advice she decided to try the unimaginative local dish, sadza, and furthermore at the table insisted on drinking her beer straight from the bottle – I have a suspicion that she would have liked to taste the poisonous Kachasu brew as well, out of sheer ethnological curiosity. While we were eating, we talked without interruption, or to put it more precisely: we talked past one another. Since I had studied a bit of anthropology in the last few years, for fun rather than anything else, I tried to steer the conversation to some controversial ideas of Lévi-Strauss and Malinowski, but she just brushed me off with one-word replies. Not even when, out of my unspoken conviction that this was a golden opportunity for a fruitful exchange of views between two enlightened human beings from different cultures, I shifted the conversation to Shakespeare's "Othello" and furthermore attacked Sartre's opportunistic negrophilia, did she allow herself to be drawn in. She was deaf or, rather, she just wanted to talk about Africa. When I finally did say something about Africa, her whole buttoned-up manner changed and she sat there all agape. I had the definite impression that I could tell her anything whatever, that secretly we filed our teeth, that we performed barbaric sexual rites in the open air by moonlight – the silliest kind of Negro myths – and she would buy it all. I was surprised that she who, with her pointedly sophisticated manner of dress, was ostensibly a critical young woman with a razor-sharp mind, could sit there asking for fairy tales and lies, mumbo jumbo about rain gods and totemism, instead of wanting to discuss something essential, like the issues concerning a one-party or multi-party state, or statesmen: Kwame Nkrumah, Leopold Senghor, Robert Mugabe. But it sounded as though she had never heard their names, even though she professed an ardent commitment to things African. I was all the while exasperated by the marimba orchestra in the background, which was murdering English evergreens, while she, for her part, was rocking back and forth, apparently entranced by the music and the rhythm, at the same time as I noticed how she was scrutinizing me, my body, as if I were a first-rate research object. And then of course – I should have foreseen it – came the question about the n'angas. In a studiedly calm voice I told her about my father, who was a doctor, and about how he struggled to remedy the appalling damage caused by these "witch doctors" – or what was her opinion of people who in deadly earnest believed that, even at the end of the twentieth century, disease was caused, behind all the symptoms, by spirits and black magic? She wasn't listening, she just wanted to talk about the positive aspects: how these n'angas commanded a knowledge forgotten by us, about botany, about man's inner self, the value of conversation, dreams. Did I know anything more about them? She was begging. Sitting there on that warm evening, I almost found it touching. She was running on empty as far as Africa was concerned, and she wanted me to fill her up. Despite the manipulation I couldn't help giving way, with the result that I really served up some nice tidbits about the n'angas since, thanks to my father, I knew quite a lot about their practices. I can't be sure, but I think it was for this reason, namely, on account of something I said almost involuntarily, because I felt she wanted some kind of confirmation, that later, on leaving, she showed me her room key, the number, looked deep into my eyes and said, "Be there in ten minutes". I should of course have understood where it was leading, but – I swear – at that moment I was caught completely off guard.

*

And then the morning at the Falls, I'm totally unprepared, the sight grips me mightily, in an almost physical way; this world of wetness, this big, inconceivably big, deep world, the whole of Africa in one picture, almost two kilometres of frothing bodies of water that crash one hundred metres down; black and white, white water over black basalt—wet, I stand there facing this wildness, facing the foaming, boiling bodies of water, the overpowering sound, a sight and sound that exceed the boundaries of the real. I have walked through the rain forest on the far side, on a path under dripping trees, surrounded by lush vegetation that gets showered continuously by the waterfall. I know its sweet, warm scent, I recognize the place, I have dreamt about it, I'm suddenly finding my way back to something lost, I'm standing directly in front of the Main Falls, only a few wild rose bushes between me and the abyss, I'm getting drenched as I stand there shouting for joy and letting the water moisten me. There, on the other side, on the little island at the very edge of the drop, Livingstone had stood and seen the waterfall for the first time, and now, unbelievably, inconceivably, I am standing here myself, I too an explorer, a woman mapping white spots. I follow the path farther on, all the way to Danger Point, and stand on the border between two countries . . . I feel how I too am balancing on a borderline, go as far out as I dare and see how the water is squeezed through a narrow gorge far below, wildly, infernally, I perceive the pull from the abyss, the uncontrollable desire to hurl myself over, down into those terrible whirlpools, the Boiling Pot, where the water from both sides of the Falls meets, cruelly, temptingly, I look down, can't get enough, so brutally, so darkly, so deeply, so grandly, so dangerously, how insignificant, I think, how small a human being becomes confronted by the power of nature. I walk all the way back in the opposite direction, to Devil's Cataract, the falls farthest west, where I meet a young African, I take him as a matter of course for someone from there, in short trousers, barefoot, well-formed black torso, long, strong legs. He seems modest, I take a liking to him, ask him to take a picture of me at the statue of Livingstone, we strike up a conversation, his English is amazingly good, he tells me about the waterfall, that the true magnificence of the Falls can only be experienced at full moon, he is very likely one of those poor people who, by entering into conversation, try to obtain a "grant" for their education, but he is proud, noble. I look at his shorts, the crotch, is it true what they say, that Africans have . . . are so much bigger? I brush the thought aside, but I'm wet, wet all over my body, wet everywhere.

And before that, how I stood by the waterfall in the morning. As I didn't see any reason why I should get all my clothes wet, I had put on just a pair of shorts and even walked barefoot for the first time in many years. I don't quite know what I had expected, but I wasn't immediately overwhelmed by the waterfall, perhaps from an ingrained scepticism of letting oneself be impressed by pure nature. For me, the aspect of the mighty Zambesi river that had excited my imagination had never been the Falls themselves, but the power stations below and the Lake Kariba dam and the barrage, so that if I felt in awe of something it was because of the human hand – of electricity and the fishing industry – not because of nature, though, needless to say, the phenomenon interested me in a purely professional way. From that viewpoint I was lucky with the time, since the not too great rate of flow made it possible to appraise the Falls as a geological phenomenon. So that when I stood directly face to face with Main Falls studying the hard, black basalt behind the bodies of water before me, my mind inevitably latched on to erosion, this patient but invincible power. Similarly, I was captivated by the way the river, behind me, zigzagged through narrow canyons, which thereby revealed that the waterfall had moved upwards in the course of time. I stood and contemplated the fact that 30,000 years ago the waterfall had been situated eight kilometres farther down and that, since then, there had been seven different falls, in different places, with the logical consequence that in a few thousand years' time the Falls would be farther upriver. While standing there I took immense comfort from this, that things were in motion, the earth's crust itself included, the mountains – in fact, for a moment I saw the zigzag shape of the chasms as a concrete symbol of Africa's complicated path towards the future, a future that had to be built, not least, on just that geological wealth, on mountains abounding in minerals that were simply waiting to be brought forth: gold, platinum, cobalt, chrome, the white metals. In spite of these optimistic vistas, I could not avoid feeling a shuddering uneasiness for a few seconds as a little later I stood at the edge of the abyss, all the way over at Danger Point, with nothing between myself and the roaring walls of water. The Falls suddenly took on a frightening and ruthless quality, as if they wanted to saddle you with something, moisten you against your will, indeed, as if they wanted to swallow you. Even so, going back along Rainbow Falls, I could not help seeing how beautiful they were, how infinitely beautiful, and I understood in a sort of flash that aesthetics too must have been a motive, an underestimated motive, behind imperialism. I was engulfed in thoughts such as these when I met the white girl right up at Devil's Cataract, by the statue of Livingstone, the man who discovered the waterfall, as if there were no people in the country before he came, and almost had to laugh, since to me she embodied – in her colourless khaki uniform and dripping funny hat and with her eyes popping out – the very archetype of a tourist, a person who would swoon at the sight of a jacaranda tree in bloom, who fell on her knees before a completely ordinary baobab and was willing to pay anything for a stone with a bit of carving by a simple-minded native on it. There was on the whole something so virginal and chaste about her – a Victoria from the protected North – that, out of sheer pity more than anything else, I said a few friendly words to her, whereupon she cast such a strange, almost fearful, look at me, who for my part could not resist looking at her breasts, clearly silhouetted under her wet khaki shirt. I also noticed how she gradually examined me, as if I were a statue, as if I represented something she had travelled far to see, or as if I were an exotic dish she did not quite know whether she dared to dig her teeth into.

And then the evening, the dinner on the terrace, a sumptuous *braai*, the smell of grilled food, coloured lights in the trees, a charming marimba band playing traditional music. I meet him again and am astonished that he is a guest, like me, and wearing an elegant tweed jacket, white shirt and tie. He tells me he is a geologist, one year remaining of his studies in London, and begins without ceremony to hold forth on the metals, the shining wealth in the depth of the mountains, says he is going into the mining industry, looks forward to it, that he hopes specifically to join the endeavour to extract platinum, the white, soft metal which his country abounds in but hasn't yet taken a chance on, is unstoppable, says that Africa possesses almost the entire world reserve of cobalt and chrome, half of all the gold and platinum. I'm not interested, what power, he says, I indicate that the subject bores me, what a foundation for a new future, he says, everything will change, he says, lectures, as if to prove it, about how the waterfall has moved through the millennia and about how a time will come, thanks to the geological conditions farther upriver, when there won't be a Victoria Falls at all, when the natural phenomenon the tourists come to see will be gone. He laughs, I don't like it, feel that he's teasing me, wants to take the adventure away from me, to relativise it. We go and help ourselves to some grilled food, he chooses almost nothing but fruit, papaya, melon, pineapple, but orders wine, an expensive one even, French. We talk, he starts by bringing up topics that do not interest me, scientists and thinkers who are required reading for me, something I've had enough of, I've come here for something else, to learn about everything we don't have; about this simple love of the red earth, about Africa's supreme natural ability, its capacity for intuition, spontaneity, the wisdom of its customs and instincts, the extended family, care, the joy of life, the warm physical contact: "feelings are black, reason is Greek". I am on African soil, it's night, dark, warm, the marimba band takes a break, one can hear the faraway drone of the waterfall and, hard by, the crickets, millions of crickets, I perceive how my senses are opening up, I discern something great, a golden opportunity, but he falls back, is stingy, doesn't want to share his knowledge, his life in Africa, with me, doesn't want to draw upon his experience, is fascinating just the same, proud, handsome, different. After a while he tells me something about his country nevertheless, delves into its history, the oral tradition, the past as present, he touches on those wonderful ideas about the relationship between people and animals, tells about the soul of a tree, a mountain, about the power that unites, permeates, all of nature, the ancestor cult, the rites of passage, the ceremonial hunt, some piquant details, such as the fact that the men have to undergo a fertility test in some places, squirting their semen into water to see whether it sinks or floats. The more he tells, the more handsome he becomes, I think he must be a descendant of a powerful chief, I am on African soil, it's night, dark, warm, I perceive the suspense in my body, that I am attracted by him, in fact, that I sit here wanting him. He begins to talk about the statesmen, political problems, but I manage to turn the conversation back, ask him about the *n'angas*, is it true that they use the heart of a lion? I ask him nicely, he gives in, is handsome, that noble face, I'm horny, try to restrain it, but I'm horny, he tells his story, I try to listen, he speaks of the contents of the bottle gourds, the use of talking pictures, about how they throw oracular bones or shells on the ground like dice, about the tattoos, the decorated horns full of powder and herbs, I listen, looking at his slim, strong hands, want him to touch me, he speaks Shona for me, quotes some proverbs, I clap my hands, have to laugh, I look at his mouth, his lips, those perfect teeth, notice my desire increasing, I must have him, now, right away, don't know what is the matter with me, it must be the place, Africa, the heat, the faint rumble from the waterfall, I show him my room number, ask him to come, insist that he come, notice my voracity, how irresistibly I want his body.

And before that, how I walked around Victoria Falls shaking my head over this hole of a place that showed in an exemplary way how greed for hard currency could transform any idyll whatever into a society utterly without charm consisting of smart hotels and a bustling shopping street where you could buy hamburgers and all sorts of sham souvenirs but could barely find a book. And I almost had to pinch myself in the arm and ask myself where the low point of self-respect would be reached when I walked through the group of grubby buildings that supposedly represented a sort of folk museum and glanced in disbelief at a moth-eaten stuffed lion in a window, a half-dead crocodile in a muddy pond, and a carved monkey god with a fumed gorilla skull for a head. In time with my steps through the dusty, filthy African village – a reconstruction of nineteenth-century huts – where you could study some not particularly impressive things like wooden bowls and jars, pestles and mortars, I noticed how I was slowly overcome by despondency, how I was thinking that this might be alright if only it was a museum about life a thousand years ago – the trouble was that people lived like that today too; they were still eating ants, larvae, and dried grasshoppers and were still living in huts made of cow dung and blood. I wandered around in a monument to stagnation, walked around feeling like a stranger, or at least I *wanted* to be a stranger. For could anything be further removed from what I was striving for, what my nation was striving for, what Africa was striving for? I was hunting for the future, but everywhere I met only the past, and I noticed how the expectation and impatience I had been filled with before my trip were slowly but surely replaced by shame.

And then my room, alone, this expectation once more, this shameless impatience, the fear that he will not come, that he begrudges me his power, his potential, he *must* come, comes finally, shuts the door, hesitates, come, come, why this stinginess, this resistance, you want to, I know it, why pretend otherwise, his steps in the dark, he approached the bed, an unfamiliar smell, exciting, numbing, I'm wet,

wet; wet as at the waterfall, I pull him down, my shyness all gone, I'm about to succumb to forces in my own body, I did not know I had them, that they were so strong, it must be the place, the situation, this smell, him, I pull him down on to the bed, his sinewy body, I should have had the light on and seen that black skin; come my *n'anga*, show me your tricks, your secret wisdom, your . . . wildness; no, don't stop, please, not so slow, no foreplay, you don't have to show that you are a modern man, cultivated, I want to be like you, we are alike, two warm individuals, two steamy bodies, don't hold back, just take me, hard, right away, come into me, yes, there, oh God, so . . . big, so brutally different, so . . . dark, so deep, so great, so . . . dangerous, he almost lifts me, the violent movements squeeze sounds out of my mouth, I can hear myself shouting, I don't know what, I can't get enough, I love this strength, this aggressiveness, this anger, this seriousness, this . . . hatred; a hatred that brings out kindness in me, gratitude, the wish to reciprocate, give him all, body, soul, ask forgiveness for something, I don't know what; just come, take me, enlarge me, this rippling sensation as he penetrates me, deep, digging up layer after layer in me, layers I don't know, right down to the authentic, deepest me, the abyss, I know, for the first time, what I am, this naked, innermost, simple thing that cannot be explained away or drowned out, like the roar from the waterfall: sheer current, sheer rhythm, sheer . . . feeling.

And before that, how I arrived at Victoria Falls Hotel filled with ambivalent feelings, but still could not help being cheerful, indeed, mirthful at the thought of finding myself a tourist in my own country. Like the majority of my countrymen I had never seen our greatest attraction, frankly I had not had any desire to. But since Father had so convincingly argued that I ought to visit the place, also on account of my studies, and had treated me to the trip to boot, I will not deny that I felt a certain satisfaction at setting foot on this symbol of white power and colonial recreation, a sort of sadistic glee that was reinforced when I sat down on the terrace with a dry martini and surveyed the landscape that, as it happened, once more, perhaps because of the almost too perfect angle of vision – the location of the hotel was supposedly determined by Rhodes himself – gave an impression of being unreal, that it had nothing to do with Africa. Notwithstanding, I enjoyed the illusion of being on a level with Rhodes himself, or at least on a level with the white tourists, not to mention the experts on the developing countries with their tennis rackets and golf clubs and four-wheel-drive Toyotas, even though some of the enjoyment evaporated at the sight of the servants, who despite their white jackets expressed a sort of humiliatingly servile, if not cowed, attitude. Nevertheless I did not get seriously depressed until the evening when, as a sort of joke, I attended the unbelievably boring and monotonous dance exhibition with the scandalously unsuitable name, Africa Spectacular. It was as I sat there, saddened to the core in the midst of a flock of camera-sporting whites, observing this hopelessly inauthentic dance that consisted mainly of stomping and howling, while studying simultaneously the enthusiastic, almost ecstatic white faces around me, that I really understood how far, for how long, we still had to go before we would be taken seriously. For these people didn't want to understand, they only wanted to be seduced.

And then this uplifting, falling experience, the decisive thrust that tears down the last wall, plunges me into the fantastic, unexplored unconscious, a brief but eternal journey to the heart of darkness, to the end of the night, to a place where everything stands still; a glide from Danger Point down into the whirlpools, the entire waterfall in a crash of thunder above me, before I get sucked down, drowned, boiling white water over hard black basalt, white and black, black and white, oh come, my Africa, my beloved Africa, plunge your warm torrents down into my dark, deep cleft, a pleasure out of all bounds, to be totally powerless, submerged, swept along in nature's overwhelming embrace, becoming part of something never-ending, incomprehensible, forgotten, pristine, yes, yes, yes, ye-e-e-e-e-es.

And before that, the landing and the misgivings that showed the moment the wheels thumped the ground. I was home, and all the same I strongly suspected that this would be a mistake, that I ought to have waited until I was entirely done with my education. As I descended the aircraft steps, I cursed the cocky impulse that had led me home, made me tempt fate, exposing myself to the danger of being sucked in, back. As I was sitting in that rattletrap of a taxi, which had scarcely seen a spare part in a decade, I was increasingly plagued by a sense that those unreal ornamental trees that covered the landscape formed a false surface, like a continuous picture postcard; a varnish over hidden dictatorship and a catastrophic economy, bureaucratic corruption and a decaying infrastructure, ethnic clashes and a health problem no-one dared to think about. I had wanted to forget it, but I had not forgotten it. And at the same time I tried to think about all that was positive, the possibilities, about all the riches that lay buried in the earth's crust – the white metals – which were just waiting to be bored, so that they could form the basis for a new future. The taxi moved at a snail's pace. I leaned back in the ruined seat and tried to stem my fatigue at the thought of how far we still had to go. So much nature and so little civilisation. I could see the high-rise buildings in the capital rear up ahead of me and knew I would be disappointed. Nor could I help thinking, at the sight of a Land Rover with some well-known emblem or other on the door, about the myriad of relief organisations and all sorts of research fellows who were having a fling with our problems, or about the flock of anthropologists hunting for bizarre phenomena. What should we do, how were we to be able to resist all this good will, all this guilt that was only yearning to meet us, that wanted to *possess* us, crush us in its embrace? Already as I sat there in the car and half-apathetically established that the door handle was broken, I pondered how I was to get away from here, out again, as soon as possible. I had to get back.

Translated by Sverre Lyngstad

BEATE GRIMSRUD

The Long Trip

"We're doing the long trip," Mother tells them.

She had been making the same comment ever since they set off. All of them are suitably dressed.

"That's where we're going," Mother says and points.

However, it is obvious that the youngsters, especially the smallest ones, are so small that they see nothing. They can't see that far as they are too small. The day is still young and they are suitably well: The tiny one, the little one with the red bobble hat, the medium-sized one with pigtails, the big one and the biggest one. They are dressed for the long trip. Water trickles and flows, and far ahead the path narrows and is barely visible, but they know it is there and they are on their way.

"When will we be there?" says the medium-sized one with pigtails.

"We're doing the long trip," Mother replies.

Water flows and trickles, and the songbirds screech in the open moorland.

"Come on. Let's build a house," the little one with the hat says. "A stone house."

They stop. They collect stones, and the contours of a room emerge from the mossy ground.

"Heather," Mother says. "This is heather." She points as the children energetically carry on building.

"Look! A tin can!" says the tiny one. And the big one admires the discovery.

"It's the stove. You've found a stove," the big one says, while the biggest one carries a heavy stone towards the dwelling.

"Did you used to play like this when you . . ." the biggest one has turned to Mother's mound.

"No, no, we didn't play like this." Mother looks towards the eventual destination of their long trip.

The biggest one doesn't hear, but has lifted a hand and pulled a medium-sized pigtail. A scream is heard. A scream from someone who always has someone above and below her, someone older and someone younger.

"We need to make tracks now, and it's not for my sake, children."

They have already left. They run off enthusiastically.

"I don't want to. I want to live here." The little one with the bobble hat is still sitting in the stone house.

"*I* built it. It's mine."

"Come on," shouts the biggest one.

"I want to take it with me. The house . . . I want to take it with me or I'll stay here for ever."

The others are gone and the little one finally comes trotting up behind. The red bobble hat bounces between the heather-clad mounds and the tin can is clutched in one hand. The sky is a canvas of friendly grey-blue patches and far in the distance it sinks away and merges with the mountains. The little one trails behind, or is a little to one side, a little ahead, clutching a tin can.

"I'm tired." The tiny one looks at the biggest one.

"Over there, Tiny," says Mother . . . "Over there, just past that nearest mound . . . oranges are growing. Glorious ripe, golden oranges perfect for a long trip."

The tiny one purses her lips and can only see the hill closest to her. Her short legs climb the shallow slope and the tiny one counts each step.

"Oh my goodness, look!" Mother pulls an orange out of a bush. "This one's for Tiny." She stretches out an arm and the orange is grabbed by a small, surprised fist. Mother picks more oranges, she picks lots of oranges and says: "Don't throw away the peel."

And under the feet of the orange-peeling children, mountain cranberry plants are trodden into the moss, to bounce back into place later.

"Ambiosis," says Mother. "Moss is ambiotic."

They have finished eating and the biggest one is already back on the path, a little ahead.

"Throw away the peel," says Mother. "Orange peel is actually very useful. It rots and becomes fertile earth. But it must always be hidden, always hidden, children . . . because it takes time. The rotting process is like . . . like a slow self-eating. Like a complete union of external elements. Only the ink on the label is dangerous."

The biggest one digs a trough with bare hands. The children put the peel with the label face down in the trough, and then the biggest one hides it by putting a big stone over it. And then they trudge on.

"I feel sick," the medium-sized one with pigtails doubles up and whines: "My tummy hurts. And my head hurts."

"Sick! No, you can't be sick, not now everything's going so well. Look at the little one . . . Show me how clever you can be." Mother walks beside the medium-sized one and chats.

"I don't feel well, at all, at all, at all . . ." the medium-sized one persists, eyes to the ground.

"Come on! I'm going to tell you a story."

The medium-sized one peeps up at Mother and takes her hand.

"Once upon a time, there was a tiny kingdom. Once upon a time there was a princess. She was called Princess Don't-Want-To and she lived in the tiny kingdom. She was beautiful. Very beautiful. But stubborn. She was so stubborn that as soon as someone opened their mouth to say something, she contradicted them. She was so used to shaking her head that the movement had got stuck. Her head rocked from side to side."

"Even when she was sleeping?" asks the medium-sized one with pigtails.

"But she was so beautiful . . . What's that? . . . Yes, even when she was sleeping. The king was beautiful too, but at his wits' end. The queen could not sleep at night. 'What will become of little Princess Don't-Want-To?' the king said every morning as he opened his eyes. 'Good night! Sleep tight! . . . Oh dear! Oh dear! Oh dear! . . . What are we going to do with Princess Don't-Want-To?' the queen said, sighing, before the servants turned off the lights at night and everyone in the palace fell asleep."

"Everyone apart from the queen," corrected the medium-sized one.

"But then one day . . . it was such a lovely day, when the sun had woken up in the east as it did every morning. And the king had summoned all the sons and daughters in the kingdom, all the wise ones and the learned ones of the kingdom, the talkative ones and the taciturn ones. And they came riding through the bright day from all corners of the kingdom. Everyone so loved Princess Don't-Want-To, and wanted to do all that was in their power to make the beautiful princess stop contradicting everything and everyone. They gathered expectantly in the great hall of the castle to hear what the queen had to say."

"That's mine!" screams the tiny one and interrupts their mother's tale. "It's mine. Mother! The little one's taken my tin can."

"Give it back," Mother says quickly, but then she changes her mind and says, "No, wait, I mean . . . It belongs to the little one now. Can't you see that the little one's got it . . . and you've got no use for it."

Mother bows down and whispers to the tiny one: "That tin can is ugly and it's not worth dragging it along with us."

"It's mine. I found it," the tiny one says, slapping her chest.

At the same time, the little one has slowed down and is trailing far behind, to one side.

"Don't scream!" screams Mother. "It's worth nothing. Tiny!" her storytelling voice returns. "Over there. Behind that one, I do believe there is a chocolate tree. I can smell it." Mother sniffs the ground. "Come on, Tiny," and from the sparse foliage of the tree, two squares of creamy, nutty chocolate appear.

Tiny's eyes follow the piece of chocolate before it disappears into his mouth, leaving only a taste – a secret taste about which the others know nothing.

"Let's eat here." The largest one shouts from the crest of the next hill. "Come here!"

"But I thought . . . is it really time to eat already . . .?"

Mother is interrupted.

"I've found the best picnic spot in the whole wide world just here. Of course we're going to eat here." The biggest one welcomes them with open arms.

Thermoses full of hot chocolate and goats' cheese sandwiches emerge from the rucksacks of Mother and the biggest one. Munching and slurping noises rise into the canopy of blue merging with white, indicating that it is still day.

"Bloody hell! You clumsy idiot!" the biggest one shouts at the little one with the red bobble hat as they watch the hot chocolate running down the stone and disappearing in the soft moss. Greaseproof paper rustles, and Mother says, "Don't throw the greaseproof paper away. As well as its natural components, paper also contains dangerous chemicals."

Stomachs are full and a red and a blue thermos are packed away in their rucksacks.

"The long trip," Mother says. She gets up and sets off as she looks into the distance and continues on the long trip.

The tiny one runs a bit. But then says, "I'm tired." And drops to the ground.

"Tired, not now, Tiny, not yet."

Mother takes the tiny one by the hand. She sets off, and in this way the tiny one is tugged along, eyes turned towards legs which are mechanically and jerkily advancing.

"This must be the last dwarf birch tree," Mother says. "Yes, it must be because I haven't seen any others for ages. Listen, children! We're now passing the last tree. We're crossing the treeline. Can you see how this tree is struggling to remain standing with every ounce of its being? How the trunk is turning away from the wind, how flat and horizontal the branches are as they grow as close to the ground as possible? And look at the long roots clinging to hold the tree in place. They've covered almost the entire mountainside here."

They walk and are walked along. The little one with the red bobble hat has been allowed to sit on the shoulders of the big one.

"Me too," says the tiny one. "Me too."

"Look at me! Giddy up!" shouts the little one and a red-hatted head bounces from side to side while the big one gallops along the narrow path.

"Me too," the tiny one looks at Mother. "Me too, I want a ride."

Mother lifts the tiny one, who is carried up the steep mountainside on top of a blue rucksack. It gets steeper, the steps shorter, and legs grow more tired.

"We're on the long trip," Mother says.

And the mountains in the distance are splashes of colour. The heather is darker and its shades of red have duskier hues. Mountain tops can be just made out in the far distance as they all but merge with the sky.

"I'm thirsty," the medium-sized one with pigtails has fallen behind and shouts at the backs of the rest of the group.

"Come on, there's probably a stream up here somewhere. We can all have a drink there. Come on!" Mother has turned to the medium-sized one who has picked up speed and is catching up with the others.

"Is this the right path?"

"Of course it is," Mother answers the question of the biggest one.

"Are you sure? Are you really sure? I think . . ." The biggest one looks around suspiciously.

"Don't nag, please. I'm doing the best I can. And this is the right path," says Mother and walks on.

"The stream. Where's the stream? I'm thirsty," says the medium-sized one.

"Me too," the tiny one announces from Mother's shoulders.

"Thirsty, so soon . . . Good God. I said that we'd find a stream soon. This high up, the water is crystal clear, newly melted, ice-cold, as clear as can be," Mother waves a hand. "Wouldn't you like to walk for a bit?" She lets the tiny one down to the ground. "And then you can run ahead and find the stream. Listen out for the gurgling of the water and you'll surely very soon find a stream."

They continue. No gurgling is heard for a long while. But the tiny one runs ahead. Runs and runs with eager, short steps. The biggest one is the one who finds the water. Who hears the gurgling first. And they gather, and they kneel on the slippery rocks and slurp. Their teeth freeze. The tiny one laughs.

"Don't put your whole head in. Your bobble hat will get wet," Mother says to the little one.

"Do raisins grow here, Mother?" the medium-sized one with the pigtails asks.

The tiny one looks around and Mother says, "Not just here, I don't think. But maybe up there." She points at the next summit. They trudge on.

"Look, a big trench," shouts the big one.

"It's a reindeer trap," Mother says when they have all reached the place and stand, peeping down into the enormous hole. "They used to chase the wild deer into the mountain ridge. First they dug out a big trench like this. And then they laid branches over the top, so when the terrified flock rushed through, there were always some that fell in. That's how they used to do it, children. And then they dragged the dead animals up here."

"And they ate . . . didn't they, Mother? They ate them," says the big one.

"Yes, they ate the bodies and the skins were used as warm fur rugs." They go on and leave the animal trap far behind.

"Were you alive then, Mother?" The little one with the hat looks at Mother.

"No, it was before my time."

"Before your time," repeats the little one, stepping carefully on the ever steeper mountain track.

The air around them becomes thicker by imperceptible degrees. And cool breezes brush past the climbing figures.

"I don't want to," the medium-sized one with pigtails has made up her mind. "I don't want to go any further and definitely not up here. Can't we stop, Mother?"

"But we're on the long trip," says Mother. "I'm doing this so that all of you can see. You'll all be so pleased when we reach the top. I'm sure it'll be beautiful. I know, and you'll all thank me for having managed it and for reaching right up to the top."

"I don't want to. Don't want to, not me." The medium-sized one pouts and stamps the ground.

Mother is exhausted too, but she can't tell them. She says, "But look at the big one, look at how the big one walks . . . and look at the little one with the hat, the little one isn't crying . . ."

"I'm not crying, and I don't want to go any further." The medium-sized one whines.

"Come on, darling. Come on, don't ruin everything. Show us how big you are and stop mucking about . . . I mean, I mean, darling . . . I think there might even be raisins growing here too. Aren't we lucky?" she says as a hand dives to the ground and the fistful disappears in the mouth of the medium-sized one.

Mother's movements are quick.

"There are loads growing here," she says and picks small piles of raisins for all of them.

The big one takes the lead. The tiny one has grabbed Mother's hand, the medium-sized one with pigtails holds the biggest one by the hand and trudging a little behind is the little one with the bobble hat. The path has veered off in another direction, or maybe they have left the path. The mountains in the distance have disappeared altogether and the sky is a vacuum which can only just be made out.

"Ow! Ow! MO-OTHER!" The little one has fallen to the stony ground. They stop and the little one screams, "I'm dead! I died, Mother."

Mother picks up the living bundle and carries it over to the others where the little one's grazed hands are wiped and Mother says, "Remember, on the long trip you have to put in a bit of work, fight a little with yourself."

They carry on.

"I've got blisters," the biggest one removes shoes to reveal a bloody blister on one heel. While a plaster is applied, the biggest one says, "Were you really born up there Mother?"

"What are you talking about? What an imagination," she sighs. "We have to go on."

"Were you thrown down from the peak, down into the deep valley?" the biggest one continues, "Mother, where's this from . . .?"

"Now we're on the long trip," Mother takes a break. She turns away from the children and says, "Not for my sake, children, not for me, I just wanted . . ." She walks on.

The well-dressed children follow.

"I'm never ever, never ever going on a trip," the words of the medium-sized one are carried away into the thin air.

"We're nearly there, soon," says the big one. "Come on, we're nearly there."

They climb.

"Come on," shouts Mother. "Come!"

Mother runs ahead. "Co-ome!"

And then they are there. All of them together. The biggest one, the big one, the medium-sized one with pigtails, the little one with the red bobble hat, the tiny one and then Mother. They stand close together and Mother says, "Look. Look here."

It's completely dark. Nothing can be seen. But the cold wind gives them the feeling that everything else lies below them. That a world about them lies at their feet.

"I want to show all of you the view," says Mother.

And five children stare into the darkness. They can scarcely see each other and their eyes are heavy.

"Here," says Mother. "Here . . ."

The biggest one interrupts. "Are you sure that . . . Mother, are you absolutely sure?"

"I'm absolutely sure," says Mother. "Absolutely sure."

Translated by Angela Shury-Smith

INGVAR AMBJØRNSEN

Skulls

One day, several summers ago, he had been on the point of smashing her head against the dashboard. They had been stuck in a queue of cars just outside Toulouse. The air shimmered in the heat and they had wound down all the windows; she was sitting there with the steering wheel in one hand and a cigarette in the other. She had been irritable and impatient; he still considered that they had enough time. Besides, he was aware that a rush of adrenalin would not get them to the hotel any quicker. So, to calm her down and to avoid using words – something told him that words might be risky at precisely this moment – he put his left arm around her shoulders and ran his fingers up her neck, until the back of her head rested in his hand like a large, warm rock. She had smiled. She understood him well enough to know that he understood her.

But he hadn't understood himself. The impulse to thrust her head away from him with all the power he could muster took him totally by surprise. In a flash he saw all the blood in front of him, the look of disbelief in her eyes, heard her scream. He had withdrawn his hand. He had seen the thin membrane between everything and nothing. The experience had done something to him – what, he wasn't sure.

He lay on his bed, smoking. The bathroom door was ajar and he could see her standing in front of the mirror, putting on her lipstick. An ill-becoming pale pink which always made him think of the Sixties, of blondes with beehive hairstyles and of black and white checked collarless suits.

"Are you ready?" She slipped her lipstick into her bag and stood pursing her lips at her reflection.

Yes, he was ready. The breakfast room was almost empty. It was ten to ten and they were the last. A single fried egg was floating in bacon fat on a white plate, the juice was lukewarm and the percolated coffee undrinkable. He drank it anyway as he watched in disgust while she dragged her knife through the egg yolk and the yolk ran into the fat. He watched her soak everything up with a piece of bread and put it all between the pink lips. He shuddered as her tongue collected a small fragment from the right hand corner of her mouth.

"You'll have to try to get *something* down you," she chewed. Now the knife and the fork tackled the bacon. Limp, covered in fat, not salty enough.

"Don't start on that again." He lit up a fresh cigarette, the third. "I'll eat when my stomach tells me to. Right now it's issuing the severest warning."

He rested his head on his shoulder. "I don't appear to be on proper speaking terms with my stomach today. But if I don't get *something* down me . . . My God, what was in those drinks last night?"

"Whisky and ice in mine. I think yours was a bit more of a mixture."

The night before was bathed in a sheen of unreality. They had taken almost a week to drive the length of Scotland, caught the ferry from Thurso to the Orkney Islands and reached Kirkwall early in the afternoon. They had eaten boiled cod and scallops at a small fish restaurant and wanted to spend the evening in the hotel bar. They had come to the end of their journey – the green island in the sea to the north of Scotland, the playground for the Picts and the Norwegian Earldom – and they were exhausted.

It turned out, however, that the islanders, or perhaps it was some unimaginative hotel manager, saw fit to organise a "Bermuda Night" in the bar on the very day they arrived. Hordes of Kirkwall's youths piled in wearing Hawaiian shirts and Bermuda shorts. Out of the driving wind and rain they came, into a bar where unsuspecting tourists were sitting over a drink, unable to believe their eyes. A drunken lad with a pimple the size of a thrush's egg on one cheek had plied her with the first sea-green drink – and then the race was on. They had woken up lying diagonally across the double bed; she still with her stockings on.

"People have lived up here for five thousand years," she said, pushing the plate to the side. "Did you know that?" She took one of his cigarettes. "My God, isn't that when the Egyptians were building the great pyramids?"

"Don't remember," he said.

"Burial grounds," she said. "The whole island is full of burial grounds. Pass the coffee over, will you?"

*

They reached the farmstead at about twelve. A farmhouse, the brickwork well worn, a double garage, an outhouse. A solitary hen pecked indiscriminately with its yellow beak at the gravel; shadowy figures moved behind the thin curtains as they parked the car in the drive.

A private museum.

They had no idea that this kind of thing existed until they caught sight of the sign a couple of kilometres towards the north of the island.

The land came to an end a few hundred metres away in the east. White gulls soared and plummeted in the wind above the jagged black cliffs.

The woman who came out on to the step was tall and thin, almost gaunt, closer to eighty than seventy. Her eyes were sunk deep into her face, but they still sparkled with life. She must have a young soul, he thought: banal thought, but that was what went through his mind. As she proffered her hand, he had the feeling that he knew something about the soil out here.

Burial grounds? On this property there was only the one. Joe would show us the way as soon as he had had his lunch. She didn't eat lunch herself; no, there was no question of them waiting outside in the wind.

They entered a covered veranda which ran the length of the house. On the wall and beneath the row of window-panes there were glass showcases. Her bent index finger pointed out the arrowheads, stone axes, skulls and remains of bones. She talked about a lifetime of digging in the "garden".

And then what he had always secretly yearned to do every time he visited a museum actually happened. The old lady raised the glass lid of one of the showcases.

She turned round. "It has been my experience that no-one can understand history without touching it. It is the same as . . . death." Now she was smiling like a little girl, a little girl who had been given an unexpected present.

A moment later each of them was standing there with a skull in their hands.

"I call them Lucie and John," she said, gingerly running a finger across the yellow brown surface she was holding.

"They're bonny. I think they're bonny. They're more than four thousand years old. I like to imagine they shared a life together. They were like us. Hatred. Love. Happiness. Sadness. What you are holding there in your hands is all that they have left behind them."

He hefted the skull in his hand. There was no real weight to speak of. When he held it up to the sun and looked through the eye sockets he could see the yellowish light falling through the thin membrane of bone. The teeth were white and strong, no sign of wear, only one tooth was missing, a canine.

John? What had his real name been? What kind of dreams had flickered brightly behind that thin skull? Over his thoughts, in the background, he could hear the old lady holding forth about the people who settled out here on the remotest rocks facing the ocean. She called them the "eagle claw folk" because their burial chambers had contained eagles' claws. It was a hierarchical society: one person was buried with three claws, another with eight. They had opened one man's grave and found twelve claws. They reckoned he was the tribal chief, but there was a crater at the back of his head.

"And this one? John?"

She laughed. "A worker. A farmer. A dreamer. We didn't find any claws next to John. Not next to Lucie either."

He put the skull down carefully, observing at the same time a reverence in his behaviour which surprised him. He shot a glance over at the person who shared his life and saw that she had reacted in the same way. He stood gently stroking Lucie's forehead as if he were comforting a child from the past or perhaps more probably a sister. This skull had strong white teeth, too, a complete set. But several of the teeth were worn down to roughly half their length; he saw the hunter's wife sitting by the fire, chewing leather until it was soft. A continuous process, like digestion, breast-feeding or constant mental activity.

The old lady took his hand in hers: "You're right-handed, aren't you?"

Yes, he was.

She stood so close to him now that he could tell her smell apart, a slight aroma of lavender and something else which he could only define as the smell of an old woman. He noticed her skin was as taut as a drum skin over her nose and forehead. A thin blood vessel descended her left temple; her eyes were open and blue. There was a light about her like the one he had seen in the skull he had just put down.

"Look at this. You think you're looking at a stone, but what you see in reality is a masterpiece."

He saw a stone. A grey, oblong stone weighing around half a kilo, irregular in shape, but honed smooth, the way that the sea shapes stones against other stones.

"No," she said, as if reading his thoughts. "It wasn't the sea that did this; it was one of your erstwhile kinsmen."

She placed the stone in his hand and his heart gave a jolt as his hand closed around it. The grey stone resting in his hand was perfectly weighted; it became part of his hand, an extension of it: a lethal weapon.

She nodded. A weapon.

He couldn't let go of it. It made him think of his grandfather as he lay on his deathbed. Ninety-two years old, a sparrow almost denuded of plumage, the huge workman's hands reduced to colourless claws. The old man asked him to fetch the plane. The long plane. He had assumed that the old fellow had gone senile just before departing on his final journey, but he had done what he was asked. His grandfather had sat up in bed and placed the long plane that *his* grandfather had made during *his* lifetime across the white duvet cover. Grasped the handle. Not with much strength, it was true, but he had grasped the handle. His hands were above the darkest part of the wood, the part where a couple of generations had stained the tool with their own sweat.

"It no longer fits," Grandfather had said. "The plane has outgrown me."

But the stone fitted. It fitted the hand of a grown man. Today, as it had done four thousand years ago. A shock ran through him, he was touched, felt tears fall like a veil in front of his eyes. He thought about what the old lady had said about no-one being able to understand history without touching it. This was an encounter with a perfectionist from the time before everything.

Joe didn't say much. He held out his hand when he saw them coming towards him with hands outstretched, but he was not curious about where they came from or who they were. A short stump of a man, though he moved over the ground lightly.

He showed them the settlement. A circle of stones in the sodden earth.

It hadn't been like this "in olden times". It had been woodland. Warm. Traces of four types of corn had been found in the piles of waste.

He appeared with a leather bag containing six batteries. They had to remember to change the batteries in the torch and wear knee-pads as they entered. He pointed to the path which led to the cliffs and the sea. They couldn't go wrong.

Then he went back the way he had come.

They found the burial place. A mound overgrown with grass. Barely thirty metres from the edge of the black cliffs. Down below, the green sea crashed against the rocks, throwing up white spray; from above they could see the sea birds.

Rocks laid upon rocks up to the turf covering, one and a half metres off the ground, formed the end of the burial place facing them. The entrance was a square hole.

They took out of the bag the knee-pads and the lamp. And they found the answer to the question neither of them had asked. They had to crawl on all fours to pay their respects to the dead. The damp corridor that led into the mound was barely a metre in height and much the same in width.

He changed the batteries in the lamp. "I'll go first."

She looked sceptical. "I don't know if I want to. Yes, I do. Right, you go first."

It was tight. Tighter than he had imagined. He was sweating; water from the stone roof dripped on to his face. Cold drops of water. He was reminded of water torture, regular drops on to your skull hour after hour, day after day, until every drop felt like a hammer blow.

After ten, twelve metres he came to the burial chamber itself. Inside here the roof was high enough for him to half-raise himself. He did, felt his back approach fifty degrees and fell back on to all fours again.

Rocks. Layer upon layer of rocks. The roof was cast in concrete. It irritated him, ruined the view of ancient times.

The graves were oblong niches in the layers of rocks protected by glass against souvenir hunters. Skulls. Little heaps of yellow brown skulls. And bones. Legs, thigh bones, hips, vertebrae. Loose jaws, teeth. An entire small community was at rest here.

What had the death ceremonies been like? He seemed to remember reading somewhere that the Picts had laid their dead out for birds of prey and ravens. Then they collected the bones, which had been picked clean, and piled them up later. A splendid custom. What you hunted you gave back to your prey.

He looked at the skulls. He felt his own brow with his fingers and contemplated the space around him. Stone walls. The skull. The bone membrane under the skin – the soft brain. Inside, inside. In the room, in the brain. Outside, the others, the otherness, the changing images.

The space shrank, the walls came in, moulded his reactions in the way that a blow to the head changes thoughts, consciousness, how you perceive the external and internal worlds.

He had to leave here. Hitherto in his life he had had a theoretical standpoint regarding claustrophobia; now he was immersed in a new experience, panic was driving him, he had difficulty breathing, nausea was rising, he hadn't eaten a thing, he had nothing to sick up. With his heart pounding in his chest, his pulse throbbing in his temples, he began to crawl back. Something was not right, he should be able to see the light now, the grass and the sky, but it was dark, something was coming towards him, she was coming towards him, he screamed at her to back away. She, frightened by the panic in his voice, the fury, screamed back that she couldn't. He interpreted *couldn't* as *wouldn't*, thought that she wasn't taking him seriously. The narrow space closed in on him, he was being suffocated, he began to shake his head from side to side, into the stone walls, the skin under the roots of his hair tore, he felt the blood begin to flow, warm, sticky to the touch, he lost the lamp, the beam of light hit him in the face, she invoked a God she had never had any time for, he shouted at her that for the same God's sake she should shut up, his eardrums . . . She edged closer, placed her hand over his and whispered words he had not heard for ten years. Her face was close to his. He banged his head against the wall again. She took his face in both her hands and began to cry. He butted her in the middle of the face with his head as hard as he could. He heard her nose crack and had her blood all over his hands as he reached out to break her fall.

Later, much later, she said, "I'll never forget what the old lady said about no-one being able to understand history without touching it. I don't know why, but the words are seared in my brain."

They had just finished washing the dishes together. He straightened the drying-up cloth for the glasses and hung it over the stove to dry. He went to the bathroom and stood there staring at himself in the mirror. His hairline had receded further, his eyes searched deeper and deeper into himself. He rested his forehead against the cool glass and for one tremulous moment his mind went blank.

Translated by Don Bartlett

MERETHE LINDSTRØM

The Sea of Tranquillity

There has been a traffic accident. The face of the old man lying in the road belongs to a stranger, but it's still somehow familiar, because I've seen him before. Long after passing the scene of the accident, the onlookers and their vague speculation about what happened in this street, I muse: who could he be? Someone was probably sitting and waiting for him, not knowing that he was lying in the road. Why didn't he walk on the pavement? Why did he walk right out into the middle of the road as he did? It was almost as if he were asking for it. An old man. A grey coat. I can't get it out of my mind and decide to call my father, even though he lives elsewhere, in another town; it has nothing to do with him, but I ring him anyway. He's in, of course. But he asks if we can talk later. If there's no hurry. "Not at all," I say. But it makes me uneasy. I call from a bar. It's still early for a place like this, only a few customers; an elderly couple in conversation with the man behind the bar. I put the phone down and decide to stay. They're playing bar billiards in the back room. Three men. I'm warm, it's been a hot day, but it's going to rain soon, the weather's going to change, you can feel it in the air on days like this. I'm well into my beer and I haven't eaten a great deal. Perhaps that's why I have this feeling of well-being, it's like velvet, like touching velvet, and before the game I'm watching from the corner is over, I know that one of them will be accompanying me home afterwards. Or to be more precise: I'll be accompanying him. It happens slowly, everything has begun to happen slowly now. He has shaved his hair off, and he has this strange tattoo, which he shows me even before we leave his friends at the bar. In the taxi, we don't say a word to each other. We don't speak, or we hardly speak. I can already imagine his shaven head between my legs. I know such things are not spoken about, but I can't help thinking it. I can't be the only person who thinks about such things, and since there doesn't seem to be anything alien about the thought of the man with the shaven head, and since, still sitting in the taxi, I can imagine him with his head facing my abdomen, there must be a chance that he has been thinking about the same thing. I don't say this to him, though. The house we go to is cold, even though it is still summer. It seems empty in the way that a house can seem empty, even when it is inhabited, as if an important item in the house's inventory has been removed, or as if someone has left in a hurry. I can see photographs on the shelf in the living-room, a framed photograph of a woman sitting with both hands between her thighs. Judging by the background and the way her hair is blowing in all directions, she's sitting somewhere desolate, the top of a mountain perhaps. There's also a photograph of a young girl, in her first years of schooling. She's holding a pencil out in front of the camera, showing it off with a weary, forced gesture, as forced as her toothless smile. Notice board in the background. School photograph. He's gone to find a drink for us both. I could have told him it wasn't necessary, that we could have started right away if he'd wanted to, but, of course, I can't say that now. In fact, I couldn't have said it anyway, such things remain unspoken, much the same as what I think of him and what he thinks of me. I could have put the framed photographs face down. Not that I minded having them there. But I wondered what they would have thought of me, these people whom I have never met. In a way, I'm sorry that we've ended up together here in the same lonely, miserable room.

Now.

He smells exactly the same as my father. After he comes back, after we have drained our drinks, after we have settled down on the sofa, after we have got closer to each other. That's what I mean. Now he smells like my father. Of course, he has always smelled like that, but I didn't notice or I didn't think about it.

I have a childhood memory of my father. We were watching television together. The moon landing in July, 1969. The first glorious steps when everything was new and the whole world was following the crackly reports. He was drinking beer. Nothing particularly unusual about that. He was wearing a T-shirt; he smelled of unadulterated beer and sweat. I sat on his lap as we watched the men making their way across the bare surface of the moon in their clean white uniforms. The memory saddens me; I think I have an inkling why. Somewhere, there is a photograph of my father with a shaven head, taken several years before man had first set foot on the moon. He was about twenty-five years old in the photograph. The time when he was admitted for the first time – electric shocks, pills, his hair shorn only for fashion reasons. A stiff tie, a grey suit, short trouser legs, hitched up slightly because he was sitting, a starched white shirt, sleeves rolled down properly. We used to visit him when he was hospitalised. My mother was wearing a particularly short, tight skirt; she had a new hairstyle and was carrying a wrapped present, usually a book about space travel. Some novels. Henry Miller. She told me to remember not to worry him so that he didn't become sad. What she meant by that has always puzzled me. If I asked, she always answered the same. "Oh, you know well enough," she said to me, although I was just a young girl at the time. We sat waiting for him to appear. Years went by. That's him, coming down the corridor, that special way of walking he has, they all walk like that in here. I want to run over to him, to give him a hug. Remember he doesn't feel good. Use your head now. So I sit on my hands, watch him coming to the door, his eyes meet mine, barely a smile, as though I am a little too far away, as though he had caught sight of me somewhere out of his range. I am not allowed to ask how he is.

When I became older, I used to take boys with me, boys I was with for short periods as a teenager, and later men. Sometimes he played cards with them. After a while he moved home for good, but I can still see him in front of me in the rooms, walking down the same corridors, down to where I was waiting. I took him flowers; I took books and chocolate. I waited for him to speak first.

He never asked how I was. And yet he must have noticed my companions, seen it as more than merely a coincidence that they were there, because, later, he often asked what I had done with them, or what they were doing now. And I always answered that I wasn't sure. They could have disappeared from the face of the earth for all I knew.

Mare tranquillitatis, my father said as we watched the spaceship that stood erect on the moon's surface that special day in July, 1969.

They call it a sea although I assume it is completely dry up there. I asked him why they had called it that of all things, and he said that once people believed the dark patches on the moon were sea. He thought it sounded appealing, he said. The sea of tranquillity.

"Neil Armstrong is no wimp," he kept saying that morning. And since he said it aloud, I thought that it was directed towards me. I thought it was important. That I shouldn't forget it.

The man with the shaven head, whose bed it is I'm lying in, can't wait. Perhaps he believes that I might disappear or assume some other, less tangible form if he doesn't act quickly. What drives him to do the things he's doing now I can have no idea about, of course, so I assume that they are the same motives that drive me; they feel like a covering of perspiration and hunger across my skin. And after that? Tranquillity. And he moves to the other side of the bed, and I also move away, much as if we were now two poles forced apart by the same powerful energy that drew us together. He gets out of bed, and I can hear him in the bathroom. On his return, he is wearing a dressing-gown. It seems natural after the urgency to be naked. He switches on the little lamp on the bedside table. Offers me a smoke; I say no and he takes one.

"So, what's your story?" he says, seeming to need to, or, more likely, merely wishing to listen to my thoughts. Naturally, I don't reply, or I answer a different question he might have asked. I tell him nothing, anyway, nothing of any consequence, because there's not much to tell. And what there is to tell can't be told. I say I'm a journalist; it's not so far from the truth. An hour's time. That's how long it takes to talk about nothing. Afterwards I sleep heavily, badly; on the shelf there are portraits of the woman and the girl with the pencil. Captives of time. *Mare tranquillitatis.*

"Nothing is as beautiful as the earth seen from the moon," my father said.

He wants to see one particular film. That is before we go to sleep. He asks if I mind. Since we don't know each other.

The film opens with some men talking in a hotel room; they're talking about the chances of finding – I think the words they use are *getting hold of* – of getting hold of some girls. They're on the beach now, talking to some young women in bikinis. The women shoot sidelong glances at the camera. Later, they're in the hotel room with some of the girls. No-one is talking any more now. They seem to have lost any interest in or any need for words. They take off their clothes. They take each other, or rather: the men take the girls. One of the male participants in this odd company pushes a metal object up into the body of one of the girls. It's a strange instrument for the purpose. There's something about the chilly, frozen, stiffness of the object and the softness of the girl's skin. That he does this is strange. Apart from the husky moans, a couple of cries of Yes-Yes and No-No, there are no words, only the sounds of bodies in motion, rubbing up against the bedding. Now that they are here, they don't seem to have anything to say. There is nothing else to say. Or: there are no words for it.

The last time I went back to my hometown I visited my father. He showed me a picture, a photograph of the moon which he had cut out of the newspaper. And he appeared to be happy. He appeared to be happy, not sad as he often was when I visited him.

"Do you remember the time when we were buying a Jack Russell terrier," I asked him, "and you rang the kennels and enquired whether they were the people who bred Jack Daniels?"

He sniggered. "Don't think I do," he said, suspicious now. He didn't like talking about the past.

He asked where I lived. I answered, "In a hotel."

"Come back soon, Miriam," he said.

He meant to the town. He never liked people getting too close to him. I knew it would be a while. My letters would reach him, my voice on the telephone, remote as far as he was concerned, as remote as if it had been hurled out through the atmosphere, out into space, our voices, like the voices sent back from the moon, reproduced through a crackling receiver. Somewhere out there a whole avalanche of words was lying in wait.

"Are you afraid of the dark?" he asks after the strange film is over. While laughing? Is he laughing?

"No," I answer, lying. "No, I'm not afraid."

But I am. It's not the dark as such, not the absence of light. It's just something you don't understand, something which is never said, something you can't understand, like the silence, more the silence than the darkness, but suddenly everything seemed to make sense. When he asks me, I know that he doesn't actually mean the dark. Not exactly. I know what he means, that there are two different things. I could have answered that there are two things. One is my father and the other is this man in the road, the casualty. They have nothing to do with each other, and yet. The man in the road. And my father an onlooker. As I am myself.

But I don't say that. I don't say that.

"Can you see?" my father said. "Can you see the landing gear? The machinery is unbelievable. "

"It certainly was," I said, looking at the old photograph of the moon landing he had hanging on the kitchen wall, cut out of a newspaper, covered in transparent adhesive paper. "Things are different today."

"I know," he said. "But it was fantastic back then. Quite unbelievable. Imagine standing on the surface of the moon. The surface might be illuminated, but when you look up, it's simply black, there's no atmosphere, just total darkness. But then you suddenly glimpse the earth, and nothing is as beautiful as the earth when you see it from the moon."

I looked at him. At his eyes, as though he had been there and had seen it. We sat in his kitchen. That was when I visited him last. I often think of how he made me feel so secure the times I used to sit with him. I thought of the exact time when he was drinking beer and wearing a T-shirt, and how I could smell his anticipation even though I was only small, the anticipation that something fabulous was about to happen, how he made me feel it too, the excitement he felt about the occasion, as he called it, that was taking place on the television screen.

"But we are here," I said.

I visited my father last Whitsun.

I had the impression that he was well. I watched him walk down the garden path, stop and look at the lawnmower at the bottom of the garden; he remained standing there for such a long time that I thought he wasn't going to stir from the spot. I never ask what he thinks about. I don't know what he does when I'm not there. He just stood in the same place, staring at the lawnmower. I could have asked.

I wake with a vague memory of having called my father again. He picked up the phone, it was a strange conversation. "What are you doing now?" he asked and I answered that I was just a little worried, and he said that there was something he had to do. In the garden. He couldn't speak any more. "There's just something I have to say," I said.

He repeated that he couldn't speak for long.

"All these years I have gone home with men," I said. "I have stayed with some of them. Their furniture has become mine, the pictures on the wall, the videos. The windows, the views, their friends. I acquire other people's lives. That's what I do. That's what I'm doing now. I can't help it. When I'm not doing this, I watch television."

"I don't think it will ever change."

"What?" he said. "I don't understand. I don't understand what you mean."

Translated by Don Bartlett

DAG SOLSTAD

Shyness and Dignity

He was a rather sottish senior master in his fifties, with a wife who had spread out a bit too much and with whom he had breakfast every morning. This autumn day, too, a Monday in October, not yet knowing as he sat at the breakfast table with a light headache that it would be the decisive day in his life. As every day, he made sure to put on a sparkling white shirt, which alleviated the distaste he couldn't help feeling at having to live in such a time and under such conditions. He finished his breakfast in silence and looked out of the window, on to Jacob Aall Street, as he had done innumerable times throughout the years. A street in Oslo, Norway's capital, where he lived and worked. It was a grey, oppressive morning, the sky was leaden, with scattered clouds drifting across it like black veils. I wouldn't be surprised if it rained, he thought, picking up his collapsible umbrella. He stuck it in his briefcase, together with his headache pills and some books. He bid a markedly cordial goodbye to his wife, in a tone that seemed genuine and sharply contrasted with his irritable, and her rather drawn, expression. But this is how it was every morning when he composed himself, with great difficulty, for this cordial "take care of yourself", a gesture to this wife he had for years been living so close to and with whom he consequently had to feel a deep solidarity, and although he could now, on the whole, feel only remnants of this solidarity, it was essential for him to let her know every morning, by means of this cheerful and simple "take care of yourself", that in his innermost heart he thought that nothing had changed between them, and while they both knew that it didn't reflect the actual situation, he felt obliged to force himself, for the sake of propriety, to rise to a level high enough to make this gesture possible, not least because he then received a goodbye in return in the same simple and genuine tone, which had a soothing effect on his uneasiness and was indispensable to him. He walked to school, Fagerborg Secondary School, situated only seven or eight minutes from his residence. His head felt heavy and he was a bit on edge, after drinking beer and aquavit the evening before, a little too much aquavit, about the right amount of beer, he thought. A little too much aquavit, which was now pressing on his forehead, like a chain. When he reached the school he went straight to the teachers' lounge, put away his briefcase, took out his books, swallowed a pill for headache, said a brief but unaffected good morning to his colleagues, who had already taught one period, and went to his class.

He entered the classroom, closed the door behind him, and sat down behind the teacher's desk on the platform by the blackboard, which covered most of one long wall. Blackboard and chalk. Sponge. Twenty-five years in the service of the school. As he stepped into the classroom, the pupils hastily sat down at their desks. In front of him, twenty-nine young men and women about the age of eighteen who looked at him and returned his greeting. They removed their earplugs and put them in their pockets. He asked them to take out their school edition of *The Wild Duck*. He was once more struck by their hostile attitude towards him. But it could not be helped, he had a task to perform and was going to go through with it. It was from them as a group that he sensed that massive dislike sent forth by their bodies. Individually they could be very pleasant, but together, positioned as now, at their desks, they constituted a structural enmity, directed at him and all that he stood for. Although they did as he told them. They took out their school editions of *The Wild Duck* without grumbling and placed them on the desks before them. He himself sat with an equivalent copy in front of him. *The Wild Duck* by Henrik Ibsen. This remarkable drama that Henrik Ibsen wrote at the age of fifty-six, in 1884. The class had been taken up with it for over a month, and even so they were only in the middle of Act 4 – that was doing things in style, he thought. A sleepy Monday morning. Norwegian class, two in a row, in fact, at Fagerborg Secondary School, with a group of seniors. Directly outside the windows, that grey, oppressive day. He was sitting behind his lectern, as he called it. The pupils with their noses and eyes turned towards the book. Some were slumped over rather than seated at their desks, which annoyed him, but he didn't bother to take notice of it. He was speaking, holding forth. In the middle of Act 4. Where Mrs Sørbye appears in Ekdal's home and announces that she is going to marry Werle, the merchant, and where Ekdal's lodger Dr Relling is present, and he read (himself, instead of asking one of his pupils to do it, which he did at times for the sake of appearances, but he preferred to do it himself): "Relling (with a slight tremor in his voice): This can't possibly be true? Mrs Sørbye: Yes, my dear Relling, it is indeed." As he was reading he felt an unendurable excitement, because all at once he thought he was on the track of something to which he had not previously paid any attention when trying to understand *The Wild Duck*.

For twenty-five years he had gone through this drama by Henrik Ibsen with eighteen-year-olds in their last year of high school (or secondary school), and he had always had problems with Dr Relling. He had not fully grasped what he was doing in the play. He had seen that his function was to proclaim elementary, unvarnished truths about the other characters in the play, well, actually about the entire play. He had seen him as a kind of mouthpiece for Ibsen and been unable to grasp why that was necessary. Indeed, he had been of the opinion that the figure of Dr Relling weakened the play. What did Henrik Ibsen need a "mouthpiece" for? Didn't the play speak for itself, he had thought. But here, here there was something. Henrik Ibsen lays his hand on his minor character Dr Relling and, within parentheses, makes him speak with a slight tremor in his voice as he asks Mrs Sørbye if it is really true that she will marry Werle, the powerful merchant. For a moment, Henrik Ibsen pushes Relling into the drama on which he otherwise exclusively comments with his sarcasms. There he is, caught in his own bitter fate as a perpetual, unsuccessful admirer of Mrs Sørbye, throughout her two marriages, first to Dr Sørbye, now to Werle, and for a brief moment it is his fate, and nothing else, that is frozen into immobility on the stage. The moment of the minor figure. Both before and after this he remains the same, the man who reels off those smart lines, one of which has acquired an immortal status in Norwegian literature: "If you take the life-lie away from an average person, you take away his happiness as well."

It was this he now began to expatiate on to his pupils, who were partly sitting at, partly slumped over their desks. He asked them to flip their pages to Act 3, where Dr Relling enters the stage for the first time, to read what he says there, and then move ahead to the end of Act 4 (he assumed that the pupils were familiar with the whole play, although they had only reached the middle of Act 4 in their examination of it, for their first assignment had been to read the play in its entirety, which he presumed they had done, regardless of what the pupils themselves, individually or as a whole, had accomplished in that respect, thinking, with the hint of an inward smile flickering through his rather – after yesterday's meditative little drinking bout – shivery body, that there was no reason why he should act as a policeman in class), the very place where Dr Relling, among other things, expresses his subsequently so immortal statement about the life-lie, and he said: There, you can see, Dr Relling is just chattering, all the time, except for one place, and that is where we are right now. Now we've got him, you see, he is in the drama for the first and last time. The pupils did as they were told, leafed back, leafed forward, leafed back to where they were, namely, where they had Dr Relling in the drama for the first and last time. Did they yawn? No, they didn't yawn, why should they yawn, this was not something that called for a demonstration so violent as to necessitate a yawn, this was a perfectly ordinary Norwegian class for a group of seniors on a Monday morning at Fagerborg Secondary School. There they sat, listening to the teacher's interpretation of a play that was a prescribed text for their final examination in Norwegian, *The Wild Duck*, named after a wild duck that lived in an attic, a dark attic as it happened, some looking at the page, some at him, some out of the window. The minutes were ticking slowly away. The teacher continued to talk about the made-up character, Dr Relling, who has evidently spoken an immortal line in a play by Ibsen. Here he is, he said, frozen firmly to his own bitter fate. Bitter for him, on the verge of the ridiculous for the rest of us, not least if we were to have him presented to us by way of Dr Relling's own sarcasms.

But, he added, and now he pointed his finger straight at the class, which startled a few of them, because they did not like to be pointed at in that way, what would have happened if this scene hadn't been included? Nothing. The play would have been exactly the same, apart from the fact that Dr Relling would not have had his quivering moment. Because it is completely superfluous. It does not affect the development of the plot in the least, nor does it change, as we have seen, Dr Relling, the minor figure. He is exactly the same character, with exactly the same function, both before and after his quivering moment. And when we know that this play is written by the masterful Henrik Ibsen, who carefully lays out his characters and scenes and leaves nothing to chance, we have to ask: Why does Ibsen include this superfluous scene, where Dr Relling, a minor character, speaks a line "with a slight tremor in his voice" and is suddenly pulled into the play as someone with a destiny? There has to be a reason, and since the scene is superfluous, well, in reality wasted, there can be no other reason than that Ibsen wants to show this made-up minor character of his, Dr Relling, a great gesture. But then the question arises: Why . . . In that moment, however, the bell rang and the pupils instantly

straightened up, closed their school editions of *The Wild Duck*, got up
and walked quietly and confidently out of the classroom, past the
teacher, whom they did not take notice of for a moment, not a single
one of them, and who was now sitting on his chair, all alone, annoyed
at having been interrupted in the middle of a question.

Ten years ago, he thought, as he too got up, they would at least have
let him complete his sentence. But now, as soon as the school bell
rang, they closed their books and left the classroom, confidently and
blamelessly, because it was beyond doubt that the ringing of the bell
signalled the end of the period. The decision was made by the bell,
such were the rules whereby the instruction was organised, and one
had to follow the rules, they would have said, calmly and
convincingly, if he had said it was he who decided when the period
was over. They would have looked at him and asked, Why, then, do
we have a bell that rings when, after all, it is you and not the bell that
decides. Then it would have been useless for him to mention that the
bell was simply a means of reminding a teacher that it was time to
stop, in case he became so fervently elated by his teaching that he
forgot both time and place. He went towards the teachers' lounge.
He was a bit irritated. Not least because he had looked forward to the
recess even more than they, and he certainly needed it more, tired as
he was, both beforehand and after talking for three quarters of an
hour almost without a break. He needed a glass of water and he
needed a headache pill. And as he stood there in front of the drinking
fountain and poured cold water into a glass, sneaked out a pill and
swallowed it, he thought that, by Jove, just the way I feel right now,
Dr Relling felt throughout the play, with a pressure on his forehead,
all shivery, slightly weary of body and soul; yes, it was precisely in this
condition he found himself as he went about uttering his semi-elegant
(yes, he had to admit that was the way he viewed them) lines, of
which at least one had been made immortal, and he had to smile to
himself. He sat down in his usual place at the large table in the
teachers' lounge and talked a little with his colleagues about the
football results over the weekend etc. Since the teachers were
originally from widely different parts of Norway, every team in our
two upper divisions was represented by at least one fervent fan, and
those who had won over the weekend never failed to make everyone
aware of it. He himself was in Division III, at the top of the division,
to be sure, with the hope every year of moving up to Division II, but

when they asked him questions it was still mostly out of politeness and pity, which he couldn't find any fault with. (His female colleagues didn't take part in these discussions, though they sat at the same table, beside the men, but they were knitting, as he used to tell his wife with a sly little laugh.)

Translated by Sverre Lyngstad

PER PETTERSON

The Moon over The Gate

Sometimes I go out walking at night. Not only in the summer when
the light comes down from the sky the whole day and night too and
it's easy to see for a great distance even well after midnight, and not
just in winter either, when the snow lies thick, oozing light from a
vertically opposite direction, from the ground up, like the
discotheque floor in London where I once danced (but that's a long
time ago now). If it is cold enough it makes you want to dance, it's
true; to hear the dry grating sound when your boots meet the snow
with each bounce you make. The sound of tap shoes on the country
road on a January night! It's a good thing then to have your cap on, a
good thing that no-one can see you blushing. The darkest time in the
valley here is in late November, before the snow settles, when all I can
see when I open the door and go out on the doorstep are the outside
lights of one other farm on the opposite hillside, and all round me the
autumn-ploughed fields swallow and smother – each glimmer, each
flicker, each flame, and give nothing in return. Then I will probably
put my jacket on, most often the pea jacket from the novels I have
written, and go out into the yard when I cannot sleep or do not *want*
to sleep. I leave the torch inside. The contrast it creates when I switch
it on, and the ray of light cutting through the night dividing everything up into a *here* and a *there* may reawaken the fear of darkness I
had when I was small, which has almost quite vanished now, but in
certain situations, at certain mental and geographical points of
intersection I cannot calculate or beforehand see coming, it strikes me
heavily and leaves me so stiff with terror that in my bad periods I
bring my knife from Crete out with me. I grip it tightly round the
handle with the naked, sharp, metal blade ready for use against all
those that crawl around and fill the darkness completely with their
slimy, raging, wild bodies, and will do for me at the first possible
opportunity.

Then I feel a burning stab of cold in the back of my neck, and
nevertheless set off, all the way down through the valley.

Usually it is not like that. On the contrary. Without either knife or torch I walk down the slope from The Gate (as it is called, the place where I live). Sometimes with one of my dogs for company – preferably Laika, who is youngest and least inclined to laziness – sometimes on my own, if I suspect my special moose is standing where it usually does, chewing and dozing in the bushes beside the road through Dæsjroa, or *Dalsroen*, as it will say on some maps. Not that the moose has any fear of Laika. It does not move an inch no matter how much the dog barks, and Laika knows the moose is not afraid, and as it does not take flight, Laika cannot chase after it. This is so frustrating to her, that she gives voice to that until she almost splits in two. So do I then, I split in two; all this is far too noisy and not how I want it at night. Then I'd rather walk alone. I do not necessarily need company. The moose can stand there in the bushes, that is fine with me, and I would like to know it does, and maybe even be able to hear it, but then as a *part* of the night I am moving through as *I* too want to be a part of that night.

What I want is the pitch-black night as a *condition*, as something to sink and dissolve myself in; what I want is for the darkness to gush in through my eyes and my body to float out so it no longer is as distinct, as *important* as it often may seem to me, it must be admitted, that I can be found listening to its signals in monomaniacal and hypochondriacal ways; what I want is for the severance of body and non-body to dissolve a little, maybe accomplish some slight osmosis where the one ends and the other begins; to *erase*. That is what I want when I am sick of myself, of my face in the mirror, of the words I put on the screen, sick of the metallic taste in my mouth I get through staging myself each single day, when the proportionate relationship between me and *me* is almost 1:1, but not quite, and disgust and self-contempt ooze out of the cracks along the edge where the disparity prevents the tape of life from sticking.

And I ponder: was this how it was for those who felt themselves drawn to the great desert, the Sahara, in Sven Lindqvist's book *Desert Divers* (which I have just read for the third time and think about often); was it like that for Saint-Exupéry, for Isabelle Eberhardt and the others in that book, that they too wanted to be erased, and that the Sahara was their night, and what they did was to think with more ambition, with a stronger will than I have done, standing out here in the cold, restless and itching all over, with only this late autumn night at my disposal and maybe I'll restrict myself to that. But I understand the craving, that attraction, at those times when I find myself on the roads in the dark, as now, with my arms stretched out to both sides like the wings of an aeroplane, a mail-route plane maybe, on its way from Casablanca to Dakar, like Saint-Exupéry's plane; the vibrating machine, so warm and close to my body, but also a great silence enveloping my head, my thoughts, and I walk this way through the darkness to confirm the space around me. To sense how it is potentially infinite and thus can give an almost overwhelming freedom, just like the desert is potentially infinite, and *was* for Sven Lindqvist when he read and dreamed about the Sahara as a boy, and still was when as a middle-aged man after the break-up of a marriage he travelled there for the first time. That break-up gave him the freedom, the point-zero, the possibility he needed to be able to look back and see who he was when as a child a long time ago he gazed towards the point in time where he *now* found himself, prompted by circumstances he suddenly turned and looked back, and one can picture how the gazes of the two met, one clear and blue, the other perhaps a bit more pale, and the elder one saw the question in the young one's eyes: who have you become, what have you managed to do? And he would have to reply: No, I have not been to the Sahara yet. I have travelled everywhere, I have written numerous books on what I have seen, I have posed many important questions, but I have not been to the Sahara yet. I can go now. I will go now. I know I must.

I float around in the dark like a man blindfold though with eyes wide-open, my arms out in front of me now, as in films I have seen. The Sahara may seem a bit much, a bit large; were there *so* many things that needed erasing for Lindqvist and his divers? Do *I* need the Sahara, or is this November night in Dæsjroa sufficient? It is hard to tell. It depends on whatever is the matter with me, if you can say that anything is.

In his book *Bench Press* Lindqvist writes: "Sahara means 'emptiness'. It also means 'nothing'. It is that great empty nothingness that lures me. I am leaving tomorrow." And I understand that, I know where he is heading, and yet I think: how can such a well-travelled, such a wise and well-read man with so much at heart, long for "nothing". Or why do *we*? Because we do. And if the Sahara is his night, does he and all those he is writing about, Michel Vieuchange, for instance, want morning to come at last? Vieuchange died of the Sahara. Isabelle Eberhardt died of the Sahara. It was definitely not what they wanted, but they died all the same. *I* do want morning to come. Of that I am certain. If I search my mind. I do not want to float around in this night for ever. Only those times when I feel the need to be erased, until my body again is like the floating bubble in a spirit-level lying in its right position, *in its place*, and with that what we call our soul.

In *Bench Press* the middle-aged Lindqvist lay on the couch in a gym trying to lift his father's death away, as well as his own divorce, with the sweat running down his face. But it had to stop with death, he did not get any further. Not all pain can be lifted off. I have tried it myself, though not in the same way, not by lifting. What *I* do is I walk away, and then not only at night, but I walk, quite simply, both fast and far; faster and faster, kilometre after kilometre, until what I am trying to forget lies behind me, until the dogs refuse to go on any longer, especially Lyra, my oldest, who has started to tremble now each time I put on my brown running shoes. *Oh no, oh, no,* I see in her eyes, *not those shoes, not again!* And it does work, with dark glasses against the daylight, as long as you keep moving, as long as your breath comes fast and drowns out all other sounds, and the pain in your legs increases uphill, but if you stop and feel you cannot take one step more, a sharp-edged stream hits you hard and fast, and makes it difficult to swallow, to keep that down which wants to come up. Then the contourless black night is your only source of rescue, the night through which you can dance if you like, as in slow motion, move through like water, through the Hemness lake maybe, somewhere ahead in a landscape I cannot see now, where an otter lives on an islet; to move slim and beautiful through the dark water like that, it would be something, or through the night here where even my age is hidden, a fifty-one-year-old Billy Elliot dancing down the road through Dæsjroa. And Lindqvist leaves his gym and goes off, from *Bench Press* to *Desert Divers*, on a cheap flight first to Agadir in Morocco, and then eastward on to the desert in a small rented Renault to keep a promise he made to himself almost forty years earlier.

"In *Bench Press* today there is a sandstorm brewing," he had written. "It is the same one that used to blow in my childhood, just before I fell asleep. It envelops me where I lie on the bench, like a shrieking, biting fog." And then he drives into a real sandstorm. Visibility shuts down, the car lurches as in snow, sand seeping through every crack, he is chewing sand, he rubs his eyes, he longs for a bottle of mineral water, Oulmez brand, and he is not unhappy. Neither am I. That's not what I am saying. But maybe I can say there is something the matter with me. For I should have been indoors now, in my house, in a different darkness than this, in the bed my wife has so beautifully constructed, asleep and resting out before a new day's work at the keyboard and maybe an hour or two with an axe in my hand. But I cannot settle, the bed becomes my mind's prison, the house becomes too small, and so I go out into the hall, put my dark-blue pea jacket on and think: I do not fear anything, and go straight out into the night.

"The Oblivion Seekers" is the title of one of Isabelle Eberhardt's stories, the greatest desert diver of them all, and maybe there are many who *do* that; seek oblivion, for reasons I shall not pass judgment on now, not out here alone on the dirt road, but to find that oblivion, to be forgotten, they may let the desert be the great eraser, be the sponge on the blackboard so thoroughly that in the end nothing can be heard in the emptiness except the fragile sound of "nothingness bells". Others seek change, desire to change themselves completely, and to achieve that they must go through the night, go into the desert and perhaps let the burning dry wind of change blow through their bodies and blow their souls clean; let the desert re-educate them in elementary things. In any case, they came, the desert divers, from their various positions, each with their own longing for some part of this, all pointing to the same centre, to the Sahara, with their strength of mind and courage depending on how great their sincerity was. Did they try to be brave, perhaps, so they did not have to be afraid ever again? Did they want what Bob Dylan sings of in "It's Alright, Ma (I'm Only Bleeding)": "You lose yourself, you reappear, you suddenly find you've got nothing to fear." To dare lose yourself and then possibly find yourself again, and to have that necessary courage, because you can never be certain whether you will ever surface again. When you once have let go. That weightless moment! And do you really dare be the one you then become, whom you cannot know beforehand? Like Rimbaud after he made a clean break and stopped writing the poetry that revolutionised French and European literature and just disappeared at the age of twenty-five when he went off to Yemen and to the Horn of Africa, and resurfaced as a different person, with apparently new qualities and new skills and said: "*Je est un autre*," which in fact is grammatically wrong, for of course it is, "*Je suis un autre*," *I am another*, but by saying it with the verb in the third person, he objectified and alienated himself. Then he *forgot* himself, then he lost himself, that is the suggestion made by my friends who know French.

It does sound right, I agree, but to walk through the night here, that too is to lose yourself a little; to move along when you can barely see your own hands: to exist, to think, but to be invisible to others, to yourself; almost deleted. Then I even close my eyes, which is not really necessary, and leave the road to take one of the paths across The Gate Ridge, which is hard enough to see even with your night-sight intact, but I know the directions and I know where to take the turns; step by step I have measured it all up during the years, and the whole circle of movement is lodged in my body with a shining compass at the centre. There is also a detector in there somewhere, near the heart maybe, and in any case I close my eyes because it feels right.

Some way along the path I feel the pressure of the trees on each side, more and more of them; the terrain rises, I let my feet feel the stones and the roots on my upward path, and they make light of that, but I swallow and think, what is really the matter with me? I am fifty-one. The space around me is no longer infinite. That is what's true. Eternity has crashed, and suddenly disgust may come like a malicious wind and make everything you want to do, all your aims and intentions, crumble between your fingers, in your mind, and blow away like a dry, grey powder. Then what matters is to walk quickly by day and walk dark by night, or must I turn and look back, as Sven Lindqvist did, and meet my own gaze at the other end of the time tunnel? I open my eyes and stare into the darkness, and immediately close them, for it does no good, it makes no difference. I see just as much or just as little. Open or closed.

Open or closed; it's the same shit, I think, and feel myself working up a fury, which is often the case when something comes over me that I cannot do anything about. But of course I *do* see him, though his eyes are hard to catch. "Hey you, look over here!" I shout between the pine trunks I know stand all around me, and my voice sounds sharp and very strange in the dark night. But he will not reply, he just stares bashfully down at the pavement on his way up from the station on Railway Square to the Narvesen shop on the corner of Parliament Street opposite the parliament building. That shop was more proletarian, was my opinion then at the end of the Sixties, than Cammermeyer bookshop on Karl Johans Street, for we did have a Narvesen shop in Veitvet too, which was where I lived on the outskirts of Oslo, and you could be anonymous in Stortingsgate the narrow and shady Parliament Street, while Karl Johans Street was wide and always bathed in light. But they had masses of books in the Narvesen shop too; I could buy Keats there, and Shelley and Poe in cheap American editions (instead of Cammermeyer's English), and that I did, for I was a romantic that year, and what I read should above all be beautiful to read, and I bought a book of Chinese poems in English called *The White Pony*. There I met Li Po and Tu Fu for the first time, and there was such a sky above their poems I had never seen the like of anywhere else, and no doubt some of that was due to their strangeness and my incorrect reading; a kind of orientalism on my part, but what the hell did I care? And I bought Obstfelder's poems in a pocket edition, and I bought Gunnar Larsen's novel *In Summer*, and sat in the tube train reading all the way up through the Grorud Valley past Hasle and Økern and Vollebekk and all the other stations. I was the only person I knew who read these books. I did not make a secret of them, but neither did I talk about them to anyone else, and there was no-one who knew that on certain Sundays I went into town on my own and walked from the central station to Møller Street to sneak into the little Presbyterian church there, and sat down in the last pew so I could listen to the archaic English they used in the liturgy. I did that because I felt it resembled the English in a lot of the poems I was reading and resembled the way they spoke in Zefirelli's film of *Romeo and Juliet* I had seen that year at the cinema. It was the strangeness again, the beautiful, that which was different from anything I saw around me in my everyday life, that was what I wanted, to find out if it might lift me away to a different place. And at the same time I did not want to go anywhere, I wanted to stay where I was, and I wanted *where I was* to hold all that I needed. But it did not! And if it did, it was invisible to me, and at least once each day it felt as if I might split in two, as Laika does when she realises she cannot be an obedient and happy dog and at the same time chase the moose.

I see him sitting in the back pew, in the Presbyterian church on Møller, with the navy-blue pea jacket on his lap, his eyes slanted towards the pew in front, and his cheeks slightly flushed, and it does look odd, I readily admit, because he is not even a Christian. He has tried really hard to be one, out of pure need, with his utmost will-power, but he has not succeeded, it merely brings embarrassment and distaste. So what the hell is he *doing* there? What am *I* doing there? Why do I sit there for so long?

I sit waiting to become whole. But I do not become whole. It just gets worse, and it's the same when I am at home, when I walk past the house I live in, where the neighbours sit out on the doorsteps the whole way along, having coffee and talking, and I pass them with my pea jacket on and my long scarf thrown over my shoulder as an artist would. No-one else wears a scarf that way, and they call out to me: "How goes it, Persha, you take care of your eyes now!" For they know I read a lot, my father has told them, they have seen it themselves, and they think it might possibly be bad for me. And I do like them so, these people in this long house and in the houses surrounding it; I know them so well, they really want the best for me. They care about me, and I wish I could talk to them about Tu Fu, about Obstfelder, and about this new book I have read called *The Myth of Wu Tao-tsu* by Sven Lindqvist from Sweden. It is about a man who longs so much to immerse himself in art, as something perfect and flawless; a fulfilment of the need for harmony and beauty and at the same time an emergency exit from the world, as the wise man and artist Wu Tao-Tzu could do when in his prison cell he climbed into his own wall-painting and vanished. But it does not work, there is no way he can do it, for the walls of the world are tumbling down around this man, around Sven Lindqvist in the 1960s, and anyway I cannot talk about these things, I have no words for them yet, not even for my own use. So I call back: "Just take it easy, my eyes will do for a while still," and I blush and wave to them and walk along the house and out on to the road and up past the shopping centre to take the train into town where all the bookshops are, and all the record shops, and the Presbyterian church. But right up the hill, out of sight of my house, I split in two and stand there breathing heavily with my hands on my knees before I can walk on. I don't know why I am like this, don't know if it is common, whether others feel the same, or if it is something that happens to me only, but quite honestly, I cannot take it. That the world is not one, that the world is not whole, that perhaps I must decide to get away from all this, that if I want to make something of myself, then at the same time I must leave all that is mine behind me, all I can do and all that I know; leave these people sitting on the doorsteps outside the house where I live, having coffee and talking about all that *they* know; say goodbye to them for ever. And if that is what I must do to develop myself, as they say, then what is the point of it all?

Jack London's Martin Eden did that, he left behind him all that was his to acquire the culture he saw that the educated classes, the bourgeoisie had – the poetry and philosophy, the whole thing – because it seemed so attractive, so wise and so beautiful and necessary; he wanted to raise himself, he wanted to have what *they* had. He wanted to cross the line. So when the opportunity arose he went ashore at San Francisco and into the mansions of the prosperous districts to talk to the people living there, to converse (as they put it), to listen, to borrow books, to be instructed, and he was afraid his shoulders would send all the porcelain crashing just by moving through their living-rooms in his seaman's way, and he could not even hold a knife and fork as they did, but he was determined to learn what they knew, and even more. And he managed that, through such an effort that it still moves me when I think back and remember myself with my head buried in a book that most certainly is unreadable today but which shattered me then, because when he made it to his goal, when Martin Eden had his hand on the innermost door, he realised that the people he looked up to and respected so highly, really did not care as he did, that this culture was not important to them at all other than as a façade, as varnish, as a veil over what was really important – to own, to have power – and otherwise their world was an empty, barren and hard place. In disgust he turned away and fled back to the parts of the city that once were his own, to the sailors and the factory workers. But it was too late, the string was cut, they could no longer understand each other, there was a glass wall there that he could not penetrate, and in despair he went aboard his boat and sailed out on the San Francisco Bay and jumped into the water, and he swam down, down, until the pressure above him was stronger than the one that pushed him up, stronger than the will to live.

It is easy to see now that this book has greatly influenced my life although I have never really been aware of it, and there is of course something terribly wrong in Martin Eden's reasoning; it is obvious to everyone, and to me as well, but precisely *what* it is I have never quite discovered, for in a way he is right too. But not for anything in the world would I share this fate, not in despair end up among seaweed and kelp in the Bunnefjord, or in the Alun lake among perch and pike, and it is possible I lack the necessary courage, but neither would I do as Rimbaud did and become *an other* in that way, become an arms dealer and possibly a slave trader in Africa, and so I have tried to gather it all into my own body, both sides at once, both me and *me*, the one I was and the one I could have been if I had once let go, tried to cast it into one person that I *am*, but I seldom succeed, for there is really not room enough; I might split in two. But as long as this is how I am, I shall walk out here in the night, almost forgotten by myself, with the darkness pouring in through my eyes, with my hands stretched out to the sides like the wings of an aeroplane, dancing down the path when no-one can see.

And then the clouds above me crack open, they rush away from each other at great speed, as if something important were about to happen, and I see the moon over The Gate ahead of me; a luminous round moon over the barn, and the house that I live in showing white and clear in the bluish gleam, and when I turn and look back at the forest, I throw a clear, demarcated shadow. I feel it at once; the severance of body and non-body is as sharp as a knife. It hurts.

Translated by Anne Born

LIMERICK COUNTY LIBRARY

NOTES ON THE AUTHORS

INGVAR AMBJØRNSEN (b. 1956) is one of the most popular storytellers of contemporary Norwegian literature. His books are characterised by well-informed, realistic descriptions of the seamier side of life. The protagonists are often outsiders – described with sympathetic insight and warmth. Since his literary debut in 1981 Ambjørnsen has written sixteen novels and three collections of short stories, as well as several books for children and young adults. The author's breakthrough came in 1986 with the novel *Hvite niggere* (*White Trash*). His most successful novels in recent years are the quartet about the oddball Elling, critically acclaimed and well-received among Ambjørnsen's wide readership. His stories contain less external plot, but proportionately more wild inventiveness and absurd humour. The *Elling* movie was nominated for an Oscar for best foreign film in 2001. He has received several awards, including the Brage Prize in 1995 for *Fugledansen* (*The Bird Dance*).

Most recent title: *Innocentia Park*, 2004.

KJELL ASKILDSEN's (b. 1929) first book was a collection of short stories published in 1953. In Norway today he is commonly regarded as the master of the short story. In the Sixties he asserted his influence through a collection of short stories, *Kulisser* (*Scenery*), 1966, and a novel, *Omgivelser* (*Environment*), 1969; both titles suggesting modernist stylisation and human constraint. In his fictional work Askildsen explores how individuals become imprisoned by other human beings, especially through the glance of their eyes. Everyday prose is combined with chiselled precision and the use of under-statement is traceable everywhere. Since the publication of *Ingenting for ingenting* (*Nothing for nothing*), 1982, all his books have been volumes of short stories – five in all. His work has been adapted for the stage and screen. In 1996 he won the Brage Prize's Honorary Award.

Most recent title: *Hundene i Tessaloniki* (*The Dogs in Thessaloniki*), 1996.

TOR ÅGE BRINGSVÆRD (b. 1939) is an author with a wide-ranging oeuvre. He has written plays for the theatre, television and radio, essays, children's books and novels. His trademark is his great curiosity, leading him to the far reaches of the reader's expectations, where he finds motifs from most areas of life, most cultures and indeed from the sources of myths, in particular northern mythology and history. In 1970 Bringsværd started his writing career as science-fiction author with *Bazar,* followed by *Den som har begge beina på jorda står stille* (*He Who Has Both Legs on the Ground Stands Still*), 1974, offering rich doses of satire and humour. *Minotaurus,* 1980, derives from the mythical Crete. In *Ker Shus,* 1983, Bringsværd describes our world after a catastrophe. From 1985 to 1997 he published five volumes in the *Gobi* series, in which he delves deeply into Eastern and Western cultures. Bringsværd has been translated into twenty-three languages and his plays have been performed in fourteen countries. He has been awarded numerous prizes, among them the Critics' Prize in 1985 and the Ibsen Prize in 2000.

Most recent title: *Kaptein Puma og det farlige romuhyret* (*Captain Puma and the Awful Space Monster*), 2005, a children's book.

LARS SAABYE CHRISTENSEN (b. 1953) is a gifted storyteller, a narrator who is imaginative but at the same time down-to-earth. His realism alternates between poetic image and ingenious incident, conveyed in supple metropolitan language and slang that never smacks of the artificial. Since his debut in 1976 Saabye Christensen has published ten collections of poetry, four collections of short stories and twelve novels. He came to prominence with the publication of the novel *Beatles* in 1984. The short story collection *Den misunnelige frisøren* (*The Jealous Barber*), 1997, is about people who are about to lose something – neglect, egoism or envy. The title story is published in this anthology. In 2001 he published the internationally successful novel *Halvbroren* (*The Half-Brother*). The author won the Brage Prize and the Nordic Council's Literary Prize in 2001.

Most recent title: *Oscar Wildes heis* (*Oscar Wilde's Lift*), 2004.

GRO DAHLE (b. 1962) made her debut with the collection of poetry *Audience* in 1987. Since then she has published two story collections, poetry collections and children's books, in addition to textbooks in Norwegian language and literature for primary schools. Dahle stands out as a stylistically naive, quick-witted and burlesque writer – a poet treading her own path. She has received several awards for her work.

In 1999 she was the official festival poet at the Bergen International Festival. Gro Dahle was awarded the Ministry of Cultural and Church Affairs' Prize for best children's book, for her picture book *Sinna mann* (*The Angry Man*), 2003.

Most recent title: *Djevletanna* (*The Devil's Tooth*), 2004.

KJARTAN FLØGSTAD (b. 1944) is regarded as one of the most important and influential Norwegian writers today. Since his debut in 1968, he has published eight novels, several collections of poetry, essays, mysteries, short stories, travelogues, plays and non-fiction. In 1977 he was awarded the Nordic Council's Prize for *Dalen Portland* (*Dollar Road*). His novels always demonstrate a global awareness and a strong sense of solidarity with the oppressed. He seeks to expose the forces that shaped the industrial and post-industrial society, and to convey his belief that a wealth of knowledge and indispensable strategies for a meaningful existence can be found in different forms of popular culture, both traditional and modern. *Fyr og flamme* (*Fire and Flames*), 1980, *U3*, 1983, *Det syvende klima* (*The Seventh Climate*), 1986, *Kron og mynt. Eit veddemål* (*Heads or Tails. A Wager*), 1998, are among his most important novels. Fløgstad has won several awards, among them the Critics' Prize in 1980, the Brage Prize in 1998, and the Medalla de Honor Presidencial Internacional Centenario Pablo Neruda in 2004.

Most recent title: *Snøhetta: A Monograph on the Norwegian Architectural Firm Snøhetta*, 2004.

JON FOSSE (b. 1959) grew up by the Hardanger fjord on the west coast of Norway, and now lives in Bergen. Since his debut in 1983 with the novel *Raudt, svart* (Red, Black) he has become one of Europe's most widely performed dramatists and his books and plays have been translated into more than thirty languages. Jon Fosse's oeuvre encompasses novels, collections of stories, lyrical poetry, essays, children's books and plays. In most of his work he explores the human condition in an everyday setting, writing spare, elliptical prose, abundant in repetitions. The distinctive feature of his writing is the suggestive musicality of his rhythmic language. His breakthrough novel was *Naustet* (*The Boathouse*), 1989. Widely acclaimed recent novels are *Melancholia I* and *II*, 1995–6, about the Norwegian painter Lars Hertervig, and *Morgon og kveld* (*Morning and Night*). Since his first play *Nokon kjem til å komme* (*Someone Is Going to Come*) in 1993 Fosse has written some twenty dramatic works. His plays are highly readable, telling of love, blame, loneliness, jealousy and loss. Jon Fosse has received numerous literary awards, including the Ibsen Prize, the Austrian Nestroy Prize, the Scandinavian National Theatre Prize and the prize for best foreign playwright in Germany.

Most recent title: *Det er Ales* (*It's Alice*), 2003.

KARIN FOSSUM (b. 1954) made her literary debut with a collection of poetry in 1974. This was awarded the Vesaas Prize. She has published a second collection of poetry and two short story collections. The short story collection *Søylen* (*Pillar*), 1994, is about the drama and intensity that may suddenly appear in everyday life – often from a child's point of view. She gained a wide readership, both in Norway and in translation for her highly unusual crime fiction beginning with the novel *Evas øye* (*Eve's Eye*) in 1995. Her language is precise and plain, effectively conveying the characters and the riveting stories. Fossum's novels have been filmed and made into television series. She has been awarded the Riverton Prize and the Glass Key for *Se deg ikke tilbake!* (*Don't Look Back!*), 1998, and the Booksellers' Prize in 1997 for *Den som frykter ulven* (*He Who Fears the Wolf*).

JOSTEIN GAARDER, (b. 1952), came to international acclaim with his novel on philosophy, *Sofies verden* (*Sophie's World*), 1991. His debut was a volume of short stories, *Diagnosen* (*The Diagnosis*), 1987, followed by several books for children and young adults. In Norway he had his breakthrough with *Kabalmysteriet* (*The Solitaire Mystery*), 1990, which won the Critics' Prize. Both here and in *Sophie's World* he shows his skills in constructing intriguing, multi-layered stories combining reason and fantasy. His style is somewhat postmodern, yet his message is deeply rooted in the humanist heritage. This also applies to his four published novels for adults. *I et speil, i en gåte* (*Through a Glass, Darkly*), 1993, and *Sirkusdirektørens datter* (*The Ringmaster's Daughter*), 2000, have proved hugely popular and have confirmed his international reputation.

Most recent title: *Appelsinpiken* (*The Orange Girl*) 2003.

BEATE GRIMSRUD (b. 1963) is a creative and versatile writer. She made her debut with the short story collection *Det fins grenser for hva jeg ikke forstår* (*There's a Limit to What I Don't Understand*) in 1989. The curious and experimenting self at the heart of her stories makes them both strange and thought-provoking. She has also written the novel *Continental Heaven*, 1993. *Å smyge forbi en øks* (*To Slip Past an Axe*) was nominated (by Sweden) for the Nordic Council's Literary Prize. She has also written a number of radio dramas and four stage plays, film scripts and dance productions.

Most recent title: *Hva er det som fins i skogen barn? (Children, What Do We Know That Lives in the Woods?)* 2002, the free-standing sequel to *Å smyge forbi en øks (To Slip Past an Axe)*.

FRODE GRYTTEN (b. 1960), formerly a newspaper journalist, has achieved considerable success as an author. After making his literary debut in 1983 with *Start*, a collection of poems, Grytten has published volumes of short stories, two novels and two children's books. He grew up in the small industrial community of Odda on the west coast of Norway, and Odda forms the backdrop to the greater part of his stories. Many of his characters live there, and are portrayed with humour and deep sympathy. His stories often tend to the fantastical and burlesque. In his prose, Grytten frequently incorporates a British-American subculture connected to film, music and television. The novel *Popsongar (Pop Songs)* is based on Grytten's own selection of pop songs. His novel *Bikubesong (Beehive Song)* won the Brage Prize in 1999 and was nominated for the Nordic Council's Literary Prize. *Bikubesong* has been adapted, very successfully, for the stage. It has also been translated into several languages.

Most recent title: *Hull & sønn (Hull & Son)*, 2005.

JONNY HALBERG (b. 1962) is one of the major exponents of Norwegian dirty realism and is renowned for his script to the critically acclaimed and popular movie *Junk Mail*. He has published two short story collections and four novels. His prose is concise and clear with pertinent speech and a strong verbal touch. His characters are often tormented by pent-up feelings, sometimes giving way to aggressive behaviour, but warmth and aggressiveness belong together and the author supports his characters instead of compromising them. His major novels are: *Trass (Defiance)*, 1996, *Flommen (The Flood)*, 2000, *Gå til fjellet (Go to the Mountain)*, 2004. Halberg has been awarded several prizes, among them the Critics' Prize in 2000 for *The Flood*.

Most recent title: *Gå til fjellet*, 2004.

HANS HERBJØRNSRUD (b. 1938) made his literary debut when he was forty-one. When he moved back to the family farm in 1976 the author in him was released, and he took up farming and writing. A door was opened to a linguistic storytelling energy and a profound knowledge of the human mind, a belief that each human being is a separate universe and the author the explorer. Often he balances the rational and the incomprehensible and there is no final answer to the question: Who am I? He focuses on the division between our different selves and is inspired by the local landscape, which is recreated in evocative language. His first collection of short stories *Vitner* (*Witnesses*) was published in 1979 and since then he has published five more collections, and been awarded several literary prizes, including the Vesaas First Novel Prize in 1980 and the Critics' Prize in 1997. He was nominated for the Nordic Council's Prize in 1998 and 2002 and, in 2005, he was awarded the Aschehoug Prize, judged by the Literary Critics Society.

Most recent title: *Vi vet så mye* (*We Know So Much*), 2001.

RAGNAR HOVLAND (b. 1952) grew up on the west coast of Norway and now lives in Oslo. He made his debut in 1979 with the novel *Alltid fleire dagar* (*Ever More Days*). His literary cornucopia contains books in all genres and for every age group: poems and stories for children, plays, poetry, essays, short stories, novels and thrillers. He has translated poetry and prose by French, Irish, Spanish and German writers and written both for the screen and opera. Hovland's books are often inspired by his own childhood and young manhood and by mass culture influences from film, pop music and popular literature, blended with fantastic elements into what has been called "west coast surrealism". The journey or rather the dream of breaking up, the modern myth of life on the road, is often the setting of his novels. Major works are *Sveve over vatna* (*Moving on the Face of the Water*) and *Ei vinterreise* (*Winter Journeys*). He has been awarded a number of major Norwegian and foreign literary prizes, including the Critics' Prize for *Ei vinterreise*.

Most recent title: *Finske dagar og netter* (*Finnish Days and Nights*), with co-authors Per Olav Kaldestad and Dag Helleve, 2003.

ROY JACOBSEN (b. 1954) is an author who in recent years has gained considerable recognition from the critics and the literary milieu as a whole. From his debut in 1982, with the collection of short stories *Fangeliv* (*Prison Life*), he has developed into a versatile, investigative and analytical author with a special interest in the underlying psychological interplay in human relationships. The short story collection *Det kan komme noen* (*Someone May Come*), 1989, does not have clear solutions, but an uncompromising search for truth.

Jacobsen has written four collections of short stories and nine novels, among them the modern family saga *Seierherrene* (*The Conquerors*), 1991 – his most successful novel – a biography and a children's book. He received the Booksellers' Prize for *Seierherrene* and the Swedish Ivar-Lo Prize in 1994.

Most recent title: *Frost* (*Frost*), 2003.

JAN KJÆRSTAD (b. 1953) graduated as a Master of Theology from the University of Oslo, and made his literary debut in 1980 with *Kloden dreier stille rundt*, (*The Earth Turns Quietly*), a collection of short stories. He has also published picture books and essays. As a novelist, Kjærstad is both innovative and experimental. He strongly holds that literary form is productive in creating new means of understanding in a changing world. Thus his novels are stimulating, showing mastery in the construction of intriguing and playful fictional worlds. His major work is a trilogy with the media figure Jonas Wergeland as its central character. The first volume, *Forføreren* (*The Seducer*), 1993, has been translated into English. In 1998 he was honoured with Germany's prestigious Henrik Steffens Prize for *Forføreren*. Jan Kjærstad won the Nordic Council's Literary Prize for *Oppdageren* (*The Discoverer*) in 1999, Part III in his trilogy.

Most recent title: *Menneskets nett* (*The Web of Mankind*, essays), 2004.

MERETHE LINDSTRØM (b. 1963) made her debut with *Sexorcisten og andre fortellinger* (*The Sexorcist and other stories*) in 1983. She has published five collections of short stories and five novels. Among her novels, *Steinsameere* (*Stone Collectors*), 1997, earned the widest acclaim and won her two awards, but her main contribution to contemporary Norwegian literature rests upon her outstanding skills as a creator of short fiction. The experience of irreparable loss and guilt often sets the tone, the fictional universe revolving painfully around moments of sudden change.

Most recent title: *Ingenting om mørket* (*Nothing about the Dark*), 2003.

ØYSTEIN LØNN (b. 1936) made his literary debut in 1966, and was for many years a favourite among the literary critics and an author's author. *Thranes metode* (*Thrane's Method*), 1993, was awarded the Critics' Prize as well as the Brage Prize, and it opened the door to a wider audience. In 1996 followed a new collection of short stories,

What Should We Do Today?, awarded the Nordic Council's Literary Prize in 1966. Lønn's prose is clean, concise and stylistically neutral. Although free from idiomatic expressions, it is full of double meanings and long dialogues that are at once simple and mysterious. Lønn has always dealt with the ways in which we manage our small private lives within complex societal processes. In his later publications these issues are dramatised in step with the disintegration of the welfare state, where most people are confronted with a new and insecure way of life they have not yet mastered with explicit words. Selected novels: *Tom Rebers siste retrett* (*Tom Reber's Last Retreat*), 1988, *Maren Gripes nødvendige ritualer* (*The Necessary Rituals of Maren Gripe*), 1999, *Ifølge Sophia* (*According to Sophia*), 2001.

Most recent title: *Simens stormer* (*Simon's Storms*), 2003.

TRUDE MARSTEIN (b.1973) won the Vesaas' First Book Award for *Sterk sult, plutselig kvalme* (*Strong Hunger, Sudden Nausea*), in 1998. The sixty-five short prose pieces in this book are minimalistic in scope and literary style, apparently trivial pieces about young girls and boys living seemingly secure, dull lives, but they also reveal tragic patterns in the incessant business of (post) modern dating. Marstein has also written novels and books for children, and she has won the Sult Prize and the Doubloug Prize.

Most recent title: *Konstruksjon og inderlighet* (*Constructed and Profound*, essays and articles), 2004.

HANNE ØRSTAVIK (b. 1969) made her literary debut in 1994 with the novel *Hakk* (*Cut*). Her considerable reputation rests in part on the novel *Kjærlighet* (*Love*), 1997, a story of a modern, narcissistically obsessed mother and the resulting, fatal neglect of her child. Ørstavik's authorial voice is a distinct and insistent one, following her female main characters into dark regions of anger and despair in their search for authenticity in life. Her four subsequent novels have attracted great attention among the critics and are widely read. Ørstavik's work has been awarded important prizes, among them the Brage Prize.

Most recent title: *Presten* (*The Priest*), 2004.

PER PETTERSON (b. 1952) was a librarian and a bookseller before publishing his first work, the volume of short stories *Aske i munnen, sand i skoa* (*Ashes in the Mouth, Sand in the Shoes*), 1987. Since then, his novels have established him as one of Norway's most significant novelists. As a realistic storyteller he sets his characters against the background of working-class life, often with an emphasis on bitter family relationships. He won the Booksellers' Prize and the Critics' Prize for his last novel, *Ut og stjæle heste* (*Out Stealing Horses*), 2003. His books have been translated into several languages.

Most recent title: *Månen over porten* (*The Moon over The Gate* essays), 2004.

DAG SOLSTAD (b. 1941) made his debut with the volume of short stories *Spiraler* in 1965. Since then he has published numerous novels, as well as articles, essays and plays. Solstad is widely recognised as one of the most influential and outstanding novelists of his generation. A modernist of scope and feeling, his novels also maintain an accurate, realistic record of past and present development of the Norwegian community. Some of them are openly politically engaged, but an overall disappointment is the hallmark of his ingenious, later novels. He is the only Norwegian author to have won the Critics' Prize three times, and he was awarded the Nordic Council's Literary Prize in 1988 for the novel *1987*.

Most recent title: *Artikler 1993–2004*, (*Articles*), 2005.

LAILA STIEN (b. 1946) is one of Norway's most distinguished short story writers. She published her first collection in 1979, entitled *Nyveien* (*The New Road*), and has since published novels and poetry for readers of all ages: adults, children and juveniles. Stien's writing is best described as everyday realism, and she is known for her unsentimental but very sensitive description of "ordinary" lives. Her stories are like finely-honed instruments set to register the small but vital changes in the human mind. Stien has contributed generously to the translation of Sami literature, chiefly the poetry, into Norwegian. The prizes she has been awarded include the Aschehoug Prize in 2000.

Most recent publication: *Veranda med sol* (*Veranda with Sun*), 2003.

KARIN SVEEN (b. 1948) is a diversified author. Since her literary debut in 1975, she has written poetry, novels and short stories, and she has also published factual prose books. Much of her writing is about childhood and the transition into adult life. Her collection of short stories *Døtre* (*Daughters*), 1980, concentrates on relationships between daughters and their mothers. The conflict between locally rooted, rural life and modern openness is at the core of her writing, and her storytelling varies between realistic representation and poetic, legendary imagery. Strong girls fighting their way towards an independent life are an important motive in novels like *Utbryterdronninga* (*The Escape Queen*), 1992, and *Hannas Hus* (*Hanna's House*), 1991.

Most recent title: *Klassereise. Et livshistorisk essay* (*Class Travel: An Essay about a Life Story*), 2000.

TOR ULVEN (1953–95) is regarded as one of his generation's most influential authors. He died by his own hand at forty-one. He published the first of five collections of poetry in 1977 and became an almost mythological author and the standard-bearer of poetry writing in Norway in the 1980s. After 1989 he wrote prose, but the poet was still holding the pen. Ulven's texts are exceedingly precise and full of nuances, merciless in their existential quest, and at the same time pervaded by musicality. His poetry contemplates the existence of death in all things. Ulven believed that the text should speak for itself without any comment from the author, and did not give any interviews. A selection of titles: *Gravgaver* (*Gifts for the Grave*), 1988, *Søppelsolen* (*The Garbage Sun*), 1989, *Vente og ikke se* (*To Wait and Not to See* stories), 1994, *Stein og speil, mixtum compositum* (*Stone and Mirror*), 1995 . Ulven was awarded the Obstfelder Prize in 1993 and the Doubloug Prize in 1995.

Most recent publication: *Prosa i samling* (*Collected Prose*), 2001.

BJØRG VIK (b. 1935) has made her mark on Norwegian literature over a period of more than thirty years. She has published twenty-five books, including novels, short stories, plays and radio plays. Her work has been translated into a number of languages. During the Sixties and Seventies, Bjørg Vik's writings conveyed an unusual and provocative image of the erotically active woman, including *Fortellinger om frihet* (*Tales of Freedom*), 1975, and *To akter for fem kvinner* (*Two Acts for Five Women*), 1974. Then, at the end of the Eighties, she published the Elsi Lund trilogy, which made her work popular among readers of a new generation. In many ways, Bjørg Vik's literary career is a mirror image of the developing debate on women's issues in Norwegian society – from the oppressed S.O.S. from the deep couch, via the more articulated battle-cry of the women's movement, to the deepening understanding of both sexes which is a trademark of the acute psychological descriptions contained in her prose. She has received several awards, including the Critics' Prize in 1979.

Most recent title: *Forholdene tatt i betraktning* (*Given the Circumstances*), 2002.

LARS AMUND VAAGE (b. 1952) has written novels, short stories, plays, books for children and poetry, and has been awarded several important literary prizes, among them the Scandinavian Dobloug Prize and the Critics' Prize for the novel *Rubato* in 1995. As the title of this novel indicates, Vaage's mode of writing is inspired by music, both in his way of composing story patterns and his use of rhythmic style. Thematically he often reflects on the cost of shallow, modern prosperity, confronting it with the power of his sensual, lyrical prose.

Most recent title: *Kunsten å gå* (*The Art of Walking*), 2002.

HERBJØRG WASSMO (b. 1942) has earned her popularity in Norway and abroad through her ability as a storyteller with a special concern for exposed and vulnerable characters. She made her debut in 1976 with a collection of poetry. Her first novel about Tora, *Huset med den blinde glassveranda* (*The House with The Blind Glass Windows*), 1981, was followed by two volumes forming the *Tora* trilogy, which contributes to a Norwegian realistic tradition about the coming-of-age of the unusual and artistic child. The voice of Ms Wassmo has a poetic intensity, taking the reader close to the disintegration of the small human being and her fight for dignity. *Dina's Book*, 1989, is a novel with a wide canvas from the middle of the nineteenth century, set on the coast of northern Norway. A dramatic accident in Dina's early life follows her for ever and she becomes a woman who challenges, astounds and bewitches her surroundings. In 1992 came *Lykkens sønn* (*Dina's Son*), and in 1997 *Karnas arv*, (*Karna's Legacy*), forming the *Dina* trilogy. The collection of short stories *Reiser* (*Journeys*) was published in 1995. The author has won awards in Norway and abroad, among them the Critics' Prize in 1981, the Booksellers' Prize in 1983 and the Nordic Council's Literary Prize in 1987.

Most recent title: *Flukten fra Frank* (*Running from Frank*), 2003.

NOTES ON THE TRANSLATORS

MAY-BRITT AKERHOLDT grew up in Norway and lives in Sydney, Australia. She taught Theatre History at the National Institute of Dramatic Art, was Dramaturge at Sydney Theatre Company and, for ten years, Artistic Director of the National Playwrights' Conference. She has translated twenty-two plays which have been produced by theatre companies around Australia. Her translations of Jon Fosse's plays are published by Oberon Books, London. Other publications include a book on Patrick White's drama and two volumes of translations of plays by Ibsen and Strindberg.

JAMES ANDERSON was born in Great Britain in 1951 and was trained for the stage at the Webber-Douglas Academy of Dramatic Art in London. He learnt Norwegian while working in Norway and subsequently studied at the Polytechnic of Central London. He has translated novels by Thorvald Steen, Jostein Gaarder, Jon Michelet, Morten Harry Olsen and Kristin Valla and Atle Næss' biography of Galileo, *When the World Stood Still*.

DON BARTLETT lives in Norfolk and works as a translator from German, Danish and Norwegian. His translations and collaborations include novels by Pernille Rygg, Ingvar Ambjørnson, Jo Nesbø and Jakob Ejersbo.

ANNE BORN was born in England and spent seven years with her Danish husband in Denmark. She took an MA at Copenhagen University and later an M.Litt. at Oxford. She has translated many books from Norwegian, Danish, Swedish and Finland-Swedish, mostly fiction and poetry, three of which were longlisted for the *Independent* Foreign Fiction Prize; she has also published thirteen collections of her own poetry and four regional history books. She lives in Salcombe and in Oxford.

NADIA CHRISTENSEN holds a Ph.D. in Comparative Literature from the University of Washington and currently heads a US-European university student exchange programme. She has translated more than a dozen books by contemporary Scandinavian authors. Her translation of *Tales of Protection*, 2003, by the Norwegian novelist Erik Fosnes Hansen was a finalist for the 2003 PEN Translation Prize.

PETER CRIPPS studied philosophy in London before moving to Munich to work in the theatre. In 1990 he moved to Norway, where for ten years he worked at the University of Bergen and as a stage director. He lives now in Berlin and is a translator specialising in philosophy and contemporary art.

ROBERT FERGUSON is a novelist, dramatist and biographer of Knut Hamsun, Henrik Ibsen, Henry Miller and T.E. Hulme. He has also translated and adapted for BBC radio works by Ibsen and Hamsun. He has lived in Norway since 1983.

ODDRUN GRØNVIK was born and grew up in Norway and lives in Oslo. For six years she lived in England, taking a degree in English Language and Literature at Oxford. She worked as an editor in Norwegian publishing houses and took an MA in Nordic language at Oslo University. She was a consultant on the Norwegian Language Council (1979–87), and since then editor of *Norsk Ordbok* and a member of the Project steering group since 2002. She is also Coordinator of the University of Oslo African Languages Lexical Project since 1991.

KATHERINE HANSON was born in Seattle. She received her Ph.D. in Scandinavian Languages and Literature from the University of Washington in 1978 where she is an Affiliate Associate Professor in the Department of Scandinavian Studies. Her translations include four novels by Amalie Skram in collaboration with Judith Messick and numerous short stories. She was editor of *An Everyday Story: Norwegian Women's Fiction*, and co-editor with Ia Dubois of *Echo: Scandinavian Stories about Girls*.

AGNES SCOTT LANGELAND was born in Scotland and studied Anthropology and English Literature at the University of Edinburgh. She also has an MA in English Language and Literature from the University of Oslo. Since 1971 she has lived in Norway, engaged in teaching and translating. Her translations include a novel by Hanne Ørstavik, a novel by Dag Solstad and poetry by Rune Christiansen.

SVERRE LYNGSTAD, Distinguished Professor Emeritus of English at the New Jersey Institute of Technology, Newark, New Jersey, received his Ph.D. in English from New York University. He is the author of many books and articles in the field of Scandinavian literature and has published numerous translations of classic Norwegian fiction. Dr Lyngstad is the recipient of several awards and has been honoured with the St Olav Medal and the Knight's Cross, First Class, of the Royal Norwegian Order of Merit by the King of Norway.

STEVEN T. MURRAY was born in Berkeley, California. Learning Danish as an exchange student, he later worked in technical translation doing Swedish, Norwegian, German, and also Dutch. He founded Fjord Press in 1981 to publish translations of northern European fiction. His translations include Henning Mankell's *Sidetracked*, which won the Macallan Gold Dagger for best crime novel of 2001. He is married to the translator Tiina Nunnally; they live in New Mexico with their two Spanish cats.

LIV IRENE MYHRE was born and raised in Norway. She has lived in the United States for the last forty years. She received her MA from Syracuse University, and worked in the publishing business at John Wiley and Oxford University Press. Her translations include *The Honeymoon* by Knut Faldbakken and *Westward before Columbus* by Kåre Prytz. She was the editor of *Norwegians in New York, 1825-2000*, published in connection with the 175th anniversary of organised Norwegian immigration to the United States.

ANGELA SHURY-SMITH lives in Surrey and has grown up within the Norwegian community in London, teaching for many years at The Norwegian School and lecturing in translation. She has worked as a freelance translator mainly within video documentary since attending Folk High School in Finnsnes, North Norway some twenty years ago. Previous literary translations include work by Bjørg Vik, Svein Nyhus and Lena Steimler.

KENNETH STEVEN was born in Glasgow. He lives in Highland Perthshire and is a full-time poet and children's author, as well as being a translator. He translated the Nordic Prize-winning novel *The Half-Brother* by Lars Saabye Christensen, which was also long-listed for the *Independent* Foreign Fiction Prize.

DONNA H. STOCKTON is a graduate instructor in the Scandinavian Studies Programme at the University of Colorado in Boulder, where she is completing her work on a Ph.D. in Comparative Literature. The focus of her academic studies is English and Scandinavian languages and literature, with an emphasis on literary translation. She spends half of each year in Norway.